ALL
FIRED UP

Also available from Lori Foster and HQN Books

LORI FOSTER

ALL
FIRED UP

HQN™

HQN™

Recycling programs
for this product may
not exist in your area.

ISBN-13: 978-1-335-14639-7

All Fired Up

www.HQNBooks.com

Printed in U.S.A.

To Lowell Bower.

Thank you for all the terrific prison info
and the many questions you answered. I appreciate it greatly.

Any and all errors are my own.

ALL
FIRED UP

CHAPTER ONE

The warm, muggy night closed around him, leaving his shirt damp in places. Sweat prickled the back of his neck. Inside Freddie's he'd find air-conditioning, but he'd never again take fresh air for granted. He valued every single breath of humid air that filled his lungs.

The moon climbed the black sky as time slipped by. How much time, he didn't know: he'd stopped keeping track the second he saw her.

Headlights from the occasional passing car came near him but didn't intrude on the shadows where he stood.

Transfixed by *her*.

Damn, he wanted that mouth.

In the short time he'd locked eyes on her, a dozen fantasies had formed—most of them based on her naked lips, the way she occasionally pursed them, how she twisted her lips to the side in frustration, even how she blew out a breath. The whole package was nice…but it was her mouth that kept him unmoving, staring. Imagining.

Slight of build, she served as a bright spot in the dark gloom. Understated and yet something struck him as undeniably sexy.

Once he'd noticed her, he couldn't look away.

After speaking softly into a phone, she bit her plump bottom lip, and her expression showed frustrated defeat.

The lady had made several consecutive calls. Was she in need of assistance? Given the way she'd circled a car, occasionally glaring at it, he thought she did. Judging by her frown, there wouldn't be any help on the way.

Since getting out of prison a year ago, Mitch had spent an excess of time with women. Hell, next to fresh air, freedom and steak, sex topped his list. He'd immersed himself in human contact, the gentleness, the carnality.

He'd taken satisfaction in pleasing someone else while abating a base need. Hell, watching a woman come gave him as much pleasure as his own release.

So he'd gotten his fill and then some—all while making plans to change the course of his life. To make it better. To carve out a meaningful future.

Here he was, where he needed to be, determined, resolute… and sidetracked by a gorgeous woman.

That in itself left him edgy with curiosity. No other woman had snagged his attention this way. He knew zip about her, and yet seeing her had heat building beneath his skin.

He tried to look away, but his attention kept zeroing back.

Freaking bizarre.

It was like seeing something you hadn't known you wanted, but immediately recognizing it as necessary.

Even dressed in jeans, a T-shirt and flip-flops, he knew the lady had nothing in common with him. Innocence all but screamed from her slender body and reserved manner. To someone with his jaded background, that put her in the "do not touch" category.

His fingers curled and his palms burned. Yeah, he wanted to touch her despite that.

And he didn't look away.

From the shadowed corner just outside the bar, he watched her thumb dial another number into her phone. While holding the phone to her ear, she paced. The overhead glow of the security light touched her in select places, alternately highlighting and then shadowing her understated curves.

High cheekbones framed a slender, straight nose. She tucked a few drifting curls behind a small ear. Though rounded, he saw the mulish determination in her stubborn little chin.

And that mouth…thoughts of it under *his* mouth—and on his body—tightened his jaw until his molars ached.

For the first time in years, he wondered if he could put off his agenda for a bit, say something to her, see if there was something between them despite the seemingly obvious roadblocks.

Opposites attract, and all that.

He'd made this trip a center point for a new future.

In this Podunk town he'd subtly uncovered what he could about Brodie and Jack Crews. That was the priority after all. Moving forward, leaving the past behind. It started with the Crews brothers. Hitting the bar tonight might have gained him more insight into them.

But would a slight detour—the type with long curly brown hair and a sweet little body—matter so much?

If he listened to his dick, the answer was no. His balls were giving a resounding "go for it" as well.

His head though… Hell, his head claimed he could afford a delay. In the grand scheme of things, it wouldn't matter.

Since arriving in town, he'd discovered that the men were well liked, each of them married, and they had an odd but interesting business called Mustang Transport. Locals claimed they dealt with mundane shit as well as serial killers and psychopaths. Somewhere in the middle, the truth lurked.

He'd also heard about their mother. He'd been hearing about her for as long as he could remember. For very different reasons she interested him almost as much as Brodie and Jack.

He had no connection to Rosalyn Crews, but meeting the men felt important in a way nothing else ever had. He couldn't explain it, even to himself. He'd gone through life making damn sure he needed no one, and that he wanted only for things he could get for himself.

Now, much as it chapped his ass, he wanted something else—and it depended on Brodie and Jack Crews.

It didn't have to happen right away, though. He wouldn't mind burning off some energy before making that initial contact—especially if he could convince *this* woman to give him a few hours of her time.

He noted every small movement as she spoke into her phone. He couldn't catch every word, but the low murmur of her voice stroked over him. He was pretty sure she left a message.

Suddenly she held the phone back and stared at it. Hot annoyance tightened her mouth and brought down her brows.

"Perfect. Just freaking perfect."

He heard that loud and clear.

Jamming the phone into a back pocket—a tight fit over that sweetly rounded backside—she dropped her head with a throaty groan that traveled along his spine like a sensual stroke. Her eyes closed, her mouth flattened, and the damp night drew her long, light brown hair into coiling curls.

He'd love to tangle his fingers in her unruly hair.

As if spurred by her innate energy, the curls moved, bouncing a little, drifting with the breeze. Judging people had kept him alive. With this woman, he sensed she didn't indulge in downtime very often. Even standing still, she seemed to…spark with energy.

Curiosity cut into him, mingling with the carnal interest.

Had she been stood up? Walked out on a date?

Just then she growled, "Dead. Stupid phone." The thump of her hand to a metal lamppost sent a dull clang ringing over the area. "Now what?"

Ah, well that answered his question.

White teeth nibbled her bottom lip in consideration. Considering, she glanced at the bar, shook her head once, and returned to pacing.

Clouds covered the moon, amplifying the darkness. She was far too petite to be stranded alone.

Doesn't mean she wants a quick fuck, he argued with himself.

The young woman stewing in front of him might be more likely to sell brownies at a local bake sale, but engage in a hot one-night stand? Probably not.

Sure, she was standing outside a rowdy bar all alone on a late night—but then, so was he.

So what should he do? Be smart and turn away, or see if she needed help? He remained undecided when two men exited the bar with a lot of noisy fanfare.

Drunken asses.

The woman glanced up, then quickly away with a roll of her eyes—but not quickly enough to avoid notice.

"Charlotte, hey! Whatssup?" With a leer, a mop-headed man added, "You waitin' for me, sugar?"

Mitch caught the way his unshaven bud snickered, proving the irony in the question.

"Definitely not," she replied, her tone crisp and clear.

Mitch liked the sound of her voice. Not all girly or too sweet, but firm and no-nonsense.

He did *not* like how the two dunces eyeballed her anyway, stumbling in her direction despite her preferences.

"Ah, c'mon now, don't be like that," the talkative one said.

His idiot friend guffawed, stumbled and heckled some more.

Charlotte—*nice name*—propped her hands on slim hips and issued a dire warning. "You'd be smart to keep walking, Bernie."

"How come you're here alone?" He tried a teasing voice that Mitch suspected did the opposite of entice. "You know where to find me this time of night."

"Drunk, as usual. Yes, I know." Annoyance squared her nar-row shoulders. "Not that it's any of your business, but I finished a late delivery and was heading home, then had car trouble." She added with menace, "Help is on the way."

"I'll keep ya company until then."

"No, you will not."

"But I'm already here." Intent brought Bernie closer.

She didn't exactly look afraid, but more like fed up. Before Mitch gave it enough thought, his feet carried him out of the shadows and immediately drew her attention.

Soft blue. Now that he saw her eyes more clearly, he found them every bit as compelling as her mouth.

Alert, maybe a little wary, she zeroed in on him. Her lips parted and she blinked twice.

You're sealing your fate, sugar. He tried a smile of part interest, part reassurance.

Her gaze went beyond him, searching the darkness, and then snapped back again. "Where did you come from?"

With his attention only on her, Mitch held up his hands and avoided a direct answer. "Just seeing if you need any help."

Emboldened by liquid courage, the two men blustered at him. "G'lost, asshole. She don't need nothin' from you."

As if Bernie and his bad grammar didn't hover there beside her, Charlotte asked, "You're new around here?"

Mitch gave her a long look. What, did she know everyone in Red Oak, Ohio? Probably. He could jog the main street, one end to the other, without breaking a sweat. "I've been here a few days." Whether he was passing through, or sticking around, wasn't her business. Besides, for now, he wasn't sure.

Brazen stupidity urged Bernie to step up in front of him. "You ain't listening. I told you to—"

Disgust curved Mitch's mouth into a mean smile meant to intimidate. "You're right. I'm not listening to you." Insulting disregard took his gaze over the smaller man before he dismissed him. "I'm talking only to her."

By size difference alone, it was beyond ludicrous for Bernie to issue a challenge.

And yet, he did. "Are you fuckin' stupid?"

Charlotte's voice, now edged with anger, interrupted anything Mitch might have replied or done. "You've been warned, Bernie. If you don't knock it off right now, you are *not* going to like the consequences."

Still, the fool didn't listen. "I said," Bernie blasted, his breath putrid, "for you to *get lost*." A scrawny fist, aiming for Mitch's face, swatted through the air.

Bad move, asshole.

Instincts could be a son of a bitch. Mitch leaned away from the weak hit…and at the same time automatically jabbed with his right.

His fist landed right on Bernie's chin.

Eyes rolling back, the smaller man started to drop.

Infuriated that he'd lost his grip in front of Charlotte, Mitch caught the front of Bernie's shirt and held him on his tiptoes. "You," he whispered between barely moving lips, "need to learn when to quit." Familiar anger surfaced despite his efforts to tamp it down…

And a small, cool hand touched him.

Struck clean down to his toes, Mitch peered first at those pale, tapered fingers with short, neat nails resting lightly against the roped muscles of his sun-darkened forearm.

Fucking sexy, that's what it was, highlighting all their differences, especially those of strength and capability.

Her face drew him next, the delicate lines, smooth skin…that mouth and those eyes.

That wild hair.

"I think," she said softly, a smile teasing her mouth, "if you let Bernie go now, he'll make a hasty retreat." Slanting those mesmerizing eyes toward old Bernie, she added with silky menace, "At least, he better."

Keen awareness nudged out anger.

Everything about her appealed to him.

She stood to his left, and the heady scent of her skin and hair—like baby powder and flowers—teased his nose.

He drew a deeper, fuller breath, filling his lungs with her and knew he could happily drown on that scent.

Slowly, wanting to keep her close, Mitch unclenched his fingers and allowed Bernie to stumble back to where his buddy helped to prop him up.

Unconcerned with that, Charlotte's fingers shifted in the lightest of explorations before she snatched her hand away.

Interesting—especially that splash of color on her cheeks.

She looked up at him, gave a wan smile, and whispered, "Thank you."

"For popping him?"

Curls bounced as she gave a quick shake of her head. "For not doing him more damage." She wrinkled her nose, leaning closer to confide, "You could have, I know."

Huh. No recriminations?

She actually *thanked* him?

Not what he was used to, but he'd take it. "So—"

Eyes almost crossed, Bernie spat. "You used ta be such a nice girl."

And just that easy, he fractured Mitch's newfound calm. Fury brought him forward a step. "You'd be wise to leave now."

Too drunk to see the danger, Bernie glared at Charlotte.

In what felt like a gentle reminder, she touched his arm again.

Their eyes met—and she smiled.

Son of a bitch, how had she known? No, he didn't punish smaller men for idiocy. He didn't settle things with his fists— unless he had to. Annoyance narrowed his eyes, but otherwise, he hid the churning confusion.

"You okay?" she asked, her eyes big and sincere.

Jesus. She wanted to soothe him? An abrupt nod eased her worried frown.

"Good." She gave him a pat.

Mitch stewed. It grated that even out of prison, some things hung with him. Like react first, think later, rather than take chances.

Behind bars, it was safer that way.

I'm no longer in prison. Eventually that'd sink in. Coming here, to this small town, would be yet another step to ensuring that it did.

Bernie's friend, helping to hold him upright, muttered, "Fuck 'em. Lez go," in an effort to save face for them both.

"Do," Charlotte said in quiet command, and with audacity she shooed them away.

Un-fucking-believable. But what mattered to Mitch was seeing them go.

And that left him alone with her.

After a second deep breath, something new occurred to him: Charlotte had gotten dangerously close to a volatile situation.

She didn't know him—if she did, she wouldn't have dared.

She shouldn't trust him—but she hadn't hesitated to intercede.

Ballsy. Also foolish.

And why that impressed him, he couldn't say.

Even though she now stepped out of reach, Mitch *felt* her, her concern, the sizzling contact where her flesh had met his—*on your arm, you ass*—and the inquisitiveness in the wide eyes that kept peeking at him.

Get it together. To help with that, he watched the two men travel the sidewalk until they disappeared out of sight.

Would they come back? He didn't think so.

Cowards never did.

"Sorry about that," Charlotte offered, her gaze probing. "Bernie is stupid when he drinks."

Mitch had the distinct impression Bernie was always stupid, but whatever. "You scared him." He tried a smile to put her at ease, even though he hadn't yet relaxed.

Her laugh was as nice as her voice. "Oh, it's not me he has to fear."

Well, shit. She meant him? Had his harsh reaction bothered her after all? "I didn't mean to—"

"You were justified, but I really was impressed with the way you pulled the punch. Not many men could do that."

Unsure what to say, he tugged at his ear. It wasn't bragging to say he could've destroyed Bernie with very little effort. Instead, he'd left him with a face, so maybe his reaction wasn't so bad after all.

"I wasn't talking about you, though." Charlotte's lips teased into a small smile and her voice went husky, as if to share a secret. "Bernie didn't want me to tell on him."

Barely able to get his gaze off her mouth, Mitch asked, "Because.?"

"He'd get more than a punch."

Well, if she had someone that protective, she had to be in a relationship, which meant he shouldn't be flirting with her. Disappointment settled in his gut, but hell, he was used to disappointment. As cavalier as he could manage, he asked, "Husband?"

"Men I work for, actually." She tucked back a curl, hitched her purse strap up her arm, and laced her fingers together. Watching him, she stated, "I'm not married."

A charge of relief rocked through him and he knew right then, he'd figure out a way to have her. With new intent, he stepped closer. "Glad to hear it."

His nearness caused a catch in her breath. "You?"

"Free and clear." *In more ways than one.* Shifting closer, Mitch deliberately inhaled her scent. God, he'd missed that, a woman's musk, the fresh stirring fragrance of her skin and hair.

Maybe sensing his intent, Charlotte touched her throat, flustered, surprised, and if her smile was anything to go by, pleased with his interest.

"I look forward to getting to know you better." Right now would suit him fine. "Hopefully sooner rather than later?"

"Oh." Surprise had her blinking fast, and turned her smile shy.

Was she unused to men coming on to her? Hard to believe. She was one of those perfect little packages, sexy, sweet, reserved—at least with him.

With Bernie, she'd been bossy and bold.

She tantalized him.

"I'd like that. But unfortunately…" She flagged a hand at her side. "I was expected home a little while ago."

Deciding to move cautiously, rather than chance scaring her off, Mitch nodded at her ride, an older blue Ford Focus in great shape. "You mentioned car trouble?"

The car drew her scowl. "Yes, and I'm never going to hear the end of it."

"Why's that?"

More at ease now that he'd retreated a bit, she relaxed her shoulders. "Those men I work with? They've tried to talk me into a different car for a while now." She shrugged. "But I like this one. She and I…fit."

Her blue eyes and a pretty blue car—yeah, they did fit.

Adorably, she screwed that killer mouth to the side and blew away a curl. "I left messages with a few people before my phone died. It's only a matter of time before one of them shows up, but I don't know how long it'll take. Most places around here are closed now, and I don't relish the idea of going into Freddie's to wait."

Mitch sent a derisive glance at the bar. Yeah, after already seeing two obnoxious drunks spill out, he didn't want her in there either. "You probably shouldn't be out here alone."

She tipped her head in challenge. "I'm not alone, am I?"

Probably shouldn't be here with me either. Needing a different direction, he glanced at her car. "I could take a look." Not like he had anything else to do, now that he'd veered off his plan.

His nearness brought her face up so she could look into his eyes. Hers were big and unblinking, and as he watched in fascination, her lips parted.

Damn, she needed kissing. Bad.

As if coming out of a daze, she blinked again, released a shaky breath, and let her busy fingers toy with one long curl draping her shoulder. "You, um, know cars?"

Getting his attention off her mouth proved a challenge. "I know enough." As in, *everything.* But at this point, he wasn't willing to share any part of himself or his background. It'd be too dangerous in this town, at this time, with so much on the line.

The slip of her tongue over her lips made his nostrils flare. God, he had it bad.

Before coming to Red Oak, he'd gotten his fill of sex, or so he'd thought. A five-year dry spell did that to a man, made him insatiable.

Then again, she wasn't like other women. Sweet, yes, but he sensed a fearlessness about her that equaled her pride. No one skated through life unscathed, but some people got beat down more than others.

He was glad that whatever mundane hardships she'd faced, they'd apparently made her stronger.

He was stronger too—but not in the same way.

"Actually," she said, oblivious to his darkening thoughts, "it's just a flat tire, and that's on me, not the car. I think I ran over a nail or something. I should have learned how to change it myself, but I never seemed to have the time."

A woman like her, with delicate hands and a smile that warmed his frozen heart, should never have to struggle with a flat.

"You got a spare?" As he asked it, he circled the car and saw the back passenger side tire completely flat.

Charlotte followed, but didn't crowd too close. "In the trunk."

"Keys?"

"I already opened it." She gestured. "I had some vague notion of attempting it, before I realized I had no idea what to do and I'd just look foolish. Soon as I'm back to work, learning is on my agenda."

Mitch wouldn't mind teaching her that, and a whole lot more. Of course, she didn't yet know he was an ex-con, and finding out would obliterate her tentative kindness.

Getting down to business, he dug out her jack and the spare. Caution kept her in the light of the streetlamp, but curiosity brought close enough to chat. Smart. She probably figured if he got out of line, she could be in the bar in seconds.

Not that he would. His gentleness toward women went bone deep, as much a part of him as his face and physique. To him, all women deserved care.

Then again, most people would probably consider an ex-con talking to a nice woman as totally crossing a line.

He blew out a breath, the reality of his situation never far from his mind.

"I'm Charlotte, by the way," she said. "Charlotte Parrish."

"Mitch." He didn't give his last name. He couldn't. Not yet. "Nice to meet you."

Instead of pressing it, she did the usual chitchat, asking him if he was staying in the hotel—he wasn't.

If he liked the town—he said he did, but honestly, it didn't matter to him.

How long he'd be around—and he said he didn't yet know, because it wasn't really up to him.

Just as he finished tightening the last lug nut, she asked, "So what brought you here?"

He was scrambling for a believable lie when he heard a car approach and park, then the closing of a door. He assumed it was a late arrival for the bar, until a deep voice called, "Charlotte?"

Fast footsteps approached along with that male voice. "I just got your message, hon. Sorry it took me so long. I tried to call you back, but didn't get an answer and…"

One of the guys she worked with?

Not wanting his time with her to end, Mitch kept his head down and gave all his attention to lowering the car and removing the jack.

The footsteps stopped. Mitch knew someone was close, especially when he heard, "What's going on here?"

Charlotte groaned. "My phone died. I'm sorry, Brodie, but it's already handled."

Shock sent a tidal wave of heat rushing through his system.

Brodie. Disbelief prodded his temples; he closed his eyes and gave a muttered, "Fuck," that luckily no one heard.

There couldn't be two men with that same unique name in such a small town.

He wasn't ready yet, but then, when would he be ready?

He'd wanted to do more research, to learn more, to better prepare—and now he wouldn't have a chance.

A heavy, suspicious pause filled the air. "Handled how?"

"Mitch helped me."

Seeing no way around it, Mitch uncoiled from the ground until he stood. Automatically bracing, he slowly turned to face Brodie Crews.

And damn near whistled in surprise.

Why had no one mentioned that Brodie was a hulk?

At six-three, other men rarely looked Mitch in the eye, but Brodie not only stood on a par with him, he was just as bulky with muscle.

Worse than the height similarity, though, it unnerved Mitch seeing a nose exactly like his own, a similar jaw, forehead, cheekbones—

Brows up, arms crossed, Brodie asked, "Any reason you're eyeballing me?"

Jesus, he had been. Feeling his ears go hot, Mitch scowled and shook his head. "No, I just—"

"You wanna drop the tire wrench too?" As Brodie spoke, he lightly nudged Charlotte behind him to block her with his body. "Or is there a reason you have a stranglehold on it?"

Stupidly, Mitch looked down at his hand. Yeah, his white-knuckled fist wrapped tightly around the iron.

Disgust made him laugh before he could stop it. Shaking his head again, he gingerly placed the wrench back in her car and bent for the jack.

The deafening silence made him uneasy. "So Charlotte works for you, huh?" His bad luck grew by the second.

"Works for, works with, bosses me around—take your pick." Brodie moved closer and lifted the flat tire. "You just happened along, is that right?"

Something like that. "Yeah." Nodding at the bar, Mitch gave a believable lie. "I was checking out the nightlife."

Brodie snorted. "Not much of that around here. So why are you sticking around?"

A female gasp had both men turning their heads.

"Why the third degree, Brodie?" Fists propped on slim hips, Charlotte scowled. "He *helped* me. You should be thanking him."

Shrugging, Brodie offered, "Thanks?" in dry irony.

Before Mitch could reply, another voice intruded, asking, "What's going on?"

Instinctively knowing what he'd find, Mitch looked toward another man fast approaching. He had the same height, the same damn nose and jaw, but a leaner physique.

This, then, had to be Jack.

"Brodie's being an ass," Charlotte accused.

"Tell me something new." Though the words were light, the same caution that Brodie expressed showed in Jack's dark, direct eyes.

Unfamiliar emotions had a stranglehold on him. He hadn't

expected that, had only planned on what to say and do—but not what he'd feel.

If it weren't so damned dangerous, it'd almost be funny.

The brothers now flanked him, Brodie behind, Jack in front, and it made his skin itch. He didn't like having anyone at his back, ever, but most especially not *them*, not *now*.

Not when he wasn't himself, and wasn't even sure who he should be while with them.

Shifting, Mitch considered his options, then decided: screw it. He walked out from behind the car so that he could face both men. Let them make of that whatever they wanted.

In the middle of all that excess of sentiment, Charlotte's gaze scorched over him. Confusion, yes, but also something more shone in her eyes as she visually dissected him.

"She called you too?" Brodie asked.

Jack nodded. "I was just getting back to town and was in an area with no reception. Soon as the call came through, I headed this way."

Brodie explained before Charlotte could. "She had a flat, he changed it, her phone died or she'd have called us back. That's all I know."

"Huh." Now that Mitch had moved, Jack came to stand beside Charlotte. "So if her phone hadn't died, we'd never have known she met someone?"

"That's the gist of it, yeah."

"Oh, for crying out loud." Her elbow caught Brodie in the gut. He *oofed*, then gave her a little space. Jack wisely retreated, but only a step. "It was just a flat and he's already finished, so—"

"New to town?" Jack sized him up.

Charlotte threw up her hands. "He's already been grilled."

Appreciating how both men protected Charlotte—even if it set her off—he shrugged. "I've been here a few days."

Suspicion lifted Jack's chin and narrowed his eyes. "Passing through?"

Waiting for an answer, Brodie studied him.

Resigned, Mitch accepted that they'd force him to do this here and now.

In front of Charlotte.

Not what he'd wanted, not what he'd planned for.

Damp, oppressive air closed around him. Muscles jumped and twitched in that familiar way that happened whenever he felt uneasy.

In prison, he'd felt uneasy a lot.

This was different, sure—so why were his molars grinding together?

Brodie aligned himself with Jack, *as brothers should*. Shit, shit, shit. Together the men presented a united front. Not exactly hostile, but definitely not welcoming. And why would they welcome him? A total stranger talking to a woman they cared about?

Once he explained, they'd both want to run him off.

They'd find out soon enough that he wouldn't go easily, not after he'd finally gotten here. He'd worked too damn hard for this. Deserved or not, he had a plan and he'd damn well stick to it.

"Why," Charlotte demanded, an edge of desperation to her tone, "are you two doing this?"

"They're astute, that's why." Let them hate him if they wanted—but they would not consider him stupid. There was nothing friendly in the way he showed his teeth. "They sense things are off."

Jaw tensing, Brodie straightened even more.

Misgivings bunched Jack's shoulders.

These men were impressive, and a small part of him felt pride.

"Mitch?" Compassion, confusion, softened Charlotte's expression.

He'd felt many losses in his day. This one smarted more than most. "Sorry." Working the tension from his neck, determined to get through it, he said, "The thing is—"

And yet *another* voice intruded, this one strident, a voice of authority, used to being heard—and obeyed.

The voice of a *woman*. "Brodie, Jack, behave yourselves."

As if aggrieved, Brodie rolled his eyes. "Our mother," he said in an aside to Mitch. "And if you think we're distrustful, prepare yourself."

Their mother.

Rosalyn Crews.

Something uncomfortable shifted inside him, making his heart kick. Breath held, Mitch turned—but of course he wasn't ready, hadn't even come close to preparing himself.

His gaze clashed with hers.

CHAPTER TWO

The revered matriarch of the Crews family. Mitch knew of her, but he hadn't counted on meeting her, definitely not now, late at night, in the middle of town with not only Brodie and Jack right there, but Charlotte too as a witness.

Surprise brought Rosalyn to an abrupt halt, her lips parting, her eyes flaring. Beautiful eyes. Dark, thickly lashed.

The same as her sons', Brodie and Jack's.

Very, very different from his own.

Muscles strained in the back of his neck. He didn't run from anyone, ever. Never had.

God help him, he wanted to run from the morass of things this woman made him feel.

Instead he planted his big feet, locked his knees, concentrated on slow, steady breaths, and held himself stock-still.

"Mom?" Jack moved toward her with concern.

Mitch couldn't help looking at her. He'd heard so much about her. In his mind, she represented ethereal ideas that he'd rarely experienced. Kindness. Compassion. Loyalty and affection.

Things a mother gave a son, things his own mother hadn't

shared with him. Mitch wasn't sure she even possessed those emotions. If so, he'd never seen them.

"What is it, Ros?" After shooting Mitch a brave smile, Charlotte hurried to her.

And just like that, Charlotte's brief nearness shook his resolve. His jaw clenched tighter, his lungs constricted. *Don't be a fucking coward.* He wasn't, so he held his ground and continued to watch the two women, mostly because he couldn't have looked away if his life depended on it.

He knew she went by Ros, a shortened version of her name. He'd heard it many times. Hearing it from Charlotte seemed as natural as the sun rising.

She wasn't quite what he'd imagined, but then, he'd built her up a lot in his head. Reality, he decided, was actually nicer.

Instead of wispy and angelic, she looked substantive. Warm, comfortable. Motherly in some intrinsic, indefinable way.

Real. Flesh and bone with a fiercely beating heart, instead of the paragon his imagination had conjured over the years.

And she continued to stare, her expression arrested, still.

"Are you okay?" Charlotte asked her.

Briefly glancing at her, Ros nodded in reassurance, an uncertain smile pushing dimples into age-softened cheeks. She took a tentative step closer to Mitch, and he forced himself to stay silent when the urge to turn away beat inside him.

Jack and Brodie matched Ros's every step—for her. As her sons, their protectiveness expanded beyond just Charlotte.

Over and over, he'd been told they were the type of men to impulsively protect anyone smaller, weaker, or in need, so of course they'd be especially vigilant for those they loved.

They loved their mother.

Fingertips touching her mouth in a show of wonder, Ros visually explored his face. With a short laugh, she said, "I'm sorry for staring."

His eyes never leaving hers, Mitch gave one sharp nod. He understood, even if no one else did.

Yet.

"It's just…you look very much like someone I know. Or rather how someone I know looked when he was a man your age."

His automatic swallow sounded audibly in the quiet night, as did his short indrawn breath. "Yes, ma'am." Mitch knew exactly who he favored.

With new concentration, Brodie asked, "Who?"

"There is something," Jack agreed, minutely reviewing each of Mitch's features.

Sweat broke out on his neck and his skin felt too tight.

Screw it. He couldn't take the suspense a second longer, so he stated the undeniable truth.

"I look like Elliott Crews."

Seconds clapped by like mini explosions, but at least he breathed easier.

It was done. No taking it back, no retreat.

Forward. That's the direction he had to go. Relentlessly, deliberately forward.

Drawing a cleansing breath, Mitch took his own turn studying expressions.

Mouths had dropped open, but now snapped shut. Charlotte, bless her generous heart, was the only one to blink.

Not the way he'd wanted to do things, but fuck it. Falling back on old ways, he faced the coming censure.

Out of the four people now gawking at him, it was Charlotte's gaze that burned the most. Putting the pieces together, thinking it through, she saw things now that she hadn't before.

What did she think of him now? Her gaze seemed almost… admiring, but he wouldn't buy into that.

With a knowing and self-deprecating smirk, he briefly met her gaze. *It all looks different now, doesn't it?* And she hadn't even heard the worst.

He could almost see her interest going up in flames—and he didn't blame her. He was a bastard for being here, a real prick for what he was about to do.

He looked away, yet every fiber of his being chafed at her nearness.

Locking on Rosalyn was easier than seeing Jack's or Brodie's disdain. If he gave in an inch, it'd only derail him.

He wouldn't let that happen.

"I know," he quipped into the silence. "Hell of a shocker, right?"

Eyes going liquid, Rosalyn drew a shaky breath.

Oh, shit. He locked his jaw and tried not to care…but yeah, that proved impossible.

Jack flattened his mouth.

Brodie asked, "Our *dad?*"

With one terse nod Mitch confirmed, "Yup. He's my father as well."

Talk about an incredible bombshell. Shock constricted Charlotte's lungs, so how must the others feel?

Instinctively wrapping her arm around Ros, she turned to Brodie and Jack. They appeared utterly dumbfounded.

Did neither of them see what it cost Mitch to come to them? She did. She saw so very, very much.

Like most macho men, Mitch would try to hide it, but she wasn't fooled.

Maybe because she'd already experienced his protectiveness, his concern, she felt she knew him. Knew him better than she should have in such a short time. But there'd been something— a connection of sorts—that kept her irresistibly drawn to him.

Now especially, that she knew why he was here.

Like his brothers, he was a big man, powerfully built, his wide shoulders taut with dignity and his expression one of forced arrogance. He stood alone against them, awaiting his fate.

Her heart broke for them all, but she knew the Crews family. They had each other, and that meant they could tackle most anything.

Charlotte looked at Mitch again. God help her, she couldn't keep from looking at him.

Yes, now that he said it she saw the similarities. Mitch's hair was lighter, sort of a dark blond, and unlike Brodie and Jack, he didn't have Rosalyn's dark eyes. The rest though—the bone structure of his face, that incredible body, his height, even the way he smiled…

With a sound of—*delight?*—Rosalyn pulled away and opened her arms in acceptance. "I knew it!"

Horror replaced Mitch's stoic expression as she came at him.

Matching him step for step, Ros said, "Even though I couldn't believe it, I swear I recognized you!"

Brodie tried to stop her—like that would ever work? "Mom, wait."

Ros laughed. "He's your *brother.*" Intent clear, she all but pursued him.

Oh, how Charlotte loved her. For this—and many other things.

"You're taking him on his word?" Jack asked, more with distrust than animosity.

"You have eyes in your head, son. You can see the truth same as I can."

Appalled, Mitch hastily fell back a few more steps.

If he went much farther, he'd end up in the street.

He looked back, gauging the distance, but it wasn't enough to evade Ros as she threw her arms around his waist.

Because Charlotte watched so closely, she saw something tragic cross his face.

Confusion. Torment.

Hope.

Amazing that Ros's affection could so profoundly affect such a towering, powerful man.

Typical for Ros, she didn't care. She tilted back once to smile up at him. "You look exactly like him."

Breathing a little too fast, his arms held in comically stiff angles away from his sides, doing all he could not to touch her, Mitch frowned. "I know."

Ros squeezed him again, then suddenly fury levered her back. "I'll kill him!"

Everyone stared at her.

Cautiously, Jack asked, "Dad?"

"Yes, your father!" She spun with a fist in the air. "How dare he not tell me?"

Mitch flexed his neck and his knuckles, then tried a polite smile carved from discomfort. "I should apologize—"

"Oh, honey, no." Just that quick, she reached up—way up—and cupped his face. "You have nothing to apologize for. *Nothing.*"

Thick brows leveled over his golden-brown eyes. "Actually, ma'am," he said through his teeth, "you can't know that."

"He's right, Mom." Brodie reached for her, caught her glare and retreated with frustration. "You don't even know why he's here."

Undeterred, Ros smiled. "He's here because he's *family.*"

Mitch tightened—his mouth, his eyes. His fists. Incredulity visibly warred with something more.

Alarm and sympathy brought Charlotte a step closer before she caught herself. Whatever Mitch felt, it wouldn't be improved with her intrusion so maybe she could help in another way.

Normally, directing the family fell to Ros, but yes, she was a bit distracted with hugging Mitch right now.

The loud clearing of her throat drew all eyes to her. Chagrined, she attempted an upbeat smile. "How about we go to the house and talk?"

"Yes," Ros said with enthusiasm.

At the same time Brodie and Jack tried to make excuses.

"Ronnie's waiting for me," Jack said and Brodie added, "It's late and Mary will worry."

Knowing her sons well, Ros leveled a telling look on each of them...and played dirty. "That's fine. I don't want my lovely daughters-in-law to worry. You two head on home and Charlotte and I'll visit with Mitch."

"What?"

"Hell no."

All sweet manipulation, Ros promised, "We'll fill you in tomorrow."

Charlotte laughed at Jack's horrified expression and Brodie's stubborn refusal. They both knew Ros would win, so why fight it? Feeling impish, she offered, "Mitch can ride with me."

"The hell he will." Brodie stepped forward, then grudgingly offered, "He can ride with me."

Charlotte thought that would get the ball rolling.

Unfortunately, Mitch disagreed.

With an icy growl, he asked, "Do I get a say in the plans?"

"For now," Ros said, her tone gentle as she hugged him again, "you get the biggest say. But you're here, right? You made it this far. So why not visit?"

He turned away, turned back and kneaded the muscles at his neck.

Charlotte couldn't help but notice the way his biceps bunched, the muscles that ticked in his lean jaw.

In a barely there voice, she taunted, "You know you want to."

His eyes, a mellow brown with golden highlights, flicked over to her, narrowed for a heart-stopping moment, and then shifted to Brodie. "Look, I didn't plan this—I mean, I did, but not here and not now. Not with..." He gave a vague gesture toward Charlotte.

She'd have been insulted, maybe even hurt, except that he also tried to slip away from Ros—without much success.

Keeping an arm around his waist, Ros squeezed him again. She seemed unable to help herself.

"I thought we could talk, you, Jack and me, but it can wait until tomorrow."

"You only say that," Jack muttered, "because you don't know our mom."

Charlotte grinned. No, he didn't know Ros, but he was about to.

Out of all the scenarios Mitch had prepared for, he hadn't figured on this. Gently but with firm resolve, he took Rosalyn Crews by the arms and eased her back, giving himself space to breathe. Though the woman was short and a smidge on the plump side, she had the fearless, in-charge attitude of a superhero.

With her fresh-faced appearance, her light brown hair in a casual ponytail, dressed in jeans and a T-shirt, she didn't look old enough to be mother to two grown men.

In every way that Mitch could observe, she was the opposite of his father, Elliott.

Done dwelling on Rosalyn—something he hadn't meant to do—Mitch said to Brodie, "Could I talk to you and Jack privately just a minute?"

Brodie opened his mouth, but it was Rosalyn who said, "No," in a way that closed Brodie's mouth and made Jack sigh.

To Mitch, she said, "We're a family. You can talk to all of us."

Unwillingly, his gaze sought out Charlotte. Was she related too? Jesus, if he'd almost—

"Not me," she said fast, flustered, maybe knowing his thoughts. "I mean, they're *like* family to me, because my parents passed away. But we're not blood related."

Brodie cocked a brow. "Any reason you offered up that little clarification?"

"Shush," Rosalyn told him. She laced her fingers together and studied Mitch. "As I'm sure you know, I'm Ros, their mother, so what concerns them concerns me."

Mitch tried to stare her down. "It could concern you tomorrow instead of right now."

Ros didn't flinch. "We're all here now, so come to the house. I'll fix coffee, and Charlotte made cookies earlier. We'll get acquainted."

Her goodwill bombarded him, destroying his resolve—and yet, that little tidbit distracted him. So Charlotte baked?

What the hell did he care? He *didn't*. If he wanted a cookie, he'd damn well buy a package at the grocery store.

Squaring his chin and looking down at Ros, he said, "To be honest—"

The look she gave him had to be some patented maternal expression that conveyed disappointment, determination and a donkey's stubbornness to have her own way.

He'd never seen it before, but then, he'd had a different type of mother.

The look was effective. The longer she gave it, the more powerless he felt.

Why would she welcome him when her husband had cheated? Why act as if she was *happy* to meet him?

He heard himself mutter, "This is not a good idea."

As if she'd already won—and maybe she had—Ros smiled. "Of course it is."

Without meaning to, Mitch glanced at Charlotte, saw her distracting, sexy mouth curled in a sentimental smile, and quickly looked away. Time to obliterate all those scorching fantasies because now more than ever she was off-limits to him.

Easier said than done. He was aware of all of them, but Charlotte most of all. Her attention soothed and incited in equal measure. The sooner he got away from her, the better.

For them.

Rubbing his chin, Mitch considered his options.

Because her sons were big and capable, Ros might think she understood him.

She did not.

From all he knew, Brodie and Jack were nice guys who could, when necessary, adequately kick ass. Clean fighting without any dirty tricks. Measured and civilized.

Survival had honed Mitch. No irony, no showmanship. Just pure, basic nature learned from birth, every day over twenty-nine years. Prison had sharpened his few blunt edges.

He wasn't naturally cruel, but could be the cruelest bastard around when provoked.

He knew right from wrong, but damned if that line didn't sometimes blur.

He valued life—and yet, he'd take it if necessary. Had tried to take it a few times. Left in prison much longer, who knew how many would have died?

For him the focus had been the same: his survival. He'd wanted to live, and to ensure that he did, he would have killed others.

None of that applied here, though, and he absolutely couldn't take advantage of Rosalyn's kindness.

That meant coming clean. Laying it out there.

"Let's roll credits on the drama, okay?" Head-on, he met the dark gaze that matched her sons' eyes. His face felt hard, his intentions harder, but he admitted, "I'm an ex-con."

He was ready for recriminations—yet none came.

Brodie and Jack did shift closer.

And Mitch didn't have to look to know they'd blocked Charlotte completely while standing at their mother's back.

An ex-con was a threat. He got it.

But no bitching? No demands that he hit the road?

Showing his teeth in a mockery of a smile, he said, "Yeah, I figured that'd get your attention." Now to cut past the absurd reception and lay it out there, before they all got the wrong ideas. "I don't want anything from any of you."

"You're here," Brodie said, his tone congenial even though he'd gone caveman in "protecting the little women." "Gotta be a reason."

"Sure." Like the fact he had no one else, and now that he was starting over, he wanted to do it right and he figured family couldn't hurt.

He had to reevaluate that, though, because right now, he was in fucking misery.

"So let's hear it," Jack said. "What's the reason?"

This bizarre calmness of theirs was more unsettling than rage. "Look, I have no intentions of imposing, or using any of you, or...any of that. I just..." Shit, this was not how it was supposed to go.

He wasn't a man to trip over his words. He stated his case and took the response on the chin. That's how he'd handled getting a job as an ex-con, how he'd slowly rebuilt his life over the past year, ignoring rejection, stepping around obstacles and refusing to give up.

He wouldn't give up now either, but damned if he knew how to proceed.

Everyone waited, silent, expectant.

He ran a hand over his face. "Is Elliott around?" Their father was the last person Mitch wanted to see, but maybe he could be a buffer.

"We're divorced," Rosalyn explained. "Have been for a very long time."

Well hell. Elliott had kept that tidbit to himself. Guilt made it hard to swallow. "I hope it wasn't my mother—"

"No." Rosalyn stepped closer again. "Elliott doesn't understand fidelity, and never did. That's not on you or your mother."

Un-fucking-believable. So she knew Elliott had cheated with

his mother, and she still stood there smiling at him? How the
hell was he supposed to deal with that?

Not by looking at Charlotte. Bad mistake, he looked and then
didn't want to look away. Those playful curls teased her cheek,
the corner of her gentle smile—

"You were in prison?" Brodie prompted.

Feeling like he'd tripped into an alternate universe, Mitch
dropped his head and half laughed. Brodie hadn't sounded appalled. Mostly he just seemed curious. Curious about Mitch's
cursed life and the fucked-up decisions he'd made.

Like banked embers in a fire, familiar anger stirred, trying
to spark back to life.

It was self-directed.

God knew he'd wasted so much time, made so many unfor-
givable mistakes. The future would be different, one way or
another. Even if he had to face it alone.

Prison was behind him and that's where he'd prefer to leave
it, but he knew before coming here that explanations would be
needed, so he sucked it up and schooled his features.

Not easy, but he'd learned to compartmentalize. He did that
now, shoving the shame and regret to the recesses of his mind
as he met Brodie's gaze without flinching. "Five years."

As if they discussed the last place he worked, rather than
prison, Jack asked, "What was the charge?"

Mitch resisted the urge to look around, to see if anyone else
on the street would hear. He was an ex-convict, plain and simple. No way to hide it, so no reason to try.

He opened his mouth—

And Charlotte surged forward, her tone brisk and her attitude
practical. "For heaven's sake, stop badgering him. Did you want
his life's story right here, on the main street?"

Startled by her attempt to defend him, equally resentful that
she thought it necessary, Mitch frowned. "Badgering me? With
a single question?"

Their reactions were a hell of a lot more tempered than he'd expected.

But then Rosalyn joined in. "Obviously he didn't murder anyone."

Brodie smirked. "Yeah, pretty sure a murderer would serve more time than that."

"Did you hurt anyone?" Jack pressed, ignoring the frustration Charlotte threw his way.

Trying to present the facts in a nutshell, Mitch shook his head. "I was nailed for complicity in a drug deal. My mother's boyfriend was the seller, not me." *Never me.* To this day, he despised drugs, would never touch them, and pitied anyone who got hooked. "It was Newman's drugs, his deal and his buyers."

"Complicit how?" Jack asked.

Aware of Charlotte tensed beside him, her arms folded, her gaze probing, he shrugged. Facts were a hell of a lot easier to convey than feelings. "I was the driver for the delivery. There was no one else to do it, so I filled in."

Without accusation, Brodie asked, "Why?"

I felt hemmed in.

I couldn't come up with another solution.

And his mother...

No, he wouldn't share any of that. It added nothing to the explanation. "Newman was arrested and no one knew how long he'd be held." Mitch had prayed it'd be for life, but as usual, his prayers went unanswered. "His cronies found me, explained that without the deal there'd be no money for my mother's electric, groceries...anything." *Everything.*

His jaw ached as he forced out the words. Hearing them aloud, he sounded even more foolish. "I offered to take care of those things for her, but the deal had already been made. The exchange needed to happen to avoid repercussions. So I drove."

Memories sank in, burning his gut, squeezing his heart. "One damned time, I drove." Talk about stupid…he met Charlotte's gaze, and somehow felt better for it. "I got busted."

"Five years for that?" Brodie asked.

Tension coiled and knotted in his neck, making him stiff. "I could have done three years if I'd named other people, but that would have implicated my mother too so…"

Why didn't he just tell it all and get it out there?

Because he wasn't a fucking criminal and he needed these people to know it.

He needed them—because he didn't have anyone else.

For some reason, it was Rosalyn he turned to this time. "With her boyfriend, Newman, in trouble, she had no one else."

"No one but her son," Rosalyn said.

Her understanding damn near crippled him. "She was…difficult." Weak, dependent, selfish. *She wasn't anything like you.* "I wanted nothing to do with her lifestyle, so I'd lived away from there from the time I was seventeen."

"Where?" Jack asked.

"Here, there. Doesn't matter." He'd often been homeless on the street, but it was better than being Newman's punching bag.

Brodie scowled. "She let you go?"

Yeah, he could see why that seemed so far-fetched to Brodie. But for him? His mom had usually been too doped up to notice he was missing.

Saying, "She couldn't have stopped me," seemed like a simpler explanation than the pathetic truth.

Charlotte touched his arm. "But she was still your mother, so when she needed you, you were there."

Unable to face her, Mitch turned away, and in that moment he hated himself. Hated what he'd done and why, hated his mother's choices and the consequences. Hated the fucking emptiness that had him here now, seeking impossible things with people who didn't deserve someone like him in their lives.

He hadn't been able to protect his mom from Newman, so

in the end it hadn't mattered. "It was stupid of me to get involved. I know that."

"Maybe," Ros said. "Also a little desperate?"

Her pity stung. "As an addict, Mom was totally reliant on Newman." He shrugged as if it didn't matter, when at the time—and still—it mattered too damn much. "If the deal had fallen through, they'd have snuffed her without hesitation."

"Jesus," Brodie murmured.

Mitch faced them again, ready to coast through the rest while he still could. "So I did it, I got caught and I served my time." Digging his keys from his pocket, he said, "I gotta go."

"Wait," Charlotte said, reaching for him.

He back-stepped before she could touch him. He had to leave, and he had to leave *now*. "My dog is waiting for me." He gave his attention to Brodie. "I'll call your office tomorrow, see if you want to talk. If you have the time." Tension dug into his neck, but he kept stepping away. "If not, I understand."

"Wait." Brodie strode after him.

Not knowing what to expect, Mitch braced himself.

Brodie stopped in front of him. Without Rosalyn's show of emotion, he said, "Show up at ten and bring the dog. We'll get to know each other over coffee."

Disbelief stole his voice. *Show up at ten.* Just like that? He admitted to prison time, to taking part in a drug deal, to being a brother they'd never known because of their father's indiscretion—and he got invited over for coffee?

Could it really be that easy?

Yeah, right. Nothing in his life ever came without a lot of sweat, hard work, and sometimes blood. It had taken him a while, but he'd learned patience—and so he stood there while his heart punched against his ribs.

With a crooked grin, Brodie settled a hand on Mitch's shoulder in a firm clasp. "Welcome home, brother."

CHAPTER THREE

Charlotte didn't want to think about the fact that she'd taken extra care with her hair, smoothing out the curls that would no doubt return before the afternoon, thanks to the humidity accompanying their current summer heat wave. She'd also put on a touch of makeup the way Jack's wife, Ronnie, had taught her.

Thankfully neither Jack nor Brodie seemed to notice, which was unusual in the extreme since they rarely missed anything, ever.

She thought Ros might've noticed, given the small smile she'd sent her way, but she didn't say anything.

It wasn't that Charlotte wanted Mitch's attention. She had, before he'd disclosed his relationship with Brodie and Jack.

But now?

Well, she loved them like brothers. She admired them in so many ways.

But never, ever, would she get involved with a man like them.

She wanted, needed, someone more settled. A homebody who'd be happy without excitement. A guy who'd enjoy quiet dinners at home, who'd welcome children, who'd share a contented life with her.

Yes, the brothers had married and somewhat settled down, and they were definitely dedicated to their wives. But they'd always be adventurous alphas who didn't blink at signs of danger. That wasn't the life she'd wanted.

She wanted a man who *would* blink, one who'd avoid danger so that he'd never cause her to worry.

Not that Mitch was knocking at the door, begging her for a date anyway. Last night, after everyone started showing up, he'd more or less frozen her out. Yes, there'd been the occasional long look—but with Mitch, she wasn't even sure what those looks meant.

In many ways, he reacted like any other guy—and yet, somehow she knew he wasn't. It was probably the intensity.

Oh my heavens, the man was intense.

Brodie and Jack had facets to their personalities, shades of humor, sensuality and loyalty that rounded out their protective natures and added interesting nuances to their alpha ways.

Mitch should have had the same, and yet it was as if someone had stolen those things away, leaving only stark determination and raw pride to keep him going.

He fascinated her.

He made her think things she hadn't really thought about before.

He had her fixing her hair and playing with makeup. Crazy.

Coasting through the offices, Charlotte adjusted the plate of cookies, set out napkins, ensured mugs sat by the coffee. Damn, she felt at loose ends but she wasn't about to dive into work, not until they all met with… Oh, wait.

Mitch was here to unite with his *family*, or so they all assumed since he hadn't yet stated his purpose.

She, however, was not family.

Nudging her hard, Brodie said, "No brooding. I have a feeling the man has indulged enough of that." On his way back out, he added, "Bring on the smiles. That's what he needs."

Charlotte bit her lip, then called, "Brodie? Hold up a second."

He stepped back into the break room doorway. "What's up?"

Clearing her throat didn't help her find the right words. "It's occurred to me that I'm not related, that Mitch might not want me—"

"He wants you. You're not dense, Charlotte. Now that we know he's a brother, he'll have to reconsider that." Brodie gave an exaggerated shudder. "I don't even want to think about—"

Horrified by his thought process, Charlotte gave him a shove that didn't budge him at all. "Don't be an ass!"

On his way past, Jack said, "Tell him not to breathe, why don't you?" and continued on to the front glass door, peeking out, then looking at the clock.

"Five more minutes," Brodie told him, rubbing his hands together.

Charlotte realized they were both anxious, more so than she was. Made sense. It wasn't every day a brother you knew nothing about showed up in your life. Add in that he looked so much like them, that he carried himself the same way—well, you'd think she'd have noticed, right? But she didn't know they had a brother, so she hadn't paid any attention.

Since Mitch seemed to need them, she completely understood why Brodie and Jack were so anxious to see him again.

Luckily for Mitch, these brothers were big on family, and even bigger on protection. Somehow, they'd make it all okay.

And then Mitch would, could…well, she didn't know. Stick around? Become a part of things?

Was that even what he wanted?

As if there'd been no interruption, Brodie added, "You had to have noticed how he looked at you, right? I know interest when I see it. The man was all but—"

"I *meant*," she said, speaking over him before he could embellish his nonsense, "that I'm *not* family, so maybe I should make myself scarce."

Brodie's brows drew together. "You're family."

Jack stuck his head in. "You're family." With a scowl at Brodie, he asked, "Did you say she's not family?"

"Not me, no." He nodded at Charlotte. "She said it."

Ros shoved both her sons out of her way—and for her, they actually moved. "You are family in all the ways that matter."

Since she'd lived with them for quite some time, ever since her parents had passed away, she knew that was how they felt—and she loved them for it. "I'm not *Mitch's* family."

"I'm not either," Ros said, "but I'm not about to budge and neither should you. We'll all accept him, because we're all involved."

Jack and Brodie shared a look, then Jack came on into the room. Brodie remained lounged in the doorway.

They tried to appear nonchalant, but Ros knew them too well. Folding her arms, she speared each of them with her narrow I'm-your-mother frown that put them on guard. "*What?*"

Sitting down, Jack crossed his arms on the table. "I did some research."

Disbelief took out her knees and Charlotte dropped into a chair opposite him. "You couldn't have waited to hear what he has to say?"

"He'll be here today," Brodie pointed out. "He'll know where we work, and in this town, he could easily find out where any one of us lives. Ask a farmer, a grocery clerk, someone at the bar—hell, he could probably talk to a cow and get our entire backgrounds. Everyone knows us. It's smart for us to understand what we're dealing with."

"If it was just Brodie and me," Jack continued, "that'd be one thing. But you and Mom live alone—"

"We live together," Charlotte corrected. "Just because a man isn't there, doesn't mean we're alone."

Brodie and Jack shared a look, and prepared to argue the point.

"So?" Ros released a deep breath without censuring either of them. "What did you find?"

"Ros!" Charlotte couldn't believe she'd be a party to them snooping. "He came here in good faith."

With a pointed look, Jack said, "Actually, we have no idea why he's here. Last night he left without saying."

"Damn near ran," Brodie added with a smile. "I think Mom spooked him."

"Or maybe it was Charlotte jumping in to defend him," Jack mused. "He didn't seem to like it."

"Oh...shut up." Charlotte folded her arms and tried to deny the heat rushing to her face. She *had* defended him.

If need be, she'd do it again.

"He clearly had eyes for you." Ros patted her hand. "Brodie and Jack are being protective. Nothing wrong in that."

Ros probably felt that way since they'd learned it from her. Rosalyn Crews epitomized the alpha woman. She'd fight the devil himself to defend her boys—and then she'd go after them with the same energy if she thought they deserved it.

Charlotte didn't like the snooping, but then again, she understood. They'd worked too hard to build their business, they had reliable reputations in the town.

"For what it's worth, all I found was that he'd done the time and why. Other than getting busted that one time, his record was clean." Looking down at the table, Jack traced a scratch and cleared his throat. "Also, his mother passed away a few weeks before he was released from prison."

Hand to her throat, Ros frowned. "That poor boy."

"Not a boy," Charlotte protested. Somehow she knew Mitch would hate being pitied, either for the boy he'd once been or the man he was now. "He's—"

"Alone," Ros said. "Or at least, he was."

Brodie nodded. "Other than Dad, it doesn't look like he had anyone."

"And we all know what that's worth," Jack said with disgust.

Charlotte agreed. Elliott wasn't exactly a bad person, but he was a terrible father, and he'd been a worse husband. Whatever he lacked, though, Ros more than made up for it. It was because of her that Brodie and Jack had grown up with love, security and guidance. Charlotte knew it, because she'd worked with them from the time she was sixteen, and they'd moved her in at eighteen when her mother passed away.

"Well, he has us now," Ros announced with conviction. "Whatever problems might arise, I expect you all to help work through it."

The rumbling purr of a car engine outside froze everyone for a second, before they scrambled en masse to their feet. Brodie led the pack as they paraded down the hallway for the entry door. At the last second, Ros took the lead, with Brodie and Jack at her back, leaving Charlotte to peer around them.

Mitch parked a sleek black Mustang.

"When I see Elliott again," Ros growled, "he's going to catch hell."

Charlotte almost grinned. No one knew how to pitch a fit like Rosalyn. What a surprise Elliott would have when he deigned to show up. They didn't know when to expect him, but they knew he'd eventually put in another appearance.

He always did.

"Looks like a seventy-two." Even while scowling, Brodie admired the car.

"Birthday present." Jack worked his jaw. "The bastard."

Charlotte knew he meant Elliott, not Mitch.

Elliott liked to gift his sons with Mustangs that they could fix up. It was a gesture meant to make up for all the many times he wasn't there—which was more often than not. No doubt Mitch's car had been a rusted pile when he'd received it.

What upset everyone, though, was the proof that Elliott had

known Mitch was his son; he wouldn't have given him the Mustang otherwise.

Peeking around big shoulders and long arms, she saw the fury darkening three Crews faces. "Smile," Charlotte reminded them, and the two brothers deliberately lightened their frowns.

Ros had to draw a deep breath.

As Mitch opened the passenger door and a black dog came out of the back, Brodie shook his head. "Looks like Dad, drives a Mustang, and has a dog in tow. He's not only related, but we have a lot in common."

Oh, how Charlotte hoped that was true. She already liked Mitch, and already wanted the best for him.

This family was it.

Surprise and unease showed in Mitch's frown when he looked up and found them all gawking. Today he wore a white pullover, faded jeans and black sneakers. Morning sunshine put a golden glow in his dark blond hair and slanted over his high cheekbones, emphasizing his clean-shaven jaw.

Only a man with his chiseled build could make casual clothes look so mouthwateringly sexy.

Pushing the door wider, Brodie stepped out. "Welcome, to you and the dog."

Seeing Mitch again lit an ache deep inside her. But he wasn't here for casual dating.

The man needed family.

And she needed to stay out of the way.

Realization of that wrought a sigh—and Mitch's attention zeroed in on her.

She felt…well, caught. Literally. As if she couldn't look away. His attention lingered a heartbeat more, just long enough, really, to make her breath thicken and send a flush to her face.

He didn't quite smile, but still she sensed his satisfaction before he drew his gaze away to take in the sprawling building for the Mustang Transport Courier Service.

Able to breathe again, she inhaled deeply, and took advantage of his distraction to enjoy a longer, more thorough look at him. His mussed hair looked as if he'd run his hands through it a few times. Faded jeans displayed the strength in his thighs, and the soft cotton shirt molded over his shoulders and chest before hanging more loosely around his narrower midsection.

No man should look that good—and yet, she couldn't stop staring.

When Mitch lifted a hand to shade his eyes, she stared at the flexing biceps.

Brodie nudged her, hard enough to make her stumble. "You're about to drool. Honest to God, it's almost embarrassing."

Afraid Mitch might hear, Charlotte hissed back, "Shut up," while managing a smile for Mitch's benefit.

Brodie snorted, but didn't say anything else.

Nervousness welled up as Mitch strode forward, and that irritated her. She didn't get nervous around men. One benefit of spending so much time with Brodie and Jack—she was usually immune to big, badass guys and their overly intent, intrusive ways. Next to them, she barely noticed other guys.

Not so with Mitch.

To cover her reaction, she concentrated on greeting the dog. "Who's this handsome fellow?"

Brodie said, "We already know his name is Mitch."

Jack choked on a laugh, but Mitch stalled, his gaze again snapping to Charlotte.

Heat scalded her face as she contemplated strangling Brodie's thick neck. "You *know* I meant the dog!"

"Yeah, I did." Brodie grinned. "But I figured we could lighten up the moment a little, you know?"

Wary, his jaw tight, Mitch put a hand to the dog's thick neck. "This is Brute. He's shy."

At the mention of his name, Brute looked up at Mitch with

adoration, then sat on his left sneaker with his shoulder pressed to Mitch's right leg. His tongue lolled out and he panted.

Charlotte couldn't help but be charmed. "He's gorgeous."

And Brodie, the never-ending ass, said, "Thanks. He looks a lot like me, don't you think?"

"The dog?" Charlotte snapped back. "Yes, given the slobber and open mouth, I see the resemblance!"

Jack decided to chime in with, "Comparing that animal to Brodie is an insult—for the dog."

This time, Mitch cracked a smile, and oh, it did devastating things to his already gorgeous looks.

Yes, he did look like Brodie, but not enough to bother her.

Ros said to Mitch, "We're surrounded by toddlers, and this one—" she swatted Brodie "—is the worst. If he doesn't knock it off, he'll be in a time-out."

"Yes, Mom," Brodie said dramatically, not the least concerned.

Hands in his pockets, Jack nodded at the black Mustang. "Nice car."

"Thanks. I only recently finished with it. A month ago, it looked like a quilt with one door and the hood in different colors, and all the primer in between."

One eye narrowed, Jack said, "I suppose Dad gave you the car?"

Mitch opened a hand over Brute's neck. "When I was fifteen."

"Figures." Holding the door wider, Jack indicated he should head down the hall. "He gave us Mustangs as well."

Surprise arched his brows. "Yeah?"

"It's his grand gesture," Brodie explained. "The only birthday gift I can remember from him."

"He thought it was my eighteenth birthday."

Mitch's half grin did crazy things to her stomach. She tried not to stare, she really did, but it took a lot of effort for her to give her attention to the dog.

The young pit bull kept pace with Mitch while avoiding everyone else.

"Did you tell him?" she asked, curious about his relationship with Elliott.

Mitch shook his head. "No. Getting it early worked out. It gave me a few years to work on it so it was running and road-safe before I had my license."

Brodie gave a gruff laugh. "Dad always shot for the eighteenth birthday—and always missed it by a few miles. I got mine at twenty-one and Jack got his at twenty-four."

That threw Mitch, interrupting his perusal of the offices. He went from curiously glancing around to perplexed. "But…he's your dad."

"Yours as well," Brodie said, urging him forward and into the break room. "If he led you to think he was a doting dad to us, he lied."

Brodie sprawled into a chair, and Ros seated herself across from him. Charlotte slipped in behind the others, hanging back so she wouldn't interfere, and wishing Brodie and Jack would lighten up on Elliott.

None of them knew how Mitch felt about the man.

It was one thing for family to air Elliott's faults, but if anyone else chimed in, Brodie and Jack naturally defended him. It came down to him being their father, and that broad sense of loyalty.

Did Mitch want to defend Elliott? Or did he want to do his own complaining? It wouldn't hurt to give him time to settle in so they could find out.

He glanced back at her. She smiled. He frowned and turned back to the others.

But he didn't take a seat.

A gentleman? How sweet.

"Mom raised us," Jack said as he too sat at the table. "Even before they divorced, Dad wasn't around much, and when he was, he was distracted with other things."

"And other women." Brodie's fingers drummed on the table-top as he looked up at Mitch. "Only useful thing he taught me was how to work on cars."

"Same here," Jack said.

As if unsure what to believe, maybe in deep thought, Mitch frowned. "I didn't realize…" He hesitated, one hand on the back of the chair. "Guess I had a different impression."

"Never mind them," Ros said, giving Brodie and Jack an effective glare. "Join us. Get comfortable."

Glancing back at Charlotte again, he gestured at the chair. "Why don't you sit?"

Now with everyone looking at her, she felt conspicuous. "That's okay. I might need to answer the phone or something." Her flustered laugh sounded ridiculous. "The office won't run itself."

Brodie snorted. "What she means is that Jack and I are idiots and didn't offer her a seat."

"You don't usually need to," she assured them. "I know how to sit myself down." And since the four of them were the only ones who used the break room, there'd always been enough chairs.

"One of us should have thought to get another chair," Ros said.

"I'll stand," Mitch said, again offering the chair.

Gawd, now she wanted to groan. "No, seriously. I'll be in and out, so…" She flapped a hand in insistence. "Sit."

The dog gave her a look…and sat.

That made them all chuckle.

Unconvinced but going along, Mitch patted Brute and then settled into a chair. The dog scooted over next to him.

The position near the door suited Charlotte. It was bad enough that she kept staring at the back of his head. She didn't need to sit at the table where he'd actually see her staring. Where she could look into his eyes. And at his mouth.

Awkwardness filled the space. She cleared her throat, earning another quick look from him.

"So." Brodie regarded him. "Did Dad teach you about cars too?"

With a laugh that he quickly cut short, Mitch shook his head. His succinct, "No," made it clear the idea of Elliott teaching him anything was pretty ludicrous.

Never in her life had she felt such a driving urge to hug a man.

He rubbed at one ear. "Thing is, when he visited, we usually went somewhere. For a burger or something, you know?"

"He should have helped you work on the car," Brodie said.

"Naw. He knew he couldn't. We didn't have a garage or anything, and out front of my house wouldn't work."

Charlotte wanted to ask, *Why not?* She opted to stay quiet instead. But she did scoot to the side a little, so she could see his profile. He had the same sharp cheekbones as the brothers, the same straight nose and squared chin.

"Elliott got it towed to a friend's house for me and I worked on it there."

"Alone?" Ros asked.

Muscles flexed as he lifted one shoulder and grinned. "Don't make it sound all tragic, okay? It gave me something to do, kept me busy." As if just remembering, he added, "He got me tools too to help me get started."

"Who taught you?" Jack asked.

"Trial and error, mostly." Definite humor lightened his tone. "I helped out at various garages from the time I was ten, and I guess I picked up a few things. My friend, Lang, had a cell phone, so sometimes he'd look up YouTube videos and stuff."

Mitch tried to paint a nice picture, but judging by expressions, no one bought into it.

He'd worked in garages from the time he was ten?

More softly, Ros asked, "How often did you see him?"

"Elliott?" Stalling, he sat back and pretended to consider the question, his posture relaxed but his expression tense. "I guess four or five times a year, at least until I was fifteen or so."

Charlotte could hear her own heartbeat in her ears as she waited to see who would ask.

Scowling, Jack took the honors. "And after you were fifteen?"

Smile sardonic, Mitch said, "Newman—my mom's boyfriend—became more of a regular deal."

"What did Newman have to do with it?" Brodie asked.

"Well, see, he was a grade-A pr..." He glanced over his shoulder at Charlotte, then Ros, and cleared his throat. "A real jerk. He and Elliott got into it pretty good a few times."

"They fought?" Brodie asked.

"It never quite came to that. I guess Newman ran him off."

"Pfft," Ros said. "Elliott could handle himself."

Amused by that, Mitch said, "You don't know Newman."

She smiled. "No, but I know Elliott."

Charlotte watched the curve of his mouth, heard his short laugh as he shook his head.

"If you say so. Thing is, Newman carried a knife and liked to use it."

"My wife carries a knife," Jack said. "And trust me, she likes to use hers as well. But I don't run from her."

That disclosure left Mitch brows-up and blinking. "Your wife?"

"She has deadly precision." Disgruntled as always when he discussed Ronnie's ability, Jack muttered, "Thank God she uses her powers for good and not evil."

Chuckling over that, Brodie told Mitch, "Wait until you meet Ronnie. Then you'll see what he means."

"Well..." Repeatedly, his gaze came back to Charlotte, and each time it felt like they connected physically.

At least to her. She had no idea what Mitch felt.

"Newman might not have that much power, but he's evil

all the way. He threatened to neuter Elliott if he came around again."

"He should have anyway," Ros stated, her tone gaining heat. "He should have done *something*."

"Yeah, well…" Again, he glanced at Charlotte, then blew out a breath. "Honestly, it makes me nervous having someone at my back."

"Oh." Once more the focus for everyone, she straightened away from the wall. "I'm sorry. I didn't—" He started to stand, but she quickly waved him back and moved more to his side. Now she could see all of his face—and he could see hers. "Is this better?"

Reluctantly, he sank back into his seat.

"If not, I could just go—"

"I'd rather you stay."

Every gaze in the room fixated on him this time.

As if he didn't care, he quirked a smile. "I don't mean to run you off. I'm just not used to sitting while a woman stands, and after prison—"

"You're a gentleman," she said fast, not wanting him forced to explain himself. With a look at Brodie and Jack, she teasingly added, "Unlike *some* people I know."

"She rarely stays in one spot for long." Brodie winked at her. "This is the longest, and it's because of her curiosity about you."

"Brodie!"

Jack rolled his eyes. "We're all curious about him, Charlotte. Don't screech."

Ohhh, when she got them alone, she'd…well, she didn't know. But she'd think of something.

Making a rewind gesture with her finger in the air, Ros said, "It's not right that Elliott didn't take care of you and your mother.

"He never gave you jack-shit," Brodie pointed out.

"I didn't need it." Ros looked at Mitch. "But his mother could have used money to—"

"She would have fed her addiction with it. That is, if Newman let her have any, which is doubtful." All seriousness now, he sat forward. "Giving my mom money would have been a pointless undertaking—worse than pointless because Newman would've used that money. I told Elliott so."

"So he'd offered?" Ros asked, slightly mollified.

"We talked about it, yeah. He compromised and occasionally gave me cash instead."

"How much?" Ros demanded.

For the longest time, Mitch just looked at his hand on Brute, rubbing over and around the dog's ears, along his scruff and down his back. When he finally looked up, somber and sincere, Charlotte held her breath.

She didn't know what he would say, but she knew it was important.

"The thing is, you're pissed at him. I get that. Not every day a man shows up and says he's a brother to your sons." The smile he flashed held no humor. "But you have to understand… Elliott's visits were a highlight for me. I don't know how much he gave me, but it doesn't matter." With his gaze direct, he said, "It was more than I got anywhere else."

"Then he should have—"

Cutting Ros off again, Mitch added, "I'm not mad about it. I'd rather you weren't either."

She subsided, but then reached for his hand. "I'm going to tell you the same thing I told my boys, okay? My relationship with Elliott is none of your business."

Those words, said in such a kind voice, startled Charlotte. Seemed they had the same effect on Mitch.

Brodie and Jack just smiled.

Apparently they'd heard this conversation more than once.

"He was my husband. He gave me two sons. Cheated on me

more than once. Let me down too many times to count." She squeezed Mitch's hand. "If I want to give him hell—and you can bet I do—then I will. It doesn't affect your relationship with him any more than it affected Brodie's or Jack's."

Seconds ticked by before Mitch finally grinned. "Yes, ma'am."

"Good." With a final squeeze, Ros released him. "One more thing—no more ma'aming me. Just call me Ros. I feel like we're already getting along."

CHAPTER FOUR

"When's the last time you saw him?" Charlotte asked, just to keep the conversation going now that it was so amicable.

"It's been a while. After that last big blowup with Newman waving around his knife, Elliott was real cautious whenever he came around. Usually he'd catch me on the street when I was away from home."

"But he did still come around?" Ros asked.

"Couple of times." Weighing his words, Mitch said, "Those last few times, he talked a lot."

"About what?" Jack asked.

"Newman, my mom." Mitch shrugged. "Mostly he talked about all of you."

Charlotte's jaw loosened at that disclosure. Of all the outrageous, callous...

Everyone seemed to straighten, drawn up by fury.

"He *talked* about us?" Jack asked, and although Charlotte saw the banked rage on Jack's face, she didn't think Mitch noticed.

"I liked hearing it." Mitch's hand idly stroked over Brute's ear again, and his voice lowered. "He especially talked about you, Ros."

"*Me?*"

"Yeah, all good stuff, I promise." He gifted Ros with a charming smile that made him appear more boyish. "Actually, the way he told it, I half expected to see a halo over your head."

"That son of a bitch," Brodie growled.

Yeah, there was no way Mitch could mistake the mood now. He gave Brodie a narrow-eyed stare. "He sang your praises."

"To *you,*" Brodie threw back. "I always knew he was flawed, but that's low even for him."

Charlotte touched Mitch's arm. "They're furious on your behalf, not at you."

For only a moment, he stared into her eyes, and his expression softened with some anomalous emotion that she couldn't read.

Scowling, Mitch turned away. "It was a mistake to mention it. I never meant to cause strife."

Thankful that no one else seemed to notice that short, heated connection she'd just had with Mitch, Charlotte retreated to let the others convince him.

"Don't apologize." A muscle ticked in Jack's jaw. "Dad should have told us about you too, but he…"

"Didn't." Mitch nodded, then explained, "He couldn't."

"Bullshit." Brodie's hand curled into a fist on the table. "We're related. He damn well should have introduced us."

That actually made Mitch laugh, the sound more incredulous than amused. "How do you think that introduction would have gone?"

Without missing a beat, Ros said, "Brodie and Jack, meet your brother." Her hand slapped the table. "Done. That's how."

Edgier by the second, Mitch shook his head. "It would have complicated things."

"For him," Jack said.

"And for me. You think my mother or Newman wouldn't have used me to try to extort money from you? They'd have seen this—" he gestured at the office they sat in "—and figured you had plenty to share. Anything was more than Newman had, because he destroyed everything around him."

Concern brought Charlotte a step closer—until Mitch pinned her with his incendiary gaze.

He appeared desperate...and determined to deny it.

Seeing that she wouldn't touch him again, he returned his attention to the others. "You think Newman wouldn't have threatened all of you, stole from you, or worse? Believe me, he would have." Sitting forward, Mitch folded his arms on the table. "If Elliott had introduced us when I was younger, I wouldn't be here now, and that's the truth. I'd have been too ashamed to ever show my face again."

Unable to stand it a second more, Charlotte stepped close and, reaching past the dog—who watched her—put her hand on Mitch's shoulder.

He went stiff, his breath catching.

Did she affect him as strongly as he did her? It seemed so.

Quiet settled in around them.

He shifted back—and effectively removed her hand.

It burned her, that rejection, but she would not let this be about her. Especially since she understood his need to keep control—of his emotions, and the situation. Softly, needing him to accept it, she whispered, "You have no reason for shame."

Mitch laughed. "That's ironic, right? I'm an ex-con, but I'm less ashamed now that my mother is gone and Newman isn't involved in my life anymore." He ran a hand through his hair, leaving it messy. "If nothing else, that should convince you that Elliott did all of you a favor, keeping quiet about me."

Anyone could see that Mitch believed what he said, one hundred percent. Somehow, that made it worse.

Though it was unlike her, Charlotte didn't know what to do or say. She wasn't good with awkward silences, excesses of emotion, or idle time, and she especially didn't like it now.

She didn't dare touch him again. He might tolerate Ros's affection, but he'd made it clear where it pertained to Charlotte.

Trying to find her usual manner, hoping it would help restore some balance, she blurted, "Coffee, anyone?" She already knew what Jack and Brodie would say, so she glanced at Mitch. "I made it right before you got here."

As if he couldn't help himself, his gaze went to her mouth—and stayed there a few seconds too long. "Sure, thanks."

More confused by the second, scorched by that intimate look and still reeling from being rebuffed, she had a hard time finding her voice. "Um…cream and sugar?"

"Black is fine."

Filling the mugs gave her a second to regroup. It wasn't long enough, not with the silence in the room. Trying a smile that didn't feel too steady, she set a mug in front of Mitch, then turned to get more for everyone else.

Ros fussed at her, saying, "You should let these slugs get their own."

Mitch went still, but Ros smiled at him. "You're a guest, so you weren't included in the slug insult."

"No, that was strictly for us," Jack said, blowing on the coffee Charlotte handed him before taking a sip.

"I don't mind." She gave another to Brodie and one to Ros before placing a plate of cookies on the round table. Brodie grabbed two, Jack took two, but Mitch hesitated.

God, he had beautiful eyes. Not sinfully dark like Ros, Brodie and Jack, but more of a golden brown, and so very intense.

Stop it. Ogling him would not help the situation one iota. And hey, if he didn't want her cookies, it was his loss. Personally, she'd found a good cookie helped everything.

"Charlotte's a terrific cook," Brodie said, lifting the plate to hold it under Mitch's nose. "When was the last time you had homemade chocolate chip cookies?"

Deadpan he said, "Let's see, it must've been…never?" Giving in, he accepted one, took a bite, and made a rumbling, sexy sound of pleasure. "Damn, that's good."

"Right?" Brodie still held the plate. "Grab a few more before they're gone."

With that same irresistible grin, Mitch took two more and nodded at Charlotte. "Thanks."

Blink, she told herself. Breathing would be good too. She gave a ridiculous little laugh that had both Jack and Brodie eyeing her, but thankfully they didn't say anything.

Ros asked, "Would Brute like a treat? We keep them around the office since Jack and Brodie have pets."

The dog leaned against Mitch's chair, his furry chin on a denim-covered thigh. "He might." Mitch stroked down his back, then patted his muscled shoulder. "Want a treat, Brute?"

The dog's eyebrows beetled and he slanted a look at Ros.

"He understands the word *treat*," Mitch explained. "And he knows you said it first."

"What a smart guy," Ros praised, scratching under his chin.

"My dog, Howler—who's aptly named, by the way—understands any mention of food. You can't ask for an orange highlighter because he thinks you're getting out fruit and he's always hopeful there'll be cheese or meat to go with it."

Half grinning, Mitch asked, "You're serious?"

"He's the biggest mooch—"

"The biggest *everything*," Jack interjected.

"—that you'll ever meet." Brodie smiled. "Long legs, long face, long tail...he's a lovable goofball who tries to mother other animals, especially when they're shy or timid. You can trust him with Brute."

Needing something to do, Charlotte said, "I'll get one of Howler's favorite treats and we'll see if Brute feels the same." The dog tracked her as she ducked out of the room...and so did Mitch. That hot gaze made her skin tingle.

This was crazy! Never in her life had she been so aware of a man. Some looked at her, yes. A few had asked her out, but it never lasted long. She'd known for a while that she didn't have "it," whatever it was—that elusive something that drew in people from the opposite sex.

Most in this town only remembered her because of Brodie or Jack. *"You work with Brodie Crews, don't you?"* or *"Jack Crews treats you like a little sister, right?"* There were even a few women who'd tried to get her to set them up with the guys before they'd married.

Now everyone knew both Brodie and Jack were off the market. Some still flirted, but the guys pretended to be oblivious to the attention.

They caused a stir—not her.

Never her.

Sure, she figured she'd eventually find a guy who was equally unassuming, just as business-minded and…boring.

Bleh.

Instead, she had *this* man, looking at her *that* way, and it made her giddy with the pleasure of it.

To make it worse, she was equally drawn to him.

She didn't know how to stop it, and wasn't sure she even wanted to. You only lived once, right?

When would another man like Mitch come around? If she had to wait another twenty-five years, she'd be fifty.

Not an encouraging thought.

Newly determined, Charlotte returned with the flavored bone-shaped treat from the desk in the main office. When she stepped back into the break room, Brute immediately sniffed the air.

Sitting on the floor yoga style, Charlotte patted her thigh to beckon the dog. Everyone watched her while Brute hesitated, then reluctantly ambled over. She held out the treat on the palm of her hand, and Brute oh-so-gingerly took it from her. Instead of hurrying back to Mitch, he stuck close, sprawling on his stomach to start crunching the bone.

Charlotte wasn't sure if he accepted her or forgot all about her.

"Huh." A mix of pleasure and fascination warmed Mitch's smile. "He rarely leaves my side."

The dog's short black fur was soft and shiny as Charlotte stroked along his strong back, proof that he was well fed and cared for. Splotches of white whiskers decorated the left side of his nose and trailed upward like a streak between his brown eyes. Two toes on his front left paw, his belly and the tip of his long skinny tail were also white. Powerful jaws made short work of the snack. When Brute finished, he snuffled her fingers as if looking for more, then rolled to his side and stretched.

She couldn't hold back a grin as Brute gave a groan and closed his eyes. "Such a heartbreaker."

As a true animal lover, Brodie watched it all with a grin. "He's a pit bull?"

"The vet says he's actually a Pitterdale, like a Pit bull–Patterdale Terrier mix."

"Where'd you get him?" Jack asked.

"I inherited him." He looked over the dog and Charlotte both, then turned to Brodie. "It's a shit story." To Ros, he added, "Apologies for the language, but it's true."

"Pfft." She waved that off. "We know something about rescuing animals."

"Yeah?"

By the minute, Mitch relaxed more, his wide shoulders not as stiff, his muscles less bunched. Charlotte imagined the idle chitchat helped. He'd probably been expecting an immediate round of skeptical questions fired in rapid succession, along with anger and resentment.

Instead, this wonderful family did the same thing for Mitch that they'd done for her: they offered patience, understanding and acceptance.

She understood their ploy now too; it'd be easier for him to chat about the dog than all the family issues, so she did her part to help that conversation along. "Brodie rescued Howler. It's still hard to think about how he was treated."

"Chained out in the heat, without water or food." The memory left Ros scowling. "We were all so glad when Brodie brought him home from there."

"After busting a few heads," Jack interjected, and when Mitch gave him a questioning look, he clarified, "The abusive bastards weren't happy to have their day interrupted."

Mitch grinned at Brodie. "Good for you."

Brodie shrugged. "It was my pleasure."

With a short laugh, Mitch said, "I get the feeling you enjoy a brawl every now and then."

Good grief, but the smile added a dangerous edge to Mitch's appeal, almost making Charlotte sigh. She kept herself in check with an effort. "Jack adopted Buster, a young Lab retriever, right after he and Ronnie had also rescued a kitten."

Jack sipped his coffee. "They're all good friends."

"And part of the family," Brodie added as Brute began to snore. "He's good with other animals?"

"He's a big baby." Smile fading, Mitch stared toward the dog with affection. "Given how I found him, it makes sense."

"You mentioned inheriting him?" Charlotte wasn't sure how that would work, especially since he didn't sound close to many people.

"Something like that." His brows came together and his mouth firmed. "I told you I left my mom's place as soon as I could. I didn't visit often either, usually only when I knew Newman wasn't around—or if she'd been hurt." Muscles flinched his jaw, as if he ground his teeth. "That's probably why I didn't know the bastard had been breeding dogs."

His expression didn't change, but Charlotte saw his hand clench, and she saw him deliberately relax again. He put on a front of control but she knew every second of this was difficult for him. Naturally so. He was a grown man seeking his roots with strangers while sharing an unpleasant past.

"How did you find out?" Charlotte asked, hoping to keep him talking so they could all get through it.

He didn't look at her this time, choosing instead to keep his attention on Brute. "Mom died before I was released, but no one took over the house. I didn't realize it was in my name until the city contacted me. They wanted to demolish it, along with several others, to expand the highway that ran behind it. Not a big loss since it was a dump and always had been." Derision curved his mouth. "Probably put a bunch of dealers out of business though. For as far back as I could remember, they were always there, on every corner." He gave a rough laugh. "Hookers too actually."

That disquieting revelation hung in the air until Ros asked, "You didn't get to attend your mother's funeral?"

He shook his head. "Probably just as well, though. If I'd seen Newman, I might've been facing the inside of a cell again." He released the coffee cup and blew out a breath. "Five years was long enough, and Newman was never worth it."

Sympathy crowded Charlotte's heart. "How did she die?"

"Overdose." No emotion showed on his face. "She was dead a week before anyone found her."

Another stunned silence preceded Brodie's burst of anger. "Where the hell was Newman?"

Mitch shook his head in dismissal. "Don't know, don't care." Studying Brute again, he drew a slow breath. "Anyway, I went over to the house to see if there was anything to salvage. You know, pictures or anything."

Jack nodded.

As if he heard something in Mitch's tone, Brute sat up, his ears going back and his furry little brows twitching. Mitch automatically reached down, his fingers open—and Brute went to him, fitting his square head into Mitch's palm.

She couldn't miss the dog's apparent understanding for Mitch's emotions.

Glancing around at the others, Charlotte was willing to bet a few hearts melted. Hers certainly did. If nothing else spoke of Mitch's character, the closeness he had with his dog sure did.

"So," Jack prompted. "Did you find anything?"

"Not what I'd hoped." Mitch looked down at Brute, his dark expression at odds with the gentle way he touched the dog. "What wasn't stolen was destroyed. There were four people passed out around the floor, squatters too stoned or drunk to even know I was there. The smell was unbearable." Pain and regret showed in the stillness of his face. "I almost walked out."

Charlotte watched his Adam's apple move in his tanned throat. She hugged herself, knowing it wouldn't be good.

When Mitch looked up, it was her eyes he focused on. "I heard something that didn't sound right. Like a cry, you know?"

Eyes already burning, she nodded.

"The dogs were in the basement."

Her breath shuddered in. *Dogs*. Oh, God. She heard Brodie and Jack stirring, hear Ros's small gasp.

"The mother was chained to the wall, in her own filth." His jaw worked. "Starved to death. One of her pups was dead too." He drew a fresh breath. "The only one alive was Brute."

Almost overturning his chair, Brodie pushed to his feet, drawing attention from both Mitch and Brute.

Jack went completely quiet.

Charlotte couldn't move.

Scratching Brute's ear, Mitch continued. "He was thin, but I saw a few dead rats. I think that's how he managed. The lid on the sump pump was moved, so he must've been drinking water from there."

Water that the mother couldn't reach. In that moment, Charlotte wished she could chain Newman in a basement. Let him eat a rat and suffer dehydration. *Bastard*. Miserable, awful bastard.

She loved animals, always had and always would. Hearing the story was devastating enough—but knowing Mitch had suffered Newman as well? Unbearable.

Just as he'd rescued Brute, she wished for a way to rescue Mitch. He was here now, with family.

Would that be enough?

"Brute was a little thing, his bones showing under his flesh. I thought he might bite, not from aggression but more out of desperation, you know?"

Biting her lip, Charlotte nodded her understanding. Desperation made animals—and people—do things they could regret.

"Instead he literally crawled to me on his belly, begging for everything. Affection, food, water." Mitch curled his fingers against Brute, then gave him a firm pat that made the dog's tail wag. "He was the only thing I took from the house. I went back later and buried the other two dogs before unloading the house on the state. Brute and I... Well, I'm all he has."

"Not anymore." Swiping away a tear, Ros smiled at the dog. "Now you both have family."

Mitch's frown was more ferocious than ever.

After refilling coffee cups, whether anyone wanted more coffee or not, Brodie paused by Mitch's chair. His expression firm, his tone somber, he stated, "We're glad you're both here." He clasped Mitch's shoulder. "*Glad*."

Taken aback by that, Mitch shook his head. "I find that so damn hard to believe."

"Only because you don't know them better." Charlotte swiped at her own damp cheeks. "They're all pretty terrific."

"Right—they're terrific, but my past..."

"Is in your past, right?" Brodie put away the carafe, and on his way back to his seat, he added, "We start now."

Not buying it, Mitch looked from one face to another, and

seemed distrustful of the encouraging smiles. "I appreciate... whatever this is—"

"Acceptance," Jack said simply. "You're a brother. Our brother. End of story."

"—but you have to have more questions," he finished firmly. "A ton of them, I imagine."

"Expect us to grill you, huh?"

"Of course I do." With palpable frustration, Mitch rubbed the back of his neck. "Unless you tell me half brothers pop up all the time, none of it makes sense."

"Fine," Jack said, all accommodating and smooth. "I have questions."

And, Charlotte thought, here we go.

No matter how Mitch tried to resist her, Charlotte drew his gaze, again and again. He fought it, and still it happened.

He hadn't come here to see her. Hell, he hadn't even known she was in the picture. Elliott mostly talked about his perfect wife and the two sons he was so proud of.

Unlike him, Charlotte wasn't an outsider.

But she wasn't family either and maybe that made a difference. With her, he didn't feel as cautious. She was too friendly, too...soft, for him to see her as anything other than a woman.

The fact that she openly stared at him didn't help either.

Even now, she watched him like she'd never seen a man before—or she liked what she saw.

Absurd. If big muscular guys were her type, she had two sterling examples that she worked with every day.

As Rosalyn had said, Mitch looked more like Elliott than they did. Also, neither of them wore the taint of imprisonment, an invisible filth he could never wash away.

That made them more appropriate for Charlotte, and yet they'd married other women.

If Charlotte hadn't been interested in them, why was she devouring him with those sky-blue eyes? He glanced at her again, caught her gaze, and damn it, he felt a connection sizzle along his spine.

He'd never felt anything like it, a combo of sharp awareness, affinity, and...need.

He looked away.

Even though Brute had returned to his side, Charlotte stayed on the floor. It was distracting as hell, that was the problem. What woman sat on the floor while the men all sat comfortably in chairs? Neither Brodie nor Jack seemed to notice or care, and it wasn't Mitch's place to get her sweet little butt in a proper seat—though he had tried.

And failed.

When Jack hesitated, Mitch decided to get the ball rolling. "Seriously. I didn't expect to get this far." In their offices, sitting together with coffee and cookies? Nope, not something he'd ever imagined. "You got questions, go for it."

Brodie turned his chair to straddle it. "I'll go first. What *did* you expect?"

Damn. He couldn't say for sure, but based off his usual experiences... "Anger. Disinterest." He glanced at Rosalyn, but that remarkable lady left him humbled so he looked away. "Maybe resentment."

Earnest, Brodie nodded. "Yeah, I get those expectations. But know this, the only reason anyone's pissed is because Dad never said anything."

"I'm *definitely* furious about that," Rosalyn said. "Elliott has a lot of failings that I've overlooked through the years. This crosses a line, though."

Of course it did, and he hated that his actions might have caused Rosalyn discomfort. "I hadn't planned on meeting you, so I didn't think you'd ever know." He also hadn't counted on meeting Charlotte. Whenever Elliott had mentioned that name, it was only in the context of an employee. Eliott had called her sweet, but that didn't even begin to cover it. Since he first laid eyes on her, his plans had gone off the rails.

Add in this uncomfortable stuff with Rosalyn, and he wasn't sure how to proceed.

As if avoiding his mom was somehow hilarious, Jack laughed. "So what was the plan?"

"Meet the two of you. Really, that's all there was to it. I thought I'd introduce myself, and take it from there. But then I met her—" he shrugged toward Charlotte without quite looking at her "—and everyone showed up. If I'd realized the association, I wouldn't have—" He tripped over his own tongue, drawing to a fast halt.

"Hit on her?" Brodie prompted.

And predictably, Charlotte growled, "Why can't you stop being an ass for five minutes?"

"What? It's been half an hour."

Jack grinned. Even Ros smiled. Mitch had a feeling that if he gave in and looked at Charlotte, she'd be blushing again.

Were they really amused instead of furious that he'd come on to her? Or maybe they thought his interest had died—as it should have—the moment he realized the connection? "That's not exactly what happened." He hadn't officially come on to her—although if he'd had a little more time… "I saw she had car trouble, and then two guys from the bar—"

"He offered me help," Charlotte blurted. "That's all."

But Jack and Brodie had already stiffened, their gazes turning on her with accusation.

It was Rosalyn who asked, "What guys from the bar?"

Charlotte groaned, and he realized she'd wanted that part of the evening kept private.

Obviously, these two were the men she'd used to threaten Bernie. She might have qualms about outing the little weasel and his pal, but Mitch didn't.

His look warned her of what was to come, then he said to

Brodie, "Squirrelly little dude named Bernie pressed her. He and a pal were stinking drunk and saying things they shouldn't."

Brodie's eyes narrowed. "What *things*?"

Jack snorted. "You know Bernie, so you can imagine. I'll have a talk with him."

"You had your chance and he's still an ass-hat. This time I'll talk to him."

"Yeah," Jack conceded. "You may be right."

Shooting to her feet, Charlotte startled them all. "Neither of you will do a damn thing. God, is it any wonder I'm ignored around here?"

Ignored? Seriously? Were all the men in town—present company excluded—total fools? What red-blooded hetero dude would meet Charlotte and *not* want her?

Rosalyn examined a nail. "Mitch didn't ignore you."

Oh, shit. All eyes turned on him so he held up his hands. "That's because I didn't know."

"*See?*" With a growl, Charlotte stormed out.

Curiosity, that odd connection, *something* glued his gaze to her and he swiveled on his seat to watch her go. Anger added an extra sway to her hips.

She reached the end of the hallway and instead of pushing the doors open and going outside, she suddenly stopped. Narrow back going stiff, she jerked around to stare toward him.

He recognized mortification when he saw it.

So she'd blown up and stormed away? Big deal. Did she think he'd consider it childish? Petty? She shouldn't.

The lady could make an exit or an entrance, and he'd only notice her softness, her appeal.

Her sensuality.

He excelled at making women feel good.

With Charlotte, he could make her weep with pleasure. That's what he thought about, nothing else.

Blindly reaching behind her, she braced a hand on the door.

Yeah, Mitch thought. *I'm not going anywhere.* New possibilities occurred to him, ideas beyond family.

Carnal ideas—wait, *what?* Slamming the brakes on that heated line of thought, he jerked around to face Brodie and Jack, knowing they'd see his guilt.

Knowing they'd want to run him out of town to protect Charlotte.

They still watched *her*, not him.

"That's right," Brodie said low, as if speaking to himself, "now you gotta come back."

"She'll strangle you if she does," Jack warned. "I might help."

Mitch let out a breath.

At least they weren't thinking of strangling him.

If he kept fantasizing over her, then they might…and yet, he wasn't sure he could stop.

CHAPTER FIVE

Rosalyn pushed back her chair. "I'll go talk to her." She pointed at Jack and Brodie. "You two better knock it off."

Brodie said, "Yes, Mom," while Jack asked, "What did I do?"

To Mitch, Rosalyn said, "Don't go anywhere." She patted his shoulder and then she too left the room.

Since the brothers still stared down the hallway after Charlotte, Mitch gave in to the urge to do the same. He turned in time to see her plow out the door, Rosalyn following close behind her.

Seeing her grit left him with a stupid smile on his face. The brothers treated her like a little sister, but he saw her as so much more. Last night, she'd held her own against Bernie. Hell, she'd known exactly how to handle him too—until the rest of the family had shown up.

He'd like the opportunity to learn more about her. She was an amazing cook, an energetic dynamo, a woman with great intuition and a heart so big, even his apprehensive dog had fallen for her. All in all, she fascinated him—and she made him forget his troubles.

When was the last time he'd smiled so much? Too long ago to remember.

"If we don't get coffee tomorrow," Jack grumbled at Brodie, "it'll be your fault."

"Yeah, probably." He dropped back in his seat and said to Mitch, "It's like she grew up overnight, you know?"

Uh, no, he didn't, but Brodie's comment reinforced the idea that he saw her as a sister—which Mitch appreciated. "She has to be mid-twenties, right?" *Please* let her be mid-twenties.

"Twenty-five," Jack confirmed. "Though Brodie likes to think she's still sixteen."

"Twenty-five," Brodie mused. He rubbed his face and added, "Damn."

With no idea of the problem, Mitch waited for Brodie to continue. Didn't take long at all.

"She was always quiet, not really shy but super self-contained. Guys didn't pay much attention to her, which was fine by me, and then *bam!* All of a sudden every jackass around is eyeballing her, and they're all wrong for her."

"Including Bernie?" Not that it was in question. Charlotte herself had set Bernie straight, and made her disdain loud and clear. The lady didn't suffer fools—or drunken idiocy.

"Bernie is definitely not for her," Jack confirmed. "But Brodie doesn't think anyone is good enough."

"And you do?" Brodie challenged.

With a shrug, Jack said, "Up to now? No."

They both looked at him.

Mitch didn't know if that was a warning or a question.

He did know, without a single doubt, that he wasn't good enough for her—but acknowledging it rubbed him wrong. Did she deserve more? From what he knew of her so far, hell yes.

Would he let that stop him?

Hard to say.

He wanted to know his brothers, to maybe be a part of their

lives. He had a hunger inside him, a desire to belong. As a young man, he'd refused to acknowledge it.

Prison hadn't been good for much, but it did give him time to prioritize, to do some soul searching and come to grips with his life, his mistakes... It helped him put things in perspective.

He wanted family. Today, at least, he'd made progress on that, more progress than he'd dared to hope for.

Letting brothers dictate to him though? Yeah, not sure how he felt about that one.

"How old are you?" Jack asked him.

"Twenty-nine." Not too old for Charlotte, though sometimes he felt ancient.

"Ever been married?" Brodie asked.

The line of questioning had taken a sharp turn. He shook his head. "Never been all that involved with any woman." He looked them in the eyes and gave an uncomfortable truth. "When I think of the future though, what I want and what I'm willing to work for, settling down seems the logical way to go."

"Logical?" They looked at each other and laughed. Scooting his chair, Brodie got closer and then slung an arm around his shoulders. "Let me tell ya about marriage, okay?"

Odd, how comfortable Brodie felt with him. On the one hand, he could count the attitude as progress. On the other... he wasn't big on people touching him.

Except maybe Charlotte. Her touch had been both a balm and enticement rolled into one.

Jack guffawed at Brodie's show. "You? You're going to explain marriage?"

"And why wouldn't I? Mary is living bliss."

"Is that what you call it?" Jack lounged back with a secretive smile. "If you want to know about making it all work, I'm the one you want to talk to."

Brodie started to speak, then conceded the point. "Ronnie would gut me if I said otherwise."

Their antics amused him. It wouldn't be a bad idea to learn more about a normal marriage. He knew what he wanted—a place to call home, a faithful wife and a couple of kids he could love the right way.

What that actually entailed, he couldn't say. He sure as hell hadn't experienced anything like it. Hearing from Elliott was the closest he'd ever come to hearing about love—and he'd been cheating on a great woman like Ros, and ignoring his legit sons.

That negated much of what he'd said.

"I've done things…" That path would lead to more questions, some that he didn't want to answer, so Mitch switched gears. "I know I've made mistakes. Too many to count."

"Seems to me," Jack offered quietly, "you didn't have a ton of options."

Unlike some of the prisoners Mitch had known, he had no intention of using his shitty upbringing as an excuse to be a dick. Not then, and not now. "There are always options." Leaving his seat, and displacing Brodie's arm from his shoulders, he moved around the narrow free space in the room. Not really pacing, but too agitated to sit. "That's behind me now. You have my word, for what's it worth."

For him, the past would be a lesson on what not to do. Any kid of his would have it all. Love, acceptance. Security. Protection. One way or another, he'd ensure those things.

Until today, he hadn't met a woman who seemed the right type to help with that—but given their wary expressions, Mitch wasn't about to bring Charlotte into this discussion. Better to keep his vague intentions private.

"Your word is good enough."

Disbelieving, maybe afraid to believe, he stared at Jack and saw stark honesty in his dark gaze. That didn't make sense, so he glanced at Brodie…and saw the same.

Shaking his head, a little in denial, partially to clear his thoughts, Mitch marveled at them. "I don't know what to say."

"You could tell us you plan to settle here," Brodie ventured. "That'd be a good start."

"I do." He didn't tell them it was a done deal—not until he had something more to show for it. "Seems like a good place." The people were casual and friendly, a little too curious about new faces, and hardworking. He liked the atmosphere. He liked the area.

He especially liked the idea of calling it home.

"Glad to hear it," Jack told him, standing also, joined by Brodie. "Why don't we show you around?"

"There's an apartment attached at the end of this building," Brodie said. "Mom raised us there, then I lived there while my house was being built."

Mitch had no problem with that. He called Brute to him, and they headed out. On their way past the inner office, he spotted Charlotte inside, on the phone, her back to them. How had she gotten back inside without him hearing her?

The answer, of course, was that she'd been sneaky.

Pausing outside the door, he watched as she alternately shuffled papers and jotted notes, all while talking. Brodie and Jack stood by the door, waiting for him. But screw it.

He wouldn't be sneaky. Raising a hand, he lightly rapped two knuckles on the window.

Jerking around, she stared at him, blinked…and summoned up a smile. Without leaving her seat, she stretched for the door and opened it. For only a second she covered the phone. "You're not leaving, are you?"

If she wanted him to stay, she had a funny way of showing it. "For now."

Into the phone, she said, "I have you down for Thursday the second. Yes, of course. It's my pleasure." Absently she disconnected the call and put the phone on the desk.

Still with papers in hand, she said, "I don't mean to be rude, but it's busy today."

"No problem." He lingered a second more, then leaned in through the doorway. "Plenty of time for us to get acquainted."

"Oh...okay." Her smile brightened several watts. "Yes, I'd like that."

His gaze moved over her face, and he felt himself smiling too. Amazing. "Thank you, Charlotte."

Her brows lifted. "For what?"

"The cookies. The company. Befriending my dog." *And for making me lighthearted enough to smile.* "A dozen things." He gave her a look she couldn't misinterpret. "I'd go into it more, but the guys are waiting for me."

Happiness seemed a part of her, especially here in this moment. "You are very welcome," she said with soft sincerity, then added with her own meaning, "Anytime."

Ros returned from the store with premade sandwiches for lunch. Though Charlotte was invited to join in, she stayed busy with work, bustling around the offices from one room to the next, eating half a sandwich and some chips on the go.

Not for a single second was she unaware of Mitch, but she did her best not to ogle him—or to acknowledge when he seemed to ogle her.

No man had ever taken such personal notice of her.

She was both flattered and thrown off guard.

A jerk like Bernie she could handle. But a man like Mitch?

Fanning her face, she detoured into the storage area for more file folders. Unfortunately, Mitch consumed her thoughts.

It was odd to see someone so big and capable, with such obvious strength, and yet...shades of vulnerability surrounded him. He'd probably deny that—he was enough like Brodie and Jack that she instinctively knew he'd rebel against admitting a weakness.

"Busy again?"

Spinning around, she found him standing there in the doorway, watching her. With his presence alone, he got her heart thumping.

Trying for a light laugh, she said, "Work is never done it seems."

"Or," he countered softly, "you take your responsibilities very seriously."

"Of course."

His mouth curled as if she'd given the expected answer…and it pleased him. "I thought you'd join us for lunch."

"I wanted to." That admission had her flushing. "I mean…"

"I wanted you to," he said, before she could take it back or give it different meaning. "Are you ever not working?"

When she faltered, he stepped away from the door and shoved his hands in his pockets.

Thinking he got the wrong impression, she nodded fast, realized what she was doing, and made herself be still. "I have free time every now and then."

"Good to know, because I feel like we got interrupted before. By Bernie, I mean."

"Bernie is an idiot."

Humor glittered in his eyes. "Agreed." He looked over his shoulder toward the hallway, then back to her. "See you soon, then?"

Again, she nodded, but followed it up with, "Yes. Definitely."

He returned to the others, and she dropped back against a file cabinet. She needed to get a handle on her over-the-top reaction to him. To call it embarrassing would be an understatement.

As she passed back out to the hall, she heard Ros inviting him to dinner.

And she heard him finding reasons to refuse. Funny that he wanted to see *her*, but not the others. Funny—and also wrong. Maybe, if she handled things the right way, she could help him to be more at ease with them.

Things were probably moving a little too fast. He'd expected one thing, and had gotten something altogether different.

From what they'd learned already, she knew Mitch was a survivor, but a cautious one—when caution was unnecessary, even unwanted, with his family.

And yes, with her.

Damn it, in many ways meeting him reminded her that she too was an outsider. No, that wasn't the right word. In every way that mattered, the Crews family had made her part of their inner circle. She didn't share their blood, but she shared their lives.

She could show Mitch the way, explain to him how remarkable and warm this family—*his family*—could be.

Though she hesitated to intrude, she knew the others would willingly include her.

A few minutes later, Brodie found her standing there, staring into space and eavesdropping. With a dry grin he caught her arm and urged her back into the storage area.

Voice low, he asked, "You're okay?"

"Why wouldn't I be?"

"Well." He eyed her. "There's that bit with me being an ass?"

God, he was such a big, lovable oaf. "Yeah, there's that—but it's not a big deal. Just you being you."

His expression softened to tenderness. "I'm sorry if I embarrassed you."

She peered at the door, decided no one could hear them, and blew out a breath. "I was embarrassed, but more by my dumb reaction." She ended up smiling too. "Ros gave me hell."

"No kidding?" Propping one boulder shoulder on the wall, Brodie guessed, "For being a wimp?"

Slapping a hand over her mouth barely stifled her laugh. She *had* been a wimp, and Ros didn't mind telling her so—especially since it was so unlike her.

Struggling to keep her humor under wraps, she whispered, "She basically told me to gather my gumption and quit hiding."

In a tone far too sweet for a guy like Brodie, he asked, "Were you hiding, hon?"

"Maybe. For a few minutes." Putting her shoulders back, she said, "Not anymore." Especially not after Mitch made his interest plain. "Now I'm just busy."

Guilt put a frown on his face. "You shouldn't be too busy to visit."

If only that were true. She'd picked up what she could to free up time for Brodie and Jack. If she told him that, he'd really feel bad. "Mitch isn't going anywhere, right? I'm sure I'll see him again soon. For today though, let me do what I do best, okay?"

"Keep the business running?"

Already on her way out, she tossed a smile at Brodie. "Exactly." This time she didn't glance in the break room at Mitch as she hurried along the hall to the inner office.

But heaven help her, she felt his gaze—and she was pretty sure it moved all over her.

Over the next few days, Mitch made up his mind to go at his own pace. It'd be better, easier, to move slowly—for him, and for them. They needed time to get to know him, to understand his intentions, to know he wasn't trying to use them.

And he needed time to trust the whirlwind acceptance.

Having a junkie for a mom had made him cautious, especially when her chosen boyfriend took pleasure in trying to break him—and she hadn't cared. Or at least, hadn't cared enough to change things. That had set the standard for his life, and he'd made his way by not trusting anyone—yet now he'd met the most insanely trusting people ever.

He almost felt like *he* had to protect *them*—because they didn't seem to be protecting themselves. At the very least, they should have put him on a month-long probationary period.

Instead, they'd opened their arms and were doing their damnedest to open their homes.

Crazy, that's what it was.

He didn't need cozy family dinners. He didn't need hugs—

not that Ros ever listened to his objections—and he didn't need sympathy.

He didn't need anything, wouldn't ask for anything—except acknowledgment.

Time. Opportunity.

Eventually, yeah, he'd love to join them as family.

For now, he took pleasure in getting to know them better— especially when that meant getting to know Charlotte more too.

His brothers shared facets of their lives, which included a lot of anecdotes about Charlotte, all of it nice.

He also answered a million questions.

Funny thing though, the questions were all superficial. Made them easier to answer, sure, but also kept a cloud of unknowns shrouding them.

Unfortunately, he hadn't had enough opportunity to visit with Charlotte. Oh, she greeted him when he came by, and her smiles were friendly whenever he could pin her down. She offered him coffee and food, she doted on Brute.

But she was being cautious.

For her benefit or his?

No way to know—yet. So for now, while he got better acquainted with his brothers, he didn't push it.

Even though he liked having her near. In an uncomfortable, and surprisingly pleasant way, she stirred long-dormant emotions, feelings he'd forgotten and now wanted to refuse.

When he put his head down for the night, it was Charlotte and that stirring touch of hers, the curve of her luscious mouth and her soft blue eyes that consumed his thoughts.

She kept him in a fever.

He had a feeling she was adjusting to things too. Did the strength of the attraction throw her for a loop? It wasn't his nature to pressure a woman, but soon, very soon, he'd see where he stood with her.

Earlier today Brodie and Jack had worked, so it was late after-

noon, nearing suppertime when he arrived at Mustang Transport. He anticipated at least seeing Charlotte, even if just in
passing, but the brothers had just gotten there themselves, and
they compared Mustangs. Brodie's was red, Jack's yellow and
his black. Restoring cars was something they had in common,
sort of a natural talent to make an older classic shine like new.

Talk of cars led to the name of the business—which now made
sense to him—and they explained details on the transportation
business, which he had to admit, sounded fascinating.

Today alone, Brodie had driven to Corbin, Kentucky, and
back again, which meant seven hours on the road at least, traffic
pending, just to grab some weird little art sculpture for his em-
ployer. If it weren't for this meeting, would he and Mary have
spent the night? Seemed likely.

At the very least, there wouldn't have been such a rush.

"You know, I understand if you guys need to put me under
a microscope for a while. But on busy days like this, a breather
would be fine."

Baffled, Brodie frowned at him. "What are you talking about?"

"This. Running home from a job just to grab a few minutes
to chat." He shook his head. "After all that driving, you have
to be beat. I'm not in a rush—"

"Well, we are," Jack said. "We have a lot of time to make
up for."

That attitude left him shaking his head. "We can visit another day."

"First off," Brodie interrupted, "I'd kick Jack's ass if he suggested I got tired just from a little driving—"

"He'd try," Jack amended, unconcerned, as he checked an
incoming text.

"—because my job does not leave me *beat*." Pressing a fist to
his chest, Brodie added, "I'm in prime physical condition, I'll
have you know."

Still reading the phone screen, Jack raised his hand. "Same here."

"And second," Brodie continued, "we invited you, right? Maybe if you weren't being so dodgy about dinner, we could let up a little. But until then, we plan to wear you down and fit in time to visit when we can."

Half laugh, half pure frustration, Mitch blew out a breath. They were entertaining, he'd give them that. Without explaining that his intent had been to give them time, he conceded the point. "I can reconsider dinner."

"Well, hallelujah. Mom will be thrilled."

"Dinner automatically means she has to cook?"

"Has to? Pfft." Brodie clapped him on the shoulder. "She'll insist. And Charlotte—bless the girl for her baking skills—will probably make a dessert. Don't let their backbones of steel confuse you. They still enjoy a little domesticity here and there."

"As do you," Jack said to Brodie, while thumbing in a reply on his phone.

"I'm a helluva cook," Brodie bragged. "Plus I like things tidy. Being male doesn't make me a slob, ya know?"

Since he felt the same, Mitch nodded. To Jack, he asked, "Do you need privacy for that text?"

"Privacy?" That got his head up with a bemused frown. "From you two? No."

Because…they were brothers? The continued goodwill flattened him. Mired in his own amazement, unable to think of a single thing to say, Mitch gave a nod.

Further explaining, Jack said, "Ronnie's just detailing another job." He put the phone away. "Like Brodie, I had a pickup today, but mine was in Lebanon, around an hour away. That was after a meeting with the bosses."

"They arrange meetings," Brodie said in an aside, "mostly to visit with Jack. They're taken with him."

"True," Jack agreed. "I'm fond of them as well—*now*. Wasn't always that way, though. They were disappointed that Ronnie couldn't be there because she had a separate trip to make."

"And?" Brodie asked. "How'd the pickup go?"

"Got it in the trunk." Together they walked over to Jack's yellow Mustang. He opened the back and carefully brought out an ornately carved box.

Intrigued, Mitch moved closer. He'd never seen anything like it. The detailing was amazing. "What exactly is that?"

"Coffin for a pet cat." Deadpan, Jack added, "Sans cat— thank God."

Brodie laughed.

"This guy built it for when his cat died, working on it for over eighteen years. Then his douche of a son had the cat cremated so he could sell the box instead. He knew it was quality work and didn't want to see it go into the ground."

"Asshole," Brodie muttered. "Did you have any trouble getting it?"

Placing the box back in the trunk, Jack shrugged. "Usual, when dealing with jerks." He looked up. "The son, not the owner."

More fascinated by the second, Mitch mimicked Brodie, saying, "And?"

"Since the cat's ashes were already scattered, the owner didn't want his son to have the box. Maybe from spite—and I don't blame him—he made a deal with my bosses. I got there just as the son showed up. Bastard tried to argue that the old man wasn't thinking straight, and he brought along an ape to enforce that story if necessary."

"No shit?" Mitch thought he understood their business, but maybe not. "What did you do?"

Casual as you please, Jack said, "I explained the error of his ways." Closing and locking the trunk, he stretched. "He was big and clumsy, too thick for speed. When threats against me didn't work, he tried just taking it."

Brodie grinned. "How'd that work out for him?"

Not seeing so much as a scratch on Jack, Mitch could guess, but it was still amusing to hear it.

"He limped out of there with a badly busted knee, carrying on like a baby and cursing the world. The son tried throwing a punch at me." Jack shook his head. "I dodged it, then looked at his dad, got a nod, and flattened the prick."

Mitch couldn't help but laugh.

"It gets better." Leaning against his car, Jack grinned. "The guy tried to discount the price—because he 'liked the added perk of seeing his son on his ass.' His words, not mine. I thanked him but refused. I also left him my card, in case he had any troubles holding on to his money. The son knows I'm on it, so hopefully he gives his dad a little peace."

"Can't stand a bully," Brodie muttered.

And they both looked at him.

Shrugging, Mitch said, "No argument from me." His buddy Lang, who was smaller and leaner, had often been the recipient of Mitch's protection. "I avoid trouble when I can, but I'm not one to turn a blind eye."

They each nodded in satisfaction, as if they'd expected no less. Which was nuts, of course, because they hadn't seen any examples. For all they knew, he could be a liar. Hell, he could have been a bully, a thief, or worse.

Their trusting rubbed him the wrong way. "So this is what you guys do? Buy weird shit?"

"Therman, the man I work for, who's also like a grandfather to my wife, used to be into murderabilia. Thank God he's over that."

"Murderabilia?"

With disgust, Brodie said, "Artistic shit made by convicted murderers. Sometimes while they're in prison, but also, their relatives will sell it after they're convicted. Therman collected it, along with other things, but he displayed it only for himself."

For a few minutes, Brodie shared some examples. "When

this crazy fuck went after my wife, things changed for Therman. Talk about new perspectives? Yeah, he had them. Now he's more like Jack's employers, goth twins Drake and Drew. Collecting oddities has its own risk, as you just heard, but overall it's not too bad."

"You're both exclusive now?" The people they worked for must be loaded to keep it all afloat. The business impressed Mitch.

"Overall exclusive, yeah. Therman especially wants Mary and me at his beck and call. The twins are a little less demanding. We do a variety of smaller jobs, and we donate time to local causes, like the animal shelter. That night you met Charlotte? Jack and I were already out, so she pitched in to get a little homeless dog to the shelter. She loves animals, you know? But she's especially involved with homeless or mistreated pets."

That didn't surprise Mitch. "She doesn't have a pet of her own?"

"When we keep her working all the time?" Jack huffed, then said to Brodie, "We really need to get her some help."

Brodie shrugged. "Tell her that." He added to Mitch, "She's pretty damned territorial about *her* office. God forbid Jack or I dick with her filing system."

That made Mitch grin. "She enjoys her work."

"She enjoys being bossy," Brodie countered.

Jack nodded. "She learned from our mom."

So far, Mitch had learned more about Charlotte from her family than from her. He'd like a few hours alone with her, to hear her take on things. Until then, this would do.

"She could get a pet and bring it with her to the office, but that'd make it tough for her to get everything done." Brodie looked toward the building. "She visits all the other family pets a lot."

"You mentioned a shelter?"

"We offer our services in getting animals there. The place

is great," Jack explained, "but located back on an old country road. Charlotte probably got the flat leaving there."

Far as Mitch was concerned, she shouldn't be out at night on back country roads. He wouldn't mind accompanying her when she needed him. If he got a chance, he'd make the offer, and hope she took him up on it.

One thought led to another and he asked, "She doesn't do any of the more dangerous stuff?"

"God, no," they said, almost in unison.

"Glad to hear it."

"She picks up the slack with local stuff when we're already committed elsewhere," Jack explained.

And yet every day since, she'd been answering phones, filing papers—pretty much doing everything, including fetching coffee. "You said she runs the office alone?"

"Like a five-star general," Jack confirmed. "She started working with us when she'd just turned sixteen. Mom coached her through it at first, but it didn't take long to realize she was an organizational whiz. These days, Mom happily takes her cues from Charlotte."

"You already had the business back then? Started young, didn't you?"

"I'm thirty-five, Jack's thirty-two, so we're a lot older than Charlotte, but yeah, we were young." Brodie smiled with some fond memory. "I was still actively sowing my wild oats, but Mom didn't put up with any slackers."

"Plus she figured if she kept Brodie busy, he'd have less time to get in trouble."

"Look who's talking." As if imparting a secret, Brodie leaned in. "Jack was the real Romeo, he was just more secretive about it."

"A stampeding herd of elephants would be more secretive than Brodie. Though I'll admit, he did try to keep his activities off Charlotte's radar."

"She was young and impressionable, and we were her big

brothers," Brodie said, all lofty and full of himself before he gave Mitch the side-eye and added, "same as we are to you."

The absurdity of that took Mitch from grinning to choking. Why did they keep doing that to him? Throwing him off balance with sentimental nonsense? Denial came automatically. "No."

Brow cocked, Jack asked, "No what?"

How to explain without insulting them? "The idea of a brother, any brother, is a novel enough concept. I'm not anyone's idea of a kid brother, so don't go overboard."

Unconcerned, Jack shrugged. "It's a fact, though. We're older and you're younger."

"By only a few years!"

Taunting him, Jack murmured, "We could even call you the *baby* brother."

God help him, did their heckling now include him? He wouldn't mind that so much, but not over something that left him mentally reeling.

"No." Emphatic, leaving no room for debate, Mitch said, "You can't."

"And," Brodie added, ignoring what he'd said and how he'd said it, "that makes us big brothers. And big brothers look out for little brothers."

Mitch shook his head. "You can put a stake through that idea right now." He'd always taken care of himself. He'd continue to do so.

He wouldn't be a burden to family, ever.

"Little brother." Brodie held out his arms. "The idea will wear on you."

When it had literally almost taken him off his feet? Getting used to it was doubtful.

Jack, thankfully, let him off the hook. "Brodie takes himself way too seriously. Don't let him bother you."

That made him sputter, since for once it was Jack who'd done the most goading.

"With Charlotte, though?" Jack continued. "She's always been that type of girl."

Glad to be on safer ground, and pretty sure he caught the meaning, Mitch said, "The type where you wanted to protect her?"

Jack studied him. "She's a crazy hard worker, smart, but not very experienced with men."

Talk of her brought her forefront in Mitch's thoughts again… not that she'd been far from there anyway. Glancing at the shop, he asked, "Where is Charlotte?" Once the words left his mouth, he thought to amend, "And Ros?"

Not one easily fooled, Brodie smirked. "They're both inside, probably wrapping up. When Jack and I have longer days, they do too."

Knowing Charlotte was close made him even more determined to see her.

"She's a good person, very special to us."

That particular, cautioning tone slowly brought him around to stare at Brodie.

Jack added, "She's never dated much, and she can be really naive about a lot of things."

That took his attention to Jack. "You two keep referring to her as a girl, but she's a woman now." They seemed to have missed that fact.

"Maybe." Though his tone didn't change, significance brought Brodie closer. "Thing is, I'd demolish anyone who hurt her."

Jack nodded. "Same."

Rather than let them rile him, Mitch shared his own smirk. "She mentioned that the night Bernie hassled her." He could hold his own and then some, not that he had any intention of hurting Charlotte, or fighting with his brothers. "Charlotte is… She's nice. One of the nicest women I've ever met."

They agreed.

"And I'm not Bernie." Whether these two realized the distinction yet or not, Charlotte had seemed to know instantly. He thought of how she'd touched his arm after he'd popped Bernie. Definitely a naive move, but then again, her touch had worked... so maybe she understood more than any of them realized.

"We know the difference," Brodie said.

"Bernie she'd ignore." Jack gave him a speculative look. "You, she doesn't."

"You think?" Interesting take, since he hadn't seen her much lately. "Whenever I'm around, she's busy." Or was she avoiding him? He hoped not, but he'd rather know for sure—especially since she'd seemed interested.

He wouldn't bail just because Brodie or Jack ordered him to. But Charlotte? If she told him to get lost, he'd honor her wishes. Wouldn't like it, but he'd do it.

Jack relieved him when he said, "I think she has it in her head that she shouldn't intrude."

Well hell. He *wanted* her around. "So she's not still upset about Brodie teasing her?"

Brodie smiled. "Most of the time, Charlotte doesn't get upset, she gets even. At least with us. You, though? You're new to the mix, so..."

Jack folded his arms. "She was definitely embarrassed. It surprised me, because Brodie teases her all the time. It's sort of their thing. But instead of laying him low the way she usually would, she ran, which says a lot as far as I'm concerned."

Wanting them to spell it out, Mitch scowled. "Meaning?"

"Meaning I guess I need to do the whole big brother speech."

Jack added, "Which is why we clarified first that we are, in fact, big brothers."

CHAPTER SIX

It was all Mitch could do not to groan.

Or curse.

They'd been standing around in the heat for a while now, and though they didn't know it, he had important things he could be accomplishing, work on his house, orders for his business... *and* time with Charlotte. He couldn't mention any of that because he didn't want them know the extent of the roots he'd put down here. He also wasn't keen on dissecting how he felt about Charlotte. Not when he hadn't yet gotten her alone.

When he hadn't even kissed her yet.

Cutting to the chase, Mitch met Brodie eye to eye, since he was the closest. "Let me guess. She's off-limits?"

He and Jack shared a noteworthy glance before Brodie rolled a shoulder. "See, that depends. If you're just looking for fun, yeah, stay away from her. And that's not a warning I plan to give twice."

Mitch allowed himself a slow smile, knowing it wasn't friendly, but at the moment he didn't care. "Thing is, I don't take well to threats—just as I'm guessing you wouldn't."

"I'm not messing with someone's little sister."

Though Brodie said it easily enough, without any anger in his tone, Mitch felt himself bracing. Getting into a brawl wouldn't serve his reasons for being here, and in fact might destroy everything. Thinking of Charlotte, he tried a breath and asked, "Have you ever?"

Nonplussed, Brodie stalled.

Jack snickered. "He can't answer that on the grounds it may incriminate him."

"And you never did?" Brodie shot at his brother.

Defensiveness wiped away Jack's smile. "We're not talking about any girl. We're talking about Charlotte."

Calmly, Mitch said, "I only met her a few days ago, she's an adult who can make her own decision, but so you know, I'm not *messing* with anyone either. So let me whittle this down. The problem is that you think I'd disrespect her?"

Brodie blew out a breath. "Hell, I don't know you well enough to understand what you might or might not do with Charlotte."

"When you know me better, you'll understand—"

"Exactly," Brodie said. "We've been trying, but you're holding back."

Un-freaking-believable. "I've answered every damned question you've asked."

"Because we haven't dug into anything touchy."

Touchy? Affront took him back a step. "What the hell does that mean?"

Hands in his pockets, face grim, Jack studied him. "From what we've heard, you didn't have an easy life."

Uncertainty constricted his windpipe. "It was fine." *If daily neglect and occasional abuse could be called that.* Fine? He hadn't known from one day to the next what would happen. But the past was behind him now. He would not stand around sharing shit stories with men who, thankfully, had never known what it was like to… No. Goddamn it, *no.* He wasn't a whiny bastard, and complaining about it wouldn't change anything.

He planted his feet and took a stance. "Judge me on who I am now."

Jack frowned. "No one is judging you—"

"Of course you are." Mitch wasn't fooled, and he wouldn't let them fool themselves either. "With good reason. I get it, believe me. You've already been more accommodating than I expected. You want to know my past?" Maybe if he rushed through the important parts, they'd let it go. "Not before I got busted, and definitely not after, did I do anything illegal. It was only that one time."

"We know," Jack said quietly. "We checked up on it."

Good. They weren't as gullible as they'd seemed. "So you know it's true."

Undeterred, Brodie said, "You spent five years in prison." Sympathy, or something equally nauseating, held him back, but only for a second before he continued. "What did that do to you?"

Fuck this. Mitch weighed the odds of just walking away. How would they take that? Would they see it as some sort of guilt?

Damn it…what he had with his brothers felt fragile and yet important. What would it take? How much would he have to share?

Jaw tight, remembered rage burning his eyes, he whispered, "You want the nitty-gritty?"

"We want to know *you*," Jack corrected softly.

"So yeah, that includes the nitty-gritty." Shaking off the emotion, Brodie sharpened his tone and held out his arms. "We've been sharing left and right, hoping you'd pick up on it, but you're as closed off as you were the night we met you."

"I don't want to bulldoze you."

"Dinner would be bulldozing?" Brodie shot back. "You've been invited multiple times."

Jack put a hand on Brodie's shoulder, maybe to rein him in, maybe to align with him.

"Jesus." It was almost funny. Dinner though? He could handle sitting through a meal easier than this interrogation. He filled his lungs with the muggy evening air. "I thought it'd be better to ease into things."

"Yeah, I'm not asking you to live with me." Brodie paused. "That is…you don't need a place to stay?"

Now he *did* laugh, and thankfully, it eased some of the tension, enough so that he could unclench his muscles. "No, I don't."

"You're sure?"

"Positive."

Mollified, Brodie nodded. "Good, good."

"Obviously," Jack cut back in, "this little chat was necessary because you're not denying being interested in Charlotte."

He could, Mitch thought. It'd probably make things easier to assure them both that he had no designs on Charlotte one way or the other. But he wouldn't start this new relationship with a lie. He *was* interested, damn it.

And he wouldn't let any man tell him what to do.

"Here's the thing." He again glanced toward the building, and saw Charlotte and Ros moving away from the door. Before he got too distracted with her, he turned back to the brothers. "She intrigues me."

"Mom?" Jack asked, deadpan.

It worked to lighten the mood, but Mitch answered seriously. "I meant Charlotte—though your mom is unlike anyone I've ever known."

"Before you think she's all hugs and rainbows," Brodie said, "know that she enjoys giving nonstop advice—which is more along the lines of bossiness. Plus she's a big believer in respect and loyalty."

Thinking that was all pretty damned admirable, Mitch didn't see a problem. "I noticed the bossy part." He nodded at Brodie. "Especially when it comes to you."

"Brodie needs it more than most people," Jack said. "I'm betting you noticed that as well."

Ignoring their laughter, Brodie turned his finger in the air. "Before Jack gets too deep in trashing my character, let's rewind to you and Charlotte."

Was there a him and Charlotte for them to worry about? If he could find an upside to their surprise heart-to-heart, it was that they appeared to think he had a chance with Charlotte.

Just then she stuck her head out the door. "Hey, Brodie. Therman called. He has an afternoon pickup tomorrow." Her gaze briefly touched on Mitch, but skipped away again.

For the life of him, Mitch couldn't do the same. The sight of her in a loose pink T-shirt and slim-fitting jeans felt like a balm. He wished she'd come out and chat with them. He wished... hell, for a lot of things.

And that, he knew, was what worried Jack and Brodie.

She switched her pretty blue gaze to Jack. "Ronnie said you've got twenty minutes, tops, to get home before she eats dinner without you." With an airy wave, Charlotte disappeared back inside and the door closed behind her.

He wanted her—but the brothers he'd come to find weren't entirely on board with that idea. "So I do dinner. How many times?" Would two be enough? Four? Somehow he doubted it. "You expect me to rehash life as a kid living in the slums? I won't do that. Not with Charlotte and Ros there." Not to anyone.

"Wouldn't ask you to." Brodie ran a hand over his face. "Look, we don't mean to be so pushy. You're a grown ass man, right? Charlotte is a grown woman. I get that we're coercing you and you're being great about it. It's just—"

He sighed, because damn it, he could see it from their perspective. "You care about her, and you don't know me that well."

"Come to dinner," Brodie urged. "Relax, visit. Open up a *little*. That's all we're saying."

"You don't have to relive your past." Jack leaned back on

his car. "But we need something so we can feel like we really know you. Look at it this way. As we know you better, so will Charlotte."

So they'd use her as enticement? Interesting. He glanced again at the offices. Ros paused by the door and waved to him.

Feeling somewhat foolish, he lifted his hand in return.

"You've already won Mom over," Brodie mused.

It sure felt that way. From the second he'd told her who he was, she'd been accepting. "You see the irony in that, right?"

Jack shrugged. "Yeah, but that's how Mom is." More solemnly, he added, "Give us a few weeks. Come to some family dinners. Make time."

What they asked wasn't terrible—except for the opening up part. If he could, he'd pretend his life started after prison.

"Brute is always welcome," Brodie said. "Our pets will be around too."

"It'll be painless," Jack added. "But we have nearly thirty years of history to uncover."

His history was so opposite to what they'd known. Just learning about his life from fifteen to eighteen would be enough for them to bar him away from Charlotte for all eternity. "The thing is—"

"Until then," Brodie said, undeterred, "we'd prefer you not get too involved with Charlotte."

"We can't speak for her," Jack added. "But I think you know it's right."

Yup, and that put him back to square one. The brothers wore near-identical looks of challenge. The only difference was just that Jack tempered his with civility, whereas Brodie had a tendency to use his like a bludgeon.

"Explain *involved*." If they wanted him at dinner, was he supposed to ignore her?

Jack opened his mouth, closed it—and Brodie stated, "Don't sleep with her."

Ha. So that was their worry? They thought he'd be rushing her off to bed? "Does she do that?" Again he glanced back. He could easily picture her bustling around inside the office. "She struck me as more reserved than that."

Jack's brows shot up. "Not that we've ever noticed."

"And in a town this size," Brodie said with a considering frown, "pretty sure we'd have noticed."

"Well then, since I don't go around coercing women, you have nothing to worry about, right?" If Charlotte was willing, he'd be on board with hooking up tonight. Right now, in fact. But everything he'd already learned about her told him that wasn't about to happen, so why not agree? Keep the peace with them, earn some trust, and make the headway he craved with Charlotte.

The big problem for him? No way did he want them to think they'd forced him to do the right thing. Not when he'd spent most of his life struggling to separate himself from his surroundings by being as honorable as he could be.

"Two weeks, huh?" Definitely...*probably*, he could manage that.

Charlotte stuck her head out the door again. "Sorry to keep interrupting, but Ros wants to know why you guys are hanging out here in the yard." This time Charlotte transferred her attention to Mitch. "She also wanted me to ask if you need anything?"

"What a loaded question—" Brodie started to say, until Mitch elbowed him.

Brodie ended with an "Oof."

Every time he saw her, it seemed Charlotte grew more hair. Throughout the day, those corkscrew curls expanded, going everywhere—and it was downright cute. "I'm good, but thank you."

With a fleeting smile, she went back in.

"See," Jack said. "She's interested too."

Giving Brodie a look, Mitch replied, "She won't be if you heckle her every time she speaks to me."

Brodie's mouth twitched. "You *know* that was hard to resist."

"Here's the thing." Mitch crossed his arms and gave them a germane detail. "I'm not about rushing women anyway—something you'd have learned about me eventually, even at the pace I'd set. The problem with your plan is that Charlotte also needs to get to know me. She can't do that if you make her uncomfortable when I'm around. So here's a deal—I'll chill for a few weeks as long as you stop needling her in front of me."

For a second, both brothers stared at him as if astounded that he had the gall to bargain.

Seriously, he was an interloper, the proverbial skeleton in the closet.

But they may as well learn right now that he wasn't a pushover, and he didn't take orders well. He hoped to have a positive relationship with them, and that required respect on both sides. To that end, he wanted to meet them halfway.

Jack cracked a smile. "Notice he specified *in front* of him. He already realizes you can't curb it all the time."

"Charlotte wouldn't want me to," Brodie said with warm affection. "The girl loves me as I am."

"And she enjoys taking part," Jack promised.

"She hands me a cookie and insults me at the same time. Offers me coffee and calls me names. She more than enjoys it."

"She learned from us," Jack boasted. "And we all know, between us, it's said in fun. If someone else insults us? Charlotte chews them up."

"Joining in with the banter is her way of showing she cares." Brodie shrugged. "At least, that's usually the case—though obviously not with you."

That had to mean Charlotte was as interested as he was. The brothers believed it enough to be concerned.

And I just agreed to put things on ice for two weeks.

"I'll have to take your word for it." Mitch didn't want to paint a pitiful picture, but he didn't want them to consider him dense either. Here was an opening for him to divulge just a small bit of his life. Maybe if he threw it out there in small doses, it wouldn't seem so bad. "I grew up alone, and my few friends weren't exactly from wholesome families."

Mentally jumping on that, they gave him their undivided attention. It was almost comical, the way they went so alert.

"Everyone I knew interacted more with fists than jokes." He knew brothers who'd stolen from each other, cheated each other, even taken shots at each other.

Sure, he'd seen fun relationships on TV and in movies—the same place he saw space aliens and unicorns. Overall, he figured it was BS, a contrivance of Hollyweird and their insistence on showing storybook versions of life instead of reality.

Now he had to reevaluate.

The brothers stared at Mitch with rapt expressions, making him feel conspicuous. "So brothers and sisters rib each other all the time the way you guys do, without anyone getting mad?"

"I don't know if other families are as awesome as us—"

Jack choked on a laugh.

"—but the really cool families do, yeah." With a wink, Brodie added, "And just think, you're now a part of it all."

Charlotte peeked out the window yet again. So far she'd seen Mitch laugh, scowl, and at one point he'd appeared ready to bolt.

"Snooping again?" Ros asked.

They'd both finished work twenty minutes ago, and now they lingered in the office just to keep from interrupting whatever was going on outside.

If it was anyone other than Ros, Charlotte would be mortified at getting caught spying. The fact that Ros had done the same thing several times already made her curiosity more acceptable. "Why are they keeping him out there?"

"Boy talk," she predicted.

That brought her around. She dropped the blinds and frowned at Ros. "What kind of boy talk?"

"The kind where they try to play at being your big brothers, I presume. You know they love you."

Oh, good lord. "That's just plain intrusive and not an excuse." But did that account for Mitch's earlier scowls? Were they trying to warn him off...and he didn't like it?

Grinning, Ros seated herself on the edge of the desk. "If they don't wrap it up in the next two minutes, I'll go out there and break up the party."

"Better you than me," Charlotte muttered. So far, she'd been fairly successful dodging Mitch, at least physically.

Emotionally? Mentally? She couldn't stop thinking about him. The priority was for him to get comfortable with his family. Period. So why was she so tempted to snag him all for herself?

Mired in her own confusion, she let out a sigh.

Ros pounced. "What was that?"

"What?"

"That sound. The lusty sigh."

Color climbed her neck. "It wasn't lusty."

"Oh, honey, I'm not too old to know lusty when I hear it." Her smile turned sly. "No, don't deny it."

Chin up, Charlotte said, "Fine, I won't. He's...attractive. Of course I enjoy looking at him."

"Such a weak word to describe that young hunk. He's drop-dead gorgeous—just like his brothers."

Ros said that as if she had bragging rights to Mitch too. "They do look a lot alike." Though she could have dredged up something to keep her busy, Charlotte found herself back at the window once more, peeking out at the guys.

More specifically, Mitch.

How childish was that? She should just man up and join them.

She could act all cavalier, as if she hadn't been avoiding him the last few days—

With a sharp crack of her hand against the desk, Ros said, "Enough hiding."

Charlotte nearly jumped a foot, then turned on Ros with accusation. "Good grief, you nearly startled me out of my skin."

"Because you know you're being sneaky. Go on out. Visit." Mind made up, she slid off the desk. "Come on, I'll go with you. It'll be fun."

Their ideas of fun varied greatly.

Hearing something, she put her nose to the window again, and let out a breath. "No need. I think they're finally coming in."

"Perfect." Ros bustled about, grabbing up her purse and giving Charlotte a hug. "I'll see you at home later."

Bemused, she blinked at her. "I don't know what you expect to happen, but—"

"Not a thing." She arranged Charlotte's hair, pulling a few unruly curls over her shoulders. "Don't rush. We're just having leftovers."

With it past dinnertime, anything would be perfect. "Would you rather I just pick up pizza?"

"Nope." She breezed on out the door. "Have fun."

Obviously, she did expect something. Hastily, Charlotte began tidying the desk. Her own expectations were nil, but it never hurt to be prepared.

Or at least as prepared as she could be with two hovering hulks who thought she was still a teenager.

Another glance at the office, and Mitch gave in. "Dinner," he agreed, "but not tonight. It's getting late and I need to get back to Brute." The dog had been sleeping when he'd left, so Mitch hadn't disturbed him. Still, he didn't like leaving him alone for long stretches.

"Tomorrow then?" Jack pressed. "Mom will love it, I promise."

Yeah, she probably would. So far, Rosalyn had treated him
like a long-lost son. It defied logic. He nodded, then said, "Think
I'll say hi to Charlotte since I'm here, then head out after that."

"Tell her I headed home, okay?" After digging his keys from
his pocket, Jack opened the driver's door. "And tell her everything went fine with the pickup."

"Sure."

"I'll walk up with you," Brodie said. "She needs a final re-
port from me too."

So much for trust, Mitch thought, but damn it, he was smiling. Charlotte deserved the best, and so far his brothers seemed
to be that.

Just as they reached the door, Ros came out. She smiled at
Mitch, and then scowled at Brodie. Just as quickly the scowl
turned into a blinding smile. "Brodie, I'm so glad you're here."

Cautiously, Brodie said, "You are?"

"Yes, come here." Looping her arm through his, she somehow
managed the herculean feat of dragging off her overgrown son.

Mitch watched the antics with an inner smile. Ros was one
hell of a woman and he had a feeling she always got her way
when she put her mind to it. Brodie and Jack might be concerned
with his interest in Charlotte, but Ros didn't seem to mind.

From behind him, Charlotte said quietly, "Hey."

He turned and found her framed in the doorway. A little smile
teased her sexy mouth, and he forgot about Brodie. "Hey." The
sight of her drew him closer. "I haven't seen you much lately."

"Busy, busy," she quipped, and stepped back so he could enter.

He glanced toward Brodie, saw Ros prodding him toward
his car, and gave her a silent but heartfelt thank-you. Was she
matchmaking? He wouldn't mind having someone in his corner,
especially if it was the most formidable Crews family member.

Going into the office, he said, "Jack wanted you to know everything went fine and he has the package."

She snickered. "Sounds like *Mission Impossible*, doesn't it?"

As she headed down the hallway, he followed, admiring that plump behind and the bounce of her curls. "A little, especially after Brodie and Jack explained more about what they transport. Crazy stuff."

"It is." She went into the break room and asked, "Coffee?"

"Maybe half a cup." He had enough trouble sleeping at night without loading up the caffeine, but if it'd keep her talking to him for a bit, he'd take the hit to sleep. "That is, if you'll join me."

"All right." She half filled two mugs. "Where's Brute?"

"Sawing logs, last I saw him." He waited for her to take a chair and, mindful of his promise to Brodie and Jack, he took one across from her. Watching the way she blew gently on the coffee, he tried to keep his thoughts clean.

Not easy. Her slender fingers cradled the mug and her lashes lowered as she sipped.

He had it bad when watching a woman drink coffee stirred him.

"The guys invited me to dinner tomorrow."

"They did?" Pleasure brightened her eyes. "You agreed?"

If he hadn't, he would now. The way she looked at him, with expectation and happiness, sent adrenaline pumping…but in a good way. "Yeah. They said it's okay to bring Brute."

"One hundred percent okay. We'd love to see him again."

He imagined a junkie felt like this when getting a fix. More attuned. Acutely aware of everything, including his own blood pumping through his veins.

Around Charlotte, he felt *alive*.

He didn't know if he'd ever get enough. This, this sensation is what drew him. It was all wrapped up in the way she looked, how she spoke, and the fundamentally female way she had about her.

Strong but gentle.

Intelligent but kind.

"You'll be there, right?" To make it sound more teasing, and to get to the truth, he stared into her eyes and asked, "No more dodging me?"

She started to say something, changed her mind, and looked down at her coffee. "Yes, I'll be there."

No denying the dodging part? Bracing a forearm on the table, Mitch asked, "Did I do something?" He rubbed an ear at that uncomfortable thought. "If I did, you can tell—"

"Of course not." With one fingertip, she circled the top of the mug.

To his muddled brain, it seemed sensual and provoking.

"I...you..." Huffing, she started over by putting her shoulders back and lifting her gaze.

That too was sensual, the way she found her backbone despite her modesty.

His slow smile drew her lingering gaze, and it took her a second to remember what she was saying.

Shooting her gaze back to his, she frowned in concentration. "I didn't want to get in the way of you guys catching up. That's all."

Nice, that he flustered her. It meant he wasn't the only one tangled up in overloaded sensation.

And speaking of overloaded... How often did she sit?

From what he'd witnessed so far, it rarely happened. Even now, with her foot tapping and her fingers again moving on the cup, he imagined that she fought the need to be up and moving.

The thought of having all that energy redirected to him left him scorched.

But that was only one of the things she made him feel. Around her, he focused less on goals, leaving it possible for him to indulge simple enjoyment. Instead of being a guy with a record and no family, he was just a man.

A man who could smile and relax and think about things other than correcting past mistakes.

He tried to keep his eyes on hers, but repeatedly they dropped to her mouth, making his voice a little huskier when he said, "For the record, you'll never be in the way."

Her eyes flared, and a heartbeat later her tongue came out to flick across her lips. "Okay."

Rein it in, he ordered his libido. *That lick was not meant for you.* Getting half-hard now would defeat all the promises he'd made to Brodie and Jack.

"You're staring."

"Am I?"

"Yes."

God, he did love it when she showed her gumption. "I want you there. For the dinner, I mean."

Oh, the way the woman smiled. Just barely, but with ulti-mate impact. "Why?"

No, she wasn't that naive, regardless what the guys thought. In the same sultry tone she'd used, his gaze locked with hers, he said, "You know why."

The smile warmed, but she didn't pretend to misunderstand. "It's not something I'm used to."

"Got a lot of idiots in the area, huh?"

Her laugh played over his skin like a physical stroke. His dick twitched and his balls tightened. The things she did to him...

Arms folded on the table, Mitch leaned forward. "I like you, Charlotte."

"You don't really know me."

"Bull. The guys sing your praises nonstop—"

She snorted.

"—but even if they didn't, I know plenty." Tipping his head, he pretended to study her. "You're smart. You knew just how to defuse that situation with Bernie." *And how to steal my anger—with a single touch.* "My dog adores you, so I know you're good with animals."

She laughed. "Brute was easy to win over. After all, I had the treat."

"Doesn't matter. Usually he's wary of everyone but me." He glanced around the break room. "You're super-organized, maybe even a neat freak."

"Ha! Ros could tell you different."

He liked her like this, casual and easygoing, willing to chat. "I won't believe you're a slob."

"No, not that." She wrinkled her nose. "That sounds terrible. Let's just say I'm...tidy, but not fanatical about scrubbing floors or anything." She rethought that, and added, "Well, when they need it—"

His laugh felt like the most natural thing in the world. "I also know you're cute. Kind. Loyal to your family. Sometimes funny." Appreciating the way she blushed, he added, "And sexy. You, Charlotte Parrish, are pretty much the whole package."

Eyes warming, lips parting, she whispered, "I, um... Thank you."

"It's the truth."

Before Mitch said or did something stupid, Brodie came through the entry doors and headed down the hall with set purpose. He looked harassed—no doubt from his mom derailing his plans to play chaperone—but by the time he reached them, he wore only a friendly smile.

For Charlotte's benefit.

Brodie had already proven he didn't mind putting Mitch on the spot.

"Time to lock her up and head home, you two. It's been a long day."

True. But he'd gotten to visit with Charlotte, so the ending to the day was more than a little satisfactory.

All smiles now, Charlotte scooted back her chair, turned off the coffeepot and threw away the filter, then gathered up the carafe and mugs to rinse them out.

He could tell it was a routine she'd completed many nights.

Aware of Brodie's eagle eye, Mitch offered, "Let me help."

"Thanks, but it'll only take me a second."

While she did that, Brodie leaned against the wall, a big immovable force. "Mom is happy about dinner. She said six o'clock."

Six worked for him. He'd have time to get some work done before he had to head out. "I'll be there."

"Bring Brute."

He nodded.

From the other room, presumably where they had a sink, Charlotte hummed while she took care of the few dishes. Unaware or uncaring of Brodie's turmoil—and Mitch's interest. Confident that all was fine in her world.

In his old neighborhood, girls didn't get a chance to be fresh-faced and confident. For boys and girls alike, innocence tended to flee the scene early, usually at the same time puberty hit because that's when the vultures began to notice. Those who'd been around were either mean themselves, or indifferent to the situation.

None of them had room for kindness.

But Charlotte? Her nature was a direct contrast to his, and he liked it. He liked the extreme way she made him feel.

Brodie and Jack needed time to know him. He wanted to show Rosalyn that he could be trusted.

Yet it was Charlotte who held most of his focus, because he wanted her to want him with the same intensity he felt.

Wouldn't be easy. Nothing for him ever was.

If he worked hard enough, he just might be able to have it all. Charlotte, his brothers, this life, was worth any amount of effort.

CHAPTER SEVEN

Sweat dripped down the back of Newman's neck, brought on as much by sweltering rage as the hot summer heat.

He'd been away for a few months on a piddly-ass charge. Not as long as Mitch, but apparently too damned long.

Gone. The fucking house was gone, and after cursing the demolition crew he'd finally tracked down the truth.

The conniving bitch had left it to her son, and he'd agreed to see it destroyed.

He wouldn't give two cents for the actual structure, but there were two big problems.

Whatever it had sold for, the money should have been his. He was the one who'd put up with Velma's addiction and Mitch's shitty attitude.

Second big problem? Somewhere beneath the rubble was a small fortune in crystal meth and ecstasy. At least he assumed no one had discovered it. He'd hid it well, and the bulldozer would have destroyed it.

Such a fucking waste—that put him in dire financial straits.

He couldn't complain, couldn't start digging, couldn't do jack shit without implicating himself.

"His friend lives around here somewhere," Ritchie said, peering out the window of the back seat. "I'll know the house when I see it."

He'd brought his two best men with him on this little excursion. Best being subjective, of course, but hell, hitting rock bottom made it hard to get better people.

Ritchie was all right. Dumber than a rock but loyal. The biggest drawback was his personal hygiene. Newman thought he could smell Ritchie's greasy blond hair and stringy body even with the window down.

"There he is." Lee Gilstrap, the third in their group, was a hell of a lot more reliable. Short, built like a fridge and rock solid. With his shaved and tattooed head, most people gave him a wide berth.

Lee was there once when Newman took the strap to Mitch for being lippy. He hadn't said a word.

He seldom did.

Pulling up to the curb, Lee parked and Ritchie, like an eager puppy, jumped out of the back, yelling, "Lang Hardy, there you are."

Lang looked up—and it was there on his face, the knowledge that this would not go well for him.

He dropped the hose he'd been using and tried to get into his little run-down house.

Cackling in glee, Ritchie shot out after him, tackling him just inside the doorway.

Neighbors glanced up—and away.

More slowly, Newman got out. Yeah, he was smiling. So what. He needed to get some answers, and he needed to expend his rage.

He needed to find Mitch.

And then he'd make the bastard pay—in more ways than one.

The next morning, Charlotte arrived at work a few minutes early and was surprised to see Brodie and Mitch there.

"What's going on?" she asked.

Brodie smiled at her. "Ran into Mitch in town at the hard-ware store and asked if he'd help me unload some mulch."

Mitch's gaze moved over her hair in a high ponytail, down to her comfortable polo shirt and trim jeans, all the way to her toes in her flip-flops.

Oh my. Never in her life had anyone looked at her with so much hunger. Flushed, she croaked, "Good morning."

Amusement and something more lifted the corner of his mouth. "Morning."

Rather than melt into a puddle of sensation, Charlotte looked toward the truck. Mustang Transport owned two—one a pickup and the other a flatbed. Today Brodie had taken out the pickup.

"What are you doing?"

He gestured at the building. "It's looking rough, so I thought I'd put some mulch around the area. Good thing I ran into Mitch, because he suggested gravel instead. Less upkeep and all that. Here, come look."

The path Brodie took to the truck bed brought her closer to Mitch. He stood there in torn jeans, a dirty white T-shirt and work boots. Sweat and dust left his hair sticking out in a few places.

All combined, it only added to his rugged appeal.

It was barely 8:00 a.m. What time had he started working?

Satisfaction darkened his eyes and determination curved his mouth. That compelling look made it impossible for her to turn away.

"You see?" Reaching inside, Brodie scooped up a handful of gravel and let the rocks sift back through his fingers. "Pretty, right?"

Shades of tan, gold and red glinted in the sunlight. "Very."

Aware of Mitch stepping up next to her—close enough to touch her, though he didn't—Charlotte carefully drew a breath.

The scents of sun-warmed skin and earthy male assailed her.

Brodie had a scent as well, but *his* didn't send her senses spiking or her stomach tumbling.

That was all Mitch.

His husky voice sounded right behind her. "It'll look good against the brick of the building."

What he said and how he said it were two different things. How did the man make gravel and buildings sound naughty and sexy and *enticing*?

She didn't have near enough experience to know, but her body reacted all the same.

Proving he'd heard it too—or maybe recognized the tactic—Brodie cleared his throat. He bent a look on Mitch, then asked her, "What do you think?"

Glad for something constructive to do, as well as time to recover, Charlotte glanced back at the offices and tried to envision the gravel around the perimeter. It took a second for the daze to clear and her heart to slow. Then she realized Mitch was right.

Tilting her head, she said, "Wow. It really will."

Lounging with one forearm on the tailgate, mellow brown eyes squinted at the bright morning sun, he said to Brodie, "You should really put down some weed barrier mat before the gravel, especially if you're not into landscaping."

"Yeah?" Brodie too took a casual position against the truck. "I mean, I keep up the landscape at home, but I hadn't thought about here."

"I," Charlotte interjected with emphasis, "have mentioned many times that we should add some curb appeal to the building."

"Most customers make arrangements over the phone or the internet. They don't visit the office."

"But some *do*," she stressed. "Like Jack's wife and *your* wife. I keep the inside nice, so why not make the outside nice too?"

With a put-upon sigh, Brodie grumbled, "She wants to plant

flowers, and she said she'd handle the upkeep—like she doesn't have enough to do already."

"Landscaping here would be a big job," Mitch noted. He studied the building with an evaluating eye, then gave a slight shake of his head. "Flowering shrubs would pretty it up and not require a lot of upkeep."

That disclosure drew scrutiny from her, but not so much from Brodie, who took it as more of an offhand observation.

Charlotte sensed it was more, that his input came from some level of expertise. So what did Mitch know of landscaping?

Without those persuasive eyes staring at her so relentlessly, he shouldn't have had such an impact on her senses. Yet the sharp line of his cheekbones, the straight bridge of his nose and a small dimple in his chin, all conspired against her.

When she sighed, his eyes lowered to her.

He said, "I sort of had my morning mapped out, but I wouldn't mind coming back another day to help you take care of the gravel."

Since he looked at her, it took her a second to understand that he spoke to Brodie. When she did, she flushed.

Oblivious to her inner turmoil, Brodie said, "That'd be great, if you're sure you don't mind."

With an intimate smile, Mitch drawled, "I don't mind at all."

Finally catching on, Brodie glanced from one to the other, cleared his throat again, this time with excessive force, and pulled Charlotte around to face him. "Would you mind taking Brute in with you for a drink? Since I derailed Mitch, the poor dog has to be thirsty."

Until Brodie said it, she hadn't noticed Brute, but she looked around now—and found him sound asleep in the shade made by Mitch's car. With each snoring breath, his loose lips fluttered.

Fighting her humor, she pulled a laughably sad face and crooned with heavy concern, "Oh, the poor thing looks so parched."

Brute snuffled in his sleep.

Chuckling, Mitch patted his thigh and said, "Brute. Come here, boy."

One eye opened. Brute took his time deciding, then yawned elaborately, stretched all four legs, and finally rolled to his feet. After another stretch, he padded silently over to stand by Mitch.

Before she turned to go in, she asked Mitch, "Do you need anything?"

Instead of answering her, he first said to Brodie, "Shut up."

Charlotte saw Brodie close his mouth and grin.

"I'm fine," he said to her, "but I'll walk you in and help get Brute settled."

While Brodie rolled his eyes, Charlotte narrowed hers. "What—"

"Ignore him." Wrapping warm, firm fingers around the bare skin of her upper arm, Mitch effectively stole her voice and guided her through the office door. He held it open for Brute to follow too. Letting the door close, he slid his fingers away— leaving chills in his wake.

She turned to face him.

He fought it, but his attention tracked over her, catching on her legs, her chest, and then fixating on her mouth.

"I'm sorry to add to your workload."

Scorched clean through from that thorough inspection, Charlotte struggled to catch up. "My workload?"

"Babysitting Brute. We won't be long. Half hour, tops."

Ah. She smiled at the dog, who currently sniffed around the office. "He's no trouble, I promise."

Mitch took a step closer, caught himself and frowned. "You look nice today."

Now why did *that* make heat climb her chest and bloom in her face? She looked down at her two-year-old shirt, thought of how she'd hastily pulled up her hair and… Damn it, if she'd known she'd see him this morning, she'd have tried a little harder.

"Charlotte?"

Oh, that deep voice... She bit her lip and glanced up. "Hmm?"

"Doesn't matter what you wear."

She blinked fast. "It doesn't?"

With a slow shake of his head, he said, "You always look great. Every time I've seen you, actually."

Oh my. Pleasure bloomed, making her heart feel full. "Coming from a man like you, those compliments equal more excitement than I've had in years."

He locked down—no movement, no inflection, when he carefully asked, "A man like me?"

Did he expect her to be critical of his past? "A man as big and fit and—" *Dare she say it?*

The chaotic emotion in his expressive eyes convinced her.

He might hold himself back, but she wouldn't—not physically or verbally.

Determination brought her close enough to breathe in his scent again. Head tilted back to see his face, she lightly rested her fingertips to his chest. It was a delicious feeling, the strength and heat of him beneath soft cotton.

"A man as gorgeous as you." Belatedly, she pasted on a smile. "You're a solid stack of raw power and fast reflexes and it's incredibly appealing."

Skepticism kept him searching her eyes. "I'm not sure how we got from you being so pretty, to talking about me."

Color slashed his cheekbones and she realized he was actually embarrassed. Had no one given him a sincere compliment? Huh. Apparently praise flustered him as much as it did her.

Stroking his chest the tiniest bit, she suggested softly, "Thank you."

He tipped his head. "What?"

"The appropriate response to a compliment is a simple *thank you.*" She patted his chest once, liked it way too much, and made herself step back. "Now you try it."

The glint in his eyes made her stomach flutter. "Thank you."

With a silly half bow, Charlotte said, "You're welcome. Now, water for Brute." The dog was back to sleep, making her smile widen even more. "If I know Brodie, he'll be barging in here any second."

"I'm sure you're right." He glanced out the door, turned back to her, and with fond surprise, said, "This was...interesting."

God, she hoped he didn't mean odd.

She took another step back, but it was like swimming against the tide. Regardless of her mind insisting she should get to work, her body yearned to stay near him.

He seemed to know it too.

"I'll see you again soon, Charlotte." And with that tantalizing promise, he headed back outside.

Brute did lap up water once she refilled the water dish, but he certainly hadn't been in desperate need. He followed her into the inner office, sprawled out in a ray of sunshine coming through the blinds and released a heavy sigh.

"You're living the life, bud, aren't you?" He got to hang out with Mitch all day, and slept whenever he wanted. "I'm glad."

She, herself, wasn't sleepy. Just the opposite, in fact.

She felt energized. Excited. *Alive.*

Amazing what sexual attraction could do to a body. Now she understood why Brodie and Jack had always indulged so many excesses.

She had work to do, but over the next twenty minutes she couldn't keep from watching Mitch work. Muscles flexed everywhere as he stood beside Brodie, shoveling the gravel out of the truck bed and onto a wide tarp in the yard.

The two of them chatted amicably, and once she saw Mitch laugh at something Brodie said. She'd like to see him do that more often.

It made her happy to see things progressing so nicely between them. Mitch was truly becoming a part of the family.

Now if only she knew where she fit into the equation.

"Yoo-hoo."

Snapping back from the window in guilty haste, Charlotte yelped, and then slapped a hand to her chest to keep her heart contained. "I didn't see you drive up!"

"I know." Ros gave her a sly grin. "Thinking something you shouldn't?"

"What shouldn't I think?"

Struck by that, Ros paused, gave it quick thought, and amended with firm confidence, "Not a damn thing. Look at that young man and think whatever you want."

"Ros!" Despite herself, Charlotte laughed. "He's fascinating, don't you think?"

"Likely in different ways than you, but yes I do." She hung her purse on a wall hook. "Mary was right behind me. She brought Howler, so let's go see how Brute does with him."

At Ros's arrival, Brute sat up, but otherwise he appeared un-interested in moving.

"Are you sure we should?"

"Mitch is a part of this family now, and that means Brute is too." After stroking a hand along the dog's neck, Ros cupped his furry face in both hands. "You'd like to meet a friend, wouldn't you?"

Brute cast fretful eyes at Charlotte, then back at Ros. He gave one uncertain thump of his tail.

"He's nervous, aren't you, poor baby?" Charlotte's childish tone had his tail thumping faster. "It would be good for him to have some doggy friends."

"Exactly."

Since the guys were done unloading the gravel, Charlotte patted her thigh as she'd seen Mitch do, and called the dog to her. "Come on, boy. You've got company to meet."

Good-natured as always, Brute padded along beside her—

until they stepped outside. Instinctively, he seemed to know another dog was near.

With heartbreaking—and hilarious—haste, he scuttled behind Charlotte, almost taking her off her feet. She tried to turn to Brute to reassure him, but he wouldn't let her. Nose tucked to his butt, he attempted to keep his entire body hidden behind her legs.

Her heart shattered. "Oh, honey," she said over her shoulder. "I promise it's okay."

Immediately, Mitch strode over and, kneeling, put a big hand on Brute's neck. "It's okay, bud."

Mary waited in her car, and from the back seat Howler pressed his face to the window, his baggy eyes wide as he spotted not only Brodie—who he adored—but a new dog.

The howling started, a bizarre sound of mixed glee and excitement.

Brute peeked out, appeared horrified, and tucked in again.

"Shh, shh," Mitch murmured, keeping a comforting hand on his neck. He asked Brodie, "Should I leash him?"

"Naw, it'll be fine. You'll see. Howler's good with other animals. Basically, he's an affectionate grandma in a loose suit of fur. If he could bake biscuits, he would."

Mitch snorted over that.

Charlotte said, "It's true. My money's on Howler. He'll win Brute over in no time."

Brodie strode to his wife's car, helped her out, kissed her warmly and then released Howler with a flourish.

The dog's long body unfolded in a rush from the back seat with a lot of awkward thrashing before he found his big feet and, with a lumbering lope, charged over to Brute.

Brute moved so quickly between Mitch's legs, he almost knocked him over.

The extra-sweet part, at least to Charlotte's mind, was how Howler immediately realized the problem and stopped, lowering his upper body to the ground with his bony rump still high in the air, tail flagging. He whimpered, whined, gave a few happy yaps, then army-crawled closer while Mitch tried to reassure Brute.

"Howler," Brodie said softly. "Wait."

Howler flashed him an impatient look, then rested his head on his massive front paws, his jaws lapping over, his expressive eyes constantly shifting.

"Brute, my man. It's fine, I swear." Mitch managed to peel himself away from the dog enough to sit on the ground, one leg bent, the other sticking out. Brute immediately crawled into his lap and tucked his face in his neck.

"My heart is breaking," Charlotte whispered, watching Mitch speak softly in Brute's ear while stroking all along his back and head.

"Yeah," Mitch said without looking at her. "I don't know what kind of hell he went through before I got him, but it must've been ugly."

Had he witnessed dog fighting? Tears burned her eyes and made her nose tickle, her throat thick. She wasn't a violent person, but she wouldn't mind—

"I'm just glad you got him." Ros sniffed. "Howler will be good for him, you'll see."

Finally, Brute stuck his head out and peered at Howler.

Taking that for an invitation, Howler immediately crawled closer to snuffle against Brute's foot. The dog tried to snatch his leg up as far as he could, but Howler just followed and Mitch ended up with both dogs draped over him.

He laughed quietly. "Hey there, big guy."

Howler answered with a wet lick across his face.

Brodie stood there, arms folded, legs braced apart, watching the scene and allowing Mitch to handle it.

Without his restraint, Charlotte lowered herself to sit on the ground beside him. "Come here, Howler. Let's give Brute room to breathe."

Howler didn't want to, but he twisted so that his lanky butt sat on her thighs.

"Now," she said calmly, patting Howler and then Brute, alternating until Brute peeked out again. "Such a good boy," she praised, tickling under his chin. "You're just shy, aren't you? You don't mean to make me cry."

Howler swiped her with his wet tongue too, then lavishly bestowed his love on Brute…and poor Brute couldn't dodge him. In fact, he stopped trying. He even gave Howler a tentative lick in return.

"This is getting gross," Brodie said.

"From over there?" Mitch snorted. "Try being in the middle of it."

Charlotte heard the humor in his voice, and the pleasure. "It's turning into a regular lickfest—*shut up, Brodie.*"

Both guys laughed.

"There's a lot of butt wagging going on too, so I think they're getting along now." She eased back so that Howler's weight no longer pinned down her legs. "What do you say, guys? Furry friends?"

Brute yawned, and she suddenly understood that it was a stress thing for him.

Charlotte scooted over to sit beside Brute and he gave her a happy nuzzle, looked at Howler and woofed.

Mitch's brows shot up. "Man, he's usually so silent."

"It was a happy sound," Charlotte said, thrilled to hear it.

Lunging back, Howler acted like he would pounce and instead turned a circle. Tentatively, Brute edged away from Mitch and tried to smell Howler's backside, but Howler kept jumping around to face him, and that turned into a fun game of turning circles for both of them.

Mitch nudged her with his shoulder. "Thanks for the help."

God, the way that simple touch and comment affected her, he may as well have said, *Get naked with me*, because that's what her beleaguered brain heard.

"You're good with Brute," he added. "Really good. He trusts you."

"It was either help, or really start sobbing, and I'm an awfully ugly crier."

"Yeah?" Wearing a half smile, his gaze searched hers. "Somehow I find that hard to believe."

"Stick around and you'll see what I mean." Wrinkling her nose, she confessed, "I'm one of those sappy people who get teary-eyed over dumb commercials. You're bound to witness it sooner or later."

"Thanks for the warning." Rising easily to his feet, Mitch stuck out a hand out for her. She took it, her toes curling at the warmth of his big hand as he tugged her up. Smiling warm and teasing, he said, "Crying chicks make me uneasy."

With mock affront, Charlotte repeated, "Crying *chicks*?"

She saw his grin as he...

Turned and walked away from her.

She didn't understand him, but then, when around him, she didn't understand herself either.

The time it took to catch up with Mitch left Newman stewing in resentment. He swigged more beer, swiped a wrist across his mouth and glanced around the overly lit bar.

At only 6:00 p.m., Freddie's felt like a ghost town, boring as shit. Patience wasn't his virtue. He'd rather be fucking or fighting, but none of the bitches here paid him any attention, and the dudes all avoided eye contact.

Just as well. If he started gutting people, no one would be willing to talk after that.

Thanks to one of Mitch's old pals, Newman knew he was

supposed to be in this area. Hadn't been easy to get the clown to talk, but a few gut punches worked wonders to loosen closed lips.

Punches…and the threat of his blade.

Now he needed more info on Mitch to formulate a plan. He wasn't at the hotel, the sneaky bastard—and there didn't seem to be anywhere else to rent.

So where was he holed up? *Why* was he in this Podunk town anyway?

Trying to stay off the radar? That'd make sense. Wasn't easy for a man with a record to make legit coin, and unless he'd done a one-eighty, Mitch had zero interest in the drug trade. He tried to keep things clean, the uppity bastard.

Running his tongue over his teeth, Newman thought on all the ways he'd make Mitch pay for putting him to so much trouble.

Wouldn't have mattered to Newman if he never saw Mitch again—*if* the house was his, as was right, and if Mitch hadn't let the city bury his stash in the demo.

For those things, there'd be no forgiveness.

Ritchie slid into the booth seat across from Newman. Elbows on the tabletop, he leaned in and spoke low. "No one here has seen Mitch, but one guy said his friend, Bernie, told him he'd tangled with a big guy who could've been him. Said he popped Bernie right in the mouth for no reason at all."

Newman grunted a laugh. "Getting ballsy, isn't he? Prison must've toughened him up a little. God knows I couldn't, though I tried hard enough." It never had set right with Newman, having Mitch underfoot, always judging him with his condemning stares, coming to his mom's defense whenever the bitch got what was coming to her.

A man shouldn't be questioned by a kid. Would it have killed Mitch to show a little appreciation now and then? Not like Velma could have gotten another man to do better by her. She was lucky he'd stuck around as long as he had.

Ritchie ran a hand over his greasy blond hair. "So you think it's him?"

"How should I know?" Last he'd seen him, Mitch was an obnoxious, too-proud dick—but he wasn't the type to sucker punch a person. Then again, prison changed a man. "The dude know where to find him?"

Ritchie shook his head. "Nah. Says his friend, Bernie, hasn't seen him since."

Had Ritchie asked the right questions? Who knew?

Though he was thirty-five to Newman's fifty-two, Ritchie looked older and had the thought processes of a rat. Unlike Newman, Ritchie didn't take care of himself. Too much time spent getting high had wasted Ritchie's body and his meager brains.

Newman balanced his life, hitting the weights and feeding his libido and stomach equally. Sex, good food, strength—and then a hit. That's how he'd always run it, even when Velma still hung on.

Ditching her had freed him up big-time; her whining and complaints, clinginess and constant ODs were a grind. Was it any wonder he lost his temper on occasion?

Now that he no longer had to suffer her, he should have had her house to sell as compensation, with his drugs hidden inside, and instead she'd left it to a pansy-ass son who'd run off as fast as he could.

Stupid bitch.

Newman watched as Ritchie tipped up his beer and guzzled it down, a trickle escaping the side of his mouth to catch in his whiskers before dripping along his throat and onto his dirty shirt.

Judging by the emaciated looks of him, Ritchie would burn out soon, and good riddance. But Newman planned to be around, kicking ass and fucking women bowlegged for a good long while yet.

After a loud belch, Ritchie asked, "What're we gonna do?"

"Lee's out asking around. Maybe he'll turn up something."

Unfortunately, Newman thought, he was short on comrades right now. Not that long ago he'd have pulled together a dozen men to search.

Now it was just him, piss-poor Ritchie and psycho Lee. Between the three of them, they'd eventually find Mitch, then he'd get what payment he could out of him.

And after that?

Newman smiled. He'd probably leave the bastard to die in a ditch somewhere.

CHAPTER EIGHT

After spending the rest of his day configuring his new up-and-coming business, Mitch arrived at Rosalyn's house for dinner. He was a few minutes early, but clearly that wasn't a problem.

From the driver's seat he noted Brodie and Jack's red and yellow Mustangs, parked on the right side of the driveway. Charlotte's little blue Ford was behind a newer white Mustang that he thought was Rosalyn's.

Everyone was already here...including Charlotte who sat at her leisure there on the front porch steps. Now dressed in a pink camisole with denim shorts, she showed a lot of peach skin and had a very fine set of legs on display.

Damn but the sight of her hit him like a punch to the gut. Her particular blend of sex appeal and innocence pushed all his buttons, even buttons he hadn't known about.

What would it be like to have those sleek legs wrapped tight around him while he rode her deep and fast? And after the sex, while she was still warm and damp and satisfied, he'd hold her close, see her smile, smooth that wild abundance of curls...

The fantasy drew him as much for the carnal appeal as the emotional balm. His balls tightened and his heart beat heavier.

Charlotte Parrish was the real deal, the whole package, a woman who'd make a man content just with her presence.

Course, she had a temper too—and from what he'd seen of it so far, it was just as nice.

Was she waiting for him?

The idea warmed him, but also made him wary since he had an agreement with the guys. Teasing her this morning, flirting while others were a few feet away, helped her relax with him without the risk of things getting out of hand.

She needed to know he wanted her.

This? Alone on one side of the house?

Dangerous.

Charlotte pointed to a spot behind her car where he saw just enough room for him to park.

After he let Brute out of the back, he said, "Hey."

Elbows braced behind her, legs stretched out and crossed at the ankles, she smiled. "Hey, yourself."

Was that flirting? The way she looked at him, with her eyes heavy and intense…normally he'd say yes, but with this woman? He just didn't know.

Maybe he'd been more successful this morning than he'd realized. For now, with that smile and in that relaxed position, she looked far from shy and reserved.

More like interested and on the make.

Damn, but the different facets of her mesmerized him.

Voices carried from the backyard, interspersed with happy barking that made Brute's ears perk and twitch.

As if she'd read his mind, Charlotte said, "Brodie and Mary, Jack and Ronnie, Ros and the animals are all around back setting up. Ros decided to do dinner picnic-style so the dogs had more room to play." Scrunching her nose, she looked up at the sky. "With those dark clouds moving in, hopefully we won't get rained on."

Brute looked toward the back, then walked over to Charlotte, nudging her hand for a pat. As she sat forward to oblige, the press of her breasts pressed against the lightweight material of her camisole snagged all his attention.

Did she wear a bra? While she fawned on Brute, Mitch got entirely too engrossed in studying the delicate curves, imagining how those small, soft breasts would feel in his hands—and how her nipples would feel in his mouth.

Knowing he had to clear his head before she busted him ogling her, or worse, his body reacted—*with the entirety of his newly found family on the other side of the yard*—Mitch said, "Brute likes you."

"And I like him." Touching her nose to Brute's and sweetening her voice, she crooned, "Yes, I do. I like this furry face. It's so cute."

Huh. The silly way she talked to his dog had as much effect as that body-hugging top.

Who knew it'd be a turn-on to have his dog so loved and accepted?

Sure it was different, more tender than carnal—and possibly more powerful because of it.

Desperate to get his libido under control, Mitch cleared his throat. "Coming here has been good for him."

"And you?" The tilt of her, the way she looked up at him, emphasized her blue eyes and long lashes. "So far, it's good for you too?"

What did she expect?

For him to admit how much this, an opportunity to belong, meant to him?

A confession that the prospect of *not* being alone was equally alarming to no family at all?

No, he'd say none of that. Keeping it superficial made more sense. "So far it's going better than I had hoped."

"Yeah." Her smile held secrets he didn't understand. "That's just how they are. You'll see."

In her case, he understood why. Charlotte was pretty hard to resist. "You're a part of them. If I didn't know better, I'd think you were their actual sister."

"Because we squabble like siblings?" Sighing, Charlotte braced a forearm on her knee. "There are times I want to punch Brodie in the throat, or maybe throw dirt on Jack just to muss him up a little." She flashed an endearing, impish smile. "But I love them both."

Fighting a laugh over the casual way she addressed violence, Mitch nodded. "I picked up on that right away." Little by little, he got the hang of her relationship with Jack and Brodie. He'd never been that close to another person.

For him, if he issued an insult he damn well meant it, and knew it could come to blows.

"What about you?"

Eyes squinted against the sun, she asked, "What about me?"

"Other than with the guys, do you interact with insults?" Somehow he couldn't see it. Friendliness, yes. Above and beyond with assistance, sure. But he'd bet that playful harassment started and ended with his brothers.

"Have I insulted you?" she countered with a smile, then shook her head. "I try to be nice to people, and that's easy enough around here. We have a lot of good people in town."

Her being one of them. "I'm seeing that."

"Occasionally a customer will be a butthead, but I ignore it because I know I won't see them often." Putting her nose in the air, she stated, "I can be professional."

She could be adorable—but maybe he shouldn't say that.

"The way you are with Brute...are you that good with all animals?"

Her slender shoulder lifted. "Far as I know, yeah. I love animals and they love me." Voice going softer, she added, "I visit the animal shelter when I have free time. They always need volunteers to walk the dogs or play with the cats."

So instead of dating, she spent her time with homeless animals in need? Fuck, she might as well take his heart right from his chest. "Maybe I could go with you sometime."

Admiration, and more, shone in her eyes. "I'd like that."

Standing over her, nearby but not too close, he noticed how the humidity had turned her cheeks dewy and the way a warm flush covered the skin of her throat and exposed chest. She'd caught her frizzy hair into a high ponytail but still little curls sprang out around her ears, her temples, and along her neck. "Then it's a date—when you have free time."

Her mouth twitched, probably because her free days were few and far between. "Deal."

What he wanted to do? Sit down close beside her so their hips touched. Lay his arm along the step behind her, breathe in the fragrance of that wild hair and sun-heated skin. See how she'd react, how she'd fit against him, maybe go for a kiss.

Touching her would be incredibly nice.

He cleared his throat. As much as it pained him, he couldn't break an agreement. He didn't have much, but he had his word.

So he jammed his hands into his back pockets to help resist temptation. "I should have brought something, but I didn't think about it until just now."

Remaining lazily posed on the stairs, Charlotte stroked Brute and asked, "What do you mean?"

Fighting the urge to get closer to her, he gestured toward the backyard. "A dessert or something." Isn't that what guests did? No idea. He had zero social graces.

Her smile warmed another notch. "Ros didn't want you to. Besides, I already baked a cake."

"You baked a... When?" She'd been at the office early and according to Brodie, it was supposed to be a busy day for her. Not that he knew for sure. After leaving the offices, he'd headed to his new digs to do some work of his own. God knew it'd be a while before the place would be presentable, or he could make a profit. "You didn't put in a full day?"

"I got home an hour ago."

No way. "And you decided to *bake*?" Did she ever relax? Didn't seem so. Not being great with idle time himself, her near electric vitality was another lure.

But damn it, how could he ever get a date if she never slowed down?

"Not a big deal. I enjoy baking and I had a hankering for a white chocolate cake. While it was in the oven, I showered."

"White chocolate? So…homemade? Not a box mix?"

Elevating her chin again, she said, "Wouldn't be real baking if it was just out of a box."

For someone who usually picked up a premade when the sweet tooth hit, it counted to him. "I hope you didn't go to too much trouble."

She shrugged. "The boys like it."

"Boys?" Another smile tugged at his mouth. "You're calling those Goliaths *boys*?"

"Look who's talking. You're every bit as big as they are." Pushing to her feet, she said, "Come on, they're all anxious to see you." She led him and Brute around the house.

He couldn't resist one more question. "And you? Were you anxious to see me, Charlotte?"

Over her shoulder, she replied, "I made you a cake, didn't I?"

The ear-splitting grin caught him by surprise. The cake was for his benefit, then, not Brodie and Jack's. Nice.

Suddenly it struck him: he'd just done what the *boys* had asked him not to—he'd hung around talking her up, admiring and ogling her, flirting, in relative privacy. At least at the office that morning, Brodie knew they were inside.

Damn it, he needed to avoid being alone with her or he'd never last. When he got around her, he forgot everything except getting to know her better.

When they reached the backyard, Brodie called to Mitch, "Good, you made it." And then, without missing a beat, he added to Charlotte, "Thanks for watching out for him, hon."

So Brodie had set that up? Seriously, did he not know how tempting Charlotte looked in the skimpier clothes, lounging there on the steps, her spine relaxed, bare legs stretched out, elbows braced behind her while that gorgeous hair played around her face?

Or maybe it had been a test. That idea didn't set well—especially since he'd failed it.

Or…could it have been a sign of trust?

Jesus, he wished he knew more about the inner workings of a normal family.

Having just noticed them, Howler came barreling from the back of the yard, a brown Lab right behind him.

Brute, of course, did his dodge and cower act, snuggling behind Mitch and tucking his face in his ass.

"Hey, hey," Mitch said, trying to readjust. Not easy to do with Brute so afraid.

One day soon, Brute would learn that he wouldn't let any harm come to him. Until then, Mitch would just continue to reassure him the best he could.

He'd be there for Brute…because he knew how it felt to feel threatened and alone.

"Whoa." Jack caught the Lab before he reached them. "This is Buster and he's not nearly as perceptive as Howler. He's all about playing, but I don't want him to spook Brute."

"Thanks." Mitch managed to get turned around and down on one knee.

Though Buster wiggled all over in happiness at meeting a new dog, Brute was not receptive.

Sitting on the grass beside him, Charlotte said, "Brute? Come here, baby," in a soft, throaty voice that made *Mitch's* ears twitch.

He watched, no longer amazed, when Brute switched over to

her and leaned into her side. Bare arm around the dog, Charlotte whispered encouragement while stroking Brute's neck and fondling his ears.

Stroking and fondling? Struggling to get his brain out of a sexual morass, Mitch said, "Thanks."

"My pleasure." Inch by inch, Charlotte let Howler wiggle in closer until the two dogs were happily sniffing each other and acting like friends again. "Jack, let Buster go, now. We'll see how it goes."

"You sure?" Jack asked, deferring to Mitch.

Mitch shrugged. Charlotte, with her magic touch, seemed to have it under control—which was more than he could say. "Give it a try."

"Go easy, bud," Jack cautioned Buster, before releasing his collar.

Ears flopping wildly, Buster bolted up to them, jumped on Howler, and the two spun away for a little roughhousing. Brute watched with interest and maybe yearning, his tail giving a few tentative wags, his expression alert.

"You know you want to," Charlotte whispered to him. "Why not go for it, big boy?"

Mitch stared. Hard to believe, but by the second he wanted her even more.

Bounding back, Howler gave a ridiculously high-pitched yowl, and managed to entice Brute a few feet into the yard. This time when he and Buster took off, Brute loped after them.

"Well, look at that." Brute didn't leap into the thick of the play, instead watching on the fringe. To Mitch, the important part was him being there, occasionally running alongside the others, overall looking pretty...happy.

He turned to help Charlotte up, but she'd already stood without him noticing and was moseying into the yard, keeping close to the dogs.

In case Brute needed her? Protective. He liked that.

Hell, he liked everything about her—including that lush little behind in her shorts.

"Ahem," Ronnie said, drawing his attention as she sauntered near.

During his second visit to the offices, he'd been briefly introduced to the wives, Ronnie and Mary. They were both attractive in different ways, but more importantly, they were as friendly as the guys.

"You've met the dogs, so I figured you should meet the ruler of the roost." Ronnie nuzzled a mid-sized cat with fuzzy gray-and-brown fur and wide green eyes. "This is my Peanut."

Cute. Mitch ran one finger beneath the cat's chin, earning a rumbling purr. "She gets along with the dogs?"

"Peanut is a very pretty *male* kitty, and yes, they dote on him."

"Ah, sorry Peanut." From everything he'd heard, he had a feeling Ronnie would have fit right in at his old neighborhood. He liked her *mess with me or mine and I'll land my boot on your butt* demeanor. She had an edge that promised one and all she wouldn't take any shit.

With short platinum hair and an abundance of earrings, she flaunted a style all her own. For a variety of reasons, she'd turn heads wherever she went, but she aimed all her sex appeal at Jack.

Mary, Brodie's wife, was still with Rosalyn as they carried dishes out from the house. Because her hands were full, she smiled her welcome. Despite blazing red hair, freckles and a full figure, she was a mix of elegance and business savvy.

Looking back at the cat, Mitch asked, "This is the one you rescued?"

"Yes." Ronnie rubbed her cheek against the cat's head. "My little cupid."

Rolling his eyes, Jack joined them.

"You know it's true." Then to Mitch, she said, "Some major asshole was tormenting Peanut, and I was so furious I wanted to stick my knife in his forehead."

Wow. Unsure if she was serious, Mitch glanced at Jack.

Blowing out a breath, Jack said, "I wish that was a joke, but curbing her wasn't easy."

"Ha! You didn't *curb* me." Leaning toward Mitch, she said, "You should have seen him. Jack might act all smooth and urbane, but he doesn't tolerate cruelty. He went dark and mean real fast." She grinned at her husband. "Sexy as hell, let me tell you."

"You're telling *everyone*," Jack complained, but he used one arm to pull her in for a hug.

"Pretty sure that's when I decided he was a keeper, so Peanut gets the credit. If it wasn't for this cat, I might still be under the delusion that Jack was *suave*."

The way she stated that like an insult had Mitch grinning.

From the picnic table, Mary chimed in with, "Brodie is never suave. In fact, he has one mode—caveman. It's part of his charm."

"I have *charm*," Brodie bragged.

Damn, but he liked these people. All of them. They were like mismatched puzzle pieces that somehow created the perfect picture, rough edges and all.

"What about you?" Charlotte asked as she rejoined them. "What's your usual mode?"

Survival. And with it, suspicion—of everyone and everything. *Not* something he wanted to share aloud, so he said instead, "I don't know. Definitely not suave—"

Ronnie saluted him.

"—but I hope not a caveman either. Maybe...cautious?"

Nodding, Charlotte said, "How about honest?"

The others, all listening in, gave a chorus of "hear, hear."

That probably made sense. After all, he had nearly bludgeoned them with his brutal honesty.

"Independent," Ros called out.

"Determined." Jack gave it more thought. "Stubborn."

Laughing, Brodie called from the grill, "Glad they're dissecting you instead of me."

The way they did it, he didn't mind, but he did turn the tables on Charlotte. "Your turn."

"I don't know." Her brows pinched down. "I'm just me."

"She wins people over with her baking," Brodie offered.

"And her generosity," Jack said.

"You guys." Face warm, she sauntered off again.

Watching her, Mitch smiled, and silently added "humble" to the list. Also protective, proven in the way she shadowed Brute. She knew how to take a joke, and how to dish it back.

Jack said to Ronnie, "We've lost him."

"Oh, I don't know. I think maybe we're reeling him in."

Mitch didn't bother denying that. "Her mode is subtle." He watched her pick a dandelion from the yard, then twirl it between her fingers. Subtle but effective, innately sensual, and almost impossible to resist.

With a frown, Jack started to say something, but got cut short.

"Who wants treats?" Rosalyn called out, and immediately Howler and Buster raced to her. Brute, unsure of the offer, approached more slowly, but once he caught on, he was just as excited as the others.

Using care to ensure they each only got one, Ros doled out the biscuits with affection.

Once Brute had his, he returned to Mitch, but since Howler followed, Brute whined.

"He's never gotten over being starved," Mitch explained. "Sometimes he hoards his food."

From the grill, Brodie said, "Howler's the opposite. He eats everything as fast as he can, usually in one big gulp."

True enough, Howler devoured the treat in three seconds flat, then rolled to his back, plate-sized paws in the air, his droopy lips falling back to reveal sharp teeth in an odd doggy grin. Watching Brute upside down, he wiggled closer until Mitch had to laugh.

"Cut him some slack, Brute. He wants to be buddies, not steal your snack."

Whining, Brute looked out at Buster.

"Ah, so it's the new guy, huh? Well, I don't think he'd steal your treat either."

"With Buster, we never know," Ronnie admitted. "He's sweet, but he's not as sharp as Howler."

"Don't insult the dog," Jack said, helping Brute by breaking the treat into little bites that he hand-fed to him.

That seemed to entice Brute—or else he was afraid Jack would eat it if he didn't.

After that, Brute found the water dishes on the back porch, then he headed out to the yard, the other dogs following, and they all returned to their play.

Hands on his hips, his heart oddly full, Mitch watched Brute dart around the yard.

Brodie came to stand beside him. "Howler won't let other animals be strangers. Those grandmother tendencies I mentioned? He makes sure all the kids play nice."

Mitch didn't take his gaze off the animals because he didn't want another man—his *brother*—to see how hard it hit him. He loved Brute, and damn it, he felt a kinship to him. "He deserves to loosen up." *He deserves to feel accepted.*

The thought lingered, but it was yet another better left unsaid.

"Everyone does." Lightening the moment, Brodie sniffed the air. "Hope you're hungry. I grilled corn on the cob and potatoes to go with Mom's famous fried chicken."

It smelled so good, Mitch's mouth watered.

Everyone sat at the tablecloth-covered table, and somehow he ended up between Rosalyn and Charlotte. Not that he minded bumping Charlotte every so often, feeling her thigh touch his, but damn, it worked as pure temptation. He picked up her scent without even trying.

Twice he lost track of the conversation.

No amount of distraction would keep him from noticing how they worked as a unit. Someone always had eyes on the dogs, ensuring they didn't leave the yard. Jack got up once to refill the water dishes. Mary went inside to get the salt that Ros had forgotten. Brodie caught Ronnie's napkin when it almost blew away. It was all so natural, it almost felt choreographed.

And the…affection. More demonstrative than Mitch, they openly teased each other—and him on occasion. They hugged, touched, laughed together.

When he'd come up with the idea of finding the brothers, he hadn't known exactly what he wanted. A fresh start, yes. Some semblance of family, sure. Roots. Home.

This, picnics in the yard with home-cooked food and happy animals at play…it was so damn picturesque, it didn't feel real. He'd had nearly a week with them, but it wasn't enough.

Would a year be enough? A lifetime? Would he ever be at ease in scenarios that were as unfamiliar as flying to the moon?

He didn't know, but he hoped to find out.

"Mitch?"

He looked up to find Charlotte watching him.

The quick smile didn't conceal her gentle concern. "Everything okay?"

One glance around the table showed *everyone* looking at him, making him wonder if he'd missed a question. "What—" His phone buzzed in his pocket, giving him the perfect excuse to dodge all those penetrating stares. "Sorry, I'll just be a second." As he stood, Charlotte touched his arm, her gaze inquiring.

With one step he took himself out of her reach, and her hand dropped. "Be right back."

Glad for the reprieve, he drew out the phone while walking a good distance from the table. Recognizing Lang Hardy's number, he answered with, "Hey, Lang, what's up?"

He didn't count many as friend, but he and Lang had known

each other since they were kids. In fact, Lang was the only one who knew where he was now.

"I'm sorry man. So damn sorry."

The fine hairs on Mitch's nape jumped in alarm. Anger sizzled along his spine. His breathing shortened.

He recognized those defensive reactions—learned in childhood, sharpened in prison. Walking farther away so none of the others could hear, he asked, "What did you do?"

Suddenly Brute was at his side, leaning into his leg, huffing a little with worry. Mitch automatically laid a hand on his muscled neck.

"Newman came after me."

The shock of that took a second to hit. The sound of his own heartbeat in his ears nearly deafened him. His blood chilled.

"Mitch? Let me explain."

Explanations weren't necessary. If Lang had talked, he already knew why. "How bad?"

In a rush, his voice strained, Lang explained, "He wanted to know where you were. I didn't want to tell him. I even tried to run when I first spotted them at my house—"

"Shh. It's okay." Staring straight ahead, not seeing anything, Mitch's brain was already scrambling. Calmly, with the understanding Lang requested, he asked, "How bad did he hurt you?"

"He worked me over, man. Broke two fucking ribs. Blood… The old lady found me and freaked, okay? She dragged me off to the hospital and this is the first chance I've had to call."

"When?" He may or may not have time to get away from his brothers and Ros, away from Charlotte, before trouble came bearing down on them all.

After a long pause, Lang admitted, "I figured he was there already. Not like you went that far."

Definitely not far enough. "Did he say what he wanted?"

"Your ass." Lang cleared his throat. "Dude, he was in a rage. You know how he is."

Yeah, he knew only too well. With his head dropped forward, Mitch worked the knot of tension forming in his neck. "You're okay?"

"The ribs and nose will heal."

"Nose?"

"That's why there was so much blood. You know Maria. She thought I was dying, but I've busted ribs before." After a short pause, Lang burst. "*Goddamn it*, I should have held out! I shouldn't have blabbed to him. If I'd—"

"He wouldn't have stopped." Mitch knew that for a fact—because he knew Newman. He felt a little dead inside, and also quietly enraged. "He would have beaten you until he got what he wanted, or he would have used that fucking blade." Newman looked for reasons to draw his knife.

"But I—"

"You did the right thing. Newman is my problem, not yours."

Right behind him, Brodie said, "And your problems are ours."

He jerked around…and there they were, every fucking one of them, listening in, intruding.

Even Charlotte.

"Gotta go, Lang. Take care of yourself." Fingers of alarm squeezed his windpipe. He disconnected the call, then said, "This doesn't concern any of you."

Jack shook his head. "Not how it works with family."

Agreeing, Brodie said, "So how about you tell us what we're dealing with."

Instead of backing up, Mitch took a step forward. "Sorry, no. Not this time." Briefly, he turned to Charlotte. All her earlier sass was now subdued beneath fear. He closed his eyes, drew one breath, and said again, "Sorry," before turning and heading for his car. Leaving Charlotte like that, without explanations, was one of the hardest things he'd ever done. But still he did—for her.

Brute followed.

No one else did.

★ ★ ★

Charlotte was worried.

Last night, after that awkward apology and refusal to explain, Mitch had left and no one had heard from him since. Morning had come and gone. Lunch was long over.

Where was he?

Brodie and Jack wanted to give him time. She and Ros were less convinced.

It ate her up, thinking of Mitch alone. Of him *feeling* alone. He wasn't, not anymore.

Didn't he know that?

In her heart, she knew the answer. It was all too new for him to accept it yet. A week wasn't long enough.

Would he be different after a month? A year?

Or had his life fashioned him to where he couldn't fully trust? From what little she knew, she couldn't blame him.

Even before her parents died, she'd had love, affection and attention. The Crews family hadn't missed a single step in doing all they could to keep her feeling loved. They were so wonderful, and Mitch deserved them.

But what if he left?

Her heart and head pounded in sync. He'd only just met them, only just started to relax...and now this.

From what they'd overheard last night, his mother's boyfriend was looking for him.

Newman is my problem.

Charlotte thought Newman might be capable of anything— and that scared her. Mitch needed backup, he needed support... and they didn't even know where he was.

Not within the town proper; she'd gone into town twice today on trumped-up excuses, first to get supplies, then later to deliver a contract that could have been mailed.

She'd looked for his distinctive car, but hadn't seen it anywhere. With less subtlety than she would have liked, she'd asked around—but no one had seen anyone with his description.

Had he already left?

Would she never see him again?

As Brodie passed the office, he glanced at her, did a double take, and with concern pinching his brows, stepped in to squeeze her shoulder. "I asked around. No one fitting his description at the hotel."

She didn't tell him that she'd done the same. "There's really nowhere else, is there?" Not exactly a tourist destination, one hotel was all Red Oak had ever needed.

"Don't look so glum. He'll be back."

If only confidence was contagious. "How can you be so sure?"

With a fleeting grin, he said, "You. He'll be back for you, honey."

"Me?" Surprise nearly toppled her out of her chair. "How do I factor in?"

"You're naive, but not dumb."

Her incredulous laugh sounded a little too high. *And maybe a wee bit hopeful?* "He came here to meet his family."

"Yup. But then he also met you." He brushed a fingertip over the end of her nose. "Before meeting Mary, I might not have understood. Now? Trust me. He'll be back."

A mix of emotions made her wince. "And if he doesn't?"

"Jack and I will find him. I'm willing to give him two days, so relax, okay?" With a nod at the desk, he said, "The phone is blinking."

Oh, shoot.

In a rush she put one caller on Hold and spoke with another. The afternoon got even busier, and that helped to distract her right up until the end of the day.

Then her thoughts crashed and burned again.

Damn it, how dare Mitch show up, reel them in, then just

bail over one little stupid phone call? She preferred anger over melancholy, so she dove in with that thought, fueling the flames.

How dare he flirt with her as if interested? How dare he make *her* interested?

And seriously, why did she care so much? Hadn't she known for years now that she didn't want anyone like Brodie and Jack? Yes, she had.

Mitch, being their half brother, would naturally share some similarities beyond the physical. Like his love of animals.

Given this new stunt, just disappearing on them, she knew he was stubborn and too independent as well.

Annoyed at herself, Charlotte shut down the PC, stacked the last bit of paperwork and pushed away from her desk.

By then, everyone else had already left the office. Brodie was gone overnight on a delivery and Jack wouldn't be back until late. Ros had a hair appointment. Time to lock up and stop brooding over a man who'd apparently put her—and this family—from his mind.

With one last sweep of the office building to ensure she'd turned off the coffee, rinsed out the pot and turned out the lights, she headed to the front and grabbed her purse. Stepping out of the front room, she locked the door for the interior office, turned to go out the main door—and found three men looking in at her.

Strangers showing up at the end of business might not be unthinkable in a city, or even in town, but here? Mustang Transport was located up a hill from the main road, situated on wooded acreage that suddenly seemed far too isolated.

Alarm crawled up her spine and left her trembling.

Before she even had time to plan it out, Charlotte smiled and held up a finger in the universal sign for "just a moment," then turned and unlocked the interior door. Her hands shook. She heard the main door open behind her just as she got the interior door open and hurriedly slipped inside, closing it fast and locking it again.

Alone in the dark, she backed up until her backside bumped the desk. Breath quickening and heart rapping against her breastbone, she wondered what to do now.

Knuckles rapped sharply against the door. "Hey, you okay in there?"

At the same time, a shadow moved past the window and she just knew someone was trying to look in.

Thankful that she'd turned out the lights, she withdrew her phone and darted into a corner, completely out of sight. She already felt foolish enough without anyone peeking in through the blinds.

"Little lady?" Voice mellow and calm, someone suggested, "Why don't you open up?"

That he sounded pleasant only made it more threatening. She felt like a coward and didn't care as she called the police station.

The second someone answered, she whispered, "This is Charlotte Parrish at Mustang Transport. I was just locking up when three men came in. They're knocking on my inner office door. Strangers. I... I don't feel right about them being here."

"Charlotte," said a serious but calm male voice. "This is Grant Colvin."

Oh, thank God. Grant was a seasoned cop—a good one—and a friend of the family. Always reasonable and reliable, and kind too. "Grant, I'm sorry to bother you but—"

"Have they threatened you?"

She hated to admit it, but... "No." It wasn't quite seven thirty. The sun wouldn't set for a while yet. It would literally take her two minutes to drive down to the main street—if she was in her car. And yet... "Do you think you could send someone by?"

"I'm on my way." She heard him moving, the sound of keys jangling. "Did you ask them to leave?"

She frowned, then covered the phone to say loudly, "We're

closed. Come back tomorrow morning." *When Brodie or Jack are here.*

The doorknob rattled violently.

Or maybe that was just her jangled nerves.

"Open up, girl. I only want to talk to you, maybe ask you a few questions."

She managed a breath and said into the phone, "I just did and they're not budging."

"Sit tight," he said. "I'll be there before you know it."

"Quietly, okay? If you cause a scene and they're just here for business…" *I'll really feel like a fool.*

"It'll be like a social call," Grant promised.

The call disconnected.

Leaning back against the wall, her arms hugged around herself, Charlotte tried to calculate how long it would take Grant to get from the station to the office.

And how easy it'd be for someone to kick in that door.

CHAPTER NINE

As the cop stood, Mitch did too. Two seconds into that call, his heart had lodged in his throat. "You said Charlotte."

Giving him the side-eye, Officer Colvin confirmed, "I did."

It couldn't be, yet how many women with her name would be in a town this size? "Charlotte Parrish, who works with Brodie and Jack Crews?"

"The same."

Frustration mounting, Mitch watched in disbelief and mounting terror as the enigmatic cop headed out. What the hell?

In two long strides, he caught up with Colvin. "What's going on?"

"I'm not sure that's your business." Pausing at a desk, Colvin spoke quietly to a younger man. "Charlotte has a few guests making her uncomfortable. I'm going to run up there and take a look. I shouldn't be long."

"Got it." The guy didn't bother to look up from a computer where he typed away on a keyboard.

"What guests?" Mitch demanded, striding alongside the cop as he headed outside. So far, Officer Colvin had been politely detached as Mitch tried to explain the amount of trouble that came with Newman and his gang. Unfortunately, no, he didn't know for a fact that Newman was in town yet, or where to find him if he was, or for sure when he'd arrive, or what he planned, or anything else.

But he had to warn the law, right? It was the only way to protect…his family? No, he couldn't think in those terms just yet.

In coming here, he'd also fessed up to being an ex-con himself—and although Colvin hadn't been as blasé about it as the Crews family, the veteran cop didn't seem overly bothered by it either.

"Thanks for stopping in with the info." Colvin opened his black-and-white and got in. "I'll keep an eye out." He closed the door and started the engine.

"Damn it!" In the seconds it took Mitch to jog over to his own car, Colvin had already pulled out and he had to catch up without speeding past a stop sign.

As he drove, he gave himself a pep talk. Charlotte had customers bother her all the time, but that didn't mean it was Newman. It didn't mean she was in trouble.

Where the hell were Brodie and Jack?

If Newman touches her… No, probably not him, Mitch reminded himself. He hadn't yet seen Newman, but even if he was in town, he wouldn't know Mitch was connected to the Crews family. There'd be no reason to be at Mustang Transport, hassling Charlotte.

He stayed right behind Officer Colvin, his hands gripping the wheel too tightly, until they both pulled into the empty yard.

Mitch was out of his car before Colvin had turned off his engine. Urgency pushing him, he sprinted up to the front door, pulled—and it opened.

Shadows and silence filled the interior.

Held in the grip of dread, he called, "Charlotte?"

It seemed he *felt* the pause, the suspension of time and space, and then, from the interior office, she squeaked, "Mitch?"

Relief took the strength from his legs. "Yeah." He tried the handle but she had it locked. "Shit. Are you all right?"

The door opened and she peeked out. Seeing him, she jerked it wider and demanded, *"Where the hell have you been?"*

Okay…yeah, wasn't expecting that.

Officer Colvin cleared his throat.

Wow, he'd forgotten all about him. Mitch glanced his way and found him lounging in the entry, a look of acute interest on his face.

Mitch frowned—and Charlotte rudely pushed past him.

"Grant, thank you for coming so quickly."

"Part of the job," Colvin said. "Everything okay?"

"I think they finally left." She leaned out the door to look around, but Mitch already knew the lot was empty. "There were three of them, and someone kept jostling the doorknob until I stated that the cops were on the way. I could hear them talking and laughing, but I couldn't understand what was said. Then it got quiet. I wasn't sure if they'd left, so I didn't open the door."

"You did the right thing." Colvin followed her outside.

Mitch trailed them both, his irritation ramping up.

Lifting a hand to shield her eyes, Charlotte searched the area. "It's weird, right? I mean, that they'd come here, hang around and rattle doors until I said I'd called the cops?"

"Weird enough that I think you need to give me a description of them."

Charlotte bit her lip. "I had only a brief glance."

Rather than interfere, and possibly draw her ire again, Mitch stood off to the side listening. Charlotte explained how she'd put them off and very smartly locked herself inside.

Renewed rage began to churn, because in his gut, hell, in his bones and heart and the blood pumping through his veins, he knew it was Newman.

Even before she gave the description of early fifties, brown hair pulled into a ponytail and a receding hairline, he *knew.*

Squeezing the words out through locked teeth wasn't easy. "That's him." His jaw flexed as he struggled to keep his anger contained. "It's Newman Bates and it's a serious problem that he was here."

Charlotte stiffened but didn't look at him.

He didn't look at her either. If he did, he'd grab her close, hold her tight to assure himself she wasn't hurt, and that'd blow his edge. Right now he needed to think, and Charlotte with her soft smiles and gentle nature made that damn near impossible.

Quirking his brow, Colvin glanced back and forth between them. "I'll ask around, check the hotel and such. There aren't many places to stay near here—"

"We know," Charlotte said, her tone almost sugary, "because we looked for Mitch and couldn't find him."

"A day," he said, spreading his arms in emphasis. "It was a single damn day because I had shit to take care of."

Her little nose went up and she turned away. "Will you let me know what you find out, Grant?"

Amusement had Colvin's mouth twitching, but his tone was all business when he said, "Of course." He patted her hand. "Until then, you shouldn't be here alone. And be damn sure you tell Brodie and Jack what happened. Got it?"

For *him*, she had a beautiful smile. "Of course I will."

Mitch pinched the bridge of his nose. He felt a headache coming on in tandem with the rage. Could he find Newman first? Doubtful.

This was one of Newman's favorite games. Striking from the shadows, causing worry and then terror and when his prey grew frazzled, then he would make his move.

But what to do now? He'd just met these people, and he'd brought the worst kind of trouble *literally* to their door.

Colvin turned. "You two okay here?"

Not about to speak for Charlotte, Mitch folded his arms and scowled.

She patted the cop's arm. "We're fine, no worries. I'm sure Mitch will take off—again."

Damn it, did she have to keep throwing barbs at him?

How much of that shit did she think he'd take?

But of course he knew. He'd take it all, because no way in hell was he leaving her alone, not until he knew she was home, safe and sound.

Well hell.

Well now, that had been worth the trip. He could still see the wariness in her eyes as she scuttled her sexy little ass into that office and locked the door. Smart girl.

What would he have done? No telling now, though his intent had only been to talk to her, to see if Mitch told her where he might be staying.

"She damn near fainted," Ritchie cackled, laughing so hard he choked himself.

Grinning in agreement, Newman soaked up the gleeful satisfaction over little Miss Charlotte's fear.

Pulling up to the hotel, Lee said, "It's doubtful Mitch was fucking her."

"I know. Sweet little girls aren't really his speed."

Finding Bernie had been a piece of cake. Dude spent all his free time in the bar and everyone knew him. Once Newman had explained who he was and that Mitch owed him money, they became allies in animosity—or so Bernie thought. Dumbass had blabbed about Mitch as fast as he could—and in the process, told them about Charlotte.

"Hadn't expected to find her all alone like that," Newman mused, wishing he could have gotten his hands on her. His plan had been to play the role of a doting relative looking to find Mitch.

One look at them though, and she'd bolted. At the time he

hadn't realized that was her intent. He thought she'd already locked the door and was going back for the keys.

Instead, she'd locked herself into a dark room. Terrified? Probably.

He started chuckling with the memory and that got Ritchie going again.

Lee, always a stone-faced bastard, turned off the car. "What now?"

Wiping his eyes and still grinning, Newman said philosophically, "We keep looking." Today's activity had at least broken up the monotony and offered a little amusement.

The thick balmy air assaulted him as he left the car and headed for the hotel. They wouldn't stick around forever, but for now, he planned to exhaust every effort to find Mitch.

Along the way, he'd planned to have more fun with Charlotte. Next time she wouldn't be able to dodge him so easily.

The second Colvin's car pulled away, Charlotte turned and marched back inside. Mitch half expected her to lock him out, but instead, she went into the inner office and flipped on a light.

As if he approached a wild cat, he used caution as he leaned in to see her at the desk chair, making a call.

Elbow on the desktop, the phone pressed to her ear, she stared straight ahead. The fingertips of her other hand drummed an antsy tune against her thigh.

Mitch ventured farther in. "You okay?"

"Fine and dandy."

Judging by the clip of her voice, she wasn't. She tried to hide it, but he saw the subtle trembling in her shoulders.

Suddenly she said into the phone, "Brodie, hey. Did I catch you at a bad time? No, good. You took so long to answer—oh, gotcha. Well did you want to call him back?"

Apparently Brodie had been on the phone with someone else.

Mitch got comfortable leaning against the wall and made no pretense of not listening in.

Making a face, Charlotte said, "Well, see—first, don't freak out... No, I'm *fine*. See, you're already freaking out!" She stuck the phone on Speaker and dropped it to the desk, saying in a near shout, "I should have called Jack!"

"No, *I'll* call him—after you tell me what happened."

Mitch said, "I could explain."

This pause was really heavy and fraught with suspicion.

Brodie asked, "That you, Mitch?"

Unable to stay still, he pushed off the wall. "Yeah, and I'm sorry, but three men showed up at the office a little while ago when Charlotte•was alone." Unlike her, he wouldn't waste time venting or arguing, not when they all needed to understand the situation. "Like she said, she's fine. She had the good sense to lock herself inside even before she knew if they were dangerous."

"But you figure they are?"

Dangerous didn't quite cover it. "Pretty sure it was Newman and his cronies. She called Officer Colvin. He's going to check around, starting with the hotel. I'm damned sorry, but if it was Newman, that's a serious problem."

"Couple of questions while I drive," Brodie said in an admirable, take-charge voice. "First one's for Charlotte. How did you know they were bad? Customers do drop in occasionally."

Mitch watched her fidget in her seat before she shook her head. "I didn't, I guess. But I had a feeling. They *looked* bad—and although I know looks are deceiving, there was something there. It's like I felt it."

"You have good instincts. I'm glad you used caution."

Mitch said, "Newman is one of those guys you see, and you know right off he has bad intentions."

"Sounds like," Brodie said. "So Mitch, how'd you end up there with her?"

Though he expected it, Mitch didn't hear anger, only curiosity. Was Brodie one of those guys who stayed cool under fire? Apparently. Tension gathered in his neck and crawled around to his jaw. "I was talking to Colvin when she called. I followed him here."

Charlotte spun her chair to face him. "You were talking to Grant? Why?"

"Good question," Brodie said.

They both waited.

This whole thing of answering to people… Mitch wasn't used to it, hadn't done it since he was a little kid, and he hadn't done it often even then. For as long as he could remember, he'd pretty much been on his own.

Maybe he liked it better that way. This shit was uncomfortable. Was it worth it?

He didn't know yet, but he'd hoped so.

He'd wanted a chance to find out.

Pretty sure that opportunity just died a painful death.

To loosen up the clenching of his neck, he popped his head to the side. "Like I said, Newman is a problem. He wants to see me for some reason." A few rolls of his shoulders helped to loosen him further. "He wants that bad enough that he worked over Lang—the only person who knew I came here." He stopped, his throat going thick and his muscles clenching, both in anger and fear. Fear for Charlotte. Fear for his family. Knowing he had to be brutally honest, he stared at Charlotte. "He beat on Lang until he told him where I'd gone."

Silently, her anger receding, Charlotte stared up at him.

She had reason to be afraid. He needed to get Newman away from here and fast. Only one way he knew to accomplish that.

Brodie said, "That's the call you got last night?"

"Yeah. I figured I had to do something, so I went to the township cops. I was talking to Colvin, explaining things, when Charlotte called. I'm not sure Colvin bought it at first. I mean, not many put faith in the word of an ex-con." With a gruff, humorless laugh, he said, "Seems more on board now."

"Your friend's okay?" Brodie asked.

Unbelievable. Why would he care? And even if he did, why ask about Lang now instead of focusing on the more personal trouble happening here and now?

These people…every time he thought he had things figured out, they threw him for another loop. Even stiffer, damn near brittle, he paced away and said, "He will be."

"What's the damage?"

Aware of Charlotte's silent scrutiny, he slashed a hand in the air. "Broken nose, busted ribs." Going after Lang was like kicking a puppy—total chickenshit. Lang didn't have his bulk, or his power, which was why Mitch had often protected him.

This time, he'd really let him down. Somehow he'd make it up to Lang. *Later.*

The real concern now was *this*, the tacit threat to Charlotte, the looming risk. "I can't stress this enough—Newman is not a problem you want to ignore."

"Don't plan to. I'll get hold of Jack as soon as we disconnect. He'll be home tonight and I'll be home tomorrow. Mary and Howler are with me but Ronnie's home with Buster. Jack will call her too, I'm sure. Until Jack gets there, you'll stick around?"

Not wanting to look at Charlotte, Mitch stared down at the phone, his hands in his back pockets, his jaw flexing. "Sure, for a few hours." He wouldn't let anyone hurt the women, but sticking around wouldn't solve the problem beyond this one night. "Long-term, a better plan is for me to head back home where Newman's buddies will see me and then clue him in that I'm back. Once he knows where to find me, he'll leave all of you alone."

"To come after you."

"Yeah. But I can handle myself."

Sucking in a breath, Charlotte stood.

He couldn't resist glancing at her, and he found her hands fisted, her arms stiff at her sides, her glare hot enough to fry him.

"You could do that," Brodie said in a low and somewhat lethal voice, "but then I'd kick your ass, so maybe you should worry about me instead of this Newman character."

Mitch jerked his chin back as if the first blow from that warning had already landed. "Don't be stupid."

Brodie laughed. *Laughed.* "I'm never stupid, *little brother.*"

A scowl carved its way into Mitch's aching head.

"Obnoxious, sure. Pushy as hell, usually. But I'm promising you, Mitch, if you leave, I will find you, and I'll drag your sorry ass back if I have to."

Stupidly, Mitch took a hard step closer to the phone. "Might not be as easy as you're thinking, *brother.*" In every pore of his body, he was aware of Charlotte's censure and disappointment. But fuck it. What did she expect him to do?

Maybe explaining wouldn't hurt. "I'm trying to save you some trouble. I'm trying..." *To prove I didn't come here to use you.* He closed his eyes, locked his molars, and edited that sentiment. "I didn't come here to make your lives more difficult."

"Nope, you didn't," Brodie agreed. "You came to have a family, and now you've got it. That shit doesn't change, you know. Good times or bad, family hangs on like a too-tight shirt. You don't get to outgrow it, you can't wash it when it's dirty and it clings even worse when you sweat."

Mitch stared at the phone, then shook his head. "That's a terrible analogy."

"You get my point."

He did, sort of. "I have to do what I think is right."

"So do I," Brodie said. "So do I." Ending the debate, he said, "Charlotte, you're too quiet. It worries me."

With good reason, Mitch thought. Her expression was not pleasant. In fact, it promised a whole lot of *un*pleasant.

She narrowed her eyes…and turned away. "I'm fine. Ready to get home, in fact."

"Promise me you won't buck me on this, okay? I get it that you're upset, and also pissed."

How did Brodie know that?

"But cut him a break, and make *my* life easier too. Let him stick around until Jack gets there, okay?"

"Don't worry, Brodie. He can follow me home and visit with Ros, no problem at all."

"That'a girl."

"I need to get Brute," Mitch said. "I left him behind since I was going to the station. Didn't think the cops would appreciate me bringing him in."

"How long will that take?"

"It's a few minutes out of the way."

"Done," Charlotte said before Brodie could speak. "I'll just follow you there."

Now, why did that make him suspicious? Mitch studied her, but she kept her attention on the phone.

"Any problems," Brodie said, "one of you call Grant. Now I better get hold of Jack. Lock up and, after you get Brute, go straight to Mom's." The call ended.

Mitch stood there, furious, unsure what to expect, what to do next. Brodie could bluster all he wanted, but Mitch was long past letting others dictate to him.

He would do what he deemed best.

"Stop it."

His attention snapped to Charlotte. While he'd been introspective, she'd gathered her purse and moved close. Very close.

"Stop what?" He would not step back. She'd crowded his space, not the other way around. Knowing his frown darkened, he stared down at her upturned face. "I'm just waiting for you."

"Bull." She closed the space between them even more, letting her body bump his. "You can't lie to me."

Of course he could. "Don't act like you know me, Charlotte. Take my word for it—you don't." It was dumb to hang around here, so he opened the door and stepped aside. The message was clear: let's go.

Like a small tornado, she stormed past and was out of the building before he had time to catch up. He waited while she locked the door, checked it and then looked around the area.

A track circled much of the property, maybe left over from days gone by, or used now by the brothers to test their cars. Beyond that a shadowed woods made it possible for people to hide.

Mitch didn't like it.

The one-story building was long, with an attached garage for engine repairs and more, and an apartment at the farthest end where Brodie used to live before he completed his and Mary's house. The backside of the building overlooked the hill with the town below. Dirt surrounded it, without a speck of landscaping to soften the look. Done up right, the business would look even more impressive.

But as he'd agreed, it'd be a lot of upkeep.

Shaking that off—he couldn't very well help deck out the building if he wasn't even going to be around, now could he?—he turned back to Charlotte.

Proving her nervousness, she studied every shadow.

"We're alone," Mitch said, then immediately wished he could take back the words. No threat hung around, but the idea of being *alone* with her—not a single soul around—obliterated everything else that had happened and instead gave focus to his never-ending attraction.

She shot him an impressively mean look and started for her car. "What did you decide?"

Keeping pace with her, he asked, "About?"

"Leaving."

He could wait until they heard from officer Colvin. Maybe if he located Newman and his cohorts at the hotel, he could run them off. Not likely, but it wouldn't hurt to find out how that went.

He'd tried going by the hotel himself, but of course the desk wasn't forthcoming about guests.

Could he afford to up and leave? He'd already bought the landscaping business, already put in orders for things he'd need, contacted suppliers, talked to two possible employees...

Charlotte started her car, flipped on the air-conditioning, then stepped out.

Pacing one way then another, each step a little angrier, she pivoted and stormed up to him. "You have a family now."

The pugnacious attack took him back. "I know." And he hated to lose them, but—

Her finger prodded his chest just once, giving him a little push. "Like Brodie said, you do not get to run off and sulk." With the insult out there, she went back to her car.

Disbelief and anger drew his spine straighter until it felt like his head would shoot off. He caught the door before she could slam it. "I don't *sulk*."

"Prove it," she demanded with just as much heat. "Be here tomorrow, and the day after. Trust Brodie and Jack." She drew in a slow breath, her tone softening, her eyes imploring. "Give it a chance."

He'd never met anyone so damned mercurial. She looked sweet enough, but she went toe-to-toe with Jack and Brodie, and didn't hesitate to give him hell. "It?"

"Should I have said *us*?" Her smile went crooked. "Your jaw is ticking."

Unsure what else to do, unsure how to deal with her, he settled on glaring.

"Is the idea of sticking around so awful? Or are you just afraid?"

Goddamn it, she didn't hesitate to strike—and he somewhat admired that too. But Jesus, she thought he feared Newman?

He feared what he might do to Newman, if put to the test, but that's not what she asked in that little innocent voice.

Withholding a reply, he refused to play her game. Not to-night, not when this was real—whether or not she and Brodie wanted to accept it.

Mouth flat, he closed her door without slamming it—*some herculean restraint he showed there*—and stalked over to his own car.

Yeah, part of his outrage was the situation. Newman fucking with his life again? Unacceptable.

He had to end it—but not here in Red Oak. Not with these people somehow involved.

Charlotte waited until he started out of the lot, then followed close behind. He was careful not to leave her at a light, or to let her get more than a car length behind him.

Some part of him kept expecting Newman to show up, but he saw no sight of him as he drove the short distance out of town to the ten acres he'd purchased with the sale of his mother's house.

Property in Red Oak, especially on the outskirts, was pretty damn cheap.

The house-turned-business with a small living section wasn't much to see yet, but what did he care? He'd be fixing it up and for now, when he couldn't sleep in the tent, he enjoyed using the screened-in porch. He had an eat-in kitchen, a small bath-room and plenty of land.

It was enough.

If he got to keep it.

If the past didn't come and steal it away.

CHAPTER TEN

When they arrived, Brute was in the screened-in porch and he looked thrilled to see Mitch again, his nose pressed to the screen, his body jiggling.

She'd been pretty happy to see Mitch too.

And yet she'd been terrible to him. The short drive had given her time to collect herself, to think about how she'd carried on, and now it shamed her.

She'd accused him of being afraid.

Of course he was. Family was new to him. It had to be intimidating to have them all crowding in, demanding loyalty and expecting him to understand how family worked—this family in particular.

She'd been a bitch, and she wasn't even part of the family. He literally owed her nothing. Brodie and Jack, sure. He needed to learn to trust them, to confide in them.

But her? She was...nothing to him. Not really. She'd like to be a friend. Shoot, if she was honest with herself, she'd enjoy being a whole lot more, but it wasn't fair to expect anything of him right now. Somehow she'd make herself keep that in mind. She wouldn't pressure him.

And she absolutely would not start getting attached.

She gave her attention to the farm-style house. Paint peeled and a few shutters hung loose, but it had nice bones. Mature trees surrounded it, and cattails framed a small pond nearby. Overall, it was pretty.

Without him inviting her to, Charlotte got out of her car, looking around while Mitch released Brute so he could visit several bushes.

Off to the side, a large outbuilding had seen better days. A sturdy lock kept the double barn-like doors secured.

What did he have inside there?

When a bird took flight, Brute chased after it. He ambled back soon enough, his skinny tail swinging, to give her a belated welcome.

Petting him, Charlotte said, "This is such a peaceful area," while trying not to stare at the ratty couch on the porch with the sheet, blanket and pillow haphazardly thrown across it.

Or the tent erected right there in the front yard. With it zipped shut she couldn't see inside, but her curiosity hummed.

Mitch didn't reply. Hands in his back pockets, broad shoulders stiff, he looked off to the side.

The silent treatment from a guy? Okay, definitely not the norm in the Crews family. Brodie and Jack never held back their thoughts.

Instead they bludgeoned her with them. Jack was a little smoother about it, but still...

"Are you not talking to me?"

His head jerked up. "What?"

Charlotte shrugged. "Seemed like you were mad and didn't want to chat. I don't want to bother you."

His brows came together in a ferocious look of confusion. After studying her face a moment, he shook his head. "I'm concerned, not mad."

Oh, good. Well, then... "Do you own this?"

Almost against his will, Mitch nodded. "I haven't had time to do much with it yet. Paint is bought, though."

Property meant he was settling in, and her heart rejoiced despite the pep talk she'd given herself about staying detached. "What color?"

Resistance showed in every line of his body, but finally he glanced at her. "Slate blue. I'll do the trim in white."

"That'll be beautiful."

With a grunt, he said, "Anything would be an improvement, right?"

"Homes need love and care." Just as people do. "Give it time." Until then, the surroundings would inspire anyone. "How much land do you have?"

He pointed. "See that thicker tree line way out there?" He swung his arm in the other direction. "You can just barely see a fence bordering a farmer's fields over there. I can hear his cows in the morning. You saw where we first pulled off the road— that's the front of the property, and the back goes up to the train tracks." He gave her a crooked grin and said, "Hear that in the morning too."

His smile could melt her bones but she didn't know if it was seeing him happy that did it, or the fact that he was so incredibly gorgeous and the happiness only emphasized it. "You can pretty much hear the cows and the train whistle all around Red Oak. I like it."

"Yeah, I do too."

"Mitch…" She glanced around again, thinking how isolated he was here if something happened. What if Newman found him? What if he brought all three men here to hurt Mitch? He'd be completely alone.

"What?" His brows pinched more, then rose high. "Did you just shiver?"

"No," she lied, because how could she explain that a sense of doom had chilled her? Deciding to tackle one thing at a time, she laced her fingers together. "What Brodie said..."

"Which part?" His jaw ticked again. "Brodie said a lot."

Yes, he had—and then she'd said more, all of it unkind. "About...well, coming after you. Brodie *would* track you down, that much is true. But you should know, he wouldn't actually hit you."

Wearing a mean smile, he leaned in, tweaked her chin, and said, "I wouldn't let him."

His nearness rendered her mute and sent her heart into hyperdrive. She thought he meant to kiss her and anticipation spiked... but what he did instead was a gesture for a kid.

As Mitch walked away from her, he called Brute over to his car, his tone light and easy.

Jerk.

Staring daggers at the back of his head, Charlotte accepted that in the most infuriating ways, he was too much like his brothers.

Full of arrogance, he called back to her, "We should go."

That had her searching the surrounding woods as she hurried to her car.

"Relax." Taking pity on her, he promised, "No one is here now."

"How do you know?"

Hands flexing at his sides, jaw working, he shrugged. "You develop a sixth sense when you're in prison. If anyone was lurking around, I'd feel it."

"Oh." How awful.

More gently still, he explained, "I assume Brodie made those phone calls, and your family will worry if we don't show up soon."

"*Your* family," she stressed, and opened her driver's door. "And they'll worry about *both* of us." Before he could reply, she started her car, ready to go.

Shaking his head, Mitch called, "I'll follow you," then got behind the wheel.

The return drive gave her more time to think—or stew, actually—until she pulled up to the house and found Ronnie on the porch swing, dressed in her usual black jeans with a pullover shirt, her fair hair highlighted by the setting sun. The second she spotted them, she stood and opened the front door, saying something that brought out Ros.

Both women stood there as Charlotte and Mitch parked, locked up their cars and started in. Brute kept pace alongside them.

"Jack called," Ros explained. "I was already out so I picked up Ronnie to wait here with us."

Eyes narrowed against the hazy red sunset, Mitch shook his head. "You shouldn't be outside. There's no telling if Newman might—"

"Let him come," Ronnie said, her lip curled. "I'd feed him my knife."

Incredulity freezing him to the spot, Mitch stopped and stared. His mouth firmed. His gaze hardened. "You're out here *looking* for him?"

Ronnie shrugged. "Or for you two—whoever came first."

Dumbfounded, he started to speak, but came up blank. His jaw clenched and he glowered at Charlotte.

How was this her fault?

Maybe he didn't know how deadly Ronnie could be with her knife—or how fearless she was when facing danger. She gave him a hard nudge. "Ronnie's pretty badass. The stories I could tell…"

Ros huffed a breath. "Yes, she is, but she's not using her knife on anyone tonight—and we all know Jack is going to have a fit if he finds out Ronnie said that."

"Let him." Ronnie kept all her attention on Mitch. "I want to know everything about this jerk who scared Charlotte."

Humiliation scalded Charlotte's face. Compared to Ronnie's courage and lethal ability, she was completely helpless against real danger.

The comparison sucked.

Low and mean, Ronnie continued. "I especially want to know why you haven't demolished him yet."

At that, Mitch gave up his annoyance with a short bark of humor. "Well, at least you realize I could." His gaze slanted to Charlotte. "She seems to think I'm afraid of him."

"What?" That wasn't at all what she'd meant.

"Charlotte," Ros chastised before she could explain. "Of course he's not."

Horrified by his assumption, Charlotte said, "I didn't—"

"He's smart not to tempt the law for any reason," Ronnie interrupted with a frown. "Not with a record."

"There is that," Mitch agreed.

"I didn't—" she tried again.

"But afraid?" Ronnie scoffed. "Don't forget, he's related to Brodie and Jack."

"Bravery by blood, huh?" Mitch shook his head. "Don't you think we should discuss this inside?"

"Go on," Ronnie said. "I'll stay out here, keep an eye out—hey!"

Ros locked an arm through hers, urging her inside.

"Jack is still my son and I love him," Ros explained with calm insistence. "If you're outside when he gets home, he's going to rage, then you'll rage back, and you'll both be miserably mad at each other." She shot Ronnie a stern look. "I don't want my son miserable."

"Besides," Charlotte said, hoping to help, "I'll feel safer with you and Mitch both inside with us."

"Yeah," Mitch said, deadpan. "I'll feel safer too."

Charlotte glared at him. Clearly he didn't yet realize that Ronnie, despite her petite stature, had enough daring and ability for three grown men. Jack and Brodie had learned, and eventually Mitch would too.

For her part, Ronnie just snorted.

They'd barely gotten inside when Charlotte felt compelled to explain. "I never thought Mitch was afraid of this Newman fellow."

"You thought it enough to ask me about it," Mitch pointed out.

"No, I—"

With the patter of nails on wood floors and a lot of barking, Buster came barreling around the corner. He drew up when he saw Brute, ears perking, then charged forward again with renewed exhilaration.

Typically, Brute tried to dodge him, but it didn't dim Buster's glee.

Laughing, Mitch took his spot on the floor so Brute could crawl into his lap. With one hand on Brute's collar, the other on Buster's, he corralled the dogs.

"Buster," Ronnie said in exasperation, but he ignored her. "He's so enthusiastic about everything now—especially other animals."

"It's fine." Mitch got Buster to sit long enough for Brute to warm up to him again. This time it didn't take long.

When Buster led the way toward the kitchen, Brute followed.

Standing over Mitch, Charlotte crossed her arms. "You misunderstood." She said it fast before she got interrupted again. "I meant that you were afraid…"

Ros cleared her throat in warning.

Okay, right, scratch that. "That is, I thought you might be *concerned* with the idea of a family. You know, relying on someone—"

"Not happening."

"—and having someone rely on you," she finished, deflated by his refusal to depend on any of them.

"Rely on *me*?" he challenged, his gaze holding hers.

"Yes, of course."

"Who?" With lethal grace, he rose back to his feet to face off with her. "You?"

Her thoughts went utterly blank. "I, um..."

"Them?" he continued, nodding at Ronnie who admired her knife, and Ros who smiled as she watched them.

"Yes." Elevating her chin, Charlotte gestured at the other women. "Them, Brodie, Jack. That's what family is. Give and take. Worry and encouragement. From *both* sides."

"She's absolutely correct." Pleased now, Ros nodded. "Brodie relied on you to see Charlotte home safely. Jack is relying on you to stay here until he returns." She gave him her patented *mother* look—the one Charlotte had always found to be extremely successful. "We're all relying on you to stick around."

He started to say something, but changed his mind. Lectures from a mother figure were likely a novel experience.

Charlotte figured it was good for him. He needed to know that when people cared, they sometimes intrude—all with good intentions.

To Ronnie, he asked, "When is Jack due home?"

"Soon." She put the knife in her boot. "Grab a seat, get comfortable, then tell me everything you can about Newman."

When Jack came in an hour later, Mitch released a long breath of relief. Dodging Ronnie's interrogation hadn't been easy. Bless Ros for insisting everyone eat. She'd gotten them all seated around the kitchen table with grilled-cheese sandwiches, chips, pickles and tea.

The women ate a sandwich each, but Mitch devoured the two that Ros served him. Even better, there was a piece of leftover cake that Charlotte had made, and they all decided he should have it.

It seemed to be a traditional method of coping for them—sitting together, eating, talking. Since the food was so good, and he was able to avoid a lot of the conversation, he didn't mind too much.

He'd just finished the last delicious crumb, along with a cup of coffee, when Jack came in.

There were general greetings with Jack kissing Ronnie, then lavishing some attention on both Buster and Brute before he asked to be updated.

Mitch left that to Charlotte as he helped clear the table against Ros's complaints. The sooner he wrapped this up, the sooner he could get going.

When he finished with the chore, he thanked her again for the food, called to Brute, and bid everyone a congenial good-night. Confident that he'd covered his haste to leave, he turned to go.

Charlotte gave him a disapproving frown, as if he'd let her down.

He probably had.

Everyone else looked worried. Nothing he could do about it tonight. He had plans to make, and it'd be better if he got to them now.

As he and Brute left the house, Jack said, "I'll walk you out," and Mitch realized there was nothing he could do about that either.

His half brothers were pushier than he'd ever expected.

Ros was more accepting than he dared to hope.

But it was Charlotte who took him most by surprise—maybe because he hadn't figured on meeting someone like her...and because he already liked her too damn much.

The quiet closed in around them. A deceptively peaceful night.

With new concerns at the forefront of his mind, he checked the surrounding area as he headed to his car.

It was well lit, front and back. There'd be no chance for anyone to lurk in a shadow or behind a thick shrub. "You and Brodie install the security lights?"

"And a top-notch security system." Pinning him in his gaze, Jack smiled. "We don't take chances with family."

A lot of uncomfortable meaning hung in that statement—uncomfortable because he knew Jack included him, and he wasn't sure he deserved it. "You'll stay the night here with them?"

"That's my plan," he confirmed. "So what's your plan?"

"I'm working on it," Mitch hedged, now undecided on what to do.

"I'd appreciate it if you'd consider sticking around."

Huh. A new tactic? "You're actually *asking*?"

Jack's mouth twitched. "Let me guess. Brodie threatened?"

"Pretty much, yeah—although Charlotte said he wouldn't actually—"

"Charlotte's wrong. He would." Jack put his hands in his trouser pockets and looked out over the road. "Don't get me wrong, family is important to me. Very important. But Brodie and I have different approaches to things."

An understatement. "So I've noticed."

Jack accepted that with a smile. "Brodie's always taken the role of big brother to heart, maybe because Dad was never here enough to round things out, you know? Brodie rolled with it and filled in where he could."

"Rosalyn doesn't strike me as a person who needed a lot of help from her kids."

"No, she didn't. But our protectiveness especially extended to her. The stuff Dad put her through..." Blinking away his frown, he explained, "Brodie forgave him, took Mom's advice and just accepts him for who he is. Me?" He shook his head. "It still infuriates me. When Dad comes around, he spends his time, limited as it is, with Brodie because I want nothing to do with him."

Mitch understood that, and yet, Elliott's visits had been like a treat for him, better than Christmas or birthdays since his mom hadn't celebrated those occasions much. With Elliott, he had someone who talked with *him*, who focused on him, took him to lunch or dinner. It was nice—something he'd looked forward to.

"Maybe Rosalyn's right and that's all Elliott has in him." Mitch had long ago accepted that his mother suffered dependency—on drugs, on a man, on her own wants and needs. Was she born weak? He didn't know, but for his entire life she'd been needy—just not needy of her son. For her, Mitch was an afterthought at best. "Very few people are like your mom."

"She's definitely special."

And if Mitch stayed, she could be hurt. Hell, Charlotte had already been frightened, and God only knew what could have happened if not for her quick thinking. Scaring her might have satisfied Newman's twisted sense of humor, but Mitch would never underestimate his capacity for violence.

Rather than drag it out, he met Jack's gaze. "Leaving is the best option to protect everyone."

"Actually, Brodie and I have another idea."

The front door of the house opened and Charlotte stepped out. "Grant called. He found Newman at Freddie's. He said he's staying in the hotel but isn't there much. When Grant asked him about…about his visit to the office, Newman said he didn't mean to alarm me. He claims that when I locked myself inside, he thought something was wrong and just wanted to help."

"Bullshit," Mitch growled.

Charlotte shrugged. "I agree, but he didn't actually do anything, right?"

To Mitch's attentive gaze, Charlotte now looked self-conscious and uncertain, prompting him to take a step toward her. "Don't do that. Don't ever second-guess Newman. You absolutely did the right thing."

Grateful, she treated him to a faint smile. "Well, regardless,

Grant told him to stay away from the office." She laced her fingers together. "He said he has personal business with you, Mitch."

"Yeah, I just bet he does." Mitch rubbed his face. Before he and Newman had their confrontation, it would have been better to get him well away from here. That option was gone. "I'll head to the bar right now."

He didn't want anyone else to suffer collateral damage.

"No."

Both he and Jack looked at her.

In that now familiar way, she put up her chin. "Grant said he doesn't want any trouble. He asked that you not go and start anything."

"It started today when Newman frightened you."

"Correction," she said. "It started when he treated you badly. But that has nothing to do with you looking for trouble now."

Forcing his mouth into a smile, Mitch promised, "I'll invite him outside. Hell, I'll invite him to my house—"

"Don't you dare." Coming down a step, Charlotte propped her hands on her hips. "Grant said Newman would probably take off now, and that's what we should let him do."

"If Grant thinks that, he's as naive as you are."

Her glare could have burned him to a crisp. "Naive?"

Jack said, "Thanks, hon. I'll be done here in a minute."

"No, Jack Crews. You do not get to dismiss me."

Mitch opened his mouth.

"And *you*. Why do you have to be so damn stubborn? And so *blind*?"

He had no idea what that meant. "Charlotte—"

"Unless you're staying, I don't want to hear it."

He closed his mouth again.

Shaking her head, she turned away—and no one could miss the disappointment.

For a few seconds, neither of them said anything, not until Charlotte got inside and quietly closed the door behind her.

It felt…well, final. And also devastating.

Jack cracked a smile. "Girl has a temper."

"And you don't?"

"Takes a little more to get mine going. In fact, it usually takes more to get her that hot." He looked at Mitch in speculation. "Guess you bring it out of her."

No, he wouldn't get pulled in again with outrageous observations. "I need to go so I can catch Newman before he—"

"You seem to think we're unfamiliar with danger, but we're not. Thanks to the work we do, we run into thugs, psychopaths, even murderers. We can handle one asshole." Jack put a hand on Mitch's shoulder. "So the question is—can *you* handle a little help freely offered?"

If that help didn't involve Charlotte, maybe he could. Now, though, he couldn't separate her from his brothers. She came with the family. Hell, she was the best part of it all.

Thoughts of Newman focused on her were enough to freeze his blood. And Ros…sweet, bossy Ros.

"We're not fragile," Jack said.

"Neither am I."

"No, but you are alone—and you don't have to be."

Jesus, the way his heart punched it almost hurt. Yes he was alone. Always had been. Life was easier that way—but it wasn't nearly as nice.

Accept help?

Could he? It made his skin crawl to think of it. Even before prison, he'd stood alone. After prison? He trusted himself first and foremost.

Trying to hide his reaction, he said, "It's not the way I generally roll."

"I get that. Coming here is all about adjustment though, right?"

No kidding. So far, Charlotte had been the biggest adjustment he had to make, followed by Rosalyn. In comparison, two brothers were a piece of cake. "I know Newman and you don't. I have to call the shots."

"Brodie's the one who'll have a problem with that, not me." Jack clapped his shoulder, then dropped his hand. "So, think you can put off confronting Newman for now? Maybe stick around until we get this figured out?"

Brute had already stretched out in the grass and was lightly snoring. "Right now?"

"Tomorrow. You, me and Brodie together."

Did he dare? Things might only get more complicated. Newman was unpredictable.

"You have questions," Jack said. "Give us a chance to help you answer them."

He had a gut feeling it was a mistake, but the lure of family was strong. Add Charlotte into the mix and...

How could he resist?

"All right, fine. But I won't sign on for anything that I think puts any of you at risk."

"See," Jack said, "you're thinking like family already."

Mitch woke with a faint sheen of sweat on his body, the air heavy around him. Coming up to one elbow, he listened, determining if he'd just awakened.

Or if something had awakened him.

Dawn light filtered through the tent. Humidity thickened the morning air. Brute slept near his feet, but his paws twitched and he gave a muffled woof in his sleep.

Nothing more menacing than a doggy dream.

Sitting up, wearing only boxers, Mitch stretched and glanced toward the zipped mesh screen door of the tent. The top too had vents—which made it more comfortable for him.

He preferred to sleep outside without the tent, with only the wide-open skies overhead. He breathed easier that way, but here, with woods all around him, the bugs treated him like a feast.

Stirring, Brute looked at him and did his own four-legged stretch.

"Sorry, bud. Did I disrupt your rabbit chase?"

Brute's tail slapped at the tarp floor and his tongue lolled out with a wide yawn.

"Yeah, I did, didn't I?" Mitch rubbed his ears. "Let's go take a leak." He unzipped the tent and ducked out, Brute right beside him. Automatically Mitch did a quick and thorough search, his senses alert.

All was secure, for the moment at least.

As weak daylight crawled over the woods, birds sang from every treetop. Usually the inherent nature of his surroundings brought him a sense of peace; this was his, a fresh start, a better life.

He was truly free.

But now, with Newman on the hunt, the familiar serenity eluded him.

Brute went in one direction and Mitch another, each heading to a bush. Yes, he had a bathroom inside. A bedroom too.

But fresh air and lack of restriction appealed more than a soft mattress. He had enough privacy here that he could set up a hose and shower outside if he wanted—except he appreciated hot water too much to do that.

Besides, once he got the business going, his privacy would end.

As he tucked himself away, Mitch inhaled deeply, filling his lungs with the scents of green woods, earth and a brewing storm. A glance up showed dark bloated clouds off in the distance. If a storm lasted, that could drive him inside tonight. He'd still avoid the small bedroom that felt too much like a cell, despite the window, opting instead for the screened-in porch.

Back at the tent he fetched his phone so he could charge it

while he showered, grabbed his jeans, shirt and shoes, and whistled for Brute. First coffee for him and kibble for Brute, then his shower.

He'd offered to help with the gravel around the Mustang Transport offices; he felt bad that he'd bailed on that yesterday. Newman's appearance put him in a raging tailspin and he was only now recovering.

Because of family? Possibly. He only knew how to operate alone, but maybe he'd learn.

Jack said they were putting off the gravel for a few days while Brodie considered more landscaping. Charlotte's effect on him, no doubt. If pressed, he'd put his money on Charlotte winning that debate. From what he'd seen, she was the lifeblood of the office, the critical piece that kept it all going.

If she wanted shrubbery and flowers, she should have them. He wouldn't mind offering his time for maintenance if it'd help her cause. Working with his hands was a pleasure, not a chore.

With that task eliminated, he had the afternoon to work on his own place before he'd meet with Brodie and Jack to figure out how to deal with Newman.

Not that he needed their input, but humoring them was the family thing to do.

Or so Jack had claimed.

For now, physical work would help take the edge off, at least until he could get his hands on Newman.

Standing there in the yard, his bare feet on lush, dew-wet grass, he surveyed what he owned from the pond and outbuilding to the house and yard. He had enough work to keep him busy for a week at least, and that was before Newman had showed up.

He was just about to head in when he heard the approaching car. Brute stiffened, his ears back in his usual sign of worry.

Dropping his clothes to the porch step, he locked a hand in Brute's collar.

If Newman had found him, he'd put Brute inside so he couldn't get hurt. Literally, he would die before letting Brute be badly treated again.

Expecting the worst and preparing for it mentally and physically, he waited, watching the narrow road that entered his property.

It boggled him when a blue Focus came down the drive, kicking up dust and reflecting the sunrise in blinding force.

What. The. Fuck.

His thoughts went chaotic—not unusual when dealing with this particular lady.

"It's okay, boy. It's just Charlotte."

Though his tone was gentle for Brute's sake, turbulent emotions churned. There was nothing *just* about Charlotte Parrish, not with how he felt.

Forgetting he wasn't dressed, Mitch stepped away from the porch to wait for her. Already his heart danced against his ribs and his jaw tightened. Seeing she'd come alone fired his blood even more, making his skin burn...and his balls tighten.

Why the hell does she have this effect on me?

And why did he like it so much?

After giving him a wary look through the windshield, she parked and stepped out. With a forced but sunny smile, she gave a lighthearted wave. "Hey."

Hey? That had to be a joke. If he didn't have better control, he'd be hard already. As it was, it took all his concentration to keep things in check.

Brute, of course, was happy to see her. He charged her, ran a circle around her and yapped like a damn puppy. She'd been good for the dog.

Trying to ignore the pang in his heart at how warmly she was greeting Brute, he asked, "What are you doing here?"

Her smile faltered. "I—"

"You shouldn't be." Yes, his tone sounded harsh but for her to be here at his home, alone? He'd already wanted her, and Newman's threats against her had only heightened everything he felt.

He wanted to protect her, and he wanted to fuck her. He wanted to talk with her and hold her close, and he wanted to *keep* her.

More than he'd ever wanted anything, he wanted that.

Jesus. He ran a hand over his face.

Even as they stood there watching each other, her hair curled and a flush colored her face and throat.

She looked so damned innocent—what if Newman had followed her? What if he'd run her off the damn road? What if he'd hijacked her, and worse?

Anger brought him a step closer. "Don't you realize the danger?"

Alerted to his tone, Brute's ear twitched, and he came back to sit by Mitch.

"You're upsetting the dog."

Mitch dropped a hand to Brute's neck, gently rubbing.

Eyes narrowed, she advanced a step as well. "What did you want me to do? Hide in the house? Am I allowed to drive to work? The grocery?"

"You didn't go *there*." Those places were at least in town, with people nearby. Though yes, he had a feeling she'd be at risk everywhere until he took care of Newman. Another reason why he should have handled it last night. If he'd known she'd be this reckless, he would have, and to hell with what Jack or Brodie thought. "You came *here*."

She nodded, then cleared her throat. "I did, yes. And...um. You're in your underwear."

Mitch held out his arms. "It's the crack of dawn and I was just heading in to shower."

Her gaze devoured his exposed body, moving over his chest and shoulders, down his stomach and to his thighs. Suddenly he felt naked, as if the boxers had melted away.

Liking the way she looked at him, craving even more, he came forward another step—

"Why do you sleep outside, anyway?"

God help him. At least she'd snapped him out of the fog of lust.

Clearly, she was too busy digging into his privacy to take his warnings to heart.

Sensing that the conflict had eased, Brute looked at him, looked at Charlotte and loped off to visit another bush.

Getting himself under control—*again*—Mitch asked with a sigh, "Why are you here?"

"We came to see if we could help."

The hairs on the back of his neck prickled. "We?" He no sooner asked it than he heard another car approaching. "Son of a..." Striding back for his jeans, he hurriedly stepped into them, zipping up just as a red Mustang came into view.

Well hell.

Not just Charlotte, but Brodie too.

"You brought him here," Mitch accused.

She shrugged. "He didn't know where you lived, so he asked, and yes, I showed him." With a beautiful, guileless smile, she added, "I enjoyed seeing you without your jeans, but since Ros came along too it's probably better that you're wearing them."

He opened his mouth with no idea what to say. *Was that another of her attempts at flirting?*

Snapping his mouth shut, he glowered.

Leaning toward him, she whispered, "You have family now, Mitch. You may as well give in."

Right. But give in to *what*?

CHAPTER ELEVEN

With a sense of satisfaction, Charlotte finished cleaning the large country kitchen. A buildup of dust, cobwebs, dead bugs and mustiness had collected during the long absence of use. Overall, though, it was a lovely room. The porcelain sink showed bright white again. The black-and-white floor, though slightly worn, sparkled in a streak of sunlight through spotless windows. A good rub with furniture polish made the maple cabinets glow.

She'd been cleaning for a few hours now, but so far the storm held off—both from the sky and from Mitch.

When he'd spotted Ros carrying fresh sheets and towels, and Brodie with his toolbox, a sort of shocked disbelief had kept him rooted to the spot. They'd all come prepared to help him get the place in better living condition. Obviously, he wasn't used to helping hands—but he would be, eventually.

If they convinced him to stay.

Once he'd found his tongue, he'd tried to object. Repeatedly. With lots of gratitude and an equal amount of excuses for why it wasn't necessary.

Of course Ros steamrolled right through him. She smiled again thinking of it.

Around the yard, Brute and Howler barked in play.

A warm breeze wafted in through the open window, carrying the sounds of muted conversation, hammering and sanding.

Mitch had already scraped parts of the exterior so it could be painted, but with Brodie's help, they'd finished most of the troublesome spots. They couldn't paint today, not with the dark clouds threatening rain, but she'd overheard Brodie say they'd all be back to get it done in a single day.

Loose boards in the front steps were now more secure and Ros... Charlotte turned to look through the kitchen doorway. Ros was working on the bedroom and bathroom.

Curiosity took Charlotte out of the room and down the hall.

Humming to herself, her hair tied on top of her head, Ros finished making the bed with fresh linens and a soft quilt.

"It looks great." But would Mitch ever use it?

"It does, doesn't it?" Hands on her hips, Ros surveyed the room. "He needs curtains or blinds for the windows, of course— here and in the bathroom window."

"Oh?" Charlotte peeked into the small, all-white bathroom with an ancient pedestal sink, toilet and bathtub. The tub needed new grout in places, but at least now it was clean, just like the tiled floor. Sure enough, the positioning of an uncovered window would make it easy for anyone to see Mitch while he showered. Naked.

And of course she immediately visualized that. After seeing him in his boxers, it was easy to do. My oh my, the man had an amazing body. Broad in the shoulders, thick in the chest and biceps, with a narrow waist and flat stomach, and that tantalizing body hair... It sparsely covered his chest from one flat brown nipple to the other, then arrowed down as if pointing the way to what he'd hidden in his boxers.

Oh, how she'd love a peek.

Talking while he'd stood there showing off his bod hadn't

been easy. She was rather impressed with herself for accomplishing it.

"Did I miss anything?"

Good grief. She'd been staring at the bathroom too long. Charlotte shook her head and smiled at Ros. "No, it's spotless."

"He could use a rug for the floor. Help me remember to take care of that."

"Sure." Shortly after they'd all arrived, Mitch had come in to brush his teeth but he hadn't yet showered or shaved. His toiletries were now neatly arranged on the side of the sink. If he exchanged the chipped mirror for a medicine cabinet, he'd have a little more storage. She'd mention it to Brodie and Jack.

Would Mitch stand here in only a towel while he shaved? Did he use any cologne? She looked around, but saw only soap, shampoo, toothbrush and toothpaste, a razor and shaving cream.

He was a basic guy, living the simple life. Was that a preference, or something he'd gotten used to while in prison?

Just thinking of him—and she'd been thinking of him nonstop since meeting him—made her heart pump faster and her pulse go erratic.

Now with the image of him in snug boxers? Yeah, that'd be stuck in the forefront of her brain for a very long time, fueling all her fantasies.

"You shouldn't have gone to all this trouble," Mitch said from somewhere behind her, making her jump. "I've never slept in here."

As if he could see her guilty thoughts, heat rushed into Charlotte's face. Luckily, he wasn't looking at her. He had his attention on Ros.

"It's ready now if you decide to," Ros said easily as she picked up additional linens from the chair in the corner. "I'll make up that couch out front too, though how you'd fit on there, I don't know."

Charlotte suspected that he didn't, at least not often. Would no one else ask about the tent? So far they hadn't. They'd all been too polite.

Humming again, Ros breezed out of the room—leaving them alone.

Had she done that on purpose? Ros wasn't known as a match-maker, but she wouldn't put it past her.

She and Mitch stared at each other. Again. They seemed to do that a lot and she hoped it meant something—like maybe he was as interested as she was.

"The scruffy look works for you, big-time."

The words took him off guard, making him huff a laugh and then shake his head.

In total disarray, his dark blond hair stuck up, partly, she knew, from his restless hands, but also because they'd interrupted his morning. His darker beard scruff added to his dangerous air. And the intensity in those golden brown eyes... *Be still, my heart.*

In one respect, Charlotte felt trapped in the room with him. Unlike Ros, she couldn't just sidle past, not with the way his big body blocked the door—and not with the way he made her heart riot.

On the other hand, the thought of touching him made every part of her spark with awareness in the most delicious ways. It was as if female parts of her that had been dormant were now awake and cheering for attention.

Without thinking about it, she licked her lips...and saw his gaze track the movement.

His nostrils flared.

And suddenly he turned away, striding fast from the room. *Without a word.*

Staring at his retreating back, hurt, unsure what had just hap-pened, Charlotte saw him head back through the kitchen, no doubt to go outside.

Until she sucked in a deep breath to feed her straining lungs, she hadn't realized she'd stopped breathing. Stumbling forward, she sank down to sit on the edge of the bed.

What to do now?

If she was better at these types of relationships, maybe she'd know for sure what to do. Maybe she'd know for sure what was happening.

But being woefully inexperienced with male attention, she just didn't know. Yes, she was pretty sure he was attracted to her, but that didn't really mean much, right? Her close association with the family probably put her in the "off-limits for a fling" category. Anything more?

Doubtful that he wanted that. He'd only just found his brothers, had a new house in a new location. Adding a romantic entanglement wouldn't be ideal.

Maybe she was hindering, rather than assisting, his relationship with his brothers. Over and over again, she tweaked his anger. Repeatedly she asked questions that were none of her business. She hadn't meant to be, but she was intrusive.

Should she bow out? Keep her distance? Maybe she'd talk to Ros and get her opinion. Until then...

She wouldn't cower. She wouldn't hide. No, she didn't have Ronnie's courage or Mary's polish, but she had pride enough to get her through today.

And if she wanted him more and more? She'd deal with it.

Pushing back to her feet, Charlotte followed the path Mitch had taken until she heard voices outside—not just Mitch and Brodie, but another guy too.

Newman?

Fear got her feet trotting until she pushed through the screen door in a rush, only to find Grant there. Relieved, she noticed he wore jeans and a polo shirt instead of a uniform. He stood near Ros, looking between her and the brothers as he talked about Newman.

Yup, she'd just accepted that she intruded too much, and still

Charlotte couldn't resist joining the group to find out what was going on.

"I saw him again," Grant was saying, "just hanging out at the diner. Reminded him I wouldn't tolerate any trouble and he did an impression of a misunderstood, innocent man who only wanted to see Mitch."

"Oh, he'll see him all right," Brodie said, all but cracking his knuckles.

With an eye roll, Mitch replied, "I have no problem seeing him." To Brodie, he added, "*Alone*. In fact, I could head over there right now—"

Grant shook his head. "Sorry, no. I offered to put him in touch with you today, and he said he was taking off soon on some business and didn't know when he'd be back. He asked where you lived, but I didn't know and wouldn't have told him anyway. I do know he checked out of the hotel."

Muttering a curse, Mitch said, "So now he's on the loose? I knew I should have gone last night—"

"What kind of business?" Brodie interrupted.

Grant shook his head. "No idea. He had a weaselly little creep with him who cracked up when he said it."

Mitch's mouth flattened. "Probably Ritchie. Newman is a coward who's afraid to be alone."

"This Ritchie fellow didn't look like much in the way of backup."

"He's not, except that he won't hesitate to stab you in the back." Shoulders bunching, Mitch added, "Literally."

Grant's face darkened. "I'm sorry there wasn't more I could do."

Ros put a hand on Grant's arm, which caused him to go very still.

Interesting.

Charlotte looked, but neither Brodie nor Mitch seemed to notice. Well, *she* noticed, and for the first time she realized that

Grant was a good-looking guy. Close to Ros's age, maybe a year or two older. Silver-tipped dark hair and piercing blue eyes. A strong jaw and a still-fit body. No, he wasn't as tall as Brodie or Jack, but was significantly taller than Ros.

They looked…cute together. *Huh.*

"He knows you're aware of him, and that you're keeping an eye on things." Ros's smile had a little extra wattage to it. "That matters."

"I want you to call me anytime." Covering her hand with his own, Grant looked around the circle. "All of you."

"Will do," Brodie said, and everyone knew he wouldn't. He much preferred to handle things his own way.

Obstinately silent, Mitch didn't commit one way or the other.

Leaning closer to Grant, Ros said, "We do have an idea."

"Mom," Brodie said with significance.

Unfazed by his warning, she continued. "Brodie has someone keeping an eye on Freddie's to determine if Newman visits there at a certain time each night. We already know he's hung out there twice. If we can anticipate where he'll be and when, we can all confront him—"

"*What?*" Mitch took a hard step back, separating himself from the rest of them. Muscles in his shoulders and back expanded. He sounded almost desperate when he said, "No, listen. You don't need to do that."

"It's a good plan," Brodie countered.

"It's really not." Mitch scowled at them all. "See, I'm not a kid. I don't need any of you to protect me. I only told you about Newman so you'd protect *yourselves.*"

"He needs to know you're not alone," Charlotte said.

"I don't want him to know that! I don't want him to know anything about you."

"Mitch…" Ros began.

"I'll find him. I'll talk to him." He took another step back. "I'll handle it, I swear."

"Sure you will," Brodie said. "We have no doubts on that. But we want him gone, right? For good. Like Charlotte said, he needs to see us with you."

He shook his head, rejecting the offer. "It'll go easier if you're not."

"I met him," Grant said. "One on one, you'd do fine. You know that's not how his ilk operate, though, so accept the help."

"He's up to something—I know that because I know Newman, know how he works. I know what it means when he goes to ground. It's better for all of you if he doesn't know we're…"

"Related?" Charlotte offered softly.

The look he shot her made her want to cringe, and also hurt her heart. The desperation, she knew, was to protect them—even at a risk to himself.

Sighing, she held up her hands. "It's true."

Frustration ripened to something hotter. "Jesus, I didn't come here for any of this, and I'm starting to think it was a big fucking mistake."

Firm, purposeful, Grant took a step toward him. "Calm down and watch your language."

With a humorless laugh, Mitch ignored him. "I don't need mothering. I don't need backup." He gestured at the house. "I didn't need any of this." His gaze zeroed in on Charlotte. "You shouldn't have brought them here."

Charlotte's throat went so tight she couldn't swallow, could barely breathe. He was hurting, and that hurt her too.

"You done?" Brodie asked, and in comparison, he sounded completely composed.

Mitch threw up his hands.

"I'm giving you some leeway, because one, I know my family and I are pushy as hell. We don't know how to tiptoe in, so instead we bulldoze. I hope you'll get used to it because I'm not sure we can change. Two, you're used to being alone and handling things your own way. Getting input chafes your ass, but trust me, that's not going to change now that you're part of us. Not today, and not twenty years from now. Family is there—good times and bad. Sometimes nice, sometimes annoying as hell. In the end, they're still family."

Mitch's eyes flared, then narrowed again.

Arms folded, Brodie didn't blink. "And three, at this point, it's not so much about what you want."

Fingers in his hair, Mitch turned away. The raised voices had brought Brute to his side, looking up at him, obviously worried. Howler chose to lean against Mitch's other side, almost pushing him over.

Unconcerned, Brodie smiled. "Jack and I now know we have a brother. For us, there's no going back. Regardless of what you do or how you feel about things, we'll be here, caring and concerned. It'll be easier for us if we're with you. Does that matter at all?"

If anything, Mitch only stiffened more, but at least he rested one hand on Brute. Then he rested the other on Howler.

Brodie gave her a small, reassuring smile with a wink, before he continued to Mitch. "Charlotte and Mom have big hearts. You don't know this about them because you're new here, but they'd have done the same for any new resident." He shrugged. "They help. Anyone and everyone."

"True enough," Grant said. "Folks want or need something, they usually start with Ros because she's good at figuring it out."

"And Charlotte always pitches in," Ros added. "Every single time."

A deep inhale, a slow exhale, and Mitch faced them again. "I appreciate it. I really do. But it's too much." He looked at the house. "I had plans to get it fixed up. Eventually it'll be a business. I wasn't in a big rush, so you didn't have to—"

Brodie scoffed. "You think I'd do less for a brother than I would for a new neighbor? You'd be dead wrong."

"Look at it as an opportunity. A fresh start here, with your family." Ros curled her mouth, but it wasn't exactly a smile. "And just so you know, I'll mother anyone I want to and there's not a damn thing you can do about it."

Admiration beamed from Grant's smile.

"I think," Charlotte said, "that you all need to give him a little room to breathe."

He nodded at her for that.

She wasn't done. Hung up on something he'd said, she pointed at the house. "What kind of business?"

Mitch gave her such an incredulous look, it made her defiant.

Right, she'd just asked everyone to give him room, and then she, herself, had pushed forward again. "What? Is it a secret?" When he continued to stare at her, she grumbled, "You shouldn't have brought it up if you didn't want me to ask."

Everyone waited, and finally Mitch gave in. "Landscaping."

Brodie snorted. "Why the hell are you secretive about *that*?"

He shot back, "Maybe I don't want you taking over?"

That earned a grin. "I promise my contribution will end with painting, and you can buy the paint."

"It's already bought."

"There you go."

Charlotte stepped close again. "Do you really want us all to go?" She prayed not, but if he did, she'd do her utmost to get the others to budge.

For now.

First though, she'd try to gently talk him around. "Isn't it just a little bit nice to be able to share? I mean, you've already accomplished a lot."

"I shared when I bought my land," Brodie said. Smiling, Ros looked around. "Didn't this use to be a landscaping business? I seem to remember buying flowers here once."

Appearing relieved to have a diversion, Mitch nodded. "Four years ago, the owner died. I had the money from my mother's house and everything I'd saved. This setup was cheap." He gestured at the barn. "Tools and machinery included, though the bigger equipment needs a little work." Before Brodie could get a word out, Mitch cut a glance his way. "I'll let you know if I need any help."

Pleased that he was no longer growling, Charlotte grinned. "Brodie's good with mechanics. Jack too."

This time Mitch's huff sounded close to a laugh.

"It'll be wonderful," Charlotte said, then wished she hadn't when Mitch lifted his gaze to hers, then just kept on looking. It immediately put her on the spot, and she could feel *everyone* glancing her way. "Well, it will be."

He nodded. "Hope so." Giving in an inch, he added, "And yeah, I guess sharing is nice."

"Landscaping." She liked the idea of it. "You have experience with that?"

Looking around at the yard and outbuilding, Mitch nodded. "Before prison, I worked for a self-employed guy who did landscape design with trees, shrubs, that sort of thing. That's what I've done for the past year too. In the time between getting out and coming here, I mean. I like being outside, working with my hands, seeing things grow, so…" He seemed to run out of words and turned his attention down to Brute.

Both dogs looked ready to doze off.

"It was meant to be," Ros whispered.

To Charlotte, it sounded as if Mitch had truly settled here— near his new family.

Near *her* too, though she knew she hadn't factored into his decision.

"That's why you knew about the gravel?" Brodie nodded as if just piecing that together. "Since it looks like Charlotte wants those damn bushes—"

"I do," she said fast.

"Maybe I can get your input on that too."

Instead of agreeing, Mitch said, "I'm going to go by the

hotel." Steely-eyed, he looked from Brodie to Grant to Ros. He didn't even glance toward Charlotte. "I'll leave my number for the desk clerk to give to Newman. Hopefully he'll call and I can get this resolved."

"Fine," Brodie said, as if it were still up to him. "But if he dodges you, like I think he might, we'll go with my plan. Deal?"

Very reluctantly, after a long hesitation, Mitch gave a single firm nod of acceptance. "All right, sure. But don't say I didn't warn you."

"Never would."

Progress, Charlotte thought, and it made her smile.

With that settled, Grant turned to Ros. "Why don't I drive you home? Leave the boys here to talk."

Ros actually blushed. "Thank you, Grant, I'd appreciate it." To the *boys*, she warned, "No fighting, and I mean it." She gave Charlotte a hug. "I'll see you at home later."

Then she allowed Grant to help her into the car, when she'd have smacked Brodie or Jack for even trying.

As if it only just then struck him, Brodie stood there watching them, his expression comical until the retreating car could no longer be seen. Turning back to Charlotte and Mitch, eyes wide with confusion, his jaw a little slack, he asked, "Does Mom have a boyfriend?"

All the tension building from the last hour suddenly burst, pushing Charlotte into a fit of laughter. She tried to quell it, but then she'd look at Brodie again. Eventually her hilarity affected Mitch and he joined in.

Brute and Howler started running around, barking excitedly, and that just made Brodie's droll expression all the funnier. She and Mitch were practically holding each other up.

"Wrap it up any day now," Brodie directed.

"Your face," she gasped, trying to explain why she couldn't.

"Hit ya hard, didn't it?" Mitch tried to wipe away his grin, and failed.

Deadpan, Brodie said, "You're not helping." He cracked a grin. "I call dibs on telling Jack."

"Still can't believe Mitch ratted you out to Barney Fife. What a shit move."

Hiding his ire wasn't easy, but Newman managed a grin for Ritchie. "The cop was funny, right? Trying to stare me down." He knew a clean cop when he laid eyes on one, and the squeaky-clean guy who'd approached him at the diner looked like he'd never done more than write a speeding ticket. Hell, Newman had gutted better men than him. Having a badge didn't change things.

They'd already thrown the few things they'd brought with them into duffels and left the hotel. He didn't run from any-one—but he'd told that damn nosy cop that he'd be away, so how could he stay here?

"We should gut the bastard," Ritchie said, "and be done with him."

"We?" Lee asked, once again driving.

Ritchie shot him a dirty look. "You know what I mean."

"This place is different from back home," Newman mused, watching the landscape as Lee took the long way around to their destination. "You think folks around here wouldn't notice a dead cop? They've only got—what? Three?"

"A few more than that," Lee said, since he'd scoped out the station on their first day. "With the whole town so small, they don't need many."

"Besides," Newman added, "working around Officer Colvin might even be more fun."

"Yeah?" Brightened by the prospect, Ritchie sat forward. "What are we gonna do?"

Pulling up to the far end of a wooded lot, Lee said, "We're here."

Ritchie looked around in confusion. "Here, where?"

"Come on." You'd think Ritchie would have caught on by now, but there were times Newman thought he might be too stupid to live.

His tone must have conveyed as much, because Ritchie didn't ask any more questions as they trekked through the woods with Lee leading the way.

They stopped when Mustang Transport came into view.

"Oh, shit," Ritchie whispered.

In the cluster of trees and scraggly shrubs bordering the track around the property, they could see the building—and anyone going in or out.

Lee had been here off and on all morning, waiting for the little curly-haired bitch to come to work. It was a starting point, a way for Lee to tail her, to find out where she lived.

When she hadn't showed, Newman thought maybe Lee had fucked up and missed her somehow. Then Colvin caught him at the diner, and it all went sideways.

So here he was, playing chickenshit games. No matter how he painted it for the others, it grated. One way or another, he'd get his pound of flesh.

For more than an hour they suffered the smothering heat and endless bug bites, and finally the little blue car he remembered from his last visit pulled up.

She got out, using a hand to shield her eyes as she looked around. He'd tried to find out more about her, but folks around here were suspicious as hell, and too damned protective of her.

We're behind the trees, honey. You can't see us...but we see you.

No, he wouldn't go back to the transport business. But he would find ways to run into little curly again.

Forced to reevaluate, he decided fucking with Mitch's new neighbors would be better than going after him directly. Mitch had always considered himself too good for the people from the old neighborhood. Yeah, he'd hung with Lang some, and good thing because without Lang squealing, Newman never would have found him.

Had Lang called Mitch? Did Mitch already know how he'd worked Lang over, leaving him bloody and battered on the dirty floor?

It brought some satisfaction, especially since Mitch liked to think of himself as a protector. God knows he'd gotten in the way of Newman's fist enough times, all to spare his mother.

"She's alone," Lee said, and damned if he didn't sound excited, an uncommon occurrence for Lee.

Newman wouldn't mind if Lee had a little fun—after he got done, of course.

As they watched, another car, a slick red Mustang, pulled into the lot and a freaking Goliath got out. He was as big as Mitch, and when *he* looked around, they all three ducked.

"Think he's onto us?" Ritchie whispered in breathless alarm.

"Doesn't matter." Newman watched them both go inside. "He can't be with her 24/7."

Lee spared the vaguest of smiles. "Won't slow me down. I'll still tail her."

"Cautiously," Newman warned. "I have plans for that girl. Don't get busted before I even get started."

Mitch knew what he was capable of, knew exactly what he'd do. By the time they finished, he'd be begging Newman to take back the money that was rightfully his, just to see him get out of Red Oak.

CHAPTER TWELVE

A week went by with no word from Newman. According to the hotel clerk, he'd checked out the same day Colvin had talked to him in the diner. To go where? He sure as hell wasn't gone from the area. Mitch knew better than that. So where was he?

Not knowing put him in limbo, caught between two different worlds. Right there, within his grasp, was a new existence full of possibilities, morality and honor. But every shadow held the same old ugly past filled with emotional pain, impossible choices and the reminder that life in a cell was no life at all.

A bead of sweat rolled down his neck as he struggled with a heavy rack. It was hot as Hades inside the barn, but at least it had been freshly aired.

Working with Jack and Brodie, they'd not only put bushes around the offices, they'd also gotten the house painted, the machinery in working order, and… He had a life.

A substantial life.

A basis for building more.

Little by little, it got easier to let them pitch in, especially when they didn't hesitate to ask for favors in return. While Jack and Brodie were both away, Ros asked him to pick up a stray cat to take to the shelter. During a storm that knocked out the power, Brodie asked him to check on his house.

Each day, one of them ensured that Charlotte wasn't at the office alone.

They included him, helping him—and asking for help. It made him feel less like a project they worked on, and more like an equal partner.

Actually, it made him feel like...well, a brother.

He wouldn't let Newman ruin things, but every heartbeat in his chest reminded him that he was out there, a ticking time bomb waiting for the right moment to do the most damage.

Disgusted, Mitch finished hammering the tool rack into the barn wall so he could properly arrange everything tomorrow. For once, he'd put in a full day alone while the brothers took care of their other jobs.

It felt like a reprieve, a chance to get his thoughts together without them wearing on him, making him think things he shouldn't yet think—not with Newman on the loose.

The extra hands had been great, but Mitch didn't shy away from hard work. He welcomed the stiffness in his shoulders now, and the sweat on his back.

Only downside? He missed Charlotte like crazy. She had a way of nudging him anytime his thoughts got too dark. Mitch wasn't sure if she had crazy coincidental timing—or if she was just that tuned in to him.

Jack and Brodie would have to end the "hands off" stance soon, because he didn't know how much longer he could resist.

Inside the barn, the shadows grew until he could no longer see well enough to keep working. He really needed electricity out here, but for now, the battery-operated lantern sitting on a post helped. He'd just about finished anyway.

Brute napped nearby, his head resting over a bag of grass seed that Mitch would use to fill the patchy spots in the yard.

In and around fixing up the place and trading favors, he and

Brute had hung out with *the family*. Thinking it sent the corners of his mouth kicking up.

Before actually meeting them, family had been such an elusive idea. He'd had only a vague notion of what they'd look like and how they'd react. Making their acquaintances, he'd thought, would be enough—but of course, he'd hoped for more. Occasional visits. Some common ground.

Never, not once, had he imagined that they'd be so unbelievable. Surreal. Incredibly awesome.

Hell, with his background, he hadn't trusted anything to be awesome. He'd expected to claw his way through every day.

Not anymore. Not since he'd discovered that his half brothers were two of the finest men he'd ever known. Big and solid, both in character and in build. Pushy, yes, but with good intentions. Sometimes funny, always sincere.

They were men he could proudly call family, and it stumped him that they wanted to do the same.

And Charlotte. Lord help him, but every time he saw her, his wants and needs doubled. He wanted family. He wanted that fanciful idea of home and hearth.

Now he wanted Charlotte too.

She never left his thoughts for long.

Craziest part? It wasn't just physical with her, and that was a first for him with women.

Yes, Charlotte made him nuts with her approach, pushing where the others stepped back. Tweaking their curiosity whenever she sought to satisfy her own. Anytime he and one of the brothers came to an agreement, her sweet face showed innocent pleasure, the pure kind that was all about being happy for someone else.

Being happy for *him*.

He couldn't remember anyone ever doing that before.

Absolutely, the physical attraction was stronger than anything he'd known. Hell, he wasn't used to holding back. He saw some-thing he wanted, he went after it.

It was the only way he'd ever gotten anything at all.

Now, because this was important, he had to follow someone else's rules.

How much longer did they want him to wait? How much longer could he last?

Often when Charlotte came along, she brought lunch or din-ner. The week had been filled with impromptu picnics, some-times with him, Charlotte and one of the brothers. Other times both brothers made it, and occasionally Ros was there as well.

He now had a picnic table, thanks to Jack.

And a rocker for his porch, thanks to Ros.

They overwhelmed him—and Charlotte burned him up.

He'd like to think she'd wanted to come along each time, but he knew the guys refused to let her be alone.

They were no more convinced that Newman had left than Mitch was.

After storing all his tools, he started out of the barn, calling Brute to come along. With a grumble and long stretch, the dog trotted out and Mitch put the lock back on the barn doors.

In its last farewell for the day, the setting sun left a slen-der, hazy red line bleeding along the horizon. Evening brought cooler air, but not cool enough to be comfortable.

When his cell rang, Mitch automatically hoped it was New-man. Until the bastard made contact, he was an invisible threat left unresolved. Setting the lantern on the porch and opening the door for Brute to go into the screened-in room, Mitch dug his phone from his pocket and glanced at the screen.

Jack, not Newman.

He wouldn't be disappointed that his brother was calling him. Yes, he wanted it to be Newman, but he had brothers now, and he'd never take that for granted.

Dropping down to sit on the wooden step, already smiling, he hit a button. "What's up, Jack?"

"How busy are you?"

Another favor? He'd never be too busy for his new family. "Just about to take a shower. Why?"

"Someone at the bar asked about you."

That statement put the brakes on every thought except: *Newman*. "When?"

"Not more than ten minutes ago. You have time to take a shower if you want, then head that way. We'll meet you there."

Already on his feet and striding down the hall, Mitch said, "Fuck the shower—"

"You have time."

That brought him up short. "How the hell do you know that?"

"There's a new guy working at Freddie's. Brodie and I paid him to let us know if anyone asks about you."

Son of a... "Been nice if you'd told me." Mitch grabbed a towel and stepped into the bathroom, opening his jeans one-handed. "How do you know he won't take off?"

"Our guy told us he was busy chatting up a few women. Looked to be setting things up with a barmaid who's still working, so he ordered food."

Jesus. He wouldn't wish Newman on any woman. If she knew him at all, she'd look for less lethal companionship. "I'll head that way soon as I wash off the sweat. And Jack?"

"Yes?"

"Thanks."

He showered in record time, gave a few swipes of the towel over his body, pulled boxers and a T-shirt onto his still damp skin, then rummaged through a drawer for clean jeans. By the time he was pulling on running shoes, barely ten minutes had passed.

Grabbing up his wallet, keys and cell phone, he started

through the house—and found Brute sitting in the hallway, head cocked and eyes watchful.

"You can't go this time, bud. Sorry."

Flattening his ears, Brute whined.

"Ah, damn, don't do that, okay?" Dropping to one knee, Mitch took a few minutes to cuddle him. "Every so often, I have to leave you behind, but it's temporary, I swear."

Those sincere brown eyes seemed to understand, making him feel a little less guilty.

"How about a treat?"

That got his ears back up.

"Yeah, you like that idea, don't you? C'mon, boy." Patting his thigh, Mitch went into the kitchen, forcing himself not to rush out. He found a big beef-flavored treat that usually took Brute a half hour or more to gnaw down. Hopefully by then he'd be ready for more lazing around. "Here ya go, bud."

Sitting on his haunches, his tail brushing the floor in broad sweeps, Brute accepted the treat between sharp teeth.

"Good boy."

Leaving Brute sprawled on the floor, the bone-shaped treat between his front paws while he worked it over, Mitch headed out, locking the door behind him.

Anxious to get hold of Newman before he could slither away again, he jogged to his car.

On the drive, he concentrated on clearing his head. Dealing with Newman required cold, emotionless concentration, not rage.

Unfortunately when he pulled up to park on a side street adjacent to the bar, he found Ros and Charlotte getting out of Charlotte's car. Everything in him rebelled.

Where the hell was Jack?

"There you are," Ros called. "We were waiting for you."

Utterly flattened, his gaze shot back and forth from her smiling face to Charlotte's gentle scrutiny. "Why are you here?"

Hooking her arm through his, Ros said, "For you, of course."

She tried to go forward but Mitch planted his feet and re-fused to budge. Easy enough. Incredulity left him rigid enough that his joints stopped working. Guessing the instigator of this little surprise, he frowned at Charlotte. "You actually brought her here?"

Charlotte opened her mouth—but Ros cut her off.

"I would have driven myself if she hadn't."

So not Charlotte's fault—but that still didn't explain the outra-geous irresponsibility of their presence. "Jack actually let you…"

"Ha!" Pulling away, Ros jammed her hands onto her rounded hips. "Get it through your head, Mitch, *no one* tells me what I can or can't do, where I can or can't go. Especially not my sons."

He swallowed. Ros had a mean way of staring when irate, and clearly she was. He couldn't recall his own mother ever using that particular tone with him.

Usually too lit to do more than sneer, she had rarely cared enough to put in the effort.

It was the first time Ros had been that cross with him—and some fickle part of him appreciated that she, at least, considered him worth it. "Rosalyn, listen—"

"No, *you* listen." She hooked his arm again, tighter this time. "We're here with you."

She propelled him forward three steps before he dug in again. "Where the hell is Jack?"

"Here," Jack said, coming up behind him. "And there's Bro-die."

He looked up to see Brodie crossing the street toward them. *Hail, hail, the gang's all here.*

Disgusted, he asked, "And your wives?" That's all he needed to round out this farce.

Aggrieved, Jack looked back to his yellow Mustang parked in the lot of the drugstore beneath security lights. "Ronnie's there." Pained, he added, "I convinced her we needed her to keep watch in case Newman tries to sneak out the back."

"And if he does?" Brodie asked, amused.

"She promised to call me, so…here's hoping she doesn't lose her cool and do something crazy."

That made Ros frown in worry; she hugged his arm even more.

"Mary agreed to stay home with Howler, Buster and Peanut." Brodie popped his neck from one side to the other, then rolled his shoulders and muttered, "Only took me twenty minutes to convince her."

"Well." Charlotte laced her fingers together. "Maybe we should head in?"

"Yes," Ros said. "Let's do." They started forward.

One happy little group—not that Mitch was happy. Why should Ros and Charlotte be there? Why had Brodie and Jack even told Charlotte about it? Except…they were close. Anyone could see that.

Did that mean sharing every damn thing? God, he hoped not.

They turned the corner, got halfway to the entrance and…

The door to Freddie's opened. Music and conversation spilled out with muted golden light, until the tall silhouette of a broad-shouldered man shadowed it all. With his back to them, the guy looked down one side of the street. Letting the door close, he turned the other way—toward them—and the bottom fell out of Mitch's stomach.

No. It couldn't be. *Shouldn't* be.

But it was.

"You," Ros whispered, the single word quiet with an outraged strain that grew and grew until it fairly crackled with heat—and she erupted. "*Bastard.*"

Finally, she released Mitch. Hell, she pushed away from him so hard and fast, she all but launched herself up the sidewalk like a missile with one target in mind.

Her ex-husband.

Brodie and Jack's father. Mitch's father too.

The one and only Elliott Crews.

Stunned surprise rendered Charlotte mute. The last thing they needed tonight was a visit from Elliott, yet here he was. Big, good-looking—and if she read Ros's mood right, about to get his butt kicked.

Jack rushed forward with a muttered curse. Brodie heaved a sigh and followed.

Mitch wore an expression so enigmatic, Charlotte couldn't guess at his thoughts. It was as if he'd gone perfectly still, every inch of his face carefully devoid of expression. No frown. No curiosity.

No welcome.

It had to be painful for him to see Elliott again, given their background and the way Elliott had walked away, leaving Mitch to an unthinkable fate.

Easing closer to him, wanting to offer comfort whether he wanted it or not, Charlotte nudged him and whispered, "Oops."

He didn't look down at her, but for the briefest second or two she detected a slight smile.

Everything seemed to happen at once. Brodie and Jack caught Ros in mid jump and managed to interrupt her attack on their dad. The fist that Ros swung—not an open palm, but an actual *fist*—missed Elliott by only a few inches.

"*Rosalyn*," Elliott said in alarm, reaching out to her. "Honey, what is it?"

For a second, Ros struggled against her sons. Anger seemed to have stolen her voice, but her glare was enough to make Elliott take a quick step back.

Flat, irate, Jack asked, "What are you doing here?"

"I'm visiting." But the way Elliott said it, everyone saw the lie, especially when his gaze skipped past them to Mitch. After a three-second stare and a slow blink, Elliott released a long breath. "Mitch. You're all grown up."

Charlotte felt compelled to scoot even closer to him, close enough that her hand brushed his.

Rather than take it, Mitch reached around and opened his hot palm to the small of her back, moving forward and taking her with him. "Elliott," he said with the same enthusiasm he might use to order a coffee. It was respectful but nothing more.

For her part, Charlotte was pleased that Mitch wanted her by his side.

Or was he just not thinking?

Whatever the reason, she was oh-so-keenly aware of the iron strength in his arm, the warmth emanating from his big body and the frantic pumping of her own heart.

"You look good," Elliott said, infusing some pride into his tone. "Big, strong."

"I look like you."

Elliott actually grinned. "Indeed, you do."

Ros shrugged away from Brodie and Jack, then hiked her purse strap up over her shoulder and smoothed back the long strands of hair that had escaped her ponytail.

Better composed but no less furious, she looked up at the man she'd once loved enough to marry, the man who had given her two wonderful sons. Charlotte knew that's how Ros thought about Elliott, because she'd told her so. Ros was aware of his faults but, according to her, divorcing him did not negate his paternity.

Most times Ros treated him kindly without tolerating his nonsense.

Not today.

"You, Elliott Crews, are the most reprehensible, irredeemable, irresponsible and selfish person I've ever had the misfortune to know."

Elliott frowned down at Ros in consternation. At fifty-eight, he was still a very handsome man, his bearing proud, his shoulders rock solid. He had a way of wearing his sandy brown hair that looked casual and unaffected but still drew female appreciation.

Elliott might not have it in him to ever settle down, but no one could doubt that Ros was his one true love. If he could be a better man for anyone, it would have been for her.

"Is this about Mitch?"

Agog, Charlotte's mouth fell open. Of all the stupid things to ask—did he seriously not understand the situation?

The cavalier question set Ros off again and this time, she managed to pop him one in the shoulder.

More out of surprise than pain, Elliott winced, but Ros pulled back, biting her lip and shaking her hand.

Unwisely, Elliott asked, "Did you hurt yourself?"

New fury had her drawing up until she looked a foot taller. "*You* hurt me. You hurt *everyone* who ever cared about you!" Shaking her injured fist at him, she demanded, "*How could you?*"

He leaned away from her fury. "How could I what?"

Playing peacekeeper, Brodie stepped between them before Ros could hit him again. "Don't play dumb, Dad. She has reason to be pissed and you know it. We all do."

Jack, never as diplomatic when it came to his father, said, "Even I'm surprised you'd stoop so low, and it's not like I ever expected much from you."

Aggrieved, Elliott looked at Mitch again. "This is about you, I guess?"

Mitch offered an awkward shrug. "Apparently, but that's not why I'm here. I never meant to—"

Everyone started talking at once, including Charlotte. Knotting a hand in his shirt, she drew his attention first. "Don't you *dare* apologize."

One brow cocked, Mitch looked down at her with a hint of

amusement reflected in his golden-brown eyes. His much larger hand settled over hers, engulfing her fingers in warmth. "No?"

"Absolutely not," Brodie said.

And Jack added, "Not to him. Not ever."

Mitch ignored them, choosing to keep all his concentration on her.

Floundering, Charlotte muttered, "I thought we had this settled."

He gave one small nod. "Looks a little different now, with him here too."

"They're right," Elliott said, drawing Mitch's gaze. "This is where you should be. In fact, I'm relieved you're here. I was looking for you back at your old place but the entire house is gone. Wiped away. There's nothing but an empty lot and large equipment. Something about expanding the highway." His gaze warmed. "I was hoping you'd come here."

"*You* left him there," Ros reminded him. "You left him *alone*."

Elliott shook his head. "I—"

"Your selfishness sickens me." She turned away.

"Ros, honey…" He caught her arm, but she jerked back from his touch and his hand fell to his side. "You've got it all wrong."

At that, both of Mitch's brows rose.

He, better than anyone, knew the facts. Probably because he didn't want to cause a scene, he stayed quiet and just listened.

It killed her that he felt he needed to do that. Neither of the other brothers would hesitate to give their father hell when he needed it. And he needed it now.

In her opinion, Elliott had behaved badly one too many times. But this, walking away from his son, was something that the Crews family might not be able to forgive.

"I have my faults," Elliott said, sounding annoyed. "I won't ever say I don't."

All the glares intensified—except for Mitch, who stood away from the others, both physically and emotionally. Charlotte leaned into his side. He could stand apart if that's what he wanted right now, but by God, she'd stand with him.

Accepting that, accepting *her*, he tightened his arm around her back.

"You have plenty of reason to hate me," Elliott said to Ros, "and I've been damned surprised in the past when you didn't."

"That's changing," Ros informed him.

His mouth firmed. "You know me, honey, better than anyone. Do you honestly believe I *wanted* to leave Mitch?"

"You always left us," Jack reminded him without sympathy.

"You had her!" Elliott jabbed a finger toward Ros. "Hell, I knew you were well taken care of."

"No thanks to you, Dad," Brodie pointed out.

"I know that. I know I'm a grade-A bastard. But with Mitch..." His gaze softened and he rubbed his mouth. "Newman threatened to hurt him, okay? Him and his mother. He said if I came back around it'd be them who paid for it."

"You left," Ros corrected, "because Newman threatened *you*."

"That's what you think?" As realization dawned, that they all did in fact believe it, Elliott growled. "Not fucking likely."

"Watch your mouth."

That warning came from Jack, Brodie *and* Ros, and it seemed to amuse Mitch. After shaking his head, he glanced at each of them, and shook it again. She even heard his small chuckle.

Was he finally seeing, maybe accepting, what it meant to have family in his corner? If so, hallelujah. In Charlotte's mind, it was past time.

Though that small smile stayed in place, his hand started rubbing little circles over the small of her back, sort of caressing, maybe just restless.

Whatever, she liked it.

It showed that he wasn't unaffected, but also that he felt at ease with her. Like her, he wanted the physical connection.

"I don't blame you," Mitch finally said. "Newman threatened everyone, and he often followed through. He said he'd neuter you, right?"

Surprise took Elliott's brows high. "You heard that?"

Mitch shrugged. "It explained why you stopped coming around."

"Well, understand this." He started toward Mitch, until both Brodie and Jack blocked his way. Chagrined, Elliott relented. "Newman hated it whenever I was around, and he told me so every chance he got. Big deal. I didn't care. Not until he stated that if he saw me again, it'd be you and Velma paying for it. He was damned explicit in those threats too. Said even if I called the cops on him, he had friends who'd get to you both."

Thoughtful, Mitch studied him. "Probably true. His cronies were as cowardly and cruel as him."

Elliott looked away, then back. "I talked to Velma, offered to put you both somewhere safe, but she wouldn't go. She kept saying she loved Newman, that she needed him. I told her what Newman had said and she…" His voice trailed off, then with apology, he admitted, "It didn't matter. Not enough."

The same devastation Charlotte felt was reflected in the dark eyes of Ros, Brodie and Jack.

And Mitch… Mitch's eyes held stoicism, pride and the awful acceptance of his mother's shortcomings.

"She was an addict," Mitch said, disrupting the pained silence as if her addiction explained everything—the neglect he'd suffered, the love and protection she'd withheld. "Newman supplied her fix and that made him the most important person in her world."

For him to state the truth so baldly, Charlotte imagined Mitch had accepted the crushing pain long ago. He didn't show it, but she felt it for him, so much so she had to blink back tears.

Softly, Elliott replied, "I know. I just didn't know what to do about it—except steer clear of him. That's why I started trying to see you in secret."

Still sorting it out, Mitch frowned. "He said he ran you off because you valued your…"

"My balls?" Elliott scoffed. "He threatened one ridiculous thing after another. Every single time I was there, actually. He knew I wasn't afraid of him, and that's why he switched up the threats to you and Velma." This time when Elliott pressed forward, Brodie and Jack stepped aside to let him. "I was worried about you, son. I checked in with Velma often, sent her money a few times a year. She said you were doing great, but I didn't really believe her—especially when she reiterated what Newman said, warning me to stay away."

New tension traveled over Mitch. "She never told me."

"Shit," Elliott muttered, looking away. "I swear to you—"

"I believe you."

Very quietly, Charlotte asked, "Did she tell you Mitch went to prison?"

Elliott's chin jerked up, almost like he'd been struck. He breathed a little harder, then shook his head just as hard. "No," he said through his teeth. "No one mentioned that."

For a time the two men just stared at each other, emotions, questions, grief silently passing between them.

"Newman dragged you into one of his deals, didn't he?" Sawing his teeth together, Elliott asked, "Did he make it sound like life or death?"

"Pretty much, yeah. For Mom, it would have been."

When Elliott looked at Charlotte again, she explained the details of it. At least, as much as she knew about it, given the bare bone facts Mitch had shared.

"She never said a word." Elliott worked his jaw. "Over the last year, she hasn't even answered my calls—"

"She's gone," Mitch interrupted. He filled his chest with a slow breath but otherwise maintained his statue-like stillness. "Overdosed."

"Jesus, son." Elliott looked like he wanted to embrace him,

but Mitch's stance—as cold as carved granite—shut down the idea before it could happen.

Had Elliott ever embraced him? Many times she'd seen him hug Brodie and Jack, sometimes whether they wanted it or not. But then, they had Ros as a buffer—a bighearted woman who reminded them that Elliott was their father any time they got fed up with him. She'd explain that he did love them and was doing the best he could while being the flawed man he was.

From all that she could tell, Mitch had never had anyone to nudge him along, to assure him of love.

To champion him.

Full of sincerity, Elliott said, "I'm so damn sorry."

"My mother—"

"She had her demons, son. I knew that."

Mitch nodded.

Elliott tilted his chin toward at Ros. "She could tell you I'm not the sticking around kind. I would never deny that. But I would have helped Velma start over if she'd have let me."

Mitch searched his face before apparently accepting what he said. Some of his tension seeped away. "I tried too—with the same result. No matter what Newman did, she clung to him."

No matter what Newman did... Those words covered a lot of possibilities, none of them good.

"It wasn't a healthy love."

"Not by a long shot," Mitch agreed.

Ros made an effort to calm her tone, but there was no disguising the anger in her posture. "You knew all this, Elliott. You knew what type of man this Newman person was, you knew that his mother struggled with addiction, and still you let him run you off, and then he made life for Mitch as hellish as he could."

"Ros." Though Mitch spoke softly, steel underlined the rebuke. "It wasn't like that. Besides, I told you I didn't stick around there either."

"Because you left when you were still a minor," Brodie said. "And you haven't yet said where you went."

"Here and there." Mitch's chin notched a tiny bit higher. "It's not important."

Charlotte had an awful suspicion what that might mean, as did the others. It seemed most likely that Mitch had survived on the streets. He might not want to talk about it, but his family did—and they were never easy to dissuade.

"I should have killed that son of a bitch when I had the chance," Elliott growled.

"I wish you had," Ros snapped. "You might still get your chance since he's been seen around town."

Giving Ros a sharp-eyed glance and getting her nod in return, Elliott slowly smiled. "It would be my ever-lasting pleasure to beat him into the ground."

It was the oddest thing, seeing the remoteness fade from Mitch's eyes. He didn't lower his chin and his shoulders remained stiff, but he huffed a short laugh. "All that arrogant confidence…" Glancing at Brodie and Jack, he asked, "Looks like you inherited it, huh?"

"As did you," Ros replied.

Jack smirked. "But luckily little else."

"What about a love of cars?" Elliott bragged. "You sure as hell didn't get that from your mom."

A car door slammed and someone laughed.

For the first time since they'd seen each other, Elliott looked around, and that prompted Charlotte to do the same. Good Lord, she'd forgotten they were on a public sidewalk! At this time of night, Freddie's bar was the busiest establishment in town.

She was relieved to see there were only a few people milling around: a younger couple across the street, two men standing outside the bar smoking, and a mother with her kids getting into her car.

Only a few, but enough that in a town the size of Red Oak, news of the family squabble would be the talk at every breakfast table tomorrow morning.

"We've caused a spectacle," Elliott grumbled.

"That's all on you." Clearly, Ros wouldn't give an inch. "We run a respectable business here. We're liked by the town. You're the one—"

Elliott tried to schmooze up to her. "It was a shitty situation, honey. What did you want me to do?"

As if she'd been waiting for that question, Ros shot up to her tiptoes to say close to his face, "You should have brought him to me!"

CHAPTER THIRTEEN

At first, Mitch wasn't sure he'd heard her right. But Brodie and Jack both nodded, and Charlotte squeezed closer, so…damn. He couldn't credit Rosalyn's crazy idea, but no one else seemed surprised. It was so ludicrous that he laughed, the sound choked and disbelieving.

Charlotte looked up at him, her watchful eyes full of understanding. Yeah, she'd aligned herself with him real quick. He hated to admit it, but it helped, having her close, so he was in no hurry to let her go, despite his agreement with Brodie and Jack.

Before Rosalyn resorted to blows again—on his behalf—he cleared his throat. "Look, this whole thing is…uncomfortable." What an understatement. No one had ever fought over him before, so he had no basis for how to handle it. So far, getting irate hadn't helped, and neither had distancing himself. Ros wore such a defiant look, and she could be so unpredictable, that he quickly added, "I appreciate the sentiment, I really do."

"It's not a sentiment." She returned the power of her glare on Elliott. "It's what should have happened."

He could see that she honestly believed it. "But how would that have worked?" In a mocking tone, Mitch said, *"Honey, I'm home and I brought along my bastard kid for you."* He laughed. "No one wants that."

Almost in unison, Brodie, Jack and Charlotte said, "You don't know her."

No, apparently he didn't, and he'd sure as hell never met anyone even remotely like her.

"Look, I don't hold a grudge against Elliott, okay? So no one else should either. I'd rather let it go." He was better equipped to deal with anger or rejection, not...whatever this was. "Can we just look to the future? That's why I'm here."

Grudgingly, the others gave in—except for Rosalyn and he figured she'd deal with Elliott in her own good time, just as she'd apparently been doing for years.

To switch topics a bit, Mitch said to Elliott, "You came out of the bar. I take it Newman isn't in there?"

"Sorry, no." And with a gleam in his eye, Elliott asked, "Any idea where he's staying?"

Shaking his head, Mitch said, "He's laying low somewhere, but he's still around. I know it. We thought you were him, and I have to tell you, I was looking forward to seeing him eye to eye."

Going for a joke, Elliott said, "Guess I disappointed everyone again."

It fell flat in a big way.

With no welcome to be found, Elliott deflated. "Seriously, I'm sorry." He glanced around at the unfriendly group. "Any way I can help?"

"You've done more than enough," Ros said.

"Right. True." He shoved his hands into his pockets. Rocked back on his heels. Looked around again, and gave up. "Guess I should get going then."

The ensuing silence weighed heavily on Mitch. None of them invited Elliott to stay, and he didn't think it was his place.

But damn, this all felt off. In so many ways, he'd brought trouble when that was the very last thing he wanted to do.

It also felt oddly right because he knew, suddenly knew deep down to his bones, that he had people on his side. They'd said as much, repeatedly. But now it was more than words.

Experiencing it firsthand left a funny feeling in his chest. It'd probably take time for him to process it. It was...weirdly empowering, when he'd never considered himself a man who needed that. Comforting too, though he'd die before admitting that he needed or wanted comfort.

He was strong, capable, more than able to stand up for himself in all circumstances. He'd been doing it since he was a kid.

Ten years from now he'd still be that man; he didn't know any other way to be.

And yet, now knowing it would be a choice instead of a necessity lightened something in his heart.

A heart he'd all but forgotten he had.

"So." Elliott rocked on his heels again, then nodded at the way Mitch had his arm around Charlotte's back. "Did I miss something here?"

That brought everyone else's gazes swinging toward them. Eyes widened, then narrowed, not exactly in anger but more like curiosity and sudden keen awareness.

That's right. Get used to it, because I'm done waiting.

Her graceful spine stiffened, but he didn't let her go. Nope. He wasn't about to do that.

Let them look. In fact, he brought his arm to her shoulders in a casual way that still kept her tucked close. "Guess you didn't," Mitch said, "since you mentioned it and everything."

"I shouldn't have?"

He looked at both Brodie and Jack. "Doesn't matter."

In the beginning, he'd meant to hold to their bargain, to give Charlotte space until they gave the go-ahead. But there had to be allowances for extenuating circumstances...like when a father you hadn't seen for a decade suddenly showed up and his ex-wife, who wasn't your mother, gave him hell on your behalf.

Dark eyes glinting, Rosalyn beamed at him.

In approval?

What the hell did he know about approval? He hadn't seen it often enough to be sure. Besides, Ros was a shifty one. He'd yet to understand a single thing she did.

Clearing his throat, Jack glanced around as if trying to find anything to look at other than his half brother cozying up with his pseudo-sister.

Yup, he got that it might be unsettling. Overall they still thought of Charlotte as a kid, and God knew he wasn't anyone's idea of a proper suitor. Not with his criminal record and... sketchy background.

He wouldn't blame them if they switched some of their animosity for Elliott over to his head.

What happened instead left him a little poleaxed.

Brodie said, "It's getting late. We can talk more tomorrow." The inflection made it clear he had something to say, and yet he didn't feel the need to say it now.

Meaning...he didn't mind that Mitch was still holding Charlotte? Huh.

"I'm meeting Grant inside." Ros's smile didn't dim, but now that sweet expression had a hint of wickedness to it. When she slanted her dark gaze to Elliott, Mitch understood why. "I'm joining him for a drink. Charlotte, you know where to find me when you're ready." She sashayed away, a woman without a care.

Nonplussed, Elliott looked blankly from face to face before his expression darkened. "Grant? Who the hell is Grant?"

"Officer Colvin," Jack explained with smug satisfaction. "You probably remember him. Good guy. Gainfully employed. Solid in the community."

Ouch. Seeing the incredulous shock on Elliott's face, Mitch actually felt bad for him. Then again, he'd created his own role in this farce, and for sure Rosalyn deserved better than an absentee husband.

Elliott's mouth opened twice before he managed to croak, "Your mother has a *date*?"

"Was a surprise to me too." Jack grinned. "I'm happy for her."

Brodie clasped his dad's shoulder. "Other men have eyes, Dad. I'm surprised it's taken her this long."

"But…"

"Ronnie might be creeping this way soon if I don't get back to her." Jack lifted a hand in farewell. "Good night, all."

"Mary's waiting up for me too. I should get going." Brodie let his gaze wander over Mitch's hold on Charlotte, but not with warning or anger—more like inevitability. "You'll see that she gets inside with Mom? Colvin will take it from there."

"Yes." He wasn't about to let anything happen to her.

Brodie let his fingertips graze Charlotte's cheek with affection. "You make a hell of a champion, brat."

"I just—"

"Try not to give him fits, okay? It's been a crazy night."

"I'm aware," she returned, stepping away to give Brodie a hug. "Besides, I save all my fits for you."

Laughing, Brodie looked at Mitch over Charlotte's head. "I'll be in touch." Then he turned and strode away—without saying a word to Elliott.

Left alone now, Charlotte glanced between Elliott and Mitch. "I should probably head in too."

"Not yet." Disliking the two feet now separating them, Mitch closed the distance, drawing her near and tipping up her chin to look into her eyes.

He wanted her. Now, always.

Funny how things had shifted.

It seemed with every minute that slipped past, the idea of keeping her in his life became more necessary.

As he got lost in her gaze, his thoughts forming a hazy future, Charlotte held her breath.

What was she expecting? For him to make out with her here,

with Elliott at his back? He smiled. "I need to talk to you, if you don't mind." About so many things.

Everything was different now. Elliott had come and gone peacefully for years. It was Mitch's presence that had caused the discord, or at least added to it, regardless of what they said. He needed to find a fix—for Elliott and for himself.

It felt like that should start with Charlotte, which was odd since she wasn't actually related to Elliott. *Thank God.*

Realizing she hadn't even blinked yet, he whispered, "Breathe, honey."

She filled her lungs, managed a smile and exhaled. "Thank you."

His attention moved over her face, the soft flawless skin, the narrow nose and that killer mouth that haunted his dreams. He felt like a different person when with her. Better. Less angry at the world and himself. More optimistic about his future.

A man able to deal with this awkward situation.

"Are you okay?" she whispered, glancing worriedly at Elliott, who pretended to give them privacy by studying the roof of the bar.

"I am," he replied, and meant it. The moment felt very special, an eye-opener for sure, but he'd keep from getting carried away. He owed Brodie and Jack that much. Actually, Charlotte needed to know his intent before she continued...what? Brodie had called her a champion, and that fit.

She *did* champion him, so she needed to know how much it meant to him.

He needed to know her intent too. He could read women, true, and Charlotte gave off a lot of vibes, not the least of which was mutual interest. But this whole situation put a spin on his usual perception. Damned if he'd act out of neediness, or misread compassion for chemistry.

So he'd talk to her, lay it on the line, let her know what he wanted, now and in the future.

First, he had to start with tonight. "You'll give me a few minutes?"

She nodded. "Yes, of course."

"Well." Looking around, all in all appearing a little lost, Elliott cleared his throat. "Guess I should, um, get going then."

Mitch tried to find the right words—and failed.

Deafening silence surrounded them.

"It was good seeing you, Mitch. Real good." Elliott flashed a quick smile at Charlotte, started to reach out to Mitch but changed his mind, and with a shake of his head, he pivoted and strode across the street, going fast as if he feared he might change his mind, or falter.

Mitch stared after him, emotions clamoring, loyalties divided.

Hugging his arm, Charlotte whispered, "It won't kill Elliott to stay in the hotel."

"No." Still, it felt wrong. Did he even have the money for that?

"He's brought all this on himself," she reminded him gently.

Mitch nodded. True. Very true.

With a touch to his chest, she drew his attention, her smile full of perception. "You don't have to fight yourself, you know. I understand and the others will too."

There was something amazing about that, maybe because he had a hard time understanding himself. "You think?"

"I'm positive," she promised and gave him a little push. "Go on."

Mitch believed her...because this was Charlotte and she was tenderhearted and caring, but also assertive enough that he knew she'd tell him the truth.

Plus she'd stood by him. *Literally.*

"Shit," he muttered. He clasped her shoulders. "Promise you won't move."

Her smile in place, she agreed.

"Stay where I can see you." Newman was still around and he wouldn't take chances.

She drew a finger across her heart. "I'll be right here waiting for you."

Waiting for him. That sounded nice. On instinct, Mitch leaned down and pressed his mouth to her forehead. "Thanks." Ignoring her surprise, he sprinted away.

On the other side of the street right before the corner, he caught up with Elliott. "Hey."

Still with his back to him, Elliott paused and the rigidity eased from his shoulders. Cautiously, he looked over his shoulder before facing Mitch, his expression expectant.

Shit. Mitch didn't know what Elliott hoped for, but he hated to disappoint him. "Where will you stay?"

Two seconds ticked by before Elliott gave his usual careless smile. "My car tonight—and before you think I shouldn't, it's something I've done before. No biggie, I promise. Tomorrow I'll figure out something else."

"Tomorrow?" Now that sounded interesting.

"Yeah, see, I plan to stick around for a few days at least." Briskly rubbing his hands together, he stared toward the bar where Rosalyn had gone. "This wasn't the time, right? But she and I have things to talk about."

Yeah, he could just imagine. Shaking his head, unsure if Elliott would survive another chat with Ros, Mitch offered, "You could come to my place."

"Yeah? You at the hotel?"

"No. I bought a house." Crazy how much satisfaction he took in saying that. Before everyone had helped to make it livable, he would've cringed at the idea of Elliott seeing it.

And that felt damn pathetic, like he had something to prove to the father who hadn't stuck around.

Rather than dwell on his own failings, he said, "There's plenty of room."

"A house, huh? Wow, that's terrific, son!" Genuinely happy, Elliott put a heavy hand on his shoulder, much as he used to do during his visits when Mitch was just a kid.

It felt different now, of course. For one thing, his shoulders were no longer skinny. For another, he looked Elliott in the eyes.

"So you're settling here? You'll love the place. It's always been a nice quiet little town, long as you can tune out the nosy neighbors."

"Staying is the plan." If Newman didn't screw it all up.

"It's where you belong, you know. With your brothers—and yes, with Ros. She was right about that."

But not with him? No, Mitch didn't want to think about Elliott that way. No one was under any illusion that Elliott was the "stick around" kind of dad. "I can show it to you soon as I talk with Charlotte."

"I want to see it, but it'll have to be another time, okay?"

Elliott preferred sleeping in his car? Now, damn it, that felt like a gut punch. Defensively, he cracked, "Worried about Newman after all, huh?"

A bittersweet smile curved the mouth of the man he resembled so much. "Forget Newman's threats. It's Ros I'm worried about, because she *would* neuter me for infringing on you. Besides, bastard as I am, even I know it would be wrong. Not after everything else. They're few and far between, but I do have some scruples."

So it had nothing to do with him, and everything to do with his respect for Rosalyn's will? That was sort of...charming?

Or maybe *gutless* was the better word choice. Whichever.

"We'll get reacquainted," Elliott promised. "Looking forward to it. But I can't use you."

"Actually, I'd enjoy the company."

As if he'd been thrown a lifeline, the dejection left Elliott's posture and his usual cockiness returned. "You really mean that?"

He'd said it, hadn't he? No, he didn't entirely understand it himself, except that he wanted to build more family, not discard it. That could start with Elliott, and maybe in the process he could bring a little peace between them all.

It'd be nice to do something positive for this family, instead of complicating their lives.

"I do. Understand, though, Newman really is around and I don't know when he'll show—"

"Let him. You're a grown man now, not a boy I hope to protect, so I'd be happy to *discuss* things with him." Making the threat loud and clear, Elliott clenched and unclenched his fists.

Mitch couldn't help but grin. Jack and Brodie might not like it, but in some obvious ways they were a chip off the old block. "Ros said you weren't afraid."

"Only of her." He grinned too.

"If Newman does show up, he's mine." On that point, Mitch wouldn't relent. "Just so you know."

"You look like you can handle him, so I don't have a problem with that." Elliott arched a brow. "But if I get a chance, I'm taking my turn at him too. Bastard has it coming."

Such a paradox. Mitch refrained from pointing it out. "I need a minute or two with Charlotte first." He'd kept her in his sights even while talking to Elliott. So far, she'd barely moved.

Hands behind her and ankles crossed, she leaned against the brick wall in a deliberately casual pose, probably designed to keep him from hurrying. She also made a point of not looking at them.

For such a nosy little thing, that showed real self-discipline. Mitch gave in to a smile.

The light of a streetlamp haloed her hair and created those tantalizing shadows that emphasized the indent of her waist, the thrust of her breasts and the curve of her hip.

Curves he wanted to explore on a body he wanted to get to know a whole lot better.

The picture she made reminded him of the first time he'd seen her, and it had the same effect on him now, only this was sharper because he knew her better, knew the appealing personality that went with the face and body.

One kiss, he thought. One long, exploratory kiss and then he could get it together again.

Leaning closer, Elliott promised, "I won't tell."

"What?"

"You're looking at her the way a man long-denied looks at a woman he wants."

Mitch laughed. Probably true, but… "I've only known her a few weeks."

"So? I knew Ros was the one within hours. I fucked it up, over and over again, but she's still it. I figure she always will be. If you want Charlotte, go for it. Just do it right."

Advice from Elliott? Rich, but still appreciated. "Thanks. Brodie and Jack might have something to say about that."

"Yeah, probably." He gave Mitch a nudge. "But they respect you. I can already tell. With them, that's what really matters."

Maybe Elliott knew that, because they didn't respect him. "Where did you park?"

"Down that way." He nodded toward an otherwise empty lot.

All Mitch saw was an aging pickup. "Where?"

"That's it." Abashed, he explained, "For now, I drive a truck. Don't make a big deal of it."

No, he wouldn't. A little humility would do Elliott good. "My car's around the corner. The black Mustang you gave me— but in better shape now. Give me a few minutes and then you can follow me home."

Moving to the front of a barbershop now closed, Elliott lowered onto the step and stretched out his long legs. "Take your time, son. Just let me know when you're ready." He made a point of leaning back on his elbows so he was out of sight.

Looking back at Charlotte, Mitch made up his mind. Could

he make things work with her long term? No idea. But she was damn sure the one for right now, for next week and the week after that. How long it'd take him to get his fill, he didn't know—but he wanted to find out. Badly.

She must have felt the intensity of his stare because her eyes met his and her lips parted. He could almost swear something more than sight connected them.

An edge of lust, sharp and hot, deepened his breathing and contracted his muscles as he headed to her.

In her widening eyes he saw sultry recognition. *Yeah, you feel it too, don't you, baby?* Forgetting Elliott, his brothers and even Newman, Mitch crossed the street with a purposeful stride.

Pushing off the wall, Charlotte met him at the curb.

Now close enough to touch, he took his time reading the reciprocal need in her expression, noting the rosy flush on her cheeks, the glitter in her eyes. The warmth of the night had enhanced the natural perfume of her skin and hair and he filled his lungs with that stirring scent. He wanted to taste her all over. He wanted to be inside her, stroking deep.

He wanted the right to call her his own.

And he wanted it now, more than he'd ever wanted anything, including brothers.

Meeting her had turned his plans, hell, his whole world, upside down. Best part?

He liked it.

Newman sprawled in a lawn chair out back of the ancient, creaky house, beer in hand, staring at nothing in particular and thinking of ways to make Mitch pay. That's how he occupied his time now.

It left him nearly blind with fury that he couldn't do a goddamned thing but wait.

Mitch had reduced him to this.

Mitch had forced him to hide out in the house of an old lady.

At least the little shit hotel was located close to the bar and diner, but this place?

Thinking about it curled his lip.

Fucking doilies covered every surface, the single tiny TV was without cable or satellite and all the furniture smelled like old people, a musty scent that turned his stomach.

Looking around at the dark night, swatting at a mosquito, Newman admitted that the smelly house was better than sleeping outside, or cramped in Lee's car.

Pure luck had put him in the grocery line to buy beer when the old gal told the cashier she'd be away for a month and not to worry about her. Visiting an ailing sister or something. Who cared?

The young cashier had thanked her, saying he worried about her "out there all alone." After that, it was just a matter of glancing at the address in her checkbook as she paid for a few things she said she'd be taking on her trip.

The place *was* secluded, set back on a wooded lot without any nearby neighbors. No one was likely to find him here and with any luck, Mitch would think he'd left town.

Once he let down his guard, then Newman would strike.

He relied on Ritchie and Lee poking around town to find info on Mitch, but there were only so many places they could snoop without drawing too much notice. So far, no one knew much about him. He hadn't been back to the bar, and they hadn't had a chance to get close to the little lady yet. Everywhere she went, someone went with her. And the eagle-eyed bastards were too watchful for Lee to tail her.

It frustrated the fuck out of him.

Shoving to his feet, Newman paced into the yard, lit only by a weak yellow bulb on the back stoop. Towering oaks blocked the moonlight. In the distance, insects screeched.

Rage boiling over, he pulled out his knife and took aim at a tree, throwing it hard. The knife bounced off the trunk to land in the dew-wet grass. Disgusted, Newman retrieved it, checked to ensure he hadn't caused any damage, and carefully dried the blade along his jeans.

Instead of returning it to the sheath, he closed his fingers tight around the handle.

Screw throwing it for sport. His talent was using the blade close up—when he sliced people, or sank it deep to the bone. It was those skills he'd honed throughout his life.

Mitch had seen enough to know it, but soon he'd get a reminder.

It was a relief when his phone rang because it gave him something to do other than wonder if Lee or Ritchie had discovered any news yet on Mitch.

He answered with a curt, "Hello?"

In a rushed, excited whisper, Bernie said, "Hey, guess who's here at the bar?"

Thank God Mitch had thrown his weight around that first day, because in pissing off Bernie, he'd inadvertently given Newman an ally. It had something to do with Mitch butting in between Bernie and a hot little babe he wanted.

Blood rushing through his veins, Newman said, "This better be about Mitch." If he was in the bar, he'd probably driven there. Newman could fuck with his car first, then wait near it with a tire iron and—

"No, sorry. It's Rosalyn."

Icy disappointment brought his teeth together; the name had no meaning to him. "Why the fuck would I care about—"

"She's talking to Grant—you know, the cop who hassled you? And I heard her saying Mitch is Elliott's son."

That information made his heart skip a beat. Tightening his grip the phone, he asked as casually as he could, "You know Elliott?"

"Yeah, sure. He used to be married to Rosalyn."

Rosalyn…the woman now in the bar. If lightning had hit

his ass, it wouldn't have been more of a shock. Mitch had come home to family? What laughable bullshit.

"You know what this means?"

Yeah, he did. It meant he could annihilate Mitch and Elliott both. So many times when Mitch was a kid, Elliott had poked his nose in, threatening to take Mitch away—even trying to get Velma to go too! Old animosity mixed with new, leaving Newman with volatile rage. "Enlighten me."

"Mitch is Brodie and Jack's bastard brother. I thought that might help you figure out where he is."

Oh, it'd help all right. Maybe this Rosalyn person could be another ally. Imagining her reaction turned him downright gleeful. "Guess she's fuming, huh?"

"Ros? Nah. She's good to everyone. From what I heard, she's pissed at Elliott but feeling all motherly to Mitch."

Breath strangled in his chest, and he wheezed, "What the *fuck* do you mean, she's feeling motherly? To a bastard?" Impossible. "From that cheating motherfucker, Elliott?"

Bernie fell silent, but finally asked, "Um…you know Elliott?"

Impatience mounting, Newman retrenched. Bernie disliked Mitch and probably wouldn't care if Newman slit his throat. But he spoke of Rosalyn with affection, and that made the whole scenario dangerous. After a temper-leveling breath, Newman managed to moderate his tone. "Give me a rundown on the whole family so I can figure out who's who." Then maybe he could decide his next move.

"Hold on." Background noise filtered in and out while Newman paced, calculating the time it'd take him to get to town. They'd already wasted too much time talking.

When Bernie came back, it was quieter. "Sorry, had to move to the john to hear ya. Too noisy out there." He launched into a recitation, helping Newman place all the players in this skewed family drama.

So Mitch had likely come to beg help from his brothers. From what Bernie said, they weren't exactly refusing him. And now Elliott was here too, though he and Rosalyn weren't together anymore. Interesting dynamics.

Open to a lot of possibilities.

"So, uh, how do you know Elliott?"

Pacing the yard and plotting, Newman drew another calming breath. Bernie hated Mitch for getting between him and the curly-headed gal, but that didn't mean he wanted anyone else slaughtered. Going with the truth, Newman explained, "Elliott visited Mitch a few times back when he was a kid."

"No shit? Small world," Bernie said on a laugh. "I always liked Elliott, but I can see why you'd feel different since you got stuck raising his brat."

Deadpan, Newman replied, "Exactly."

"Elliott's biggest screwup was losing Ros. She's pretty terrific. Charlotte too."

What-the-fuck-ever. Through his teeth, he ground out, "Are they still—"

Interrupting him again—something Newman would make him pay for later, after he'd served his purpose—Bernie said, "You'd have to know Rosalyn Crews to understand how great she is. Sure, she's seriously pissed at Elliott, but to hear her talk, Mitch is already part of the family."

That lucky bastard. "You said she's waiting for someone?"

"Charlotte. Pretty girl with long frizzy hair? She works for the Crews family."

Charlotte. "Wait. She's a sister?"

"Like a sister, but they're not blood. She's the one I was hittin' on when Mitch got all bent out of shape and sucker punched me."

Eyes widening, grin sliding into place, Newman murmured, "I see." Small world indeed.

The wheels churned with endless ways to torment Mitch. Oh, he had a lot of ideas now.

He headed into the house. "So they're there still?"

"Who?"

Of all the... "Rosalyn and the cop?"

"Let me look." Background noise returned. "Yeah, they're still waiting on Charlotte."

It'd be too sweet if he could get them both together. They could have some real fun, and then follow them home to see where Mitch might be. The best way to hurt Mitch was through the people he cared about. And women, more so than men, were easier to use.

Ready to put his plans into action, Newman decided to wrap up the call. "You did great, Bernie."

"Hey, I don't like the guy either, ya know?"

"Yeah, I'm aware. And that means you won't say anything to anyone, right? About this call, I mean?"

"Not a word. So what are you going to do?"

Hearing the excitement, Newman knew on a gut level that Bernie would end up being a problem.

Before he dealt with Mitch, he'd have to silence Bernie—but not just yet. Not until he had Mitch where he wanted him.

"Probably nothing, yet." Lies. He'd do plenty. "But thanks for letting me know. Keep me posted if you find out anything else, okay?" And with that, he disconnected the call.

While striding into the house, he called Ritchie. To make sure he didn't miss this opportunity, he'd send Ritchie and Lee to keep tabs on things. One of them could pin Bernie inside.

And the other could keep up with Mitch.

As the plan formed, he grinned. Finally his boredom was at an end.

CHAPTER FOURTEEN

There on the sidewalk outside Freddie's, the street quiet and the air humid, Mitch stared into blue-eyed temptation.

Like the static of an electrical storm, he felt the sexual tension ratcheting along his nerve endings, burning through his blood. Lust he'd felt before.

He'd never felt anything like this.

"Mitch?"

The husky timbre of her low voice nearly did him in. "I want you."

Happiness played with her smile and she gave a jerky little nod. "I thought so, but I wasn't sure and I didn't want to pressure you or anything."

She didn't want to pressure *him*? That was part of the lure, how she could say and do things that brought him humor when he least expected it. "So." Those silly curls drew his fingers, and he stroked along a winding tendril over her shoulder. "How do you feel about that?"

"I want you too," she rushed out, then bit her lip and shrugged. "I do."

He laughed a little, charmed by her and relieved to get her

confirmation that he wasn't in this alone. Yet there was something in her tone and in the way she watched him now.

Touching her cheek, taking in the warmth and velvet softness of her delicate skin, he said, "You seem a little worried about it."

"Not worried, exactly." She gave him a *very* worried look. "It's just that I've never..." Searching his face, she tried to come up with the right words, gave up and shrugged. "I've never."

Never *what*? His brain attempted to sort what she'd said, with what he wanted, what he'd believed, but the puzzle pieces weren't clicking together.

Maybe they weren't supposed to.

"You're telling me you're a *virgin*?"

"Sorry?"

His body warred with the idea, wanting to grab her close, claim her, be her one and only.

Another, more pragmatic part urged him to step away before he got entirely snared.

If he wasn't already.

She'd be trouble, maybe more than he could handle.

A *virgin*. How was it even possible in this day and age? She was so damned appealing she set him on fire. She wasn't withdrawn, didn't shy away from saying what she wanted, asking whatever she pleased.

Stepping back, she crossed her arms and glared. "Okay, if you're done being a jerk, maybe you can tell me the problem."

The problem was that her inexperience could change everything. It was bad enough that he, an ex-con bastard with a shady background, wanted a nice woman like her.

But a virgin? Now he understood Brodie and Jack's issue— she truly had *zero* experience.

Shouldn't her first time be with...well, someone else? *Anyone* else?

Not Bernie. He almost shuddered. Hell, he hadn't met anyone yet he thought would be good enough for her. He knew for certain that he wasn't.

As much to himself as her, he said, "It would be obscene for me to continue this."

"*Obscene?*" Her arms dropped to her sides, her hands balled into small fists. "So now my choices are obscene?" Her laugh wasn't friendly. "I'm so glad we got that cleared up."

Hurting her was the last thing he ever wanted to do. "I didn't mean it that way."

"So tell me what you did mean."

He saw the devastation in her eyes, the hope that he'd somehow make it right. But hell, he was born wrong. "I'm sorry, but I'm not sure—"

"Well, I *am*." Grabbing his shirt, she attempted to give him a jerk. "I'm very sure. About you. About...*this*. I only mentioned my lack of experience because I thought you should know so I don't disappoint you or anything." She hesitated, but made herself say, "In bed, I mean."

As if she ever could. No, he was the disappointment, more so when lined up with her.

Resolute, Mitch caught her wrists. He'd do the right thing whether she wanted him to or not. Keenly aware of her smooth skin and delicate bones beneath his rough, callused hands, he started to lever her away.

Poised on her tiptoes, Charlotte thwarted his plans by awkwardly smashing her mouth to his.

The second their lips made contact, Mitch lost the battle.

His lungs ached and his skin burned. Without meaning to, his hands slid from her wrists, along her forearms to just above her elbows.

However, he managed not to drag her close.

It was enough, almost too much, to feel her fast breaths on his cheek, her hands opening on his chest, followed by the sting of her short nails. Right as her body made full contact with his, he heard her soft, nearly imperceptible moan.

Yeah, *that*. That right there was responsible for his loss of total control. He couldn't rein it in, not with her slim little body flush to his larger frame.

By small increments, she sank back to stand flat-footed.

With her eyes still closed, her lashes sent long shadows over her cheeks. Her nostrils quivered with her deep shaky breaths. She licked her lips. "Say something."

A dozen replies came to mind, all more appropriate than what he said. "You have the sexiest mouth I have ever seen. I've been fantasizing about it from the minute I first saw you."

Her eyes snapped open. "Really?"

Were the men in Red Oak total clowns? Had none of them ever told her she was sexy from head to toes with a mouth that'd make a saint sweat?

Well by God, he'd tell her.

Cupping his fingers around her jaw, he let the edge of his thumb play over her now damp bottom lip. "Thinking about the things I want to do with this mouth, things not suitable for a virgin, keeps me awake at night."

Hot color bloomed in her cheeks even as she smiled brightly. "That's the sweetest thing anyone's ever said to me."

Sweet? Heaven help him. He chuckled. "The things you do to me, Charlotte."

Happiness danced in her eyes. "Things like?"

He put his forehead to hers. "My life…" There were so many things he hadn't said, things he didn't want to talk about. Things a woman like her should never have to know. He did his best to censor details while still giving her the truth. "There's been a lot of ugliness, especially those years in prison. It left me angry over…well, damn near everything. I walked around waiting for something, anything, to tip me over the edge."

He couldn't keep his fingers still, not with her hair draping his fingers. He toyed with a curl, fighting the urge to sink his fingers in deep.

"I thought I'd find some peace in family, you know? Brodie and Jack, even if they hated my guts on sight, I'd have met them. I'd have had a reference for things."

She kissed him again, more lightly this time. A kiss of comfort and affection. Wisely, she stated, "You'd have known you weren't alone."

Mitch leaned back to look at her. From the start, she'd *got* him, maybe understanding him better than he understood himself. "You changed that though."

"What? *No.* I didn't want to change anything." Her hands clutched at him. "You aren't alone. Don't you see? Brodie and Jack are so happy to have another brother, and Ros—"

The press of his thumb to her lips quieted her. "Let's put them aside, okay?"

"What do you mean?"

"Not to pressure you, but I know you now. It's shifted my priorities."

Her smile went crooked. "Being a priority is way better than being obscene. And for the record, whatever you've been thinking, this particular virgin is interested. When you're ready, I mean…because I'm not trying to pressure you either."

She was so busy being concerned for him, she forgot to be concerned for herself. "Doesn't it scare the hell out of you?"

"Pfft. Excites me, maybe. But I'm not afraid."

"You should be." He caressed her arms. "I swear I'm not obsessing. Tell me to get lost and I will." Somehow. But that'd be a kick in the teeth worse than any other. "I *want* to do the right thing."

"And you are. All that pulling back nonsense? Totally wrong. But this…" Sighing, she traced his mouth with a fingertip. "The kiss and the compliments get you a gold star for the day."

"You confound me, Charlotte."

"Why?" She gave his chest a friendly pat—followed by a stroke. And an experimental *feel*. "I never imagined anyone like you." Warm and sincere, her gaze met his again. "I can tell you don't know this, Mitch, but you're better."

"Better?"

"Than anything I'd ever imagined."

The sheer shock of that took him back a step.

Of course, Charlotte followed. "Silly man. You're so incredibly gorgeous that I could just look at you all day." His scowl didn't deter her. "If that wasn't enough—and at first, believe me, it was—you're so brave."

Retreating again would've put him in the street so instead he let annoyance bring him forward. "Brave?" His huff told her what he thought of that. "How the hell do you figure that?"

"Are you kidding me? What other man would have the backbone to seek out half brothers who didn't know he existed? Who would have come out of prison and still been honorable? Who would try to give up his plans to protect people he barely knew?"

If he didn't interrupt her, she'd end up slapping a friggin' halo on his head. "You don't know if I'm—"

"Yes, I do," she interrupted, very sure of herself. "I know it and so do your brothers, so don't bother denying it." Though she stood a foot shorter than him, she flattened a small hand to the center of his chest and gave him a push. "And you can forget all this bluster. You don't intimidate me. You never have."

He remembered that first night, when he'd popped Bernie right in front of her. He'd never forget how she'd touched him—and how it had affected him. "I wasn't trying to."

Her look called bullshit. "Yes, you were. It's instinctive when anyone gets too close. Big, badass Mitch comes out, all gruff and grumbling with 'back off' signals flying left and right."

That nonsense made him snort—but she wasn't done.

"The thing is, I know you're a good man. I knew that right away."

It occurred to him that part of what drew him to Charlotte was that she saw the best in him. She made him believe things would work out. She filled him with the type of peace he'd been searching for.

"I'm glad you think so," seemed like the most adequate reply. He didn't want to spoil a moment that felt more special than any other in his lifetime. Elliott waited for him, they were on the damn street, and still he asked, "How are you a virgin, honey? *Why* are you a virgin?"

Sincerity faded from her expression; she rolled her eyes. "In case you haven't noticed, the town has a shortage of hot single guys, and apparently I'm choosy."

"Yeah, I wasn't exactly looking." He'd been too focused on Charlotte to notice much else. "So it wasn't Jack and Brodie chasing guys away? I mean, since they asked me to give it time—"

"They did *what*?" Anger sharpened her gaze. "They warned you off?" Her mouth flattened. "I swear, when I get hold of them—"

Mitch ended her tirade with another kiss. Softness. Heat. This time, knowing her inexperience, he took charge. "Charlotte," he said against her mouth, because he needed to hear her name, needed to remember that he *had* promised his brothers, and she deserved his patience.

Turning his head a little, he deepened the kiss, and when she moaned, he slowly licked into her mouth, stealing the delicious taste of her.

The sound of breaking glass startled them both.

Jerking away, Mitch searched the area.

Elliott jogged across the street. "Came from over there." He pointed toward the corner.

Where Mitch had parked.

Son of a... "Take her into the bar to Ros," he told Elliott. "Now." Then he started off in a run.

★ ★ ★

Not waiting for Elliott, Charlotte ran ahead, her heart in her throat and her stomach jumping. Ignoring the way he called her name, she burst into the bar and frantically searched for Ros. She saw Bernie, the ass, waving at her, and she saw an unruly group of men and women laughing far too loudly at their own jokes.

Elliott caught up to her as she pushed forward. He latched onto her arm as if to keep track of her. "You see her?"

"I think that's her in the back." She strained away.

"Go on to her then, and I'll go after Mitch."

She didn't know if that was a good idea or not, but she didn't debate it. "Hurry." When he turned away, pressing through the crowd with far more ease than she had, Charlotte continued on. In a semi-private booth in the back, Ros and Grant talked in close conversation.

Ignoring greetings, rudely moving past people, she reached Ros and burst out, "There's trouble!"

Grant shoved back his chair and shot to his feet in a single movement. "Tell me."

"We were outside talking, and there was a crash. Glass breaking, it sounded like. Mitch ran off—"

"What direction?" Grant demanded.

"Elliott went after him." She quickly explained which direction he'd run.

Grant turned to Ros. "If you'll stay in here—"

"Forget that." Much as Elliott had, she caught Charlotte's arm and together they headed out.

Grant got to her side. "For God's sake, Ros—"

"You're wasting time!" She had her phone out already. "Learn now that you can't boss me around, or this will be our last date."

Aggrieved, he gave her a dark glare, cursed and barely managed to get out the doors ahead of her.

Trotting along, Charlotte heard Ros say into the phone, "It's probably nothing, but Mitch might be in trouble," and she knew

Ros had called Jack or Brodie. "No, don't head this way yet. I wanted you to know so you could be ready, but Grant and Elliott are both here and I'll know what happened in just a minute."

In just a minute, because she and Ros were fast-stepping toward the sound of the crash and soon would have eyes on the men. It occurred to Charlotte that the night was dark, and only a few streetlamps lit the area. She looked around nervously as they passed a narrow alley, and then, parked at the curb, they spotted Mitch near his car, Elliott and Grant with identical stormy expressions each searching the area.

Ros stopped, caught her breath, and said, "It's fine. I see them now."

"Someone vandalized Mitch's car." Charlotte watched as Mitch walked the length of the driver's side, then around the back. His shoes crunched over sparkling gravel that had once been a window.

Ros relayed that information through the phone. Frowning with concern, she approached the men at a slower pace, with Charlotte following. "No," Ros said quietly into the phone. "Elliott won't start anything with Grant. He knows I'd take him apart."

Under different circumstances, Ros's comments might have amused Charlotte. Not this time.

Breaking away from the woman she loved like a second mother, Charlotte walked up to Mitch.

He didn't look at her. "They knew I was here."

That frosty voice sent a shiver down her spine. "It's still drivable?"

"They keyed it, broke the window—" He scanned the area and shouted louder, "Then they ran like the chickenshit cowards they are."

His voice boomed over the empty streets, bouncing off buildings and echoing down alleys. In the distance a dog barked, but otherwise only silence replied.

Elliott came quietly to his side. "It can be repaired, son. Odds are the boys already have windows at the shop." He glanced at Ros.

She shrugged, spoke into the phone, then confirmed, "They do. Brodie says he doesn't have black paint but he can get it here shortly."

"There, you see." Elliott squeezed Mitch's shoulder. "It'll be a joint effort. I'm good with this sort of thing, in case no one told you."

Provoked, Mitch closed his eyes and laughed. When he opened them again, blistering rage made it clear what he thought of Elliott's offer. "You think I give a damn about a scratch or a broken window? Better that it be my car than anyone else's." His gaze flickered to Charlotte, burned there a moment, then cut to Grant. "The big picture here is that someone knew I was nearby. Since only a few people saw me, I have to wonder if Newman was lurking around the area, waiting—or if someone clued him in."

Grant, a law officer through and through, said, "We don't know for sure that it was—"

"It was," Mitch stated.

"Without a doubt," Elliott affirmed.

After he and Mitch shared a knowing look, Elliott shook his head. "Look, none of you know the prick, okay? Mitch and I do, and I'm telling you, this is his handiwork. Every damn time I visited Mitch, my car got trashed."

Mitch's brows went up. "I didn't know that."

"No reason you should," he said gruffly. "Wasn't a problem for a kid, you know? The point is, Newman likes dicking with people. He gets off on it, makes him feel like a big man."

Ros folded her arms. "And I suppose you just let it fly?"

"Now, honey, you know me better than that."

Both Ros and Grant scowled at his endearment.

Elliott didn't seem to care. "I told him if he didn't leave my car alone I'd be collecting his teeth—and meant it—but it always came back to Mitch, and Velma's refusal to leave. I couldn't risk it, so I started parking elsewhere."

"I'd have rather you made him toothless," Mitch said.

"I did bust some knuckleheaded goon he sent after my car." Elliott smiled at the memory. "Let's just say he won't be eating any corn on the cob."

"If you're done bragging?" Still holding the phone so Brodie could hear, Ros walked over to Grant. "Is there anything you can do?"

"Not without proof, no." Resentment left him taut. "I've got people watching for him, but until he shows…"

"He'll show," Mitch said. "Starting tomorrow, I'll begin a pattern that even an idiot like Newman can't miss. He'll know where to find me and when."

Through Ros's cell, Brodie said, "And we can get that trap set."

Mitch nodded.

Tired of him ignoring her, Charlotte went to his side. "In the meantime, is it safe for you to be alone?"

His laugh was harsh. "You can't know how badly I'd love for him to show up, to try something. Anything."

"From what you've told us, he won't fight fair," Charlotte reminded him.

Finally his gaze clashed with hers. "And you think I will?"

Funny, but her predominant emotion in that moment was pride. Taking his hand, whether he wanted her to or not, Charlotte smiled. "I think you'll do whatever you need to."

Her never-ending faith in his character left Mitch visibly struggling. Eventually he'd understand that *he* was the one with the bias. Others saw the truth, saw *him*, and felt nothing but respect.

Ros delicately cleared her throat. "Are you staying in town, Elliott?"

Shifting uncomfortably, Elliott said, "Ummm…"

"Because you should." With a firm nod in Mitch's direction, she explained, "He's out there all alone and I don't like it."

Mitch opened his mouth, but Ros didn't give him a chance to say anything.

"If you can resist the urge to run off, I'd appreciate it if you kept an eye on Mitch."

Elliott beamed. "For you, Ros, darlin', anything."

Mitch rolled his eyes. "It's late. I want to make sure you and Charlotte get home safely."

Grant and Elliott both jumped in, volunteering to escort the ladies at the same time.

Despite the awful circumstances, Charlotte almost laughed at the way Ros gleefully—vindictively?—chose Grant.

"We'll stay in groups. Elliott and Mitch can go together, and Grant can come home with us." She smiled at him. "You'll check through the house too?"

Now that he'd gotten his way, Grant grinned. "Be my pleasure."

After explaining the plan to Brodie, she gave the phone to Mitch. "He wants to talk to you."

Phone in hand, Mitch turned his back on everyone and said to Brodie, "Everything has changed." He nodded. "Yeah, I figured you knew—right?" His gaze sought Charlotte. He didn't smile, but there was something in his eyes that looked remarkably like deep satisfaction. "I'm glad you see it the same way I do." He nodded. "Count on it."

After he returned the phone to Ros, he walked to the rear of the car, looking it over again.

Following, Charlotte whispered, "What was that about?"

"Just setting things straight with Brodie."

The way he said that, her heart started jumping in her chest. She licked her lips, saw him track the movement, and flushed. "Meaning?"

His fingers, rough tipped but incredibly capable, drifted over her cheek. "It was either walk away—"

"*No.*"

"—which I can't do," he finished. "Or keep a closer eye on you."

Oh, great. Another watchdog? "Are you serious?"

With a slow nod, he smiled. "I'll be pursuing you with intent."

"Won't be much of a pursuit." She held out her arms, ready, willing and more than happy about it. "I'm right here."

Glancing at the others, he lowered his voice even more. "Tempted as I am to move at Mach speed, you deserve the whole deal, so that's what you'll get."

Honest to God, her heart tried to hammer its way from her chest. Butterflies unleashed in her stomach. "The whole deal?"

"Dates. Dinner, movie…" He shrugged. "Whatever's available in Red Oak. I want to spend time with you, Charlotte. Just the two of us."

"I want that as well."

"Perfect. Then we can start tomorrow—that is, if you have time for coffee before work."

"Oh." Her smile went so wide, it hurt her cheeks. "Yes, that'd be terrific. I could meet you—"

"Nope. Part of the deal is that I'll pick you up." With added meaning, he said, "I'll keep you close. I'll damn sure make certain Newman gets nowhere near you."

Aware of Ros, Elliott and Grant watching them, trying to hear, Charlotte twined her arms around his neck and went on tiptoes for a brief but stirring kiss. "If everyone thinks I need an added guard, well then, I'm glad it's you."

Mitch's hands settled on her waist. "I wouldn't have it any other way."

Fifteen minutes before Mitch was due to pick her up, Charlotte paced the kitchen. She'd thought about him all night, won-

dered how it had gone with him and Elliott, and she wanted to
see him to know that nothing awful had happened overnight.

Had he slept in that tent, vulnerable to attack? She couldn't
imagine Elliott joining him in the yard, but hopefully he'd stay
close enough to hear if there was any trouble.

She wasn't an alarmist, but her instincts screamed a constant
warning and she couldn't help but be afraid.

For Mitch.

Today, she'd dressed with a little more care than usual. Yes,
her hair was up; the forecast predicted a scorcher with high
levels of humidity, so nothing else made sense. But instead of
her usual haphazard ponytail, she'd taken the time to arrange
a careful and hopefully romantic topknot. Since Mitch seemed
to enjoy them, she'd deliberately left a few flyaway curls teasing her nape and temples.

Instead of a loose T-shirt paired with worn jeans, she chose
a fitted cream-colored camisole and denim shorts with an em-
broidered hem. Because she couldn't run around the office in
anything uncomfortable, her sandals were the same.

Hoping it wasn't overkill, that she wouldn't be too obviously
on the make, she touched one long curl that draped her shoulder.

"My, you look nice," Ros said as she made a beeline for the
coffeepot.

Turning, Charlotte laughed. Ros too had upped the ante on
her appearance. "Look who's talking."

Striking a pose, one hand holding her coffee elevated, the
other placed just-so on her hip, Ros smiled. "Is the shirt too
low? I don't want to give Grant the wrong idea."

Grant or Elliott? Charlotte wondered, but then maybe even
Ros wasn't sure.

"You look beautiful." What Charlotte lacked in boobs Ros
made up for in excess. She rarely wore V-necked shirts, not out
of modesty but more in deference to comfort. Like Charlotte,

Ros preferred jeans with T-shirts in the summer, oversize sweat-shirts in the winter.

Today she'd chosen a floral tank top and white capri jeans and she didn't look anywhere near her early fifties.

"So." Bringing her coffee to the table, Ros said, "Sit with me a few minutes."

Having nothing else to do, Charlotte took the chair opposite her.

Folding her hands on the table, Ros got right to the point. "You and Mitch."

The smile took her by surprise. "Yes, me and Mitch." Then she remembered and scowled. "Did you know Jack and Brodie convinced him he should wait before showing his interest? Mitch mentioned something about it yesterday, so I called Brodie last night."

"They love you," Ros said, unconcerned as she sipped her coffee. "You know deep down that it wasn't a bad idea to get to know him better."

Before she replied, Charlotte considered her words carefully. In the end, the truth was all that mattered. "The thing is, I already know him. I felt I knew him the second we met. There was something… I don't know how to describe it, but it was different."

"From other men you've known?"

She nodded, trying to think it though. "With other guys, I wanted to be liked. I wanted them to want me." Even with Ros, talking about this was a bit uncomfortable, but she continued anyway, wanting the feedback. "I mean as a woman. Not…not sexually. I just wanted to be involved with someone, to be able to say I had a boyfriend or that someone found me appealing."

With a tempered smile, Ros sipped her coffee before setting it aside. "That's completely natural."

Maybe… "But now, with Mitch…"

"With Mitch, it's all of the above, isn't it? You want him to

like you for the person you are, and you want him physically."
Rosalyn reached across the table for her hand. "Plus it doesn't
matter what anyone else thinks because with Mitch, it's not
about proving anything to anyone."

Overwhelmed with Ros's insight, Charlotte smiled in gratitude. She couldn't have had this conversation with anyone other
than the woman who was like a mother to her as well as a best
friend. "I know it's too soon, but I think I love him."

"A little soon," Ros agreed lightly. "But I'm a good judge of
character and I think you're perfect for each other."

When she retreated to drink more coffee, Charlotte gave
voice to the rest of her concerns. "He hasn't said much about it,
but it breaks my heart to imagine what he's gone through. Not
just his home life—or lack of one—but prison?" The awfulness
of it tightened her throat. "He spent five years locked away."

For a moment, Ros was quiet—then she thunked down her
cup and scowled. "It makes me so damn mad. If Elliott hadn't—"

"Ros," Charlotte said gently. "Don't do that, okay?"

"I can't help but be furious."

"I know. I am too. But Mitch doesn't blame Elliott and yesterday, I could see how uneasy it made him, having everyone mad.
He wants to be a part of a happy family, not one that's divided."

Ros snorted. "Honey, it's not like Elliott and I will ever get
back together."

"I realize that, and I think Mitch does too. He's not a little
kid wishing for crazy things."

"No," she murmured, letting the truth settle in. "He's a
strong, independent, capable man—who's been terribly hurt
far too many times."

Exactly. "I know it's asking a lot, but could you go back to
treating Elliott the way you did before you met Mitch? I think
that's what he wants. Elliott told him a lot about you, and knowing him as we all do, he was probably upfront about his own
lacks—and the fact that you forgave him enough to get along.

Not as husband and wife, but as mother and father. I think it would help him."

Pained, Ros whispered, "Oh, how I wish I was that young man's mother. I would have protected him."

"It's not too late to start." This was the tricky part, getting Ros to understand without inadvertently hurting her feelings. She might come off as a woman of steel, but underneath it all Ros was as tenderhearted as they came.

With her head propped on a fist, her elbow resting on the table, Charlotte smiled and explained, "You've been my mother for quite a few years now, and I love you for it. You could do the same for Mitch."

"Oh, honey." Finishing off her coffee in a rush, Ros left her seat to embrace Charlotte tightly. "This is why you're so wonderful. Believe me, loving you has been my pleasure. Not to detract from your mother in any way, I swear, but you *are* my daughter, in my heart and in my head, whether you have my blood or not."

A quiet knock on the door had them pulling apart. Both women hastily dabbed at their eyes, then laughed at each other and hugged again, a different type of hug this time.

Charlotte saw Mitch watching through the kitchen door window, a tender smile on his face, as if he already knew what they'd been discussing and found it touching.

Beyond him, Elliott looked around, trying to avoid Ros's scrutiny.

Hopefully Ros would remember what they'd just discussed.

When Charlotte opened the door, Mitch leaned in and kissed her first, a soft smooch of familiarity—because now they were "a thing." He claimed his pursuit all bold and macho, and even as an independent, intelligent woman, it thrilled her.

"Good morning," she said.

"It is now." Holding her back, he let his gaze move over her with appreciation. "You're beautiful."

Stupidly, she blurted, "I did a little more than my usual."

His smile went crooked. "Yeah?"

"For you, I mean."

That earned a soft laugh. "I'm flattered."

As a reminder that they stood in the doorway with her inside and Elliott out, Ros cleared her throat loudly.

Unfazed, Mitch stepped in, his arm around her shoulders. "Good morning, Ros."

"Good morning. Coffee?"

"Thank you, but I'll pass. I figured Charlotte and I would take off, give us plenty of time to visit before she has to clock in."

Pretending to tell a secret, Ros leaned in. "Psst. She doesn't have a set schedule. Keep her as long as you like."

"Ros!" Laughing, Charlotte shook her head. "I can show up a few minutes late, but any more than that and I'll have work piled up to my ears."

It was new, the way Mitch watched her. Sort of possessive and hungry, but also affectionate.

Because it flustered her, she turned to Elliott. "How about you? Do you want some coffee?"

His eyes, caramel colored like Mitch's, watched Ros warily. "I wouldn't mind a cup, that is, if Ros can spare a few minutes."

Her smile looked carved in stone, but Ros got it out there. "Sure, come on in. Do you still take it the same?"

Surprised by her acceptance, Elliott sauntered in and took a seat at the table. "Black, hot and with good company."

"You'll have to settle for black and hot." As soon as the words left her mouth, Ros sent a guilty look toward Mitch. "You two, go ahead and take off. Elliott can hang around until Grant gets here to escort me to work."

Mitch glanced at Elliott, then Ros. "You don't mind?"

Obviously, he hadn't expected Elliott to trail him to the house, and felt a little guilty about bringing him uninvited into Ros's kitchen.

"No, honey. I don't mind at all. Elliott and I have some things to talk about anyway." She hugged Charlotte before doing the same with Mitch.

This time he didn't go as stiff, and actually let his arms close around Ros for two heartbeats.

Beaming with pleasure, Ros stepped back and shooed them away. "Go on then. Have fun, but be careful."

"I'll get her from work too," he offered. "That is, if Charlotte doesn't mind?"

"She doesn't," Ros said before Charlotte could even blink. "In fact, why don't you join us for dinner? I'll cook something special."

"Ros is an amazing cook," Elliott verified. "You don't want to miss that."

In her efforts to ignore him, Ros went laughably still and stiff, a pleasant smile frozen on her face.

"I've had the pleasure," Mitch said. He hesitated before adding, "Actually, though, I was going to invite Charlotte to my house for dinner."

Wanting him to know she was entirely on board with that idea, Charlotte blurted, "I'd love to," before Ros could offer her up again.

Elliott winked. "In that case, I'll make myself scarce."

Ros slowly turned. "What does that mean?"

"Uh...see..."

"I invited him to stay with me." Defiant but firm, Mitch met her astonished gaze. "I'm not using the bedroom anyway, and you fixed it up so nice—"

"Ros fixed it up?" Sitting back in lazy satisfaction, Elliott smiled. "I thought it had her touch."

"*You...*" Remembering her promise at the last second, Ros forced her mouth into a strained smile. "Will join the boys and me for dinner."

"Really?" Surprise brought him forward in his seat again. "Hot damn. Thanks, honey."

Teeth locked, Ros opened the kitchen door, making it clear that this was the perfect time for them to make a hasty getaway. "Have fun."

The second they cleared the doorway, Ros closed the door. Half smiling, Mitch took her hand and led her to his car with the broken window now covered in plastic.

"Will there be bloodshed?" he asked, tipping his head back toward the house.

"Not a drop. I promise." At least she hoped the two of them would behave. Elliott could be awfully provoking, and Ros wasn't a woman to suffer nonsense.

"Good." Caging her against the passenger's door, Mitch looked at her mouth. "Because I'd rather concentrate on you."

Charlotte had no problem at all with that plan.

CHAPTER FIFTEEN

The second they heard the car pull away, Elliott held up his hands in a protective gesture. "How pissed are you? Should I run?"

Given her performance the other night, Ros didn't blame him for being wary. If she'd had a big stick then, she would have used it on him.

Now, though, with Charlotte's reminder in her head, she kept her cool. Actually, he looked so cautious, she almost laughed.

It was hard to demolish a man who made you smile at the worst of times.

That was always the problem with Elliott. He made her cry when few others could—but he also made her laugh harder than she did with anyone else. He'd shown her the greatest, most encompassing love, but also crushed her heart. He was never around, yet she knew she could count on him in a crisis.

He'd do whatever he could for her…and then he'd take off again.

Long ago she'd learned that Elliott's struggles were his own, and her happiness didn't depend on him. Still, it saddened her—

for *him*. Since he was unable to commit to anything or anyone for long, she didn't think he'd ever truly be happy.

Yes, very sad indeed.

"You're looking at me with sympathy. Does that mean you plan to kill me off? Honest, honey, I won't fight you—but I'd rather not die today."

There was no point telling him her thoughts; she'd done that before and it hadn't mattered.

So she played it off, slapping his shoulder and giving in to a laugh. "You're terrible, but I have to admit, I'm glad he didn't stay out there alone last night."

"Near enough," Elliott said, folding his arms on the table and studying her in that intense way he had that made her feel sexy and more like a woman than she did at any other time.

"What does that mean?" After refilling her own cup, she sat across from him, careful to avoid touching his big feet under the table. On Elliott, everything was big—and in her youth, that had often been her downfall. Together, they could burn down the roof. Oh, how she'd loved his big body and the way he used it when pleasuring her.

"He slept alone, honey. Out in a tent, I mean." Visibly perturbed by that, Elliott toyed with his cup. "I tried to get him to take the bedroom, but he was clear about sleeping outside with his dog."

"So you took the bed?"

"No, that was too far away. I squeezed onto that damned short couch in the screened patio. Trust me on this, it was not meant for a man of my size."

Ignoring most of that, Ros said, "I wondered about the tent. Do you think it was his time in prison?"

"Probably. He told me a little about it. Just the basics, ya know?" His hand knotted into a still credible fist. "I failed him in every way possible."

"Yup." She wasn't about to sugarcoat the truth just to soothe his conscience. Softer, she added, "If only you'd brought him to me."

"I know." Full of guilt, he met her accusing gaze. "I really did consider it, even talked to Velma about it. I didn't want to go on in front of Mitch, but she flat-out refused. Made no sense. Wasn't like she could care for him the way he needed—at least not that she showed. But she said she'd come after me, and I couldn't see bringing that much trouble to your door."

"Elliott." Over the years, they'd had similar conversations so many times that it almost felt like a waste of her breath. "You should have taken him yourself, then, and let the trouble come to your own door."

"I know. You're right." He sat back with a sad smile. "This is like old times. Me fucking up, you calling me on it."

"The big difference is that I gave up on you ever changing when you hit forty. Now when I bitch, it's just to vent, not because I think it'll make a difference."

"Maybe one small difference." He lifted his hip and drew a wallet from his back pocket, opening it and pulling out a check. For a moment he just fingered the paper, then finally put it on the table and slid it toward her.

"What's this?" Confused by the gesture, Ros picked it up, staggered to see it was made out to her—for one hundred and twenty thousand dollars. Her heart hit her feet with true alarm. "What did you do? Did you rob a bank?"

The accusation widened his eyes, but then he gave a gruff laugh. "That's actually as plausible as the truth."

Slapping the check down, she glared at him. "Which is?"

Uncomfortable, he rubbed his chin, scratched at his ear. "See, this nice gal I was seeing had an elderly neighbor. She was out cutting her grass one day and I felt bad for her so I went over and finished it up. It was odd, but we fell into a pattern. Even after Tracy and I stopped seeing each other, I went over there to check on the old gal."

"Cutting grass once, I can believe. You were never afraid of work." Still reeling from the size of that check, Ros drummed her fingers on the tabletop. "It was the responsibility and routine that made you break out in hives."

He didn't deny the truth. "The thing is, Jean appreciated me. And she respected me, even when she shouldn't have. It didn't matter if a month went by without me seeing her, when I thought of her and dropped in she'd insist on making dinner and she'd trail me when I did repairs to her house."

Ros's brows climbed all the way to her hairline. "You did her repairs?"

"Little things. Leaky sink, broken porch swing." Honest embarrassment made him duck his face. "Re-shingled her roof once."

Not a single word came to mind so Ros just sat in stupefied fascination and listened.

"I'd take her grocery shopping and she'd hang on my arm and tell me what an amazing *young man* I was." His short chuckle sounded of both discomfort and pleasure. "I, um, I found out she didn't go to the grocery store anymore, so when I didn't come by, she sometimes did without. That bothered me so I started coming around more often."

Unbelievable. "And somewhere within this incredible story, you managed to profit?"

Color slashed his cheekbones. "I don't blame you for thinking the worst. You sure as hell have every right and the truth is pretty damned bizarre."

Ros propped her head on her fist. "I'm all ears."

He shot her a disgruntled frown. "Jean didn't have anyone else. I didn't know that either. I figured her family just neglected her. God knows I understand that, since I'd always neglected you and our sons."

"No argument from me."

"Yeah, well…" He shifted. "Meeting her got me thinking

about how *I'd* be alone and neglected—because I'd never given anyone reason to care. I can't change that now. You, Jack and Brodie don't need me. But Jean did, so I stuck around and kept her company and...enjoyed being useful for a change."

Discomfort began to crowd out Ros's resentment. Elliott didn't have to say it, because she could see he was hurting. Yes, it was a pain of his own making, but as she'd always told the boys, Elliott was who he was, and they could either accept him and get on with their lives peacefully, or despise him and let his derelict ways continue to hurt.

For the most part, they'd chosen peace.

And she'd done her utmost to ensure they never felt the loss.

"The thing is," he continued, "when she passed away, I found out she'd written a will and left everything to me. I thought that meant her old house and whatever car she had out in her barn. She'd told me it was old and didn't think it would run anymore, so I just drove her where she needed to go. I figured it was an ancient Buick or something. Typical old-person's car, you know?" He looked down at his coffee, stirring the top with his fingertip. "Her tiny little house sold real fast for twenty-two grand. I used part of that to give her a real nice funeral. Her car though..." His gaze lifted to hers. "Turned out it was a '68 Shelby GT500—and it sold for a hundred and twenty Gs at auction. I'm keeping the rest from the house to eventually replace my own car, but the Shelby... I want you to have it."

What in the world would she do with that kind of money? Protests mounted—

He cut her off before she got a single word out. "It won't make up for the past. I know that. And I swear to God, Ros, I'm not trying to buy you or anything."

"So what are you trying to do?" For sure, it wasn't the usual. Not with a gesture this grand.

"I..." He rubbed at his neck. "Look, we both know I was

never going to hold down a job long enough to give you everything you deserve. To repay you for all you've done."

"What I've done?" It wouldn't kill him to spell it out.

Knowing it was what she wanted, he smiled. Elliott always
knew her—and sometimes it unnerved her.

"We have very fine sons."

"We do."

All too serious, he said, "They got their height and physical
strength from me."

As well as their good looks.

"But every other fine quality came straight from you. Their
guts, caring, compassion and backbone…that's all you, honey,
and we both know it. You're a natural-born leader and it's because of you that my sons turned out the same, and that I'm so
damn proud of them."

"I love them," she replied, then pointed out, "And I never
asked for payment." Chasing Elliott for child support would
have been a lesson in frustration. He handed over money when
he had it, but far too often, he had nothing at all.

"I know it, and I know why. You could have had my ass
thrown in jail. You could have turned the boys against me. You
could have…well, hated me and kicked me from your lives. I'm
glad you're not made that way. It's coming late. Too damn late
for forgiveness. But I appreciate you, I always have."

Agog at that ridiculous declaration, she laughed. "You took
me for granted."

"I know it looked that way." Staring into his coffee, his voice
lowered. "I used to thank God that you were a better person
than me." When he glanced up, his eyes were a little glassy.
"Take the check, honey. It's a sliver of all I owe you, but it's all
I have to give."

Because he'd never give *himself*. Not his time, not his…love.

No, that was unfair. She knew he loved her and their sons.
He just couldn't love as much or as fully as she could.

And for that, again, she pitied him.

"You said you had to replace your car?"

"Yeah. Totaled my Mustang." With a self-deprecating laugh, he said, "You know I was behind on my insurance payments."

She'd always been the responsible one who made sure payments were made, so that didn't surprise her. "How?"

"A drunk T-boned me. Fool ran straight through a stop sign and pow! Lights out for me."

Dear God. Shaken by the thought, she asked, "You were hurt?"

"Spent a little time in the hospital, but I'm fine now. They released me and two days later I found out Jean had passed." Holding up his hands, he grinned. "It all conspired against me. A taste of my own mortality, seeing how Jean died alone…"

Gripping the edge of the table, Ros ignored the panic rushing in and used her most forceful tone. "Elliott Crews, you tell me right now. How badly were you hurt?"

His gaze slid away.

"Elliott."

Aggrieved, he gave her his full attention. "Concussion, broken nose, fractured eye socket—"

"Dear God." *He could have died.*

"—but it was the cut on my thigh that was the worst." Pushing back his chair, he trailed a finger along her left inner thigh, from knee to groin. "Chunk of metal broke out of the door and got me." He flashed a quick smile. "Thank God it missed my jewels."

"It isn't funny!" Hands shaking, Ros fought the tears in her eyes.

"Yeah, laying in that hospital room and thinking of all the ways I'd screwed up, I agree. Not funny. Jean—God bless her— gave me the means to do something good for once." He reached for her wrist, prying her hand loose and pulling it toward him, engulfing it in both his much larger hands. "I want you happy, Ros. More than anyone I know, you deserve that."

Oh, how her heart broke. Very softly, she said, "I can't be happy with you Elliott."

"I know that. And if Grant's the one, then...well, I'll try not to despise him too much." His smile came and went. "But maybe I could try to correct some of my losses with the boys. They've both got beautiful wives now, and that probably means grandkids soon, right?"

"Grandkids." Indulging a watery laugh, Ros pulled away from his grasp to swipe at her eyes. "I don't know that I want to be called granny yet. I'll have to think of something better."

"You always looked beautiful with a baby in your arms."

"Oh, stop." She slapped at him.

Holding out his hand, palm up, this time asking instead of taking, Elliott waited. "Can we be friends? Do you think you can forgive me enough for that?"

"Elliott." She shook her head and placed her hand in his. "I've always done my best to ensure you have a place in your sons' lives. If it doesn't work out for you, it won't be because of me."

"They broke the mold after making you. Even Jean, who adored me to the moon and back, often said I was a fool for letting you get away." He lifted her hand to his mouth and kissed her knuckles. Wisely, he then released her. "Were you serious about dinner?"

Her hand tingled from his kiss. Damn it, why did it still have to be this way with him? Blowing out a breath, she quipped, "Why not? You can be here at six." She pushed the check back toward him. "But you can keep that. I don't want it." It was bad enough having him here, stirring her up despite her commonsense. "You'll probably need it to get yourself going again."

He snorted. "What the hell would I buy with it?"

"You could start with insurance. Maybe pay it up for five years in advance."

For a second he only stared at her, then laughed. "They won't do that. I asked."

At least he made the effort to do the right thing. "So put it in the bank and do automatic withdrawals."

"Nope." He stood without touching it. "If you have to, donate it to your favorite charity. I know you have many. But I have no right to it."

"Then give it to Mitch!" She popped out of her chair too, not about to let him get away yet.

He snorted. "You don't know him as well as you think you do. No way in hell would he accept it, but you're welcome to try. It can be a gift from you."

She grabbed his forearm. Soft hair covered firm muscles, warmed from his body. Choking back a groan, Ros snatched her hand away. "I thought you were staying until Grant got here."

"You didn't hear him pull up?" The slow smile that curved his mouth was too damn sexy. "Glad I could distract you for a minute there." He bent and put a lingering kiss to her forehead. "I love you, Ros. I'll always love you—enough to stay out of your way, I promise."

And with that parting shot he opened the door and greeted a startled Grant. "Morning, Colvin. You're just in time."

When Elliott stuck out his hand, Grant automatically accepted it.

Elliott pulled him close. "Don't let anything happen to her. Red Oak would never be the same." Whistling, he sauntered away to an old beat-up truck.

Grant's stare moved from Elliott to her in narrow-eyed speculation. "What the hell was that about?"

She shook her head. "Same old, same old." Going back to the table, she snatched up the check, folded it and tucked it into her pocket. "Coffee?"

Without asking her about the check, Grant slid his arms

around her waist from behind and nuzzled her ear. "I'd rather have you."

Oh lord.

It wasn't a total lack of interest on her part...but on the heels of Elliott being there? That wouldn't be fair to Grant. Smiling, she turned to face him. "Are you free for dinner? Mitch wants some alone time with Charlotte, so I invited Elliott here. I'll get the boys and my daughters-in-law to come over too."

He blanched. "You invited Elliott to dinner?"

As if speaking to a dunce, she reiterated, "So Mitch and Charlotte could have time alone." It was Grant's bad luck that her patience for explaining to men had already run thin.

He pondered it for far too long before asking, "Are you sure that's what you want?"

"You can behave yourself?"

"I will if he will."

Sometimes, men were just overgrown little boys. "He knows and abides by my rules."

That brought his brows together. "You sound admiring."

Oh, for the love of... Going for the quickest and easiest way of ending the conversation, Ros leaned up and kissed him, quick and light. "There's no way I'm getting hooked up with Elliott again." He never stuck around long enough for her to even consider it. "But Charlotte pointed out that Mitch came here for a fresh start with a *happy* family, not a family at each others' throats. So I'll play nice, and I expect you to as well."

Not quite convinced, he cupped her face and kissed her again. "I want you happy. You know that, right?"

That sounded far too close to Elliott's sentiment, making her testy. "I'm a grown woman who knows her own mind and I can damn well ensure my own happiness. Now will you come to dinner or not?"

"I'd be happy to."

With that settled, she put their cups in the sink and grabbed her purse. "Let's go. I want to do what I can to keep the office running smoothly until Charlotte gets in. If she shows up to a mess, she'll never again take the morning off, and that girl deserves a break."

"I have a feeling Mitch does too."

On that, they were both in agreement.

It hadn't been easy, following the cop without getting seen. Lee had to "borrow" Bernie's car, and still Newman made sure he held way back. Eagerness and anger became a volatile mixture. If he didn't get to Mitch soon, he'd lose his shit.

Once they'd gotten Bernie drunk last night, it had been easy asking him questions, finding out where Ros and Charlotte lived. Luckily, they lived alone, which made things almost too easy.

Today was all about reconnaissance, getting a lay of the land, seeing what their odds might be for gaining access later. That's what he wanted most, to terrorize them up close and personal, to smell their fear, to see them sweat.

It would eat Mitch alive when they went crying to him.

And maybe, as a bonus, it'd turn them against him. Who wanted a bastard ex-con bringing that kind of trouble to their door?

They'd know Mitch was to blame—because he'd tell them so.

And if he had to fuck with the outside of their house instead? Whatever. He could make that work too.

This early, Bernie was still crashed and wouldn't miss his car. He'd gotten so wasted that Newman doubted he'd stir until noon at the earliest. After meeting with them on the outskirts of town in a less noticeable bar, he'd nearly drunk them all under the table—until he'd finally passed out.

They'd had to haul him inside and drop him in his bed— and then they'd made use of his place, instead of heading back to the old lady's house.

Thinking of last night made Newman incandescent with rage all over again.

When they'd finished working over Mitch's car, he, Lee and Ritchie had climbed atop the low, flat roof of a hardware store where they could watch without being seen. He'd waited, almost breathless with anticipation, to see Mitch's reaction when he viewed the damage on his beloved car. He still remembered the day Mitch got it from Elliott, how goddamned happy he'd been over the pile of junk.

Sneaky bastard had hidden it away too.

The only upside had been that it kept Mitch busy and out of the way.

Lang had told him Mitch drove the car now, that he'd fixed it up real nice...but still, he'd barely recognized the sleek, shiny Mustang as the same old heap of scrap metal.

Damaging it had felt good.

But the miserable prick hadn't given him any satisfaction. Instead of losing his shit, Mitch had calmly walked around the car, checked under it as if he thought they might be hiding there, and then searched the area.

Looking for *him*, Newman knew.

For some fucked-up reason, they'd all three ducked, and the shame of it scalded his temper. He'd considered climbing down and carving Mitch's face right then and there, but Lee—always cool headed—had spotted the cop charging up the walk just in time.

No reason to get arrested just to make Mitch pay.

His day was coming, sooner than he thought.

Better to stick to the plan, to drag out the fun.

Now, as they rolled past the house, they noted the distance between the neighbors, the big wooded yard, and he knew, absolutely knew, getting inside would be a piece of cake.

They'd be back.

In the dark.

And then the fun would begin.

★ ★ ★

Cradling Charlotte's much smaller hand in his gave him a sense of peace, despite what had happened last night. With a tall sycamore tree shading them from the bright morning sunlight, they stood at the edge of a fast-moving creek. The water sparkled as it carried away a leaf. Birds circled overhead and somewhere in the distance a cicada chirped.

Filling his lungs with the fresh humid air, Mitch ordered his thoughts.

He'd brought her here to kiss her, to touch her and let her get used to him, but in a setting that guaranteed he couldn't get carried away.

Never, not in a million years would he hurt her, and that meant there were things she needed to know.

Before coming to the park, they'd gone by a deli and picked up breakfast sandwiches and orange juice, then sat on a park bench to eat. Charlotte hadn't yet said much, but she didn't need to.

He felt her anticipation.

And suffered his own.

He also felt her acceptance, and it meant the world to him, more than being accepted by his brothers, more than seeing his absentee father. More than having a house or finding roots.

He'd laid eyes on her that first night and without effort she'd turned his entire world upside down, altering his priorities and realigning his focus.

Quietly, with only the birds to overhear, he said, "There are things you should know about me."

Just as she had so many times before, she leaned into his side, her arms around him. It was a special thing to be embraced by this woman.

Hot, stirring, yet somehow also calming.

"I'd love to know more." In this light, the blue of her eyes reflected the sky. "But it won't change anything."

Anything, meaning she'd still care? He'd find out now, wouldn't he? "Let's sit." Thanks to the heat wave, no morning dew remained on the grass.

Without hesitation, she stepped out of her sandals and got comfortable at the edge of the creek, poking her small feet into the water. "There's a bigger creek that divides Brodie's property and ours. After a rain, it's deep enough to swim in." She peeked at him, watching him as he pulled off his own shoes and socks and rolled up his jeans above his ankles. "Would you like to go there sometime?"

"Sure." As he eased down beside her, he asked, "You ever skinny-dip?"

"Eeww, no. Not with Brodie around. If he ever busted me, we'd both die."

Yeah, right. "Somehow I think Brodie would survive, but you?" Just looking at her made him smile. He lightly tweaked a curl. "Yeah, you might have trouble getting around it."

"It would be awful." A breeze drifted over them, and she lifted her face. "No one has seen me naked since my mother passed."

Funny how there were things you knew, logical assumptions, but you didn't think about them. Being a virgin, it made sense that no one had seen her, and yet, until this moment, he hadn't considered it.

Finding a small rock in the grass, he tossed it into the stream. "You're putting thoughts in my head."

"What thoughts?"

"You, naked."

"Oh." And then with more meaning, "*Oh.*"

"I wanted to talk."

Glad for the change, her shoulders relaxed. "So talk already."

"Soon, I'm going to see you naked."

Clearly that wasn't what she'd expected. Tucking in her chin, she glanced at him. "You think so, do you?"

He'd fought it…a little. Not enough, obviously. But now

that he'd given in? Now he wanted to put all his concentration on her, on protecting her, making her happy, showing her how special she was. "You and me…we're meant to happen."

Pleasure slowly took away her embarrassment until she smiled. "I'll look forward to it."

That brought him full circle and he stared out over the fields. He'd deliberately chosen this spot because it was secluded, but no one could sneak up on them. He didn't trust Newman and would never take chances with Charlotte.

He protected what was his, and whether she knew it yet or not, whether she'd consider him a caveman or overbearing, she was now his.

Best to get it over with. "I almost killed a guy." He plucked a clover bud just to give his restless fingers something to do—other than reaching for her. "And so that you understand, I mean that literally. If the guards hadn't dragged me off him, I would have finished him." Sights and smells crowded his brain. The image of blood and gore, the shouts and the shock of pain that hit the back of his knees… One deep breath, then another, and he managed not to crush the clover.

Her expression searching, then softly sympathetic, she asked in the gentlest voice ever applied to him, "Why?"

Why? That single word nearly knocked his heart through his chest. She left him at a loss for words. He'd prepared for a variety of reactions, just not that one.

She didn't look appalled, or frightened. No, not Charlotte. She only wanted details. She'd withhold judgment until she knew the facts.

In this case, the facts might repulse her even more than the brutality of what he'd done.

And the reasons he'd done it.

His throat tightened, making him swallow hard.

Charlotte didn't move—so he had to. Stretching out on his

back, he dropped a forearm over his eyes. Maybe if he didn't see her, it wouldn't shame him quite as much.

"Prison… It's all about dominance."

Silence, and then he felt her settling beside him. Her hand came to his chest, right over his heart, and rested there. Her lips touched his. With startling perception and uncompromising compassion, she whispered, "Tell me."

Yeah, that was the point, right? To let her know how he was, to see if she could handle it.

To see if they had a future.

He didn't want to. He fucking *hated* the idea of repeating it. Before meeting her, he would have sworn that he never would. How to describe humiliation and rage and fear and retaliation?

Burying it, shoving it to the back of his mind, was easier.

But this was Charlotte, and she had a right to know him. "Two men pinned me down so another could rape me."

She went perfectly still, her hand on his chest heavier…and suddenly she was full against him, hugging him fiercely. So tight, as tight as a woman of her size could, he imagined.

"He didn't succeed," Mitch whispered, wanting to soothe her.

"You got hurt."

"Yes, I did." Badly, so badly that for a time he hadn't known if he'd recover. "I think that's what kicked me past reason. I was an animal fighting for survival."

"I wish you had killed them all."

The tears in her voice leveled him. "What? No, honey, you don't mean that." He locked his arms around her.

"Yes, I do," she said, without loosening her hold or raising her head, and that made it easier. "Tell me what happened."

"I was new, but my cell mate had been in and out of prison his whole life. He wasn't a bad guy." Such a subjective term, so he clarified. "A miserable thief, yes, but not a rapist or murderer or child abuser." Those were the worst, because those men had no conscience at all. They weren't even men, just monsters living in human shells. Unpredictable and immoral. At times, they'd hurt people just to break up the boredom.

A lot like Newman.

That lazy breeze shifted the leaves overhead, sending sunlight to dance over Mitch's face. It was a reminder: he was alive, free, his brothers had accepted him, and now Charlotte hugged him.

Overall, life was better than he'd dared hope a few years ago.

Coasting his hand down her back, then up again, Mitch collected his thoughts. "The first few days I was there, he explained things to me, even helped me make a shiv. I had it on me that day, but couldn't get to it. The attack came too quickly from behind me. One of them busted the backs of my knees..." Rage and terror welled up again. The feeling of being helpless.

Never again.

For the rest of his life, he'd face each day head-on. He'd learned, hell yes he had. Now he could sense trouble before it reached him.

Trying to give him her strength, she snuggled in even more.

"I thought..." Dry-eyed, he stared up at the tree, making himself see the leaves surrounded by blue sky, instead of the images from that day. "I thought they would succeed and there wasn't anything I could do about it."

"You got away?" she asked in a very small voice.

"My cell mate showed up." Mitch made sure to keep inflection out of his tone, to speak in a flat monotone—but he couldn't censor the language. "He grabbed back one of the guys and that was all the leverage I needed. I kicked that bastard in the face, dislocating his jaw and shattering his nose. Broke the other one's arm in two places, then punched him in the balls."

Nodding against him, she whispered fiercely, "Good."

It made him smile, this ferocious side of her and wasn't that crazy?

No, that was Charlotte. He turned his face to kiss the top of her head, to slowly breathe in the fragrance of her skin and hair.

"The other guy—he'd terrorized so many people, and I'd had enough. I figured I was already in prison and if I stayed there, so what. At least it'd be on my terms without some asshole preying on me constantly. So I punched him in the throat and collapsed his esophagus. While he choked for air, I kneed in his nuts—making sure he wouldn't rape anyone else."

"*Good*," she said again. Then went one further to add, "That makes you a hero."

CHAPTER SIXTEEN

Jesus, she was special, so damn special. She not only accepted what he did, understanding the reasons for it, she praised him. Complimented him.

Redeemed him.

"I left him blind in one eye," he said, desperately needing her to understand just how far his temper had carried him. "I destroyed his nose, knocked out a few teeth—"

"Good, good, *good*." As she spoke, she rose to kiss his face, her tears dropping. At first it confused him until he realized what it was, then he saw that her eyes were red, her cheeks blotchy.

She'd been silently crying that whole time.

"Oh, baby, don't. Please don't." He could deal with anything except seeing her upset. Rolling, he put her under him and brushed back those sweet flyaway curls. "I'm sorry. I didn't mean to—"

Her fingers smashed over his mouth while she audibly swallowed. "Don't," she choked. "Don't regret telling me." She struggled to swallow again, then sobbed softly and grabbed him, hiding her face against his chest.

"Charlotte?"

"I'm proud of you," she strangled out.

The laugh sounded rusty, as confused as he felt. "Proud?" He tried to tip up her face, but she resisted, and then her head bumped his chin as she nodded. "I would never—"

Her small fist thumped his chest. "I *know* that. You don't go around raging on people. You don't have a terrible temper. You defended yourself, just as you should, and probably ended up saving other people too." Gearing up for more, she drew in a breath. "So I'm *proud* of you for doing what had to be done. Proud of you for surviving." She not-so-subtly wiped her eyes on his shirt. "Proud of you for being who you are—a man who thought I needed to hear this, so even though I know it had to be painful, you told me."

Yes, very painful, but he'd felt satisfaction too. That day he had proved he could survive.

Hell of a lesson—and one past due at that point.

Sniffling, she cupped his face in her hands. "I hope I don't scare you off, Mitch Crews, but I'm falling in love."

His stomach took a free fall. She stole his breath. Hell, she stole his reason and his strength and every other damn thing he thought he had control over. "You…?"

Defiant and with her own measure of pride, she nodded. "If you can't handle that, we should probably call it quits right now."

Unthinkable. "Oh, hell no."

Her lips curved. That mouth, that incredibly sexy, scorching hot smile…

Suddenly ravenous for her, he crushed her mouth under his, aware of the wetness on her cheeks and the way her fingers tunneled into his hair.

Her acceptance.

Her *willingness*.

He could have her here, in the park, on the hard ground— but he wouldn't. He cared for her too. Love? He didn't know much about love, but he knew Charlotte was vital to him. She deserved his patience, and by God, he'd give it to her.

But he could show her how it'd be for them. He wanted her to want him every bit as much, to be just as hungry as him.

Leaving her parted lips, he kissed away the tears, opened his mouth on her throat and tasted her sun-warmed skin, filling his senses with her. God, he could get drunk on her taste.

Fingers open, he trailed his hand up her side, covering a lot of tantalizing ground from her pliant hip, the curve of her waist and up to one small, perfect breast.

Finding her nipple already stiff beneath camisole and bra, he groaned.

Charlotte squeezed her eyes shut and pinched her lips together, but he still heard the little hum of excitement. He watched her face as he worked his thumb over and around her nipple. When she involuntarily arched, her lips parting, he couldn't help but take things a step further.

"You, lady, are a scalding-hot temptation." Almost too tempting to resist. "Will you trust me?"

"I already do."

Humbled, he kissed her again, saying against her lips, "You'll like this." Propped on one forearm, he slowly tugged down the top of her camisole, taking her bra cup away as well, until he revealed her.

Creamy pale skin drew his fingertips. Gently, lightly, he explored her, circling her puckered nipple until her breaths grew uneven.

"Beautiful." Lowering his head, he placed one small kiss on the very tip. She shifted against him, bringing one leg up, hooking it around his calf. Her hips lifted.

Liking that response, he teased with his tongue, circling her, circling, plucking with his lips...

"You're right," she whispered brokenly. "I like that."

Smiling, he drew her in, sucking softly—then not so softly.

It shouldn't have surprised him; with Charlotte, she never reacted as he expected. But her immediate trembling, the way she rocked against him, told him how quickly she turned on.

Just from his mouth on her breast.

"Damn," he breathed, moving to the side of her, set on his course. "You and I are going to have so much fun."

Eyes closed, cheekbones dewy and flushed, she whispered, "I'm counting on it."

Already she appeared so aroused. *Starved.* That's what she was: a sexy, incredibly sweet woman who, for unimaginable reason, had avoided sexual involvement.

Until him.

He'd take care of her, in every way she could imagine.

A glance around ensured they remained alone. "I'm going to show you how good it will be."

She breathed faster.

Though he'd done little enough, she was already so primed his ego swelled—along with other parts of him.

He kissed her, softly devouring her mouth until her fingers clutched at his shoulders. Her shorts were nice because the leg openings were loose, making it easy for him to trail his fingertips up her satiny thigh and under the hem.

On a sharp inhale, Charlotte went still, suspended on a precipice of anticipation.

So beautiful—and meant for him, only him.

Watching her face, very aware of the differences in their sizes, experience and expectation, he explored her through her panties.

"Mitch…"

"Hmm?"

"Don't stop."

"No, I won't." As he stroked over her, her eyes grew heavier, darker and dazed, until she closed them on a shuddering sigh.

He could feel the heat of her—and he wanted more. Sliding

beneath the elastic of the leg opening, he touched *her*. Warm, damp, swollen…

Biting off a groan, he bent back to her nipple, tonguing her while sliding one finger over the seam of her sex. Her legs shifted apart. He pressed in, barely entering her. Clamping a hand onto his forearm, she tried to guide him, moving against him.

Yeah. So fucking hot.

It was a struggle not to get lost in sensation and need, but he managed to stay aware of their surroundings, attuned to any sound of approach.

All stayed quiet except for the birds in the tree, the rush of the creek and the rustle of the breeze through the leaves.

As he worked that one finger deeper, they groaned together— him in a surge of lust at her tightness, but he was pretty sure her reaction was to sensory overload of a new experience.

Going a little deeper each time, he stroked, gently in and out, until she caught his rhythm and moved with him. It was tricky because the shorts were restrictive, but he got his hand turned enough to bring his thumb up to her clit. Her electric reaction to that was one of the hottest things he'd ever experienced.

Charlotte made everything sharper, sweeter and infinitely hotter.

By small degrees, release crept up on her. He saw it in the flush of her skin, her swollen lips and labored breaths, the way she tightened, arched. Closing her eyes, she put her head back, her expression beginning to contort in signs of nearly painful pleasure.

In response, he grew so hard he hurt.

Turning her face against him with a throaty, broken groan, she let go, and the climax rolled through her.

If he had her alone in his house he'd make use of the soft bed, strip her naked and eat her until she sobbed like this with release, and then he'd ride her hard and deep, making himself a part of her.

Short of that, this was perfect. He hurt with his own need, but he didn't care. He'd see to it that they had plenty of time for the rest of it later.

Staying with her, soaking in her incredible response, Mitch felt the moment she started to ease and he lightened his touch. Her nipple was very dark and ripe when he released her from his mouth. Blowing gently on her caused a moan, and she fell flat again, legs slightly parted, breast exposed, pulse thundering.

Mine, he thought, looking at her with her displaced clothes, mussed hair and rosy skin. "You're mine."

"That goes both ways," she whispered.

Worked for him.

Getting oxygen into his lungs wasn't easy. As he looked her over from her bare feet to her twisted shorts and up to her sweetly exposed breast, throbbing need and gentle affection overwhelmed him.

"You are the sexiest, prettiest, most amazing woman I've ever known."

She got her lips to smile, but it looked like it cost her. "Mmm." Lazily, she sighed. "How am I supposed to work now?"

"You'll see." He slowly took his hand from her shorts and brought his fingers first to his nose, stirring even more at the scent of her musk, then put them in his mouth.

Maybe a little embarrassed, Charlotte watched him.

He touched her cheek with his fingers, smiling at her shock. "It'll be easier for you now. Working through lust is a bitch—I know, because you've kept me there from the moment we met. Now you'll be more relaxed."

"So relaxed I almost feel comatose."

"You'll recoup." He shifted, winced and said, "Sorry," as he reached down to rearrange himself.

That made her eyes widen. "You're..."

"Hard enough to be deadly, yeah." Also happier than he'd ever known was possible. "Don't worry about it."

She gave a short laugh. "That hardly seems fair since I..." Her cheeks warmed. "You know."

"Got yours?" Her modesty amused him. "God, I'm glad. Today, with you, will be one of my best memories ever. It was a gift, and I thank you for it."

"Pfft." Already recovering, she sat up and tucked her breast away. "I'm not a selfish person."

Far from it. "You're a beautiful person." He felt too good to move yet, so he crossed his arms behind his head. "There were more things I meant to tell you."

"Like?" She half turned to face him, tentatively put a hand on his chest, then stroked down to his abs.

Out of self-defense, Mitch caught her hand and flattened it to his stomach. "Much more of that and I'll never get things under control." To be safe, he sat up too and picked a piece of dried grass from her hair. "Will you have dinner with me tonight at the house? We'll have more privacy there?"

"Yes," she said without hesitation—and looked down at his lap. "I could maybe…?"

He almost wanted to hear her finish that thought, because he knew she'd put a Charlotte-type spin on it. "Finish that thought tonight, maybe after we've had dinner and talked some more."

"How about I finish my thought when I first arrive, and we have dinner and talk after?"

He looked at her earnest face and laughed. "Sounds like an offer I can't refuse." Wishing he could keep her here a little longer, he pushed to his feet, and helped her up next to him. "Love the shorts, by the way."

She gave him another mischievous smile. "They were a good idea, weren't they?"

"One of the best." Holding her hand and leading her back to his car, he added, "Tonight I'll enjoy stripping them off you."

She faltered a step, put her free hand to her heart, and let out a long breath. "It's going to be a very long day."

No kidding. But tonight would be the payoff.

★ ★ ★

Charlotte arrived at the office to find Ros had organized everything very neatly for her. Bless the woman, she was the only one Charlotte trusted to touch the paperwork. Brodie or Jack would have gone off course with some method of their own and totally confused her system. She'd have spent an hour fixing what they'd done in ten minutes.

Ros, on the other hand, had taught her the system and so she already understood it.

She would have liked to talk to Ros, to share—just a tiny bit—of her relationship with Mitch, but late morning things got hectic and only got crazier as the day went on. Brodie and Jack both had jobs that took them out of town until dinnertime. Mary went with Brodie, and Ronnie filled in with a few local jobs.

If things kept up like this, they'd need to hire another person.

Ros had mentioned how much she'd like to bring Mitch onboard, but Charlotte had a feeling the landscaping business would better suit him once he got it going. She could see him working out in the sunshine, sweat on his back, using his hands to build, grow and beautify nature.

His current plan was slowly unfolding, but thanks to Newman's intrusion in their lives, he had several things on his mind.

Despite the workload, she floated through the day, juggling phone calls, sending out invoices, setting new appointments and sorting files.

It was midday when Ros decided to run to the store for groceries. Purse over her shoulder, she paused in the doorway to the office, catching Charlotte on one of the few times she'd been able to sit at the desk.

"Ronnie should be here any minute. Do you think you'd be okay by yourself for a bit? I want to grab some steaks for dinner."

"What?" Looking up from the paperwork, Charlotte took in her worried expression and smiled. "Of course. I'll be fine."

"You're not nervous after what happened? Them coming here, I mean?"

"I don't think they'd dare to try that twice."

Unconvinced, Ros said, "You'll lock the door behind me? Stay inside until Ronnie gets back, or Mitch shows up?"

"Absolutely." No, she wasn't extra nervous after Newman's surprise visit, but neither would she take chances.

Ros looked at her a moment longer, and grinned. "There's a glow about you."

"You can see it?" Hands to her cheeks, Charlotte thought about the morning, what Mitch had done, how he'd made her feel, and she laughed. "I didn't know it showed."

Coming farther into the room, Ros propped a hip on the edge of the desk and touched Charlotte's hair—and came away with a blade of grass. "I take it Mitch is responsible?"

She nodded happily. In a whisper, sort of tasting the words, she admitted, "I didn't know. Before Mitch, I had no idea…"

"I'm glad you're seeing things how they should be. I'm a big believer that when the right one comes along, there's no use fighting it."

That sobered Charlotte. "The way you're fighting it with Elliott?"

"Different story." Rather than deny it, Ros said, "I've been there, done that, and know how it ends. I hope—I *pray*—that Mitch isn't like him in that regard."

Awed by the gift of trust, Charlotte stood. "He's not." She felt very sure of it. "Settling down, getting some roots and having family is too important to him. I think he wants that more than anything."

"Funny, because I think he wants *you* more than anything." She dropped her hands into her lap and studied Charlotte. "He may have first come here for his brothers, but it's you, Charlotte, who will get him to stick around."

Wow. The weight of responsibility weighed heavily on her.

"I'll certainly do my best." For her own selfish reasons, she too wanted Mitch to stay.

"Good." Ros drew her into a hug and a kiss on the cheek. "I think you're both pretty special. In the nicest possible ways, you deserve each other."

After securing the door behind Ros, Charlotte checked the time. Hopefully she got back soon because they had one last local job to fit in.

It'd probably put them over a bit, but the delivery was for a friend and neighbor, not just a customer. Charlotte couldn't wait to see Mitch again, but she also believed in great service for their return people.

Lost in thought, it startled her when the landline rang. That's what she got for imagining how things would be tonight with Mitch instead of concentrating on the work schedule for tomorrow.

She answered with a crisp, "Mustang Transport, this is Charlotte. How may I help you?"

"Sweet Charlotte."

The unfamiliar voice made her senses prickle. She pushed back from the desk, her brows pulling in a frown. "Yes?"

"I heard Mitch was looking for me."

The world came to a standstill. "Newman?"

Without confirming or denying that, he said, "Tell him not to worry. I'll find him—when I'm damn good and ready."

Drumming up meager courage wasn't easy, not when her limbs trembled and her stomach bottomed out. "He's not alone anymore."

"No, he's not, is he? Now he has you." She heard breathing, and then, "I'll be seeing you soon, and then we're going to have us some fun."

That sounded like a threat, making her mouth go dry. "So this *is* Newman. I'm hanging—"

"Don't you fucking dare!"

Alarm shot her heart into her throat and she automatically slammed down the phone—a perk to having a landline.

It immediately rang again, each loud peal jangling her nerves. She stared at it until it stopped.

Seconds later, a knock on the front door brought her half out of her seat, ready to slam the door to the inner office again.

Then Ronnie called out, saying, "Hey, Charlotte. It's me. Let me in."

Relief turned her legs to noodles. Ready, even anxious for an ally, she rushed to the door, scanning the surrounding lot through the glass as she opened it.

Dressed in black jeans and a white tank, the bangs of her short platinum hair swinging from a side part, Ronnie entered with her usual swagger. "Hey, girl, what's up..." Always observant, she took one look at Charlotte and her words died a quick death. "What is it? What's wrong?"

"A call." Locking the door again, Charlotte headed back to her desk. She needed a seat before she started explaining.

Ronnie stayed hot on her heels. "From *him*?" she asked, a sneer in her tone.

God, how she wished she had Ronnie's courage. Trying to contain her thundering heart, she flattened a palm on the desk and drew a shuddering breath. "That's what he said."

Suspicion sharpened Ronnie's gaze. "What else?"

"Maybe just nonsense, but..."

"But probably not, so spill."

Seeing no way around it, Charlotte nodded. "He...well, he toyed with me and I maybe overreacted."

"What did you do?"

"Slammed down the phone—after he warned me not to."

Ronnie grinned, and offered a high five. "Way to go."

Helplessly, Charlotte smacked her palm to Ronnie's. "Yeah... pretty sure it only made him mad."

"Too bad for him, right?"

When the phone rang again, Ronnie's grin widened. "I'm putting him on Speaker, so don't say anything." With that warning, she answered the call. "Lo."

There was a startled pause, and then: "Hmmm, no longer sweet little Charlotte, huh?"

"Nope." Sitting on the edge of the desk, Ronnie folded her arms. "So what do you want, asshole?"

"To talk to her."

"Tough titty. Anything else?"

Charlotte gaped at her. Thank God it was the same voice, and not a potential customer.

The caller laughed. "Oh, you fancy yourself a little badass, huh?"

"Bad enough to cut out your heart, if you weren't a coward who resorted to childish prank calls—and dicking with cars."

"Bitch!"

"But hey, you are, right? So how about I'll just hang up on you? Yeah, that's what I'll do." Unlike Charlotte, she didn't slam down the phone. She merely pressed the button.

"Ronnie..."

"Just wait. He'll call back. They always do."

Nails tapping on the desk, Ronnie waited while Charlotte sat there feeling...exposed. Like people could see her, could know her fear.

Trying to hide her uneasiness, she whispered, "Maybe—"

The phone's jarring ring didn't jolt her quite so badly this time.

"So," Ronnie said by way of answer. "Working up to something, are you?"

"Yes, I am." He sounded more composed this time. "Soon we'll see how good you are with that little blade."

Ronnie laughed, a sound that was both mean and anticipatory. "Anytime. Anywhere." Taunting the caller, she added a few clucking chicken sounds.

A feral snarl erupted through the line. "You just sealed your fate."

"Uh-huh. Well, thanks for hanging on the line long enough for me to trace the call." With false satisfaction, she stated, "Gotcha."

Immediately the line went dead.

Ronnie shook her head. "Idiots will believe anything."

"Oh my God," Charlotte whispered, dumbfounded by Ronnie's audacity. "You taunted him."

"Yeah, so? We need him to act. Now he'll be more inclined."

"To *kill* you!" *To kill* me *too.* But then, she hadn't yet told Ronnie what he'd said.

Hyperventilating was a very real possibility.

Giving Charlotte a long look, Ronnie left the desk and went to peer out the door. "Odds are he called from a cell, and that's a whole different matter—not that the idiot seemed to know it."

Sympathizing with Jack and his efforts to keep Ronnie safe, Charlotte followed her. "You really shouldn't have done that. I'm pretty sure the guys won't approve."

"I can guarantee Jack, Brodie and Mitch feel the same way I do. Waiting is the tough part, not knowing where the creep is or when he'll do something."

"When he does something," Charlotte pointed out, "they want it to be toward *them*, not you."

Indifferent over that possibility, Ronnie shrugged. "Once he comes out of hiding, the guys will get him." She glanced back, her gaze intent. "If I don't get him first."

Charlotte could only shake her head. "You're—"

"Yeah, Jack has a few names for it, none of them all that complimentary." Dropping back against the wall, she smiled. "At least not all the time."

"I don't understand you." In case she took that wrong, Charlotte added, "I adore you. I love having you in the family. But the things you do—"

"I know." Voice so low Charlotte could barely hear her, Ronnie whispered, "You've never been attacked—and I'm glad. But it changes things."

Gently, Charlotte asked, "Like?"

"I'll never be the victim again. I'd rather attack first." Turning back to the door, she said, "Mitch is here," as if they hadn't been discussing something so very dark.

Anxious to see him, Charlotte stepped up next to Ronnie to watch his long-legged, easy approach. Dark sunglasses hid his eyes, but his hard mouth held a sexy curve of anticipation.

To see her.

She loved seeing him like this, carefree, happy. He deserved peace and quiet. He deserved a secure life.

"God, I hate to tell him about this," Charlotte murmured, dreading his reaction. "He's already dealt with so much. Finding out about this is really going to upset him."

"Upset him?" Ronnie snorted. "It's going to piss him off," she corrected. "Besides, he's not a little kid who needs to be protected."

He was once…and he'd had no one.

"Charlotte," Ronnie said in gentle reprimand. "He needs to know."

"I know." She wished for a way to shield him, to insulate him from this new ugliness, but he couldn't guard himself unless he had all the details.

Reaching the door first, Ronnie unlocked and swung it open, greeting him with, "Perfect timing."

Arrested by the cryptic comment, Mitch stalled just inside the door, instantly alert. Pulling off the sunglasses, he studied first Ronnie, then Charlotte.

The transformation was startling. His shoulders seemed to bulge right before her eyes. He stood taller, looked more dangerous.

Ronnie shifted her gaze to Charlotte. "See what I mean?"

Charlotte nodded.

"What happened?" Striding in past Ronnie to Charlotte, Mitch clasped her shoulders. "Are you okay?"

"I'm fine." Seeking to have just a speck of the courage and calm Ronnie possessed, she told him everything that had happened, every word Newman said.

Ronnie dropped back against the wall. "You didn't tell me he was after you."

"It's me he wants to hurt," Mitch said. "But he'll use all of you to make it happen."

Charlotte twisted her hands in his shirt. "You can't leave us." *You can't leave me.*

"No, I can't. Not now. That opportunity came and went."

"At least you're clear on that," Ronnie said.

His hand came up to cradle Charlotte's cheek. "I'll see you home."

"No." She covered his hand with her own. "You promised me a date, and I plan to hold you to it."

"But—"

"I've been waiting all day." She got a smile on her face, and knew it reeked of determination. "Let's go."

CHAPTER SEVENTEEN

After following Ronnie to Ros's house, where Elliott was already camped out, Mitch drove out of town. While trying to get his rage under control, he kept quiet—and that bothered Charlotte.

He could tell by the way she kept looking at him, the way her hands knotted in her lap. "You're okay?"

Hoping his smile looked genuine rather than forced, he nodded. "Fine."

With a delicate clearing of her throat, she pointed out, "You don't sound fine exactly."

Because he wasn't. When he caught up to Newman, he'd take him apart with his bare hands. Overall he was in a killing mood—literally. Newman's threats against Charlotte were bad enough, but... "What Ronnie did was incredibly reckless."

"I don't disagree. From what she said, she's someone who needs to face things head-on."

That's not what she'd done. With Newman baiting them from the shadows, no one could face him. That didn't mean Ronnie should poke him with a stick. "Will she tell Jack?"

"Yes. From what I can tell, she doesn't keep things from him, and vice versa." Charlotte fiddled with her purse strap. "He's going to hit the roof, that's for sure. Not that Ronnie cares."

"No?" If he could keep her talking, maybe she'd relax. Dinner tonight shouldn't be about Newman. It should be about them.

"He accepted who she is before he married her."

Some of what they'd gone through sounded horrendous. He'd heard bits and pieces, and each time Ronnie's daring impressed him. He imagined Jack hadn't stood much of chance. "Had they known each other long?"

"Before he knew she was the one?" Shrugging, Charlotte gave it some thought. "Not really. But they went through enough early on to fill a lifetime."

"And here she is, asking for more trouble." It bothered him most that the trouble was attached to him.

"She could no more hide from it than you could. In some ways, she's even...bolder than Brodie and Jack."

"You were going to say ballsier, weren't you?" Her mouth twitched and he teased, "You were, admit it."

"The term suits her."

"I agree." He felt compelled to say, "I like her," so she wouldn't misunderstand his criticism. "I probably have more in common with her than the rest of them."

Her smile disappeared. "Them—including me?"

Reaching out, he caught her hand and gave her fingers a careful squeeze. "You're in a class all your own."

"That's better."

Laughing, he lifted her hand to brush a kiss over her knuckles. "I like Ronnie, but it was wrong of her to make herself a target. She might think she understands Newman's ilk, but she doesn't. I want him coming after *me*, not anyone else."

Abruptly she yanked back her hand, her frustration palpable. "Well, I don't want him coming after you! None of us want that, okay?"

"Don't get riled," he said, and that just seemed to rile her more.

"When will you get it?" In a dramatic display of temper, she leaned closer to growl, "*You matter to all of us.*"

He'd found that mattering to her was the most important. "I know, and I appreciate it—"

"Oh God," she groaned with a heavy dose of disgust, flopping back into her seat. "You *appreciate* it? Great. Exactly what a girl likes to hear."

Until this moment, he'd forgotten what a temper she had. He thought back on how she'd given Brodie hell a few times, and damned if it didn't make him smile.

He didn't want the polite regard of a stranger, or the kid gloves reserved for guests.

From Charlotte, he wanted everything, and that meant knowing her moods, understanding what mattered to her.

Relishing the fact that, apparently, she cared enough to let down her guard and be herself with him.

She'd said so. Hell, she'd claimed to be falling in love.

But then, she was new to intimacy and that could confuse anyone. Her temper almost meant more to him than anything else.

In a softly threatening tone, she asked, "Are you smiling?"

"I'm happy, so yeah." One glance at her, and the smile became a grin. "Few people have ever worried enough about me, or cared enough, to give me hell." She might be a sexual virgin, but when it came to emotional involvement, he was the inexperienced one. "It's a novel thing and I'm enjoying it."

"Mitch." She deflated, poignant insistence replacing the anger. "I care a lot."

"I wouldn't mind hearing that every day." *For the rest of my life.* "You're like a very special gift, Charlotte, one I didn't ask for, one I didn't even know I wanted." *One he would cherish.*

Cautiously teasing, she replied, "Good, because you're stuck with me now."

He hoped so. Pulling out his phone, he said, "In case Ronnie doesn't tell anyone soon enough, I'll get hold of Brodie and he can talk with Jack, okay? Between them, they can let Ros know, and I guess Colvin."

"Thank you. I do worry about her." Glancing out the window, she murmured, "I hope she's not out waiting on the porch again."

"Lord help us." He scowled. "Elliott wouldn't—"

She snorted. "Elliott would have no influence with her. No, if anyone does, it'd be Ros."

"I have a feeling that lady could tame lions with her smile."

Fond regard brightened her eyes and lifted her spirits. "No doubt."

They had a few minutes yet before they reached his house, so Mitch put in the call. Luckily, the country roads were deserted with very little traffic, and the scattered trees left no room for an ambush. He could afford the slight distraction, but still he put the phone on Speaker and rested it in the console between them so he could keep both hands on the wheel.

Once Brodie answered, it didn't take long to convey everything. He'd expected Brodie's anger, but instinctively knew the quiet rage was even worse.

"I'm done screwing around with him," Brodie stated, his tone flat. "It's impossible for him to be anywhere in the area without being noticed. Someone has seen him and I'm going to find out who."

He made it sound so easy. "If you could do that, why haven't you?"

"Because I hesitate to strong-arm friends and neighbors—"

"You try it with me all the time!"

With a shrug in his tone, Brodie said, "You're a reluctant brother, so it's different."

Mitch glanced at Charlotte. "Not so reluctant."

There was a moment of surprise. "Glad to hear it." Then Brodie added, "If I have to grill everyone from the grocery bag boys to the elders at the church, I will. I promise you, we'll find the prick."

"Sounds like a plan to me. When?"

"I'll start tonight at Freddie's."

Well, shit. Mitch rubbed his mouth, hating the idea of cutting his visit short with Charlotte, but her safety was more important.

"I'll join you." More than his next breath, he'd looked forward to having Charlotte all to himself. He'd been anticipating that uninterrupted time all day.

She looked at him, her own disappointment keen.

His number one priority had to be protecting her, and that meant doing whatever it took. He damn sure wouldn't let Brodie do it for him.

With him, maybe—but not in his place.

"You have a few hours," Brodie said. "I'm not even home yet, and then we have to get through dinner with Mom and Elliott. I'll go after that. Jack will probably want to sit on Ronnie...or maybe bring her along. With those two, it's anyone's guess how it'll go."

Mitch heard the amusement and marveled anew that this cocky, capable guy was his brother.

It gave him another new experience—pride for a relative.

"Freddie knows me, so I'll tell him to start listening. Plus we have our guy working there." On a roll now, Brodie said, "Between them, maybe they'll hear something."

"If you hear anything at all, I want to know."

"Guaranteed. In the meantime, though, you and Charlotte should enjoy your *dinner.*" The emphasis Brodie put on it had Charlotte scowling at the phone, but made Mitch smile. "Just keep your eyes and ears open, okay? You're out there alone—"

"I won't let her get hurt, I swear."

"Damn right you won't." Brodie paused, then asked, "I don't suppose you're armed?"

"Ex-cons aren't allowed to have guns." Not that he needed one. "It won't matter."

"Damn you're confident. Reminds me of me. I like it." His tone shifted. "Charlotte?"

She said, "Yes?"

"You're going to start carrying, okay? Tomorrow, before work, I'll get you a holster for your purse. Maybe a stun gun too."

Smile indulgent, she said, "Already planned on it, but the holster will be nice. Thanks."

After they disconnected, Mitch sat in stunned silence. A gun in Charlotte's hand? He couldn't imagine it. The image seemed obscene for a woman as gentle and kind as her.

Picking up on his mood, she said, "If it makes you feel better, I doubt I'd keep my wits about me enough to ever use the gun."

With his mouth gone dry, he had to clear his throat to speak. "You know how to shoot though?"

Wrinkling her nose, she shrugged. "Let's just say I know how to aim and squeeze the trigger. Whether or not I actually hit anything? That's usually fifty/fifty."

He pulled up to his house. At seven thirty, the sun still shone bright. At night though, it could get pretty dark and since he hoped to have Charlotte over more often, he'd taken the time today to mount security lights on the front of the barn, front, back and one side of the house, and another in the yard near where he parked his car. There'd be just enough shadows left for him to sleep in his tent without the glare of light disturbing him.

Never missing much, Charlotte said, "You put up the lights?"

"I won't take chances with you." He parked and walked around to her door. "When did you learn to shoot?"

As she stepped out, an uneasy breeze played with her hair. The air smelled like rain, so it was a good thing he'd put plastic over his broken window.

Looking up at the lights to avoid his gaze, she tried for a cavalier tone. "After Ronnie got attacked, I got...interested. The way she handled herself, how she held it together, it all impressed me."

"From what Jack told me, that was largely bluster. She's a proud woman and didn't want anyone else to see her shaken. Jack understood. Most people would feel the same. But he said he was a mess—and there's nothing wrong with that. Adrenaline will only get you so far, and when it crashes, it often takes your knees with it."

She smiled, but her thoughts were introspective. "That one night..." Her voice trailed off. "I know you've been told some of her past, the things she's been through. It hurt her, and it made her tough, but it also left her with crazy instincts."

He remembered hearing about a lunatic trying to kill her, her bosses and Jack. Charlotte appeared lost in comparisons, and it pained him. Twining one of her long curls around his finger, he smiled. "You're not her, babe, and she's not you. That's okay." It was Charlotte he'd fallen hard for, no one else.

"If she hadn't reacted the way she did that night, they all would have died." Hugging her arms around herself despite the heat, she turned her face up to his. "She's remarkable—a lot like you, Brodie and Jack, actually. I wanted to learn a few moves myself, but as you said, I'm not her."

"You don't need to be."

As if that didn't register, she continued, "Jack had already tried to show me a few things with a knife, but that's hopeless for me. So Brodie stepped in and taught me how to use a gun. He got me this cute little .45 with a laser light on it to help improve my aim. As long as I have time to follow that light, I can hit—or at least come close to hitting—a target. The Glock was just too heavy for me."

Mitch ran a hand over his face. "And the stun baton?"

Dropping her voice to a whisper, she admitted, "It scares me half to death."

Good. Mitch hugged her to him, holding her close, fitting her body to his. She nestled her head in under his chin and wrapped her slim arm around him. Her breasts pressed to his lower ribs and sparked a fire in his blood, making him instantly want more.

He had plans for tonight and they weren't to rush her straight to bed. Helping him to remember that, Brute gave one yap of welcome, looking at them through the screened porch.

One kiss first, he decided, tipping up her chin and putting his mouth to hers. She'd caught on quick, parting her lips and touching her tongue to his. Her enthusiasm scorched him clear down to his toes.

With a groan, he pulled back. "I have to keep it together a little longer, and that's not helping."

Expression dreamy, she touched his mouth and sighed. "I suppose we shouldn't keep Brute waiting."

"Not unless you want me to mop the floor."

Taking his hand with a laugh, she led him in.

Charlotte wasn't sure what Mitch had done since she'd last been there, but the house now felt more like a home. Maybe it was the few dishes drying on a rack beside the sink, or the packaged cookies on the counter. The area rug on the floor by the door? The blinds over the windows?

What they'd started for him, he'd finished, and in an incredibly short time.

She hoped she could motivate him that easily to other changes.

As soon as they entered, Brute lifted his head for a few gentle strokes, then stretched forward with an elaborate yawn, his hind legs out behind him, his front paws extended, his muscular neck arched. Sharp teeth showed as he uncurled his tongue. He ended the display by dropping down and rolling to his back, an invitation for her to give him a belly rub.

Little by little, the dog settled in, acting more secure with his situation. Hopefully Mitch would do the same.

"Lazy thing," he rumbled, joining her in lavishing the dog with affection. "Don't you want to go out?"

Bolting back to his feet, he shook his butt with excitement.

"I'd say that's a yes." Charlotte opened the door and followed him out, Mitch at her side.

At one end of the sky, the sun sank lower, a hazy orange ball that colored the bellies of numerous flat clouds. In the other direction, the skies darkened ominously and the occasional flash of lightning could be seen. All around them, insects sang and trees rustled.

She put her face up to the breeze and closed her eyes. "It's so beautiful here."

His arm slipped around her in a casual hold. "Private too."

It seemed so natural now, for them to touch, to be together, as if they'd had a relationship for months, even years. In some intrinsic, indefinable way, he fulfilled a part of her that had been missing until she met him.

She'd known what she wanted: physical contact, emotional closeness. Understanding and approval. Affection.

Yet no man had interested her enough to make it happen. Now, with Mitch, she constantly wanted more. More of his smiles.

More of his touch.

More of the stirring way he kissed her.

"What are you thinking?"

She opened her eyes to see him studying her, his frown quizzical and amused.

"You."

One brow went up.

"I was thinking of you and how you make me feel." Leaning into him was nice. Better than nice. Perfect even.

His brows smoothed out. "How?"

"It's hard to describe, but like—" She searched for adequate words. "This is how I should have been, but wasn't until now."

Both brows lifted, and a small smile formed. "That's...pro-found."

"Are you teasing me?" Not that she'd mind. She liked seeing him more lighthearted.

"Actually, it's similar for me." While watching the dog, he smoothed his hand up and down her back. "When I'm with you, I feel things I thought were always out of my reach."

Oh, now see. That *was* profound.

Before she could get too emotional over it, Brute trotted back to them. Eyes half closed, his tongue lolling out, he wagged his tail.

"You look happy, bud," Mitch told him, rubbing his back.

"So do you," Charlotte whispered.

He glanced at her. "You're here. Of course I'm happy."

They still had things to talk about, but she had promised a certain order to events...and she didn't think she could wait much longer. "Should we head in?"

In stark contrast to his gentle smile, hunger glittered in his eyes. "Yeah." Patting his thigh, he said to Brute, "How about dinner, Brute? You hungry?"

The dog lunged forward with a bark.

"Yeah, you're always hungry, aren't you?" To Charlotte, he said, "Dinner will keep him busy for an hour or two. He'll eat, then pass out for a nap."

"He's so chill."

"People see him and think *pit bull* and immediately expect him to be vicious." He rubbed Brute's ear. "At heart, he's a shy butterfly."

She laughed at the description. "You didn't help, naming him Brute."

"He can have his moments." Holding the door, he waited until she and the dog went in, then he secured it. "He likes to eat and then doze here in the screened room. For both of us, it's almost like being outside."

That was another thing she wanted to talk about—the reason he used a tent rather than the house he'd bought. What would happen when colder weather set in?

What if things between them progressed? Eventually he'd want her to stay over, right? Would he expect her to sleep in a tent too?

She would. In her heart, Charlotte knew she'd do just about anything for him, and that prompted her to say, "I love your house. There's so much character in the structure of it."

"I see it now, though I didn't when I bought it. The other half, toward the barn, is set up to run the business. The office there needs as much work as the rest of it, but for now there's an old desk, a filing cabinet and a half john."

"It's perfect, but I worry about you being out here all alone."

He filled a big bowl with dry food and set it down for Brute. While rinsing out and refilling the water bowl, he said, "This was a compromise for me. It's civilized, right? A house, the expected model for anyone settling down."

Charlotte loved watching him move, how easily his large hands handled the bowls, the casual flex of muscles in his forearms. To her, everything about him was beautiful and stirring, even the way he did simple chores. "But?"

Leaning against the wall, arms folded, he averted his gaze. "Sometimes four walls are a bit much for me." He flashed a twisted smile of regret. "Doesn't take a genius to know it's the residual effect of being locked up, right? It's something you don't think about—being free. It's so damn easy to take it for granted."

She went to him, snuggling in against that broad chest. His shirt was slightly damp with sweat, clinging to all the hard planes and muscled swells of his body. Even better, he smelled delicious, like earthy man, a scent unique to him.

There wasn't a single thing about his body that she didn't love, but it was his drive and determination, his basic character, that she appreciated most because it was that unique attribute that had helped him survive.

That had brought him to *her.*

Wondering how he felt about all the new adjustments in his life, she asked, "You're easing into things?"

Catching her face in his warm palms, he urged her to meet his probing gaze. In a sultry voice that licked down her spine, he murmured, "I'd like to ease into you."

Mmmm, she'd like that as well. With a slight nod, she smiled. "Okay."

"So agreeable."

"Because in this, we want the same thing." Wearing a mock frown, she added, "But don't get used to it."

She saw the pleasure in his eyes when he murmured, "Yes, ma'am." Tentatively, he touched his mouth to hers, lingered, firmed, caressing and teasing until the kiss turned soft, deep, devastating enough to steal her thoughts and her breath.

The soft cotton over his shoulders encouraged her hands to roam. Abruptly he turned her, pressing her to the wall and leaning in so that his hips pinned her while he continued to feast on her mouth.

And even that wasn't enough, apparently not for either of them, because his hands slid down her back to her bottom and he pulled her against a solid erection beneath his jeans.

She freed her mouth on a gasp.

He took it again, his tongue sliding past her teeth, exploring deeply while strong fingers kneaded her flesh, rocking her against him. Easily maneuvering her body, he led her in a tantalizing rhythm.

Nerve endings all came alive—and he pulled back to say, "The bed. Now."

Never in her life had she been called bold, but here, in this situation with Mitch, wanting him in a way she hadn't known existed, all that came to mind was, "Race you," and she slid away from him to stride down the hall.

A pleased, husky laugh followed her and just as she reached the bed, he reached her. Abruptly turning her, he stripped off her camisole in one smooth, probably practiced, move.

She didn't care. Whatever he'd done with other women, he was here now with her and she didn't plan to ever let him go.

A hot mix of determination, lust and tenderness drove his gaze all over her upper body. Hand shaking, he reached for the front clasp to her strapless bra.

Before Mitch, she'd always bemoaned her lack of boobs. With him, she felt incredibly sexy. "Let me."

Hand falling back to his side, his nostrils flared on a deeply indrawn breath.

Loving that reaction, loving him, Charlotte opened the bra… and let it fall to the floor.

"You think they'll be watching the girl?"

Newman laughed—and didn't tell them that she'd bammed him by threatening to track his call. He felt enough like a dumbass for believing it, even for those two brief seconds. "Probably. They'll be clustered around her, wringing their hands and trying to figure out how to keep her safe."

Ritchie cackled at the image. "While we're out here gettin' old Mitch."

Yes, he'd get Mitch. He remembered him as a gangly teen, full of defiance and pride, refusing to cower.

When Mitch was bleeding out, when he knew he was dying—and that the women were next on Newman's list—then he wouldn't be so damned proud anymore.

And after he finished with Mitch he'd cut Bernie's throat and leave town. Forget the women. They didn't really matter other than a means to torment Mitch.

If too many bodies went missing, he'd have the damn Federals on his ass. No one needed that.

Sitting back in his chair, Lee grunted. "It was nice of Bernie to be so accommodating with info."

They started another round of laughter.

When Bernie found out Mitch had bought an old place on the outside of town, he'd been all too excited to share the news. "I knew if we waited long enough, something would give. Towns this size spend all their time gossiping." Apparently a friend of Bernie's had been at the hardware store when Mitch bought security lights. He'd shared the info with Bernie innocently enough, never suspecting what Bernie would do with it.

Half under his breath, Newman said, "He can light the place up like Christmas. It won't change anything."

After leaving Bernie, Lee had come to him and once it was dark enough, they'd head out for some fun.

Withdrawing his blade, Newman examined the razor-sharp edge. "You remember what I did to Bill?"

Ritchie winced. "Yeah, there was so much blood, I'm not likely to forget it. You left him in pieces."

"That," Newman stated, "is what's in store for Mitch."

"Day-um. Hate him that much, do you?"

What he felt was worse than hate. From the time Mitch was a kid, he'd been defiant and full of disdain. He'd gotten in Newman's way too many times, and then he'd dared to sell his mother's house, when it should have been Newman's. In the process, he'd destroyed his drug supply and damaged his reputation. "Yeah, I hate him that much, and more." Mitch would give him his money, all that he had. And then he'd give him the satisfaction he'd long been denied.

CHAPTER EIGHTEEN

Short on words but long on need, Mitch couldn't slow down. Luckily Charlotte seemed to be with him every step. Her little race to the bedroom amplified everything—emotion, need, hunger. Sexy confidence and her own desire kept her standing before him, her gaze direct, her eyes alight with a reciprocal need that filled up all the empty places in his heart.

Drawn to her delicate curves, he watched as his darker fingers curved around her pale breasts, as his thumbs teased her dusky nipples into tight peaks.

Compliments, promises filled his head, but all he said was, "You're mine."

Her chin elevated another notch. "Ditto."

Pleasure pulsed through his system, ending as a throb in his cock. "Feeling territorial, huh?"

"Very."

"Good." He left her breasts long enough to open the snap to her shorts, ease down the zipper, and push them over her hips.

Now, finally, he'd see all of her.

Just as he'd suspected, the panties matched the bra, pure white, soft cotton, and scorching hot for being so demure.

Likely because *she* wore them. He knew he'd seen prettier women, sexier women, but at the moment he couldn't drum up a single one.

Color tinged her cheeks but her gaze remained steady. "Your turn."

That commanding tone from her added amusement to everything else she made him feel. "Yes, ma'am." Anxious to have her hands on his fevered skin, he peeled off the shirt and tossed it. Lack of air-conditioning left the house warm, even with the ceiling fan lazily stirring the air, sending her body's natural perfume to fill his head.

He toed off his shoes while opening his jeans, aware of Charlotte blindly backing up, dropping onto the edge of the bed, as if her legs no longer supported her.

Pausing with his hands on his zipper, he asked, "Okay?"

She nodded fast and hard, gesturing with impatience. "Go on."

The humor sharpened in tandem with the lust. "You want to see me, do you?"

"Most definitely." Her tongue slicked over her lips and her chest expanded before she sighed. "Seems fair."

Fair would be him dropping to his knees, pressing his face between her thighs, deeply inhaling her luscious scent and then tormenting her to a screaming climax.

If he said all that, she might faint. Already she looked out of her element—urgent, yes, but also wary.

Jeans open and cock hard, Mitch stepped closer to her, petting her hair until he found the clip holding it up. Carefully, so he didn't pull, he freed it and set it on the nightstand. His fingers slid through her hair until all those pretty curls came loose, falling over her shoulders, draping her nipples.

"Touch me." His gruff voice urged her gaze from his abs to his face.

With just her fingertips, she traced the shape of him through the denim.

That light, searching touch damn near put him over the edge. He hissed in a breath, his fingers carefully clenching in her hair, massaging, stroking. The bolder she got, the closer he came to the edge, until he couldn't take it anymore.

"Bad idea," he growled, stepping away again. "Sorry, but I'm already primed."

That emboldened her even more and she smiled. "Take them off, Mitch." Scooting back on the bed, lounged on her elbows, one leg bent, the other extended, she made a show of watching him. "And hurry it up."

God Almighty. Seeing her like this was a dream come to life. It felt like he'd waited for her forever, maybe even before they'd met because in so many ways, she epitomized everything he'd thought was too out of reach.

She was everything he'd ever craved—and everything he hadn't even known to want.

After stripping off the jeans, he turned to a dresser, opened the top drawer and took out two condoms. He put one by her hair clip on the nightstand and the other he ripped open, wincing as he rolled it over the sensitive head and along the shaft.

Closing the door to ensure Brute wouldn't find his way in to them, Mitch came to stand over her. Every breath was a struggle as he told himself to slow down—without much success.

"I hurt for you," he admitted in a growl, his hand fisting and opening with the need to touch her all over, to feel her warm silky skin, the texture of her nipples and that soft pubic hair.

Going to her back, she lifted her arms to him—and destroyed his will, obliterating his intent. Even as he warned himself not to rush her, he settled onto her body, the touch of skin to skin both easing and sharpening his ache.

The urge to devour her heated him from the inside out. Unable to resist, he took her mouth in a hot, consuming kiss.

Her lips were soft and open, warm and sweet, and the scent of her fragrant skin surrounded him.

She was both sensual and unique. He wasn't a lucky person, never had been—the opposite, in fact. Life seemed to enjoy kicking him in the nuts, knocking him backward for every step he gained, ensuring that he never got too far ahead.

But then he'd met Charlotte, and damned if the world didn't look downright promising for a change.

Since he saw her on the first night, his libido had been in a tailspin. Every memory of her conspired against him; her smile, her corkscrew curls, her defiance and compassion and backbone. They hit him like a shot of adrenaline and crushing desire.

Sweeping his hands over her, he absorbed the softness and warmth, the pliant flesh and slender bones, hollows and swells. While toying with one peaked nipple he licked her throat, sucked gently on her tender skin, grazed her collarbone with his teeth.

"Mitch…" Just that, nothing more, and he knew it was because words were already beyond her.

Like him, the mix of carnality and sentiment gripped her. This wasn't just sex, could never be as simple as sex. With her, it was more.

So much more.

Current problems, the ugly past, even hopes for the future faded away as he kissed a tantalizing trail down her body. Her legs parted around him as he paused to lick her nipples. When he drew her in, sucking gently first, then more strongly, she arched, her slender body tight as a bow.

Yes, that's what he wanted. Her mindless with need for him. Only him. Leaving her nipples wet and tight, he kissed her ribs, along her waist and the faint curve of her sexy belly. It required more attention, so he lingered there, enjoying the way she squirmed, before easing down to her hipbones.

As he pressed her legs apart, she went still, maybe surprised by what he intended, maybe anxious for it. He didn't know and it didn't matter. Tasting her was more important than his next breath.

He hooked one of her legs up and over his shoulder, opening her wide.

Enough light remained in the room for him to see her clearly, all of her, pink and fresh, wet and swollen. Groaning, he leaned in to kiss and lick, holding her steady when her hips came off the bed. "Easy."

Her panting breaths broke the silence in the room.

Scooping his hands under her rounded backside, he kept her lifted like that, open to him and what he'd do to her. "Just relax and enjoy."

Incredulity added huskiness to her laugh, but she didn't fight him. Instead she knotted her hands in the quilt as if to ground herself.

Perfect. Nuzzling against that downy little mound, he explored with his tongue, tasting her, further inciting her, treating them both at the same time. He'd been in a rush, but now, he felt like he could enjoy her for hours.

She disagreed.

Her soft cries turned broken, her movements desperate as she reacted to each prod and thrust and lick of his tongue. Knowing she was close, feeling it in the trembling of her limbs, he drew in her distended clit and softly worked it, tugging, teasing with the tip of his tongue, until the climax crashed through her.

Thank God he'd already donned a rubber.

Knowing he wouldn't last an entire minute, Mitch came up her body, framed her face for his kiss and pressed into her.

Wet heat closed snugly around his cock, making him stall and draw breath. "Okay?"

Eyes dark and heavy, she nodded. "Yes," she said in a husky whisper.

Each shallow thrust and retreat allowed him to sink in more. She was small, but wet enough that her body slowly accepted him.

Urging him on, she stroked his shoulders, turned her head to bite his biceps, then licked his skin. It was almost enough to send him into oblivion.

With one last rocking thrust, he buried himself in her.

They both gasped for breath, holding still, her trembling, him rigid with restraint.

"Mitch," she whispered, and squirmed.

Lost. Totally lost, he came up to his elbows, taking as much pleasure in seeing her as in feeling her, breathing her, tasting her. By force of will he kept control, ensuring his thrusts were smooth and steady for as long as he could until it felt like the boiling pressure would destroy him.

"Yes," she whispered, her hand to his jaw, watching him.

And he realized, she enjoyed what she saw.

Giving up, he pressed deep and let release roll through him, the hard rush taking away his strength until he slowly sank down to rest against her. Her lips touched his shoulder and he felt it in his heart.

Minutes later, his erection gone, he knew he had to leave her or risk pregnancy. She wasn't ready for that, and honestly, neither was he. He wanted the business up and running, as profitable as hard work could make it.

He wanted the house to be a home.

And he needed Newman to be nothing more than a bad memory.

Then, God yes, then he'd love to plan a future with Charlotte. The thought put a smile on his face.

"Mm," she said, her fingertips lazily gliding along his shoulder. "I think we're slipping off the bed."

His smile broadened even more. "You took my strength."

"Sorry, but I have none to spare."

Laughter with sex. Who knew that combo could be so sexy?

"Stay put a second, okay?" He straightened and removed the spent condom, wrapping it in a tissue and tossing it in a small trash can near the door.

When he turned back to her, he found her eyes barely open, languid and replete, watching him.

Honestly, yeah, since they'd started out with her sideways in the bed, she did look in danger of slipping over the side. Gently he scooped her up, but instead of reclining again, he sat against the headboard and held her in his lap.

Odd, but the bed, the walls, the closeness of the room, no longer felt restrictive. His breath didn't tighten, his guts didn't burn.

Maybe she'd worn him out too much for excesses of any kind. He didn't have the energy for angst.

She touched his jaw. "What is it?"

So damn perceptive. "Nothing."

Unconvinced, she glanced around, much as he had, and drew her own conclusions. "It's the room, isn't it? I know you prefer to sleep outside."

True, but no reason to belabor it. Talking about the past and his shortcomings would only taint their time together—

"Mitch," she quietly reprimanded, and damned if she didn't look like a tempered version of Ros. It made him grin.

And earned him a pinch. "There's nothing you can't tell me." Obviously she wouldn't let it go.

Lying to her was unthinkable, so he shrugged and tried to make light of it. "Usually, yeah." He wouldn't be a maudlin ass. He wouldn't tell her that having her here with him made it different. "I prefer to sleep outside." Before she could dig into that, he redirected her. "I wanted to talk to you about that."

"About prison?"

"About you and me, actually—and yeah, some stuff about prison."

"I've never sat naked on an equally naked man's lap talking. I like it." She stroked her fingers through his chest hair. "Go on."

It struck him that she was right. "You know, I haven't done anything like this either. Before you, sex wasn't about talking. It was just a physical release." Cold. Almost...lonely.

With her, everything felt new.

"I suppose you've been with a lot of women?"

Earlier in his life, no. But... "After prison, I was excessive." That sounded bad, so he shook his head. "Excessive on rejoicing." *Sort of.* "I ate steak every damn night, and these crazy desserts. I gained ten pounds."

She snuggled closer. "And lost it again, I see."

This was the tricky part. "I overindulged in everything I'd been denied. Including sex." He watched her, hoping she'd understand.

She tried not to scowl, but the shadows in her eyes gave her away. "Did you get involved with anyone special?"

Kissing the end of her nose, he said, "It was just sex, and it didn't matter—but none of them were you. With you, it matters. A lot."

The wary expression softened.

"That nonsense only lasted a few months and I was always safe. Once I decided to come here, I got my head on straight, got my act together. I lost those pounds, like you said, got fit again." He chewed the corner of his mouth, not wanting to be crude, but needing her to know. "I wanted to be healthy inside and out before looking up Brodie and Jack, so I saw a doctor. Not just because of the women, but prison is a filthy place." He shook his head, unwilling to talk about the often-nasty food, the unclean showers, the attacks with homemade knives. "The thing is, I made sure I was healthy."

Her palm felt cool against his jaw. "I wasn't worried."

Her gentleness destroyed him. "But don't you see, babe? You should have been."

"Maybe if you hadn't proven your honor right off. But you

did. That very first night, you offered help and nothing more. You stood up to Bernie."

He snorted. "That was like standing up to a puppy. And you should know, I was thinking all kinds of things. About you, I mean. If the guys hadn't shown up—"

"What? You would have come on to me? I wouldn't have minded that."

"Charlotte—"

She touched his mouth. "And if I'd said no?"

Without hesitation, needing her to believe him, he said, "No is no."

"There, you see?" She smiled in triumph. "You're an honorable man, and because of that, I knew you'd covered your bases."

The lump of emotion clogging his throat made it tough to swallow. Unable to pull his gaze from hers, feeling more than he'd even felt in his life, he whispered, "You astound me."

She looked a little overwhelmed herself. "Well again, I don't want to scare you off, but with you, things have felt right from the beginning."

Mitch crushed her close. "All my life, I've made a point of not wanting something that I didn't know how to get. But now I want you."

She tipped her head back to smile at him. "Seems you know how to get me."

God, he hoped that was true.

"I know how I feel," she said, lowering her gaze to his mouth, then his chest. "But are you sure it's not Brodie and Jack that's the attraction? I'm part of their lives, part of the family, and that matters, right?"

For sure, neither of them made him ache with lust. He smoothed down her wild, beautiful hair. "You have my word, I won't lie to you, ever. So yes, it matters. It's like if I painted the best possible scenario for my dream life. Having them as real family, this with you, even the atmosphere of the town, would be it." He pressed his mouth to hers, firm and fast. "But even if I lost them. If even they ended up hating me—"

"They wouldn't."

"—I'd still want you. More than anything else, it's about you. From that first night when you touched me… I think I already knew."

Happiness lit up her face, made her eyes bluer and her smile bright. "You see, that's why I've never been worried with you."

The laugh took him by surprise. He was trying to be sincere, trying to make her understand how much she meant to him. "If you won't be cautious enough to ensure your own safety, then I'll cover the bases for you."

One teasing finger touched the indent of his chin, traced down his throat to his sternum. "Hmm," she whispered, leaning in for a kiss. "How are you going to do that?"

For starters, he'd keep her near as often as possible. "You have my word, I won't ever hurt you. Not by accident, not through negligence. Not in any way."

Her smile was both tender and smug. "I already knew that."

Needing her to understand he was serious, he vowed, "No one will work harder than me either, or want to make it work more—"

"Mitch."

"I'll do everything I can." And it would have to be enough, because any scenario that didn't include her was unacceptable. He cupped her face. "I swear it."

With her eyes staring into his, she searched his face, nodded acceptance, and smiled. "Will you tell me why sleeping in the bedroom bothers you so much?"

Well hell. Not what he'd hoped to hear, but then it was better than being told to back off.

Charlotte put her arms around his neck and held him. He was warm and hard and his scent swirled around her, filling her with a mix of need and love and comforting security.

She needed to know if loving him would mean sleeping in a tent. She'd do it, if that's what he needed. But her hope was that, with someone at his side, it wouldn't be so bad.

"Sleeping in here…" He trailed off, cleared his throat. "It makes me feel like I'm back there again."

Did he have nightmares? Oh, how she wished for a way to protect him. "I understand."

Tentatively, his hands settled low on her back. "I won't describe it to you. I wouldn't even want you to know what it's like." He bent his head to her neck, and she felt his hot breath, slow and gentle. "There was one guy—he was claustrophobic and it was tough to see. He walked around like a damned zombie, always zoned, shaking, freaking out over every little sound." He pulled her tighter to him. "Easy prey."

"How awful," she whispered, her throat thickening.

"After I gained some clout—after that fight I told you about—I tried to defend him when I could. Some of the guards hated my guts for not going with the status quo. Others, a few good men, told me they appreciated me. One even reported the guy's issues, and he got some medical help because of it."

Even in prison, Mitch had tried to do the right thing.

"It was tricky, talking to a guard. Anything close to resembling a snitch was a death knell. Snitches were hated even more than rapists." He cupped her breast, then ran his hand down her side to her hip. "I did what I could on my own. And I got a terrible reputation."

"I'm not sure a rep for defending others is such an awful thing."

"Maybe not. It got to where people gave me a wider path. Some inmates anyway. Others wanted to kill me."

"Mitch." She burrowed closer. He was here now, with her, big and strong and capable. He had family and backup and he'd never again be alone. Knowing it made her feel better, so she hoped he felt better too. It'd take time, she knew.

It wasn't just his years in prison, but the years of neglect and abuse before that.

If she could, she'd demolish Newman for him. She knew Mitch well enough now to know he wanted that honor himself, but to her mind, he should be spared further violence and conflict. He needed peace to move forward.

"I shouldn't have said that." He trailed a finger along her thigh. "I told you, it's all ugly. We should get back to—"

"I want to know everything about you." She'd always found that talking about things lessened their impact. When she'd lost her parents, Rosalyn had spent many nights sitting up with her, listening and letting her unload her grief and fear.

And then she'd helped her to pick up the pieces of her broken heart.

Could she do the same for Mitch? Yes, it was different, but hurt was hurt, and in her heart she believed it would help. At the very least, it wouldn't hurt.

Looking up at him, she whispered, "Please?"

A slight frown kept his dark brows together, and he'd set his mouth in a grim line. Finally he nodded.

He didn't look happy about it, but he did continue. "I gained allies after that first attack—men I wouldn't associate with now, but back then, they watched my back like I watched theirs. Didn't matter what we'd done, why we were in prison."

"It was about survival?"

"That sounds really dramatic, but yeah, something like that."

"Earlier today, when we talked…what did you mean when you said you'd been hurt?" She'd had all day to think about the conversation, the details he'd given and those he'd glossed over. Now she had more questions than ever.

He took his time, measuring his words, until Charlotte started to think she'd pushed too much again. Then finally, after a kiss to the top of her head, he explained, "In prison, you find everything suspect, every movement, every word. At first it seemed impossible to know if someone was coming in to throw a punch, or just talk. After enough bruises, though, I learned fast. If someone tried to get me alone to talk, I kept my guard up and at the first sign of provocation, I kicked in their teeth. It became a sixth sense, knowing trouble when I saw it. Hell, I could smell it."

The swell of his chest drew her hand, and she stroked over him. He was such a dominating force, with the same physical attributes as his brothers. She couldn't even begin to imagine what that type of existence might do to a person. "Sleeping was tough?"

"You don't sleep, not really. I got to where I'd hear if my cell mate turned over." He rubbed his chin on the top of her head.

No wonder the room made him uncomfortable. It probably brought back all those tense memories. "The fight you told me about, that was the worst?" She prayed to God nothing else that terrible had happened.

"It was." Again he went quiet, but not as long this time. He spoke fast, maybe wanting to get it over with. "The minute I saw him looking at me, I knew what was going down and I started fighting." She felt the tension invading his muscles. "Back then three to one meant I'd get pulverized."

"Back then?"

He rolled one massive shoulder in a casual shrug, not bragging, just very matter-of-fact. "I learned to bulk up real quick. I learned to be fast and I learned to be stealthy. After that, I never thought about it—someone came at me, I threw a punch as hard as I could with the intent to take someone's head off his neck." He tangled his fingers in her hair, gently massaging her scalp. "I know where to kick to cripple a man. I know how to break bones quick and clean."

The shocking part for her was that he'd come through it all intact. Yes, maybe with some residual issues, but it hadn't made him cruel, and it hadn't made him a criminal. "You've done that?"

"More than a few times while in prison." Expression earnest, he touched her face. "Now I avoid violence whenever I can. But you should know, I'll take care of you. I'll protect you, Charlotte. Whatever it takes."

She wanted to spare him, not force him into a position of more brutality. Did he care even more than he realized?

Was he too maybe falling in love?

She didn't press him on it. This, today, should be about him. She wanted to hear whatever he felt compelled to tell her, to show him—in no uncertain terms—that it changed nothing for her.

It was too soon to know it, too soon to feel this much, but he was it. For her, he was everything.

So she tried a smile that had no effect on him. "Will you promise me one thing?"

His thumb brushed her cheekbone. "Anything. Everything."

Her mouth trembled—and she made her own vow: to hold him to that. "Remember that you're not alone anymore. You'll never be alone again." And she lifted up to kiss him.

CHAPTER NINETEEN

Mitch couldn't resist her a second more. There were a hundred reasons why she shouldn't be involved with a man like him. He'd tried to warn her, but her faith in him didn't waver. Unable to hold back a second more, he eased her onto her back.

Looming over her, loving the way her hair spread out on his mattress, he looked her over. Already hunger crept into her innocent expression, creating a potent lure.

Their time was dwindling tonight. Soon either Brodie would call, or Brute would come looking for them, but until then, he wanted as much of her as he could get.

He swept his gaze over her. She had a few whisker burns, making him wish he'd shaved again before having her.

"I probably need a shower."

"No." He kissed the fragrant skin of her breasts. "I'm not some refined guy who wants you smelling like perfume. Your skin is sweet enough." He pressed his palm between her legs. "Your musk… I want to fill my head with it."

And he wanted to fill his life—with her.

Now that he'd taken off the edge, he kissed her, slower this time, determined to convince her that they belonged together.

He was just taking his hand on a heated path down her body when Brute went berserk, barking and snarling in a way he'd never heard.

He reared up, reality crashing in.

"What in the world?" Charlotte said, coming up to an elbow.

"Something's wrong." Already on his feet and headed for the door, Mitch said, "Stay put."

"Wait…"

"Lock the door behind me, Charlotte. I mean it." Not bothering to dress, he rushed from the room, closing the door behind him. "Brute!"

Anyone who hurt his dog would answer to him tenfold.

In seconds he reached the screened-in room, where Brute had settled into low, disgruntled grumbling.

One entire section of the screening was ripped away. The lights outside showed an empty yard. Off in the distance, he heard a car door slam, then an engine rev.

Brute stood looking out, his entire body tensed, muscles rippling.

Mitch saw blood.

On the floor, the screen, the sill…and on Brute.

Heaving, his jaw aching from clenching so hard, he approached Brute in slow, measured steps. "Hey, buddy. You okay?"

His tail wagged.

Taking a deeper breath, Mitch said, "He's gone, bud. Now let me see you."

The dog turned…with a mangled shoe in his mouth.

When Mitch dropped to his knees, Brute trotted over, all pleased with himself.

Having no idea what to think, Mitch praised him. "That's a good boy. Come here, let me see where you're hurt."

Behind him, Charlotte whispered, "I'll get a towel."

Frustration reared up. If there was trouble still, she'd be in the middle of it. How the hell could he keep her safe if she didn't listen?

Seconds later she stepped back in, somewhat dressed, his jeans over her arm, phone in hand and a damp towel held out in offering.

He didn't know what to say to her either, so he took it and gently swabbed at Brute's mouth. The blood came away and he realized it wasn't Brute's, but more likely the owner of that shoe.

"Thank God," she said, followed by, "I called Brodie. He's on his way so you might want to put on your pants."

She'd taken over, the same way Brodie and Jack always tried to do. Charlotte's methods were more effective, but still… "I told you to stay in the room."

"I did—until I heard you talking to Brute and realized the danger was gone." Tipping her head, she studied the demolished, bloody running shoe. "You think he took that off someone?"

"Not sure what else I can think. You saw the screen?"

"Yes."

Rising, he stepped into his jeans, trying to organize his thoughts as he zipped and snapped. Brute acted like nothing had happened, staring up at them with his brown eyes full of happiness.

"You're just a badass at heart, aren't you, dude?" He stroked his head. "One hell of a guard dog."

Brute gave a single *woof* in reply.

Shaking his head, Mitch took Charlotte's arm, and led her toward the couch. "I need you to stay here, with Brute, while I look around outside. Do you think you can actually do that?"

"Sure." Predictably enough, her chin went up. "Unless I think there's something else I should do at some point—and then I'll do that." Smiling crookedly, she gave him a fierce hug. "I'm not an idiot, okay?"

He didn't know what to do with her, but holding her was a nice start.

"You think it was Newman?"

Yeah, and a hundred unthinkable scenarios crashed through his brain in the time it took him to reach Brute. "I thought someone had hurt him. I half expected to find him maimed or...or worse." Anger, as well as guilt, left his voice rough. "And then there's you. I left you alone in the room, no weapon, no landline. I figured your phone was in your purse in here and I didn't know if you'd think to—"

"I got your phone from your jeans."

Thank God she was a quick thinker. "I don't mind that you called Brodie, but we need to call Colvin too."

"Brodie will do that." She pressed away from him, then gave him a thump on the shoulder. "If you think it scared you, imagine what it did to me. Hearing Brute like that put my heart in my throat, and then you ran out there—like you said, without a weapon. What if he'd been there with a gun?"

"I've never known him to touch a gun." But she was right. He'd taken chances with her and that was unthinkable. In that second, he made up his mind. "I won't bring you here again."

Throwing up her arms, she huffed. "Next time, *I'll* have a gun."

"That you said you can't shoot."

"I can shoot—it's the accuracy that's in question."

Brute leaned against his leg, and Mitch couldn't resist lifting him up for a hug. The dog was an armful, but it didn't matter.

Charlotte dutifully sat on the couch. "Go ahead and check around outside. But be careful, please."

He set the dog down with her. Brute circled twice, dropped with a grunt and sighed.

"I think he wore himself out," Charlotte said, stroking Brute's ears. Then she too bent for a hug. "Thank God you weren't hurt."

Mitch touched her hair, something he couldn't resist doing again and again. "I won't go far."

Ten minutes later, Brodie and Colvin showed up. Jack remained behind with the women, to ensure nothing else happened that night.

Because the storm seemed imminent, thunder booming louder, closer with each minute that passed, Colvin took a series of photos showing the blood in the grass and on the outside of the building, the ripped screen and even the tire tracks in the dirt at the end of the long drive, even though the new arriving cars had ridden over it.

Colvin walked inside to talk to Charlotte, but Brodie lingered outside with Mitch. "It's getting late, but we could still hit up Freddie's."

He nodded. "I just need to get Charlotte home first."

"We could send her with Grant."

Yeah, he could do that, but it didn't sit right.

Voice lower, Brodie said, "He's a good cop. Don't let his laid-back attitude fool you."

"It's not that." Hating the truth, Mitch said, "I can't have her out here again, not until Newman is taken care of."

"Agreed, but then, I'm not crazy about you being out here either."

That sentiment caused a smirk. "I can handle myself."

"Sure, but—"

"In my shoes, would you relocate?"

Brodie stared at him a moment, then snorted. "No."

"I'll take Charlotte as far as Freddie's, and Grant can take her from there. It'll give me time to talk to her. To explain—"

From behind him, Charlotte asked, "Explain what?" The second their gazes met, she seemed to know. Glaring at Brodie, she said, "Thanks for nothing." And stormed on down the steps toward Colvin's car, Brute at her side.

"You're taking my dog?"

Spinning around, she asked, "Did you want him staying here alone? No, of course not. Especially not after what happened."

Hands shaking, she pushed back her unruly hair. "Go play vigilante or whatever it is Brodie convinced you to do."

Ah. At least that explained her ire at Brodie. "He didn't convince me to do anything. It's a good plan." The only one they had at the moment.

"When you're done," she said, opening the back door and letting Brute climb in, "you can come by the house and get him."

"And then," Brodie said low, "she'll see that you're okay." He nudged Mitch. "Play along. It'll make her feel better. Besides, Dad wants to come back here with you too. You can round him up at the same time."

Right. He'd almost forgotten that Elliott was his house guest. "Give me a minute with her," he said to Colvin, and headed after her.

He'd do what he had to, but he wouldn't leave things like this.

Watching him approach, her face set in annoyance, Mitch decided honesty was the only way to go. She didn't get out of the car, but she did roll down the window.

Hands braced on the roof, he leaned in and said, "I'm sorry tonight got ruined."

"Ruined?" Brows shooting up, she snapped, "It was the most wonderful night of my life and some stupid creep won't ruin it for me."

Always, every damn time, she took him by surprise. "How do you figure that?"

The incredulous, slightly hurt look she gave him damn near made him back up. Lips stiff, she said, "I was with you. That's what counted."

Tonight he'd run the gamut of emotions—lust, anger, frustration, uneasiness... Need. Affection. And of course whenever with Charlotte, humor.

Tension eased, and a smile crept in. "Most wonderful, huh?"

"Yes."

The way she said that, all snappish and curt... "But you're still mad?"

"Yes, I'm mad! I... Ugh. I'm mad at the situation. I'm frustrated that we got interrupted. I want to stomp Newman into the ground. And I want you to..."

When she trailed off, he prompted softly, "To?"

"I want you to care as much as I do."

Jesus. How much more could he? Already she consumed his thoughts, and he burned for her around the clock.

Leaning in, he put a firm, quick kiss to her mulish mouth. "I'm already there, Charlotte."

"You don't know how much I care."

She'd mentioned love. Is that what she wanted? He shook his head, saw she took that the wrong way, and said, "I know I'm one hundred percent committed to having you with me. Now, tomorrow, always if I can manage it."

"Oh." Her anger faded away and she smiled too. "Well then, yeah, that's enough."

Sitting around the living room with Mary and Ronnie, her feet curled under her, Brute at her side, Charlotte daydreamed.

Ros, that brave woman, was in the kitchen with Elliott and Grant both. When they'd returned at the same time for dinner, the driveway was already full, so they'd parked down the lane.

And walked back to the house together.

Now that Brodie, Jack and Mitch had vacated the driveway, there was plenty of room, but they'd return eventually, Brodie and Jack to collect their wives, and Mitch to...to tell her good-night.

Rather than dwell on how badly she wished she too would be heading home with the man she loved, Charlotte wondered about Elliott and Grant—and what they'd talked about while walking together that short distance.

Oh, to have heard that conversation! It was obvious they each vied for Ros's attention, so it could have been acrimonious—

except that they also knew Ros wouldn't put up with any nonsense...so had they behaved with false congeniality?

From what she'd seen since arriving back home, conversation was strained but pleasant. Ros looked like she wanted to boot them both out the door, but so far she'd abided by her sons' wishes to keep them around.

Charlotte would have stayed with her as a buffer, but Brute wanted to nap with the other dogs, and he wanted her with him, so rather than watch him trail back and forth, she'd settled on the couch.

In a chair across from her, Ronnie held Buster in her lap. Mary, on the floor with her back against the wall, rubbed Howler's chest. He rested on his back, massive paws in the air, velvety ears splayed out around his bony head, softly snoring.

They'd already been talking about stubborn men, which led to romantic pursuits, and ended with a rather frank and refreshing discussion on sex. Charlotte said, "It wasn't what I expected."

Ronnie eyed her. "I hope you mean it was better."

"Much. It was more natural, you know? Like whenever I used to think about sex—" though before Mitch, it hadn't been that often "—I couldn't quite imagine how two people went from a kiss to getting naked to having something as intimate as sex. In my mind it had always seemed super impersonal—remove this, then take off that, step this way, lay that way."

"Get a condom," Ronnie added with meaning.

Laughing, Charlotte agreed. "Yes, Mitch took care of that." She gave her a thumbs-up. "Knew he was a good guy."

Smiling, Mary said, "With Brodie, I don't get time to think about the process. Even though we've been together for a while now, he manages to act like each time is the first time. He gets carried away—and that gets me carried away."

"Jack is methodical." Bobbing her eyebrows, Ronnie clarified, "In a good way, I mean. He says he needs time to enjoy it all."

They all laughed.

Mary glanced at the clock, which prompted Charlotte to do the same.

It was after eleven.

"Whatever you do, however you do it," Ronnie said, "as long as it works for the two of you, that's what matters."

"It worked all right." Unable to stifle a yawn, Charlotte said, "I think I'll take a shower. That should perk me up enough to stay awake until the guys return."

"Jack said Freddie's doesn't close until one tonight. It could be a few hours yet."

Containing a groan, Charlotte stood, and that alerted Brute. He jumped up, at the ready for whatever she had planned.

"I'm used to late nights with Brodie. Sometimes we stay over at locations, but the nights we don't it's sometimes the wee hours of the morning before we get home."

"Same," Ronnie said. "It just depends on the schedule."

"Well, I've always been an early to bed, early to rise type person." She liked to get to the office promptly each day, with enough time to get the coffee going before calls started coming in.

Mary nodded at Brute. "He won't like having you out of his sight."

"I know." She stroked his head. "I'll be right back."

He gave her a long look, and then surprised them all by dropping down next to Howler. Startled, Howler lifted his head, stared at Brute, then turned to his side and snuggled around him.

Buster made note of that, and he abandoned Ronnie's lap to join the fur huddle, stretching out behind Howler's butt and resting his face over his hip.

Entwined, the dogs made quite an adorable sight.

Brute had made friends after all.

Now Mitch couldn't leave, no matter what. He'd never do that to Brute.

★ ★ ★

They'd been at the bar for hours, talking to everyone they could without being too conspicuous. Many customers remembered Newman, but hadn't seen him lately.

The hope now was that by hanging around night after night, he'd be able to lure Newman into a false sense of security, let him think that he'd catch Mitch unawares.

Wouldn't happen, but Newman didn't know that.

There'd be nights, of course, when Brodie and Jack couldn't join him, which suited him just fine. He figured Newman would wait to get him alone, because that's how cowards like him operated.

When Jack's phone rang, Mitch didn't pay that much attention—at least not until he saw Jack's expression after he'd answered.

"The john?" Jack looked around the bar. "Yeah, I can, but why...okay, sure. Hang tight." Expression grim, he disconnected. "That was Bernie."

What the hell did that little weasel want now?

"He's concerned that someone might see him talking to us, so I'm going to meet him in the john."

"He's here?" Mitch asked. Did that mean Bernie knew something important?

"Freddie let him in through the kitchen. He sounds...funny."

Just then the man they had working for them at the bar wended his way through tables and human congestion to join them. Mitch took in his demeanor and scooted over for him to sit.

"Bernie's here."

"He called," Jack said, indicating the phone still in his hand. "You didn't have to—"

"I wanted to warn you." Arms folded on the table, he leaned in and lowered his voice even more. "Someone did a number on him. He looks so bad, I almost didn't recognize him."

"Shit." Just that quick, Mitch pushed the guy back out of the booth.

"Hold up," Brodie said, also coming to his feet.

"Newman is behind this, and that means Bernie knows something."

"Keep it down," the new guy said. "Bernie's ready to jump out of his skin."

"Did he tell you anything?" Jack asked, calm personified.

"Just that they stole his car and he needed to talk to you ASAP."

Equally grim now, Brodie gestured at Jack. "Lead the way." Then to Mitch, "You and I will hold back, so we don't spook him."

Hold back when they finally had a clue? "Not my strong suit." Mitch fell into line behind Jack, struggling with the urge to push past him.

"Nor mine," Brodie said, "but we'll manage."

At the bathroom doors, Jack gave them each a look. "Stay put."

"Something's not right." Mitch had a bad feeling about this, and his instincts had never let him down. "Could be a trap."

"Could," Jack conceded. "But there's only one way to find out."

Brodie agreed, but threw in a caveat. "My foot's going to be in the door so I can hear what's happening. Anything sounds off to me, and we're coming in."

With a roll of his eyes, Jack opened the door.

And Brodie inserted his foot.

It was a strain, but they heard Jack whistle. "Damn, Bernie. Did you get hit by a train?"

"Fucking Newman and his friends." Faint with pain, the garbled voice barely reached them. "And you gotta do something."

"For you? Now why would I do that?"

Thick hesitation preceded Bernie's whine. "You're the reasonable one, that's why I asked for you."

"My reasonableness only goes so far if you hurt someone in my family. In case you haven't yet realized it, Mitch is family."

"I know—and so does Newman." Immediately he groaned, "Oh God."

Voice going tight, Jack said, "Trust me, okay? I am the reasonable one, but I have a feeling the others need to hear this before you pass out."

"That's our cue," Brodie said, swinging the door open. Mitch went in before him, determination making his stride long and hurried.

Brodie came in right behind him.

The others might be shocked at Bernie's condition, but Mitch recognized it.

Definitely Newman's work.

One of Bernie's eyes was swollen completely shut, the other opened only a slit—but in that small space, Mitch saw pure panic.

With only one thought on his mind, he stopped mere inches from Bernie. "Newman is sick and twisted and cruel. What he did to you, he'll do to others."

"I... I know. That's why I'm here."

"If you have something to share, tell me now."

His mouth opened twice without him getting out a single word. His grotesquely swollen jaw made the effort more ludicrous. Purpling bruises mottled most visible parts of his face and neck, and still Mitch saw the rise of color as Bernie flushed.

His eye slanted to Jack. "You won't let them hurt me?"

"He couldn't stop me," Mitch said, regaining his attention with sharp impatience. "But it's not you I want to hurt. Now *tell me where he is.*"

"I didn't know." With difficulty, Bernie swallowed, using one hand to lean on the sink. "I thought he only hated you."

"Hating me means hurting me—and he can best do that by hurting the people I care about."

Dropping his head forward, shoulders hunched in pain, Bernie moaned. "When I found out what he planned, I tried to stop him."

Not shaking it out of him took all of Mitch's restraint. "Tell me. Where. He *is*."

"He took my keys." Bernie wheezed. "He worked me over and threw me down my basement steps, then locked me in. Said he'd be back to finish me off but that he didn't have time right then."

And he would have, Mitch didn't have a doubt. Bernie was lucky to be alive. "Bernie—"

"Newman didn't know a bunch of boxes blocked a window. I crawled out and came here to tell someone…" With a last shuddering breath, he said, "He's on his way to see Charlotte and Rosalyn. I'm sorry—"

Terror erupted, setting his feet in motion before Bernie could finish. Slamming the door open, he barely registered Jack saying, "Go to Freddie. He'll take care of you until we get back."

"Please don't let them get hurt."

Brodie vowed, "We won't."

CHAPTER TWENTY

Even though she didn't make the shower very warm, the glass doors still steamed up, sealing her in her own little cocoon. She usually took great pleasure in her shower, but tonight, not so much.

At the opposite corner of the house from the kitchen, she couldn't hear the others anymore. It left her...antsy.

Trying to ignore the rising uneasiness, she rinsed the soap from her body. Just as she finished, she heard a noise that made her freeze. Eyes widened, ears straining, she stood beneath the spray and tried to assimilate that noise to something familiar.

Wasn't happening.

Somehow she knew she wasn't alone. She *knew.* And her heart tried to crawl up her throat.

I refuse to be a victim. Ronnie's famous words.

So what would she do right now? What would Jack or Brodie do?

Hand trembling, she turned off the water and, hoping she sounded casual instead of petrified, she asked, "Ros?"

No answer.

Pretending that didn't scare her either, she said, "Just a sec."

At the very least, she wanted a towel. It was right there outside
the shower, on the closed toilet seat.

Sliding the shower door open just wide enough for her hand,
she reached out—and thank God, she snagged it.

Wrapping it snug around herself, she searched the shower for
a weapon of any kind. All she found was a long-handled back
scrubber, but it'd have to do.

Praying she was wrong, that she'd be laughing at her wild
imagination later, she flattened her hand against the glass and
slowly, warily cleared away the mist.

Staring back at her, Newman grinned.

The scream strangled in her throat and she slipped on the tub
floor. So fast she didn't have time to fall, he opened the door
and snatched her out without concern for scrapes or bruises—
or her towel.

Instinctively she fought, but he had no problem at all locking an arm around her throat to drag her out of the bathroom
and into her bedroom.

With one hand she attempted to keep her towel in place,
and with the other she frantically tried to loosen his hold so she
could draw a breath.

When her nails caught him, he growled but finally gave her
room to gasp. The back of her remained plastered to the front
of him, her body awkwardly arched out from the position.

The security system should have signaled an alarm at their
entry.

Guessing her thoughts, he said, "One of my men is a whiz
at disabling alarms. There's no one coming to help you, so just
settle down."

"The others," she gasped.

"Don't you worry about that. I came in through your bedroom window, but the others will go around front to round up
the ladies, including that ballsy little bitch who threatened me."

Hot breath moved over her cheek when he lightly bit her ear. "And now you and me are going to have that fun I promised."

Oh God, oh God, oh God. The alarm was wired to go to the station if anyone tampered with it. Had that still happened? Would men be on their way?

Would they be in time?

While straining away, she tried to make sense of what he'd said. *Rounding up the women?* But Elliott and Grant were there too. Surely she'd have heard something if they'd been...shot.

Bile burned in her stomach at the thought. *No, please, don't let them be hurt.*

"Here now." Dragging her in front of the cheval mirror, he looked over her head at her reflection. Mouth close to her ear, he whispered, "Yeah, you're going to be a treat. Not enough to repay all the trouble that bastard's put me through, but I'll just think of you as a salty little appetizer." He trailed the flat side of a big knife up her thigh, lifting her towel as he went.

True panic set in, kick-starting survival instincts. Uncaring if she got cut in the process, she thrashed, jerked, kicked—which only made him squeeze her throat until stars danced before her eyes and her legs turned to noodles.

"That's enough of that. Conscious or unconscious, doesn't matter to me." More to himself than her, he mused, "Can't scrap if you can't breathe, now can you?"

Belatedly she remembered the back brush hanging limply in her hand. Resisting the yawning darkness, summoning one last bit of strength, she gouged it back against him, driving the handle hard into his gut.

"*Bitch.*" He loosened enough for her to gasp and choke, her throat on fire as she sucked in oxygen.

Suddenly there was a ruckus, bodies crashing, a faint scream—and maniacal barking.

Other side of the house or not, they heard it loud and clear.

"What the hell?" He caught her arm before she could get too

far from him. Frantically she beat at him with the brush, doing little damage but frustrating him more.

He yanked her forward, tightening around her neck again, lifting her to her tiptoes. This time, at least, her windpipe was in the crook of his elbow, so she wasn't strangling.

Just very, very uncomfortable.

That lethal knife flashed in front of her face. "That's not women scrapping out there. Who else is here?"

"Elliott," she gasped, "and Grant."

"Grant? The fucking cop?" Panic made his voice higher. "What's he doing here?"

Before she could answer, the door slammed open so hard, the knob stuck in the wall. Mitch stood there, a giant wall of heaving muscle, his eyes an eerie shade of amber rage.

Newman jumped so hard, she nearly got away.

"Let her go."

To Charlotte, Newman's laugh sounded strained. "Look who showed up for the party."

In contrast to the incandescent fury emanating off him, his voice sounded calm. "You have one second to let her go."

"Go fuck yourse—"

Shooting around Mitch, Brute bolted into the room. Charlotte saw fangs, heard snarling. Brute's impact against Newman got her freed real quick as Newman tried to fend off the attack.

Scrambling back, clutching her towel, she whispered through her damaged throat, "He has a knife!" If Brute got hurt, it would devastate her.

Mitch was already on him. Viciously, he twisted Newman's wrist until the knife fell to the carpet. He kicked it away—and Charlotte quickly snatched it up.

Only then did he call off Brute. Or attempt to anyway.

But...yeah. Brute wasn't trained for that. Jaws locked around Newman's forearm, he jerked and growled with no intention of letting go.

Brodie stepped in. "Son of a bitch," he whispered, sparing only a quick glance at Charlotte where she still—very stupidly—huddled against the wall.

Catching herself, she stepped forward. "I'll get Brute."

"I've got it," Brodie said, and only then did Mitch release Newman to scoop up Brute.

Once held, Brute released Newman to cuddle against Mitch. "That fucking dog is a menace!"

"Meaning it was your foot he got at my house?" Mitch asked, referring to the shoe Brute had kept from the intruders.

No wonder the poor baby had gone after Newman. Brute had probably already tangled with him once.

Brodie put Newman in a headlock far tighter than what he'd used on her, and Newman went limp. As his legs sprawled out loosely, they all spotted the bandages around his ankle.

Crooning to the dog, Mitch soothed him until Brute panted a little less, and his eyes were no longer so wide and wild. He even licked Mitch's chin. "Good boy, you did good."

When Brute squirmed, Mitch cautiously released him—and Brute went quickly to Charlotte, low to the ground, tail tucked and ears flattened.

Emotion overtook her and she carefully sat down, making sure her towel stayed in place, to hug Brute close. The dog snuffled against her, then sat at her side to watch the proceedings.

"Take Newman outside," Mitch said softly. "I'll be right there."

Without replying, Brodie strong-armed Newman through the doorway.

Crouching down in front of her, Mitch asked, "You're okay?"

She nodded, needing a second before she could get words out of her tight throat.

Lightly he touched a fingertip to her throat, his expression tortured. "Are you sure?"

"He didn't touch me except to...to choke me with his arm a little. I think he meant to, but then you got here and—"

"Charlotte."

His broken voice helped her to get it together. If she fell apart now, he'd feel worse—and he needed to finish it with Newman while he was here, with his brothers and father and Grant as backup. A deep steadying breath helped to ease the trembling. "I really am okay. I swear." Swallowing again, she asked, "The others?"

As if he didn't quite believe, his gaze searched hers. "Elliott is fine, but he got cut. It's not bad," he said when she looked up in alarm. "No one else got hurt."

"Cut? How?"

"One of Newman's buddies, a guy named Lee, came at Ronnie. She was trying to hold back the dogs and didn't see him. Elliott tackled the guy." Mitch shrugged. "If not for him..." His mouth pinched and he looked away.

Ronnie might have been killed. Glad that he hadn't finished that gruesome thought, Charlotte nodded. "He said he had others with him."

"Two guys, and they're contained, I promise." His jaw worked. "I didn't know where you were. I didn't see you or Newman." He inhaled sharply. "Finally Mary told me you were in the shower and I just...knew. That he had you, that he'd try to hurt you." His eyes went glassy and he swallowed hard. "I've never been so scared."

Why he held himself back, she didn't know, and whatever his reasons, she really didn't care. Launching at him, almost knocking him over, Charlotte squeezed him tight. "I thought I heard something but I wasn't sure and I didn't know what to do and I was so afraid the others would get hurt, and he'd have gotten to you too and—"

"Shh..." He smoothed her hair, kissing her face, her bare shoulder. "I'm so sorry, babe. So damned sorry."

With a smack to his shoulder, she tried to shove free, but Mitch held on, so she settled for snapping, "It was *him*, not you. I *love* you."

Mitch held her back, blank with surprise. "You said you were falling—"

"I was, but you can only fall so far before you land. Now I know for sure." A sob welled up, despite her best efforts to quell it. "You're the one for me. The only one."

Crushing her close again, he rocked her gently. She heard him saying, "It's all right, Brute. She's okay, buddy."

Blindly, Charlotte reached out, felt Brute's neck and stroked him.

After a few seconds, Mitch kissed her forehead. "I have to go, honey."

No. She didn't want him to. But...this was it for him. As Ronnie had said, he was no longer that little boy who'd so badly needed protection. Now he was a man who wanted to finish ugly business against the one who'd hurt him.

Drying her eyes on his shoulder, she nodded and sat back. Mitch let her. She drew a shuddering breath and said, "I need to get dressed before I go outside."

"You," he emphasized, "need to stay in here."

Determined to be at his side, she got to her feet, tossed the towel and headed for the dresser. "I love you." And to her mind, that said it all.

A few seconds ticked by before Mitch caught up to her. "Charlotte—"

"What?" She pulled out jeans.

His gaze went all over her. "I need you—"

Chin up, she said, "I need you too."

He caught the jeans, making it impossible for her to step into them. "I love you, Charlotte."

Finally. That admission gave her the boost of energy she needed.

Until he added, "That's why I want to know you're inside. Safe."

She loved hearing it, but still… "I'm safe when I'm with you." Just the thought of not seeing him, not being near him, left her shaking. She couldn't be alone, not now, not after…" Her hands clenched the denim tight. "Please understand."

So many emotions passed over his face, but in the end, he relented. "I do." He put his forehead to hers. "Promise me you won't interfere?"

Easy enough to do; she wanted no part of Newman or his henchmen. Aware of Mitch looking at her, all over her, maybe seeing bruises but, hopefully, mostly just seeing her, she pulled on jeans and a T-shirt. After she stepped into her flip-flops, she nodded. "I'm ready."

Mitch had it under control, just barely. Watching Charlotte drop the towel and dress… She'd almost stopped his heart, not only because she was beautiful, but because Newman had marked her. He spotted bruises, a scratch or two, and her cheeks were still blotchy from crying.

He wanted to pound Newman into dust, to demolish every single trace of him—but Grant was out there, so he doubted he'd be allowed that much leeway.

Touching a particularly vivid red mark on her throat, he barely managed to swallow. "I'm so sorry this happened."

She nodded. "Me too. But I'm okay now."

Me too? What the hell did that even mean?

"I'm sorry Newman touched me," she whispered. "I'm sorry he was ever in your life. We're both sorry for things out of our control." Her small, cool palm curved around his cheek. "Now though, it's over. So let's go put a period on his miserable existence and get on with our lives together."

Amazing. There couldn't be a more incredible, wonderful,

beautiful person in the entire world—and by some miraculous twist of fate, she was his.

Like his freedom, he would never, ever take her for granted. "Let's go."

Brute followed them when they left the room. Mitch wanted to reassure him more, and he wanted to pamper Charlotte, to check her head to toes and make one hundred percent certain that she was truly okay—but business first. He couldn't leave his brothers out there dealing with Newman without him.

Mary stood just inside the kitchen doorway. Buster and Howler prowled around nervously, both wanting outside. Both denied.

On a kitchen chair, Elliott sat with blood running from his shoulder down his arm. Oddly enough, both Ros and Grant tended him.

Elliott looked at Charlotte and worked up a smile. "Not as fast as I used to be. And if Grant dares to chuckle about that, I'll flatten him."

Grant grunted and, seeing that Ros had it under control, stepped back to give Mitch a look. "You have about five minutes before I'll be out there. Then it's legal all the way. You understand me, son?"

"Yeah, I do." It was more than he'd expected. "Appreciate it."

Elliott stopped him. "Hit the bastard once for me, will you?"

"Yes, sir." Brute remained on his heels. "Sorry, bud. You need to stay in here, but I'll be back."

Already on top of it, Mary said, "I'll hand out treats," and the word alone got Buster and Howler diverted. Brute she had to call twice, but he did finally give up his vigilance and follow her from the kitchen to the living room.

On the way out, Mitch remarked to Charlotte, "You have the most astounding family."

With a brief, strained smile, she replied, "Yes, *we* do." When she spotted the three men, all contained just past the patio, she froze.

Mitch stepped in front of her, blocking her view.

Newman's two cohorts were hog-tied together, sitting back-to-back on the ground. They were in better shape than Bernie, but not by a lot. "Got worked over, I see."

Brodie flexed his knuckles. "That's what happens when someone breaks into my mother's house. When he startles my wife and upsets my dog."

Standing with Ronnie, who held her knife in her hand, Jack said, "Instead of busting up your face, I should have let my wife gut you. Be glad I didn't."

"He likes to have all the fun," Ronnie said, sounding unconcerned. "But if you move, you're mine."

Newman cracked a laugh. He wasn't tied, but he was disarmed. From his elbow to his wrist, bloody tooth marks marred his skin. "You need all these people to protect you, boy?"

Mitch only smiled. Yes, he knew Newman, knew his moods and methods—and right now Newman was scared. "You're going to prison for a very long time."

Newman snorted. "Yeah, how do you figure that?"

"Breaking and entering, assault, attempted murder."

"Ha. Don't be dramatic. No one tried—"

"Bernie got out of the basement." When Newman's eyes flared, Mitch grinned and walked closer. "You told him what you planned, didn't you? The idea of him sitting busted up and broken in the basement, knowing what you'd do and what would happen to him next, gave you a few thrills, right? But now he's free and ready to tell the rest of the world."

Anger brought Newman forward a step. "You fucking sold the house," he said in a low growl, his face red, his eyes filled with hatred. "Velma loved me, not you. It should have been *mine*."

Mitch didn't lean away from his rage—no, he leaned into it. "I didn't want it, you idiot. I wanted nothing to do with you—"

"Or your mama?" He laughed. "Does your new family know you walked out on her?"

In every way possible, his mother had left him long before that day he'd decided he had enough. "They know."

Slanting his gaze to Brodie and Jack, Newman said, "Little Mitch was a real smart-ass, always butting in where he shouldn't." Gloating, he looked back at Mitch, his gaze hard. "Velma couldn't control him, but he found out that I hit a helluva lot harder than her. Ain't that right, boy?"

Brodie started to surge forward but Mitch stopped him.

Aware of Charlotte behind him, feeling her simmering animosity over Newman's taunts, Mitch kept his tone moderate. "Yeah, I did learn that. Know what, though?" His fist landed against Newman's cheek so fast and hard that no one—including Newman—saw it coming.

As he'd told Charlotte, when he hit someone it was with the intent of taking their head off their shoulders. Newman's feet literally came out from under him and he landed hard on his back. Dazed, he stared blindly into space while catching his breath.

"This Mitch," he said, moving to stand over him, "hits back. And if I'm counting, I owe you quite a few more."

Brodie was still enraged. "You cowardly fucker. You actually wanted to brag about brutalizing a boy?"

Laboriously, Newman rolled up on one elbow and spat blood to the side. He worked his jaw, winced. "He had it coming."

Jack said, "I should let him kill you. Hell, I'd be happy to help him—not that he needs it."

"No, I don't," Mitch told him. "But I appreciate the thought." He grabbed Newman by the shirt and hauled him back to his unsteady feet.

Newman tried throwing a punch, but his aim was off, with no power behind it.

"This one is for Elliott." Putting his fist in Newman's gut, he stole his air.

As Newman wheezed, Mitch said, "The rest are for Charlotte."

With crushing force, he hit Newman three more times. Since
he held him by the shirt, Newman didn't fall—which suited
Mitch. Another to the gut, and Newman's legs completely gave
out. Blood covered his face, mostly from his smashed nose and
a split in his lip.

It didn't matter. Mitch drew back once more—

And a delicate hand rested on his back. "Mitch."

That soft voice and gentle touch sank into him…and he let
Newman drop. Oddly enough, he felt nothing but impatience—
to hold Charlotte.

"You owe him more," Jack said.

"A lot more," Brodie agreed.

Ronnie asked, "Wanna use my knife?"

The humor took him by surprise, making him laugh. This
family, *his* family, was completely loony, loyal to a fault, a little
bloodthirsty and he loved them dearly.

Catching her by the waist, he pulled Charlotte around and
to his side. "I think Charlotte's gotten her fill."

"I haven't," Brodie said. "Not after he boasted of hitting a
kid."

"Get behind me," Jack argued, both of them stepping forward
at almost the same time.

Grant cleared his throat.

Frustrated, Brodie nudged Newman with his foot. "Maybe
now you understand that Mitch isn't a boy anymore, and he's
no longer alone. Mess with him and you're messing with the
whole family."

"And," Jack added, "we will destroy you."

Grant threw up his hands. "Mind if I arrest him now?"

Hearing that, Newman groaned, barely coherent.

Sirens drew near, and that got all the dogs inside howling.

With Brodie, Jack, Ronnie and Grant standing over the three

men, Mitch took Charlotte's hand and moved her back to the patio.

Near her ear, he asked, "You're okay?"

"Yes. Thank you for hitting him for me."

"That was my pleasure." His knuckles hurt, but his heart felt incredibly happy.

Newman would finally be out of his life. Charlotte would be in it, along with the family he'd never thought to have. A man couldn't ask for more than that—especially since it was everything he'd never dared to hope for.

To give herself something to do, Ros made cookies. Everyone had returned to her house after going to the hospital with Elliott. Luckily, a couple layers of stitches had mended the deep cut from the top of his shoulder to about seven inches down his back. There'd been no serious muscle damage but he would need time to heal.

Again, he could have been killed.

The boys hadn't known about the wreck yet, but the doctor mentioned it while updating them, saying it was imperative that Elliott take it easy for a while and give his body a chance to recover.

Stunned, the three of them—Brodie, Jack and Mitch—had soaked in the fact that they might have lost Elliott, and he hadn't even told them.

Because, overall, he didn't think they'd care.

That was *his* fault and they all knew it. But somehow, in the moment, it hadn't seemed to matter.

Pressing a hand to her heart, Ros waffled between fury and remorse. Fury at Elliott for creating the situation, and remorse that she couldn't somehow fix it.

"Hey, baby. You okay?"

Oh, that voice. He knew it did crazy things to her, damn him, and that's why he used it. Without looking at him, Ros snapped, "Why aren't you on the couch recuperating as the doctor ordered?

"Mitch is ready to go. He wants to drive me, even though I told him I'm perfectly capable—"

A volatile mix of emotions spun her around to face him. "You," she said in her most take-charge voice, "aren't going anywhere."

Blank surprise had him blinking. "I'm not?"

Though he might be nearing sixty, Elliott still looked devastatingly handsome and rugged with beard shadow darkening his jaw. "You heard the doctor. You'll need someone to change out the bandages each day, to apply more antibiotic ointment, to help you with your shoes and—"

Skeptically, he asked, "You?"

She swatted his shoulder, then gasped, appalled at herself. Snatching back her hand, she groaned, "Oh my God. Did I hurt you?"

His smile went crooked, his gaze knowing. "No, you didn't." Taking her hand, he lifted it to his mouth and kissed her knuckles. "You're jumpy from lack of sleep. Why don't you go get some rest? I can help the boys at the shop today."

Of all the... It seemed wise to turn her back on him before replying. "I'm in better shape than you are." Grabbing up an oven mitt, she took out the cookies. "You'll stay here, Elliott, and that's that. I'm close enough to work that I can fill in for Charlotte for a day or two, while also checking on you."

The resounding silence had her looking back, in case he'd left the kitchen.

Head down, he muttered something low.

"What?"

When he looked at her, it was with regret. "You've taken care of me long enough, Ros. I refuse to do that to you, again."

The cookie tray hit the trivet with a clatter. She threw down the oven mitt like a gauntlet. "You're leaving again, aren't you?"

"What?" His brows shot up. "No. See I was—"

"Yes, you are. That's what this is about, right? Admit it."

Charlotte and Mitch entered the kitchen, hugged up to one another. It did her heart good to see them so close. Behind them, Jack and Ronnie stepped in, then Brodie and Mary.

They all stared at Elliott.

Clearly she'd been louder than she thought.

Mitch said, "I thought you were coming home with me."

"I am," Elliott said.

"No," she countered, digging in. "He's not."

Concerned, but not really rebutting her, Brodie asked, "You're kicking him out?"

"You know," Jack said, more uncomfortable than she'd ever seen him, "he got in the way of that knife to protect Ronnie. For once, I thought it'd be okay if we lent him a hand for a little while."

"I'm not kicking him out." Did they all consider her so heartless? "He's staying here, and that's final."

"Here?" Mitch glanced around her kitchen. "You mean... with you?"

Oh, how she wished he hadn't spelled it out like that. "Yes, with me." So there'd be no arguments, Ros used her best mother's voice and crossed her arms. "You have enough to do now that Newman is out of the picture."

With a slow smile, Mitch said, "Okay."

For the longest time, everyone else just stared at her, until Elliott cracked a grin. "You heard your mother, boys. I'm staying here."

Well, damn. Now Elliott looked like she'd propositioned him! Pointing at him, she emphasized, "*Temporarily.*" His grin widened. "Until you're healed." He winked.

Oh, for the love of... "Who wants a cookie?"

After finishing a big job for a new house construction, putting in all the landscaping and laying sod, he'd taken the time to stop by a little jewelry store. Now, with too much sun on his face and shoulders, sweat gluing his shirt to his back, and a smile of anticipation, Mitch headed home.

Such an awesome thought, home. In the two months since Newman was arrested, everything had changed.

The necessary updates were done to his house to allow for a business, he'd made terrific contacts, and he had plenty of work lined up. Using Jack and Brodie as references, finding customers hadn't been difficult at all.

The best part? Charlotte had stayed over the night Newman attacked her—her decision, not that he had a single complaint—and she'd rarely gone home since, other to get a few things here and there.

Overall, she'd moved in with him.

The *funny* part? Elliott had never moved out of Ros's house. He was still there and they seemed to get along.

It surprised everyone that he hadn't taken off yet. Mitch hoped he never did. He liked having them all nearby. Knowing them, he felt a part of something bigger: family.

In his pocket, he had a modest ring. He'd shower, shave, and then the big plan was to propose. He didn't really have any doubts about Charlotte saying yes, but he'd still rest easier once he had her tied to him.

When he pulled down his long drive, he found it lined with cars—Jack's, Brodie's, Elliott's, but also an official police car, which meant Grant was visiting again.

Though things had fizzled out with Ros, Grant had remained friends with the family…which included Mitch. Whenever possible, he shared updates on Newman, Lee and Ritchie. It was a courteous, respectful thing to do, Grant said.

Friends with a cop. What a kicker. When he'd started this odyssey, not once had he seen that coming.

But then, he hadn't seen Charlotte in the equation either, and she was now the most important part.

How the hell could he propose with everyone here?

They were all outside, dogs playing, Jack and Brodie manning the grill, Mary and Ronnie sitting on the porch steps with Peanut the cat, Ros setting the picnic table where Elliott and Grant seemed in deep conversation.

He sat there, his car idling, his thoughts roiling even as he appreciated the sight they made. Family. Home.

The only thing missing was Charlotte.

He no sooner thought it than he saw her.

Coming quickly down the steps between Mary and Ronnie, Charlotte waved. She detoured to the picnic table to set down a bowl and then ran toward him.

Her wild hair danced out behind her and her smile made his world complete.

He turned off the car and got out, catching her when she jumped against him laughing.

Hugging her off her feet, kissing her warmly, Mitch cherished the moment. He looked forward to many more days just like this. "Hell of a welcome," he murmured. "I like it."

"I'm so glad you're home."

With her around, anywhere could be home—including the tent. Twice they'd camped out "just for fun," though overall he hadn't used it much, not since she'd moved in with him.

How could a room feel small and restrictive with Charlotte there, bursting with energy and lighting it up with her smile?

"I have some fun news."

"Yeah?" He looked toward the group in his yard. They were trying not to stare, but subtlety wasn't a Crews strong suit. "What's up?"

"Newman and his goons are toast. Finally, they'll get what they deserve."

His gaze automatically sought Grant's, and he got his nod. He dropped back to lean on his truck. "No kidding?"

"Grant wanted to tell you, but I insisted. He can give you

all the legal details, but the gist of it is that the seriousness of Ritchie's situation really hit home. Apparently, he got offered a plea deal and the words just started pouring out. Did you know they were staying at Mrs. Goodrich's house?"

Since he'd never heard of her, Mitch shook his head.

"She retired from working the elementary school cafeteria. A very sweet lady, but she'd gone out of town and they just set up house, living there like it was their own. Ritchie said if she'd have come back early, Newman would have killed her."

"She didn't?"

Charlotte shook her head. "No, she wasn't hurt, and when she'd reported the damage, no one put it together until Ritchie shared."

"Anything else?"

"According to Grant, career criminals always get busted for more than one thing, and that seems true for Newman. As of right now, they're tied to a murder, a rape and a whole host of drug charges." She bit her lip. "Did you know Newman had drugs hidden in the walls of your mother's house?"

"No, but it doesn't surprise me." One of the reasons he'd taken off from there so long ago was because Newman used the house for his drug deals.

"I wish I could have seen his face when he found the house leveled, the drugs lost."

Mitch whistled. "Guess that explains why he came after me."

"Ritchie said he wanted the money from the sale of the house—and revenge against you because, according to him, Newman considered it your fault."

So many times in his life Newman had blamed him, just to have an excuse for cruelty. Never again. "I hope he rots in prison." From the experience he'd had, rotting seemed a real possibility.

"Even with his deal, Ritchie is looking at twenty years, so I suspect Newman will be gone for much longer."

Charlotte hugged him, her head on his shoulder. "Understand that I feel terrible for the people they hurt, but I can't help being thrilled to know it's truly over."

"So that you and I, as a couple, can now begin?"

She went still. Casually, as if she hadn't started jiggling, she asked, "What exactly does that mean?"

"I was going to ask you tonight, but this seems like as good a time as any." He pulled out the ring. "Will you—"

Snatching the box from his hand, Charlotte squealed loud enough to bring all three dogs running, ready for some play. "Yes! Yes, yes, *yes*."

Before Charlotte, he'd never laughed this much. "Love your enthusiasm."

Holding the little jeweler's box in the air, she turned to the group and shouted, "We're getting married!"

Cheers erupted, making Mitch laugh more. "Don't you want to see the ring?"

"It could be made of clover and I'd still be thrilled."

"Well, I hope you like it." He took the box from her, opened it, and took out the ring.

"Oh, Mitch." Eyes going liquid, she studied the small round diamond surrounded by tinier diamonds. "It's perfect."

Heat crawled up his neck. The damn thing wasn't near grand enough for her. "Now that the business is going I can save more money. Later, if you wanted, we could upgrade—"

She clutched the box to her heart. "We will not. I love this one."

Like a sucker punch to the heart, she constantly devastated him—in all the very best ways. Putting a kiss to the end of her nose, he said, "God, I love you."

Suddenly they were surrounded, not just with dogs, but family too. Urged forward by congratulations, Mitch found himself seated at the picnic table, Charlotte at his side, while food and colas got passed around in celebration.

After loudly clearing his throat, Elliott said, "Well, Ros. Here's something you can do with the money. It'd make a grand wedding, don't you think?"

She choked, and both Elliott and Grant tried to pat her back. Behind her back, Elliott mean-mugged Grant until, hands in the air, he backed off, all the while grinning.

Now stroking her back, Elliott said, "I gave her a check for a hundred and twenty thousand bucks." He frowned. "She hasn't done anything with it yet."

Everyone gaped.

Brodie asked, "What the hell. Did you rob a bank?"

"Exactly what your mother asked me." That seemed to amuse him. "Actually, to make a long story much shorter, I became friends with this old gal. I'd help her around the house, she'd cook me meals. A nice trade-off. She was all alone in the world, no family to care for her, so we got close. When she died, she left her house to me. It didn't bring in that much, but in her garage she had a '68 Shelby GT500—and it sold at auction for a hundred and twenty grand."

Mitch tilted back to stare at him. "You scored that much money, and you're still driving an old beat-up truck?"

"You've always driven Mustangs," Jack said, almost like an accusation.

Brodie waved that off. "You're planning to buy one with whatever cash you got for the house, right?" Then he reconsidered. "Though from what you've said, you've had more than enough time to—"

"Yeah…" Elliott gave Ros a small one-armed hug. "Always loved those cars. And you're right, Brodie, I did mean to get another. Except…" He shrugged. "I don't know. It doesn't seem all that important anymore."

Ros leaned away in disbelief. "Oh my God. Did you finally grow up?"

"Who knows?" He took her hand. "What I do know is that

I'd rather help my boys work on their cars than get one of my own. And I'd rather not end up spending my last years alone."

With a roll of her eyes, Ros said, "You're in your prime."

"Thank you for noticing." He sent a smug look at Grant, who only snorted. "But I know I've burned bridges, plenty of them. I'm just hoping it's not too late for me."

Everyone fell silent—and it strained Mitch. Should he speak up? God knew, he wanted to.

Ros stole the moment, saying, "I still don't want your money."

"Not even for a big wedding?"

Appalled by the idea of anything that extravagant, Mitch said, "No," at the same time Charlotte said, "I only just got a ring!"

Elliott smiled at her. "Did you want a big wedding, honey?"

"We haven't even set a date." She lifted her hand to admire the glint of small diamonds in the sunlight. "But when we do, I'd prefer something simple."

Thank God, Mitch thought, though he didn't say it out loud. He'd be in for whatever made Charlotte happiest.

Jack sat forward, his arms folded on the picnic table, his probing gaze zeroed in on Elliott. "When you leave, maybe you'll need the money for yourself."

As if it didn't matter, Elliott said offhand, "Who says I'm leaving?"

Almost in unison, Jack, Brodie and Ros said, "I do." They looked at each other and laughed.

Mitch didn't, not with the expression on Elliott's face. "You're saying you plan to stay here, in Red Oak?"

Picking up a chip, Elliott nodded. "I'd like to, yeah." His gaze flicked around at the table. "If none of you mind—and Grant, your opinion doesn't count."

Grant shut his mouth, quietly laughing.

The silence wore on and again, it bothered Mitch. He wasn't an outsider anymore. He could speak his mind, same as the others. And he felt strongly about this.

When he felt Charlotte leaning into his side, he knew she was smiling, and that was all the push he needed. "I'd like it if you stuck around."

Everyone looked at Mitch.

"Yeah?" Elliott's face brightened. "Thanks, son."

"I owe you," Ronnie added softly. "So if it helps, you get my vote."

Elliott's expression softened. "You don't owe me, honey, but thank you."

Brodie rubbed his mouth. "How long do you plan to stay?"

"I wanted to settle here actually." His gaze shifted to Ros and away. "I've been looking for a job. Figured as long as I have a work truck, I may as well use it."

Charlotte coasted her hand up and down Mitch's arm. "His business is growing faster than he can keep up."

Very true. "If you don't mind that type of labor—"

"Love it." Elliott held his gaze—then he exhaled. "But I wouldn't want to impose."

"Elliott's not afraid of hard work."

When everyone looked at her, Ros shrugged. "Well, it's true. I've never seen him shun work. It's just a steady job that scares him off. The permanence and responsibility, you know. Gives him hives or something."

"Not anymore." Elliott winced after saying that so quickly, sent an aggrieved frown at Grant, and tried a smile for Ros. "I'm staying. For good." He flinched again. "That is, if you don't mind?"

"Not my business," she said loftily, standing to carry her empty plate into the kitchen.

Elliott stared after her.

Grant groaned—and pushed to his feet. "That's my cue to go." With a pat on Elliott's shoulder, he said, "She's worth whatever it takes for you to win her over. *Again.*"

His gaze never leaving the kitchen window, Elliott nodded. "I know."

"If you're sure you do, then…good luck."

Soon as he left, Elliott stood too. "Will you boys help me out?"

Caution won out. Mitch wanted to support Elliott, but Ros could make her own decisions without anyone trying to sway her. Since no one else asked it, he did. "Help how?"

"Take some money. Divvy it up however you like." He looked first at Brodie. "I know Mary has wealthy contacts, but there's probably something you'd like to do to your house, right?"

"Well…" Brodie shrugged. "Yeah, sure."

"And Jack, I know you're remodeling your house top to bottom."

"True." Jack gave it some thought. "We've also been discussing updates to the office."

"There you go!" Excited now, Elliott smiled at Mitch. "I love this place, son. You've done amazing things with it."

"With Jack's and Brodie's help."

He nodded. "How about an addition off the back? Add a bathroom to the bedroom? That'd be nice, right?"

Glancing at Charlotte, Mitch asked, "What do you think?"

"I think your father desperately wants to give you a gift, and you should graciously accept it."

"Damn." Elliott puffed up. "Always did love you, Charlotte."

"Thank you, Elliott."

Mitch laughed. "Yeah, sure. Count me in."

"Perfect! You're all, each and every one of you, perfect and whether I have the right or not, I couldn't be more proud." He headed for the kitchen. "Now for the real battle."

They all watched him go.

Shaking his head, Jack said, "Do you think he means it?"

"Means it, yes. Will he actually follow through? Who knows?"

Jack rubbed his face. "The last two months, he has been different."

"It's a little unnerving," Brodie said. "It's like he's Dad, but an improved version."

"Almost losing his life might have really changed him." Mary sighed. "I imagine that could shift the priorities of anyone."

"Maybe it's you, Mitch, that brought about the change." Ronnie tilted her head, studying him. "Against some big odds, you came home, so now he sees it's possible."

I came home. Yes, in so many ways, that's what it felt like.

Smiling, Mitch said, "Honestly, guys? I think it's just that Ros is so incredibly awesome. Who could resist her?"

"He resisted her before just fine," Jack pointed out.

"Yeah, but like fine wine, she's only gotten better." Charlotte snickered. "She's extra-potent now." That sentiment got everyone else snickering too.

Pretty soon they were all laughing—together, as a family.

In Charlotte's ear, Mitch whispered, "Can it be a short engagement?"

"Silly man," she said. "I fell in love with you that first night. If you'd asked, I probably would have married you then."

From inside the house, he heard Ros's raised voice, then a protest, and finally a giggling, girlish laugh—followed by silence.

Brodie and Jack went wide-eyed, knowing what that silence likely meant and a little shell-shocked by it. The wives thought it was hilarious, and went about kissing on their husbands, just to make sure they understood what was happening inside. With their *mother*—but also their father.

Charlotte hugged Mitch. "It's fun, right? Ros deserves to be happy, and for whatever reason, Elliott's always been the one for her."

Just as Charlotte was the one for him.

With his heart feeling crazy-full, he pulled her into his lap and kissed her, ignoring the catcalls from his brothers and the "aawwws" from Ronnie and Mary.

Even without Elliott's gift, he had a nice enough house—made better with Charlotte in it.

He had a growing business, and soon his father would work with him.

Brute was happier than he'd ever been, currently napping in the shade of a big tree with Buster and Howler in a tangle of legs, necks and tails.

He had a home. He had family.

And he had Charlotte.

Life had taught him not to expect much, but meeting Charlotte had changed all that—and now he had more than he'd ever thought possible.

With her in his life, he had it all.

★ ★ ★ ★ ★